AWARDS AND ACCOLADES FOR
KILBY BLADES

Awards for *Snapdragon* (Love Conquers None Series #1)
2018 NECRWA Reader's Choice Award 1st Place Winner - Erotic Romance
2018 IPPY Award Winner - Bronze Medalist - Romance
2018 Foreword Indie Awards Honorable Mention - Erotica
2018 Publisher's Weekly BookLife Prize Semi-Finalist - Romance
2018 Holt Medallion Finalist - Erotic Romance
2018 Holt Medallion Finalist - Best First Book
2018 Emma Award for Diversity in Romance Finalist - Erotic Romance
2017 National Reader's Choice Awards Finalist - Erotic Romance
2017 National Reader's Choice Awards Finalist - Best First Book

Awards for *Chrysalis* (Love Conquers None Series #2)
2018 Emma Award for Diversity in Romantic Literature Finalist - Interracial Romance

Awards for *The Art of Worship*
2018 IndieReader Discovery Award Winner - Erotica
2018 Holt Medallion Finalist - Best Novella
2018 Passionate Plume Finalist - Best Novella

Awards for Unpublished Titles
2018 Stiletto Contest Finalist - Mid-Length Contemporary: *The Secret Ingredient*
2018 Stiletto Contest Finalist - Long Contemporary: *Crocodile Tears*
2018 CIMRWA Elevation of Love Contest Finalist - Women's Fiction: *The Benefactor*

Accolades for Kilby Blades:
2018 Winner of the Emma Award for Diversity in Romantic Literature – Best Debut Author

SNAPDRAGON
Book 1 of 2 in the Love Conquers None Series

Copyright © 2017 Kilby Blades

Published by Luxe Press 2017
For permission requests and other inquiries, the publisher can be reached at: info@luxepress.net.

ISBN-10:0-9857983-4-3
ISBN-13:978-0-9857983-4-5

Developmental Editing: Tasha Harrison, www.thedirtyeditor.com and PlotBunny Editing, www.plotbunnyediting.com

Cover Design: Jada D'Lee Designs, www.jadadleedesigns.com

Custom Formatting: Champagne Book Design, www.champagnebookdesign.com

Cover Photography: Istockphoto.com

For the first Kilby, and for Dawn. We never stopped missing you.

PART I

THE ARRANGEMENT

CHAPTER ONE

THE WEDDING

"Can you hand me my diaper bag, Darbs? I don't think I can reach it."

Charlotte sat on the Chesterfield wearing nothing but Spanx and the frumpiest corset Darby had ever seen. The pale-pink garment sported heavy utilitarian zippers and had a complex opening around the nipple. An enormous hospital-grade yellow pump sucked and wheezed rhythmically from where it sat, plugged in, on the floor. Milk dripped faintly into twin four-ounce bottles that jutted out unnaturally from the contraption.

Darby set down her champagne. Two stylish totes sat near her feet.

"Not the Petunia Picklebottom—the Storsak."

Darby looked between the bags. "Am I supposed to know the difference?"

"It's the one that looks like a Longchamp," a heavily pregnant Jodi interjected as she waddled in from the other room. "The Petunia Picklebottom is the one that looks like a messenger bag." She shot a pointed look at Charlotte before jutting her chin at Darby. "You've got to translate when you're dealing with this one. She has no idea what any of this shit means."

At thirty-six weeks along, Jodi looked like she'd give her first born away if it meant the second one would come sooner. Darby handed Charlotte the correct bag as Jodi steadied herself on the arm of the sofa before sinking down with a groan.

A toilet flushing got all three women's attention. Iris was past her first trimester, but her morning sickness was still more like all-day sickness. It had shown no signs of letting up.

"I remember *that*," Charlotte commiserated, sharing a look with Jodi before flipping the pump off with her toes. She carefully extricated the milk bottles from the apparatus. Only when the lids were screwed on tightly and the bottles were safely set on the end table did she begin to disentangle herself.

"Next time, I'm adopting," Iris groused, looking wrung out as she walked back into the lounge. Her up do was disheveled, her face was blotchy, and her eyes looked slightly dazed.

"I know it's hard." Charlotte winced as she rubbed some sort of salve on her nipples. "But experiencing pregnancy is part of being a woman. This is *God's* work you're doing."

To prevent an unfriendly retort, Darby took a long gulp of champagne. Morning sickness and sore nipples were among the many badges of motherhood that she didn't envy.

"We got you some more Canada Dry, sweetie." Jodi patted the seat next to her, silently inviting Iris to sit while casting a worried glance at Darby.

"Thanks." Iris sat down gingerly, taking a fresh hand towel from Charlotte's pile.

Sounds from their friend Benji's wedding reception could be heard from far down the hall. The small group of women had taken over a posh ladies' lounge next to the ballroom of a South Florida hotel. They'd brought hand towels for Charlotte, cool compresses for Jodi's swollen feet, ginger ale for Iris, and two ice buckets full of champagne. They'd even brought a tray of canapés, but the smell of smoked salmon and caviar was what had set Iris off.

As the lone singleton among her old boarding school friends, Darby was used to the baby talk. By then, she'd surrendered to the idea that debates about sleep training and attachment parenting would play into many conversations. She treasured these rare reunions, but with each passing year, they left her feeling more out of place.

The wedding years had been one thing—Darby hadn't minded admiring engagement rings with FL clarity, or bearing the mild insult of repeated insistence that life was *so* much better in the suburbs. She didn't mind cooing over videos of fat-cheeked infants, and she'd quieted her judgments about how quickly the most brilliant women she knew had given up promising careers. She'd even learned to ignore the disinterest in their expressions when she spoke about her clinical research.

But even Darby had her limit. The way Charlotte talked about pregnancy and motherhood made her feel like she'd time warped back to 1954. Darby tried not to judge, but her steadfast aversion to pursuing marriage and children made these reunions increasingly hard to take. Dear God, if she had to endure one more heated debate about breastfeeding vs. formula or Montessori vs. Waldorf schools, someone was going to end up with a Sophie Giraffe shoved up her ass.

"What in the ever-loving fuck is this?" Darby had just set down a fresh glass of champagne for Charlotte when she saw the small white box on the end table.

"What?" Charlotte didn't look away from rummaging through her diaper bag, but Darby picked up the box.

"Milkscreen for breastfeeding," she read aloud. "Detects

alcohol in breast milk?" She looked around the room in alarm.

Charlotte finally looked up. "Alcohol in breast milk stunts babies' growth. If you've had too much to drink, you just pump and dump."

"Girls." Darby was matter-of-fact. "They've done studies on this, on women in France and Australia. They eat raw cheese, raw shellfish, and drink in moderation with no clinically-proven adverse effects."

Charlotte cast her a skeptical look, to which Darby rolled her eyes and brought up her second point.

"You know when our moms were pregnant and nursing, they drank and smoked, right?"

Jodi laughed cheekily, taking a sip of her champagne. "It was the late seventies. Our moms did a lot of things."

Charlotte shot Jodi a withering glare, looking between Jodi's protruding stomach and her half-empty glass. "What? I'm at the end of my third trimester," Jodi shot back with an unrepentant look.

Ignoring their exchange, Darby went back to inspecting the box before pinning Charlotte with a look of her own. "This isn't even FDA Approved."

Charlotte shrugged, plucking the box from Darby's hand as reproach for Jodi melted into pity for Darby. "You'll understand when you're a mother."

And there it was. Darby hadn't quite been waiting for it, but Charlotte had made comments like this before—more like insinuations, but none so patronizing as this. "What makes you think I want to be a mother?"

"Don't you?" Charlotte seemed genuinely surprised.

Killing the tartness that threatened her voice with a sweet gulp of champagne, Darby lithely took her seat. *And miss out on all this awesomeness?* "Frankly, no."

"But all women do," Charlotte blurted before catching herself. "You know, maybe not at first…but later. When their biological clocks start ticking."

"What are you basing that on?" Darby asked for proof she knew didn't' exist.

"History," Charlotte said with renewed conviction.

"History's been pretty shitty to women," Darby said evenly, earning a nod from Iris. "Forced marriages, non-consensual sex between husbands and wives, pressuring gay women into straight, child-bearing relationships."

"That's unfortunate." Charlotte's pitying expression reminded Darby of those old Save the Children commercials from the '80s with Sally Struthers. "But just because it wasn't on their terms doesn't mean women like that didn't want kids. Women like us—"

"Have evolved. We have access to birth control. We get to choose. And a lot of us don't choose that."

"Alright…" A glimmer of hope shone through Charlotte's disappointment. "Tell me you at least want to get married. I think you could be really happy with the right guy."

"Oh my God, Char. Leave the woman alone!" Jodi finally cut in, her annoyance obvious. "Nobody's judging you, Darbs. And if we were, we wouldn't have a right to." Jodi paused to look pointedly at Charlotte. "We sit at home on our fat asses every night, watching Netflix and folding laundry, and having bad sex every once in a blue moon with stretched out post-baby vag."

Iris chuckled a bit and shared an affirming look with Jodi. "It's like throwing a hot dog down a hallway."

Jodi nodded. "Meanwhile, Darby still looks young and gorgeous, fucks whoever she wants, and has tight-pussy sex."

Even Charlotte laughed at that, her eyes lighting and two

dimples punctuating her crooked grin. Darby's irritation faded. She rarely saw these women, and it felt good to get together
like this. Back home in Chicago, she didn't have many friends.

"You know I'm the same age as all of you, right?" Darby
reminded them.

"You don't look it," Iris admitted ruefully. "Your face has
the youthful glow of someone who's actually getting sleep."

Mention of sleep led to a conversation about how many
hours of cartoons it was okay to let your kids watch first thing
in the morning when you wanted a few more winks. When it
devolved into a debate over whether Daniel Tiger or Peppa Pig
did a better job of addressing sibling rivalry, and what Caillou
could possibly have the nerve to whine so much about, Darby
took that as her cue.

She slipped out of the ladies' lounge but dismissed the idea
of returning to the reception, eager to avoid more awkward
small talk at the singles table. Content to be outdoors, Darby
wandered to the elegant marble patio that encircled the grand
ballroom. Leaning against the cool stone wall, she breathed
away her last traces of annoyance with deep inhales of warm
saline air.

Darby liked old hotels, and secluded beaches, where blan-
kets of stars twinkled more brightly than they ever did in the
city. The ocean breeze stirred her dark-auburn hair until the
ends floated to tickle her lips. The sound of water hitting the
shore was faint against animated party sounds coming from
inside. It recalled similar evenings spent in the one place she'd
always been happy—her family's house on Lake Geneva.

"You look like you're having about as much fun as I am."

The smooth masculine voice broke Darby from her
thoughts. Her gaze fell from starry skies. Even in low light,
she could see that the man who'd appeared next to her was

uniquely handsome, his full lips and strong jaw belying an otherwise slender, heart-shaped face. His nose was uncommonly wide toward the middle, as if it had been broken at some point, but it flattered him.

"Oh, much, much more…" Darby teased. Something about the sarcasm in his voice compelled her to answer more acerbically than she normally would a total stranger. She angled herself toward him. "What gave me away?"

"Staying as far away as physically possible from the wedding party is usually a clue." Taking a better look, she saw that he was clean-shaven and tall, with a swimmer's build and a buzz cut that hinted at nearly black hair. His tanned skin offset some of the most striking dark-blue eyes she'd ever seen.

A smile hinted at the corner of his mouth. The combination of full lips and slight laugh lines that would surely improve with age elevated his status to outright sexy. The world was full of beautiful men, but it wasn't every day she came face to face with one this good-looking.

"So I guess that's what *you're* doing out here?" she countered.

He nodded slightly, as if to admit he were just as guilty. Darby took the last swig of her champagne, and for a moment they both looked back toward the party.

"Are you like this at all weddings or is there something about this one in particular?" The question drew her gaze back to his. She was glad to have an excuse to look at him again.

"All weddings. I knew it was time to get some air when my friend started needling me about when I was going to meet a guy, buy a house with a white picket fence, and have two point five kids."

He nodded in understanding. "I've been hassled about that before. Getting some air was the right call."

"She pulls the same shit on me every time," Darby complained lightly. "I should have just said I had a boyfriend, or worn a decoy engagement ring."

The man weaved his head and let hesitation paint his features. "Yeah, but then you'd have to stage a fake wedding, dig up a fake fiancé, hire an actor to officiate…"

She feigned regret and murmured, "More trouble than it's worth."

They both chuckled.

"Well, if it's any consolation," he said, "I was just groped."

She raised her eyebrows. "Groped?"

"By a married woman, no less. She spent the first two courses with her hand on my knee, then my thigh, then…"

Darby's mouth fell open.

He nodded in grave confirmation. "And her husband was sitting right there. I feel so…violated." His eyes twinkled as she laughed.

"You can't go back in there. You know that, right?"

"Well, if I can't, neither can you."

Interesting. "Isn't it rude to leave before the cake is cut?" Her protest was halfhearted.

"Maybe we could go for a walk."

Five minutes later, they were descending to the beach via ancient stone steps carved into the cliff walls. The steps were wide and steep and without a railing. Slight vertigo, plus the fact that she was wearing tall heels, had given Darby a moment of pause. But the stranger beside her gallantly allowed her to remain on the inside while offering a steady hand.

The humidity of south Florida made the air balmy, and the breeze coming off of the ocean put Darby even more at ease.

As they floated down in companionable silence, the sound of their steps was muffled by the rushing water. Why hadn't she thought of this herself? A walk on the beach was the perfect antidote to a lackluster night. And Darby loved the water. She saw it every day, but Lake Michigan did not compare to the ocean.

Before they had left the party, her new friend had slipped back inside the ballroom just long enough to procure an unopened bottle of champagne and two fresh flutes. Moments after they reached the beach and took off their shoes, he popped the bottle open and poured. When he raised his glass in a brief, silent toast, Darby did the same. He motioned in front of them, inviting her to walk first, as if champagne walks on the beach with women he'd just met were something he did every day.

"So, catch me up," she prodded lightly. "I take it you have a name. Give me the Cliff's Notes version of things you tell people you meet at weddings." Attending scores of events alone had taught Darby there were only two ways conversations between strangers could go: hitting it off quickly and connecting over something real, or dreaded, inescapable small talk.

"Michael Blaine, thirty-one. Born and raised in Chicago. Architect with Dewey and Rowe. I have a twin sister, Bex, and a niece, Ella. When I'm not at work, which isn't very often, I spend my time with them." His voice was calm and honest. "You?"

"Darby Christensen, thirty-two. Also from Chicago. Psychopharmacologist at Northwestern Memorial. No siblings, but I do have a hermit crab named Consuela. My only other family is my dad, but I don't see very much of him."

She watched him attentively. Would Michael make the connection to Frank Christensen, as so many others did? Would he ask about her father, about what it was like to be a controversial senator's daughter?

"Are you a friend of the bride or the groom?" he inquired instead.

"Benji and I went to boarding school together. I've known him since the sixth grade."

Recognition dawned on Michael's face, and he stopped walking to turn toward her. "Wait, was there another Darby in your class, or are you *the* Darby?"

His question was a formality—Darby wasn't a common name and she was curious as to what he knew. "I'm guessing I'm *the* Darby."

Michael took a sip of champagne, the narrow flute doing little to hide his knowing smile.

"I take it Ben's mentioned me before?"

"Once or twice. All good things." He said it in a way that guaranteed he was understating the truth.

Darby shook her head. "Uh-uh. You gotta give me more than that."

His smile hadn't disappeared, only softened. "I was his roommate all four years at Tufts."

"Wait, *you're* Mickey Blue Eyes?"

Memories flooded back to her as he let out a short laugh. "I forgot anyone ever called me that."

"He always talked about how women fell all over you. I remember stories about girls leaving their underwear on your door and getting into catfights over you."

"That's an exaggeration."

But Darby wasn't about to let him off the hook so easily. "Girls breaking into your room to wait for you, naked, in bed was an exaggeration?"

He cast his shaking head down, seeming embarrassed. "That only happened twice."

She laughed openly.

"Some of them were Ben's admirers," Michael insisted charitably.

"Uh-huh." His modesty was endearing. "I always thought he sounded a little jealous of you..." *And now I can see why.*

"I don't know about that. Besides, he was too busy pining over you to be jealous of me. You have to know it took him a long time to get over you. Like, years."

Darby's responding smile was bittersweet. "He was my first love," she admitted, "the first boy I ever kissed, the first boy I ever..."

By then they'd reached the water's edge. Michael freed one hand to place it on the small of her back and guided her to the left, his small gesture saving her from having to say more. He walked them along the shoreline as the moon shone brightly above them and the breeze from the ocean filled her nose with his spicy scent, which held delicious notes of citrus.

"My first time was with a professor..." he volunteered, perhaps compelled to disclose something personal about himself. "It was junior year of college."

"But I thought—"

"That's exactly what I wanted them to think. I put on a good show of confidence back then, but I was actually pretty shy."

"So who was the professor?"

"She taught French Lit. Her name was Genevieve, but I called her Gigi."

Wistfulness colored his voice as he recounted the tale.

"She asked me to be her TA the semester after I'd taken her class. We were grading midterms one holiday weekend—at her house, of course. The campus buildings were closed, and we had thirty term papers spread out all over her dining room table. We were debating the significance of one of the final lines of *Candide*, which roughly translates to 'we must cultivate our own garden'—"

"*Il faut cultiver notre jardin*," Darby translated. She'd been taught *Candide* in school. Her well-honed accent earned her a smile.

"The debate got heated—in a good way—and the next thing I knew, *I* was spread out all over her dining room table."

"Sounds hot."

The moon was bright enough to see his face clearly, and his eyes masked nothing. "It was."

A heat she hadn't felt in a very long time began in Darby's stomach and seemed to work its way down. "So how long did it last?"

He looked out at the water for a second before swinging his gaze back to her. When he stopped walking, she did the same.

"Long enough for her to give me the education every inexperienced teenage boy wants from a very experienced woman."

CHAPTER TWO

THE AGREEMENT

DARBY AND MICHAEL SETTLED INTO A CABANA NESTLED in a grove of palm trees a ways back from the ocean. Angled toward one another on terry-topped cushions, they had a view of moonlit water and clear night skies. Conversation was easy, as if they'd known each other for years, instead of merely knowing *about* each other for years.

As they meandered from topic to topic, the things Ben had told her about Michael came back to mind, leaving Darby fairly certain that Michael was understating his accomplishments. She vaguely recalled that he was a math prodigy and had received some sort of important service award from the White House, but Michael mentioned none of this, talking instead about humble beginnings on the South Side and a love for architecture that stemmed from his love of art.

He was deeply involved in charitable work and tried to attend as many of Chicago's summer food and music festivals as he could. He ran along the same stretch of Lake Shore Drive that Darby did when the weather was nice. How might he look as his torso twisted to and fro and his legs worked to propel him forward? His upper body bare, revealing a sheen of sweat…

"Where have you visited?" she asked, after he mentioned taking weekend hops to neighboring countries whenever he worked from his firm's international offices. He was a good storyteller, and she was starting to like his smile.

"From Australia, I've done New Zealand, Singapore, and Fiji… From Japan, I've done Taiwan and Vietnam. We have an Amsterdam office. I could've seen all of Europe by now, but I keep going back to Paris."

"Alone?" It was her favorite city, but so unapologetically romantic that Darby couldn't imagine going by herself.

Only after the words had spilled from her lips did she realize how much it might have sounded like a come-on. Given her current aversion to dating, it shouldn't have mattered whether he traveled alone or not.

He shrugged. "It Is what it is. Even without all the traveling, the seventy-hour work week's pretty much killed my chances of anything serious."

His words rang so true that she could have been the one saying them. "Amen to that."

He raised an eyebrow. "You, too?"

"My schedule's a beast," she commiserated. "Night shifts. Weekends. Research on top of my shifts. And it changes every week."

His smile was self-deprecating. "My sister keeps telling me to get a girlfriend. Or a boyfriend. I'm pretty sure she'd be happy with a mail-order bride by now."

"So what do you do…for company?"

For the first time, he hesitated.

She lifted her hands in a peaceful gesture. "I don't mean to pry. Really, I'm asking because I could use some advice myself."

"That would be like the blind leading the blind. You could

probably give *me* some pointers."

She nearly snorted. "Don't take advice from me. I'm days away from paying for it."

"And here I thought you were a nice girl," he kidded.

"Come on, Michael, we both know nice girls finish last."

He cocked his head and narrowed his eyes in disbelief. "You mean to tell me the good doctor doesn't get what she wants? Somehow I find that hard to believe."

"I can assure you, the woman-of-fortune-and-fame fantasy is much sexier than the reality."

"So's the one about the most eligible bachelor."

"Touché." The quickening breeze had blown her hair across her face, and she smoothed it back. "So what do you want that you can't have?"

"Companionship." He said it as if the answer were obvious.

Darby quelled her temptation to dismiss the sentiment, however improbable it sounded. "I'll bet you could find that if you wanted it. You recruited me easily enough."

Something in his gaze sobered. "You want the truth?"

"I always want the truth."

Trepidation crossed his face. He took a breath before he spoke again. "The truth is, I like you. I think you're the kind of girl I'd like to have dinner with and take to social functions. I think we'd have more good conversation, some fun times, and sizzling hot sex."

He paused long enough to measure her reaction. In the dark, he wouldn't have been able to see the goosebumps that prickled her flesh.

"I'd give a lot for a real shot at an uncomplicated relationship with an interesting, worldly woman. But I don't need to start something with you to know how it'll end. Not for lack of trying, I've stopped wanting what I can't have and dating women who want what I can't give. Sooner or later, smart women always want it all."

Darby let out a measured breath. "Wow, that's…" *Presumptuous*, she wanted to say. Instead she settled on, "Perplexing."

"It's not, Darby." His tone was disarming. "It's what happens when you're a thirty-year-old guy who doesn't want a twenty-year-old girl. Women our age want more. It's a biological instinct."

The tops of her cheeks grew hot, and her eyebrows rose. "Says the man who commiserated with me over my friend asking when I would find a husband."

But the repentant look she expected from having placed his foot solidly in his mouth never crossed his face. "Look," he began. "I get that not all women want huge diamond rings or white picket fences. But just because I know that projecting those expectations on people is wrong doesn't mean I think women want to be alone."

"And men do?"

"No. But companionship looks different to men than it does to women."

Darby shook her head and looked out toward the water. He wasn't entirely wrong, but he wasn't right, either. The assertion that wanting unattached companionship was a guy thing was ludicrous. "I know my share of women who are obsessed with getting a man to commit," she admitted.

"But?"

She swung her gaze back to his face. He smiled cautiously, seeming to sense an unfavorable reaction.

"But your view of women is short-sighted." *And borderline sexist.* She bit her tongue again. "Biological clocks and maternal instincts aren't something all women have. If you think there aren't plenty of single women who want to stay that way, you're sorely mistaken. My parents' marriage was a disaster. The career I love has me working just as many hours as you do, probably more. The last thing I need is to come home after a hard day to a man who's biologically incapable of not needing his ego stroked."

The widening of his eyes and subtle slacking of his jaw showed he was without retort.

Darby went on, bent on driving home her point. "And because *I* can't find a man who wants nothing more than to give me four toe curling orgasms twice a week and then get the hell out of my house..." She trailed off.

His Adam's apple bobbed. What other reactions had her words caused? His silence felt like victory, and she pulled the champagne bottle from his loosened grip to pour them what was left. It took him a moment to remember to hold up his glass.

Mic drop.

"Do you honestly expect me to believe that you can't find a guy who only wants to have sex with you?" he finally recovered. "Because I don't believe that." His voice had turned low, nearly husky. It wiped out any doubt that the attraction was mutual.

"I expect you to believe girls like me have only two options: one-night-stands and Romeos. I don't do one-night stands because the world is full of psychopaths who like doing bad things to pretty girls. And I stay away from Romeos because I find it insulting to watch someone go through the pomp and circumstance of 'dating' me because he thinks that's what it'll take for me to sleep with him."

By the time she finished, his eyebrows had knit into his first frown of the evening. Men could be fragile, especially the better-looking ones. What emotion had she triggered?

"So, paint me a picture," he said, "of someone who's different." His voice had that huskiness again. It made her body hum with the awareness of how quickly they were leaving the realm of the hypothetical.

"How would that someone come into your life?" he prodded when she didn't answer.

"It's complicated." Her gaze wandered to the water again. For Darby, there could be no innocent flirtations, no absent-minded affairs, no tawdry trysts. Her father was a public figure, and she had her own respectable career to protect. She wasn't like other women her age who could take to Tinder when they wanted a good time.

"I like complex things." His breath near her ear caused a tingle that morphed into a chill that traveled down the back of her neck.

"He couldn't be a complete stranger." Hearing the words issue from her lips felt strange, as if she were creating a different persona. As if she were pretending some alternative to her reality could exist. "I'd have to know that I could trust him. And the attraction would have to be real." Darby swallowed thickly.

"What else?"

His voice was gentle patience, but for a note of something bold—something that dared her to claim this fantasy that she didn't believe could exist.

"He'd respect me enough to be honest about our arrangement and respect himself enough to be mature, conscientious, and discreet." It took focus to calm her voice lest it betray her vulnerability. "And I, uh…wasn't kidding about the orgasms, either. They need to be toe-curling, and there'd need to be at least four, every time we…"

He closed his eyes for a moment, too long for it to be a blink.

"What about you?" she said finally. "If you could find a woman who was different, how would things be?"

He took his time to answer, shifting his gaze to some far point before turning back with a look of halting intensity. His deep-blue eyes reserved an ocean of secrets. It only made him more intriguing. As a psychiatrist it was her job to read people, but she couldn't read him fully.

"I want a woman who doesn't confuse me loving her company with me being *in* love with her. She has to know that whatever we have today may not be there tomorrow, not because I'm incapable of intimacy—because I choose my career.

"She'd have to be prepared for the fact that what we share won't feel transactional. It will feel intimate and intense, because I only spend time with women I genuinely like and because I take pride in doing things well. She needs to know that me showing her respect and making her feel worshipped has nothing to do with her being more special to me than a good friend and everything to do with my idea of how a woman deserves to be treated."

He let the hand that held his half-full champagne flute fall to the cushion next to him and turned his body more fully toward hers. "She'd have to understand that each of us is responsible to the other to break things off the second things get too complicated. And she has to be prepared for the inevitable. Because the end *will* come. Even if it doesn't get complicated, I'll make partner one day, or get transferred halfway around the world."

She kept her face mostly neutral even as her heartbeat quickened. She could never help vacillating between regular-girl Darby and Dr. Darby, clinically trained psychiatrist, deconstructor of everyone's problems. That line, no matter how often she tried to draw it, was made of disappearing ink. "I think I understand."

He looked cautious again.

"You're honest with the women you date, but they don't act on what you say—they act on how you make them feel. You said that being with you feels intense. A woman who believes that a man has intense feelings for her has been programmed to believe that he'll initially resist commitment but that commitment is inevitable if the feelings are real. For them, the feelings and the commitment are mutually exclusive. But for you…"

"They're not."

"Which makes you the love 'em and leave 'em jerk who breaks their hearts."

He let out a humorless laugh. "Pretty much."

She considered her glass pensively but sensed him looking at her. It was another minute before she spoke. "There was this guy…" she began, still looking out toward the horizon. In the ten years since it had ended, she'd never told a soul the story of Dave. "We hung out one summer when I was interning in Manhattan. He was a real party guy—could get you into the VIP room at any club, or the hottest parties in the Hamptons, could get you any drug… He was like the king of New York, and he made me feel like the queen.

"It started to feel like a relationship. We went everywhere together. He showed me off to his friends. His mom even served me breakfast and chatted me up every morning when we spent weekends at his parents' place."

"Were you in love with him?" Michael asked.

She shook her head. "He was a lot of fun. And the sex was good…like, *really* good." She cast him a meaningful look. "I knew dating him for real would have been a disaster. But I still pursued him. It didn't matter that I was smart and independent and didn't subscribe to all the gender role bullshit—not consciously at least. I hated myself for chasing a guy I didn't even really want, but that backwards idea that getting a guy to commit is the ultimate goal was just too ingrained."

"So what happened?"

"I ruined it. By trying to turn it into something it wasn't. I ruined something really good."

"So you're not that kind of girl anymore?" he asked.

She shook her head again. "I kind of hate that girl now. That 'first comes love, then comes marriage' mentality is toxic. The best relationships define themselves."

Michael was quick to echo her thoughts. "You can't have it all. That's the biggest lie we tell ourselves. I can't be a dedicated architect, a doting partner, a loving father, a great brother, *and* a great uncle… So I've decided what I want, and what I can be good at. I'll let the other chips fall where they may."

They held hands all the way back up the beach, feet sinking into the sand as the foamy surf lapped at their ankles. Words seemed unnecessary—perhaps enough had been said. The look he had given her when he had taken her hand hadn't been gentlemanly. He'd run his fingertips from her elbow to her wrist before relieving her of the burden of carrying her own shoes. Before they'd set off, he'd arranged a windblown wisp of hair behind her ear and grazed her jaw with his knuckles, letting his eyes linger on her moonlit face.

When they separated at the steps to brush off sandy feet and put their shoes back on, Darby almost spoke, convinced she should say something before she lost her nerve. Instead, his arm came around her shoulders, the other sweeping her up behind her knees. She drew a breath as he began to carry her up the steps.

"You didn't think I was going to let you walk up a hundred steps in four-inch heels, did you?" The vibration of his words echoed through her chest. His body was solid beneath her. His fragrance was as complex as everything else about him. She leaned her head against his shoulder and reveled in it a little. Strong arms hadn't held her in a very long time.

They reached the top far too quickly, and she was sorry when he gently set her down. Before they fully untangled themselves from each other's arms, he leaned in for a soft but thorough kiss. His thumbs caressed her cheeks as his tongue massaged hers with such expertise that she knew instantly that he'd be incredible at certain other things.

"What if I promised you five?" He pulled away only long enough to ask the question and fix her with a hawkish gaze before leaning in for seconds. After he'd gently devoured her mouth once more, he asked, "Would you see me if I promised you five?"

"Lofty goal, don't you think?" she murmured against his chin, not waiting for an answer before capturing his lips once again.

"I'm an overachiever," he said darkly as he pulled back. "Six?" He nipped at her neck.

She might have laughed at his bravado if kissing him hadn't felt so good, if his voice had held any of the humor that should have accompanied such a ridiculous dare. The idea was laughable—six orgasms? Even the four she'd mentioned had been an exaggeration. Still, a stab of anticipatory pleasure tingled up her spine at the thought that he might just deliver.

"This ends at sunrise," she managed, still out of breath as she pulled away long enough to say the words.

"I thought you didn't do one-night stands."

"It's not a one-night stand. It's an interview."

CHAPTER THREE

THE INTERVIEW

THEY WASTED LITTLE TIME ARRIVING IN MICHAEL'S HOTEL suite, ridding each other of their clothes, and fusing their bodies together. His suit had concealed baby-smooth skin. Solid, well-defined muscles contradicted what had first seemed like a leaner build. A devastatingly beautiful tattoo of she-couldn't-tell-what covered the whole of his back and some of his shoulders. The room was dim, but she didn't need full light to see that he was well proportioned, everywhere.

That they had one condom between them did nothing to prevent him from making good on his promise. He gave her her first orgasm before they even reached the bed. He stood her before a dressing mirror, one arm that felt as strong as steel holding her torso in place as his erection strained hard against her back. He opened her up skillfully, lifting one of her legs off the ground and hitching it back to wrap around his, a clever finger stroking her clit as he held her tightly.

She hadn't been with anyone in months, had known it wouldn't take much. But the image of herself spread wide open as he slowly stroked her slippery wetness, and his feline eyes watching their reflection, undid her. She came quickly, her head falling backwards on his shoulder.

As she caught her breath, she expected him to help her down, to disentangle her leg from his. But he kept her where she was, and the next thing she knew, his fingers were sweeping her long hair over one shoulder.

At first, his gentle touch on her neck simply felt nice, somewhat light and maybe even a bit tender. It was when his finger-strokes turned to kisses and kisses into nips that she began to feel it in other places. From the tips of her nipples, right down through her spine and to her core, his touch electrified her. He wasn't even touching her *there* yet, but she felt the second orgasm coming just around the bend.

Craving more, she tilted her head to give him better access. Hearing her own escalating sighs only turned her on more. When Michael began to hum in satisfaction with every delicious bite, she knew she was close.

She said his name, a plea for him to give her what she needed, and grasped the back of his head, wanted to hold onto something as the heel of his hand started moving back down. He slid a long finger inside her as he devoured her neck, his other fingers loosening their hold long enough to pinch her nipple, and that was all it took for her to come again.

They finally made it to his bed, but she ignored his outstretched hand, an invitation to join him in lying down. Instead, she straddled him, her bottom resting on his thighs. His erection stood long and thick, and even though she had just come twice, her pussy twitched at the thought of how good it would hurt to have him inside her.

But she wanted to return the favor, to repay his seduction with something equally impressive. Maybe it was her competitive nature, but she needed to undo him the way he had undone her. She touched him lightly, watching his face as her fingers roamed. Michael was at once controlled and expressive as her nails grazed lightly up his shaft. Her fingertips stroked his balls as her fist tugged gently at his head. She could tell from his breath which of her ministrations he liked, but his face didn't reveal which ones he liked the most. She wasn't so much trying to tease him as she was trying to learn him. A man's willingness to accept pleasure he couldn't control said a lot.

Lowering her nose to his belly button, she grazed against him all the way up to one of his nipples before tugging on it with her teeth, earning her a flex of his hips and a low moan. His eyes fell shut in grateful anticipation. So many men were all fuck, no foreplay, but something about the way he writhed beneath her and the small sounds he made showed that he needed this, that a slow burn brought him some deep satisfaction.

Darby was positioning herself right over him when his hand reached toward the nightstand, for the condom, but she drew his arm back. Instead, she settled her center right over his shaft, steering clear of his head, and slid up and down, spreading her wetness all over him. She lowered herself so that the tips of her nipples tickled his chest as she moved. Her mind flashed to the Vinyasa yoga class she took when it was too cold to run the lake, to all the Chaturangas that had prepared her for this moment.

On anyone smaller, this wouldn't have worked, but Michael was impressively long. And since she was still so wet, she had plenty to give him, and gave it to him painfully slow.

"God, that's hot," he breathed, maybe at the combination of things she was doing, maybe because he anticipated what she had in mind. On her last pass, she slid herself over his head before returning to sit on his thighs and beginning to thoroughly lube him up for the hand job that was to come.

Her thumb swept at his tip to make use of his precum, which she mixed with her own juices before working him up and down, with not one hand, but two. He was exquisite in every beautiful change in his face, every thrust of his hips, the flexing of his corded forearm muscles as his hands gripped the sheets of the bed.

And then it happened. Unfiltered ecstasy. She'd heard it building in his breath and felt it in the connection his hands sought out on her hips the moment before he came. It was honest and raw, and he looked her right in the eyes instead of closing his or looking away. Everything inside her tightened at the sound he made when he came, a helpless moan and a shudder that she felt all the way down to her toes.

In the hours that followed, they rolled smoothly between those moments of raw, intense pleasure and stretches of languid recovery. He took his time touching every inch of her body, learning it with his fingers and his nose and his mouth. He kissed her for what felt like hours. When the heat between them flared too high, he gave her even more. His mouth eating her pussy gave her number three. His long finger inside her stroking her g-spot as his thumb massaged her clit gave her number four. Five had been a sublime combination of both.

"Holy shit." She was breathless, the hint of an incredulous smile on her lips as she angled her head lazily back down toward him. Her long-neglected pussy felt thoroughly sated, and she fought the impulse to thank him. But the look he gave her as he rose onto his knees, wiping his mouth with the back of his hand, was just short of predatory. Five times he'd taken her to her happy place. But looking down at his cock reminded her that she'd left him in a different place entirely, straining harder than before, his tip glistening.

The smile disappeared from her face. He had more than

earned what was coming. "Don't be gentle."

She saw the exact moment his restraint broke. He was still rolling the Magnum on with one hand when he used the other one to roll her over. And he *wasn't* gentle about it, not when he pushed her legs open and pulled her up on her knees, not when he drove inside her in a single hard stroke. The strained growl that emanated from him the second he was sheathed inside her wasn't gentle, and the way he started fucking her wasn't either.

Riding her hard, he laid her out over and over, plying her body to achieve positions that opened her completely. But it wasn't mindless fucking. What she had expected—maybe even hoped for—was that he would use her body, selfishly seeking his own release. But he was with her somehow, really *with* her, in every stroke and every breath. The illusion of deep connection was terrifying and gratifying all at once.

The rhythm that overtook them was primal. Desperate and right. It made her do things she had never—not once—had the impulse to do. She bit his shoulder as he fucked her against the wall, his pelvis grinding her clit; next, she licked salty sweat off of his clavicle. And when she clenched powerfully around him, the sensation making him feel even bigger inside her, she screamed. He moaned loudly, seeming to be pushed over the edge by her display, gasping deeply before letting out a final long, deep, wobbly moan. He held her still for a long moment as they caught their breath, foreheads leaning against one another as they waited for the last of stray pulses and twitches to subside.

He was still inside her a minute later when he pulled back far enough to let his gaze meet hers. He smoothed her hair back and gave her a long, reverent kiss. She felt a sense of loss when he eased her off of him and set her down on the bed.

She closed her eyes as he walked away, then heard water running in the bathroom. She now understood better what he had said on the beach. It *hadn't* felt transactional. Though it had been fucking—shameless and wanton and between two virtual strangers—it had also felt deeply personal, as if he had unlocked some secret, treasured place within her and shared some piece of himself that nobody else knew. She understood now why women fell in love with him. When it came to sexual charisma, he was a natural.

She was seconds away from getting up from the bed, locating her clothes, asking him to zip her back into her dress, and bidding him goodbye—a goodbye that would include her leaving him her number because there was no way she would turn down a repeat performance of sex as good as that.

The bed dipped, and a warm washcloth pressed between her legs, startling her. Her eyes flew open to find Michael hovering over her on one knee, looking down to where he had cupped her and begun to clean her gently. Once he'd finished, he met her eyes and smiled. Only then did she notice the other washcloth in his hand.

Setting hers down on the bedside table, he stood up and focused on cleaning himself. When he rearranged the disheveled covers, climbed into bed, and tucked her under his arm, she abandoned thoughts of leaving. He fell asleep quickly, and though Darby was tired, her mind felt full, and she was slow to rest. The sun had already begun to rise before she drifted off to sleep.

She awoke to the regretful realization that she had to leave right away if she wanted to catch her flight. Torn between wanting to avoid a potentially awkward conversation and wanting to see his stunning eyes one last time, she decided that she didn't have the heart to wake him. So she left a note on the nightstand, jotting down her phone number on the hotel stationary, along with two simple words: *You're hired.*

CHAPTER FOUR

THE HOSPITAL

TWO DAYS LATER, DARBY'S WISH CAME TRUE WHEN SHE received a text from an unfamiliar number. She paused at a nurse's station, delaying her journey to a staff meeting she wasn't excited about anyway, to read it a second time.

Would you like to attend the Frigg Foundation Gala with me on Saturday night? If the main event is lacking, I'll make it up to you after...

She smiled coquettishly as she tapped out her reply. First, her address and then a note.

Let's hope the main event is lacking...

She was still smiling as she pocketed her phone, picked up her coffee and iPad, and continued to make her way down the hall. As hospitals went, Northwestern Memorial was clean and comfortable, with modern technology and upscale clientele. In the heart of downtown Chicago, it was a stone's throw from the Magnificent Mile and a short Uber ride to Delaware Avenue, where Darby had enjoyed many lunch hours spent shopping. But that wasn't why she had chosen it. Beyond her practice as a clinical physician, Northwestern was funding her research.

"Did you win something?" Rich asked as he fell into step with her.

"Kind of," she admitted, sipping her coffee to avoid flaunting her widening smile.

"I'm afraid to ask," he muttered. His accent made the word 'ask' sound more like 'aaaahsk'.

"You should be," she replied cryptically.

She didn't elaborate, content to maintain her air of mystery. So far as Rich knew, she could've been smiling about any number of work-related things. Darby had a reputation for shaking things up within the department and there had been drama lately around the future of their research fellowship, drama that might surface in the meeting they were about to attend.

"Ready for another episode of General Hospital?" she deadpanned.

She swiped her security badge before pushing open the double doors that allowed them to exit the patient wing. From there a walkway led them to the administrative building, where her boss was waiting.

Some days, she felt dangerously close to shoving a laryngoscope down Cesar Huck's throat to wipe the smug smile off his face—the man was a legendary jerk. Dr. Huck—and she wanted to gag every time she was forced to distinguish the unworthy man with that title—was everything a leader shouldn't be. He stood about 5' 6", which made him a solid four inches shorter than her and which came with the predictable Napoleonic complex. Posturing as the alpha typically manifested as thinly veiled misogyny with women and assertion of his positional domination over the men. This was a man who rarely spoke to Darby without being patronizing, not that he ever tried. And his ego was both so big, and so fragile that his resulting theatrics made her feel like a character in a telenovela.

"Nine months, Darby. You can survive the next nine months," Rich reassured her. Everyone expected Dr. Huck to be promoted to the hospital's next Chief of Staff, which would free her from the prison of his direct supervision.

"The question is, will *he* survive the next nine months?" Her face sobered, genuine hostility creeping into her voice.

"You've been putting up with his shenanigans for this long," Rich pointed out, referring to the four years they'd been in the hospital together.

Rich had been a godsend those past years, sympathetic when she wanted a shoulder to cry on, the voice of reason when she needed someone to talk sense into her, and a steadfast ally who was always in her corner. He was tall—north of six feet but not towering or gangly—his pale features were regal and handsome, precisely as one would imagine any highborn Brit's to be.

She'd nursed an innocent crush on him the first six months they'd worked together, which hadn't mattered because he'd been blissfully engaged. After growing up with a philandering father, Darby didn't approve of women who pursued unavailable men. Rich was the kind of guy she would have fallen for when she'd been naïve enough to think that she could juggle ambitions as lofty as hers with a relationship. After he got married, she'd lost interest completely.

And she was glad that she had. Relationships among hospital colleagues rarely survived. And it would be a shame if they'd turned out to be a failed relationship statistic rather than solid friends. Rich was an amazing young neurologist, and Darby was a well-respected psychopharmacologist, and their friendship had expanded into a business partnership as well. He was currently consulting on her research fellowship and they spent a lot of hours together. Any romance between them would only have complicated that.

Darby relied on Rich to provide her balance at work. He was practical and level-headed, whereas she could be audacious and insubordinate. And she needed all the help she could get when it came to Huck, who became more vicious every day.

"It's getting worse," she lamented aloud. She paused to look at Rich before they entered the conference room.

"I know."

"Glad you could join us, Dr. Christensen." She wasn't late for the meeting, but Huck's dismissive tone implied otherwise, and she didn't miss the fact that Rich's name hadn't been mentioned alongside hers. Huck said nothing to the remaining three doctors who arrived shortly after them. She wasn't surprised that his passive-aggressive digs had started before the meeting was even underway.

In the same moment she and Rich shared a knowing look about what had just happened, Huck started the meeting. He was the kind of man who loved to dominate a conversation. He rarely invited discussion or new ideas. Even when he gave up the floor, Huck barely let anyone get a word in edgewise. As soon as she saw that their research project was slated to be covered late in the agenda, Darby took her cue to tune out and think about whatever else was on her mind. Huck had already wasted ten minutes into a topic that wasn't even on the schedule. They'd never even make it that far.

One of Darby's many talents was to appear as if she were paying attention to Huck's insufferable monologues. Sometimes she even pretended to take notes while he was talking. When she was tired, her "notes" were her grocery list, but when she was sharp, she mapped out grand plans and thought through approaches to her research. She'd had some of her best ideas daydreaming in these inane meetings. Today, she wrote out mock interview questions she would drill herself on for Friday, when she would go before the grant review board once again.

The truth was, Darby could set up her own research institute to study opioid addiction if she really wanted to. She could think of no better use of her inheritance than to honor her mother's memory. Her egomaniacal boss's neglect of the work she was doing sometimes made her want to take matters into her own hands. But Darby knew that if she took her research to an institute she herself had funded, that act alone would give way to vicious gossip about the validity of her results.

No, she knew. She needed to prove that her research held merit, to win competitive funding from important institutions that believed in her work. She needed other people to be excited about it—for other people to associate themselves with it, and to stand by her results. She'd been careful to avoid any accusations of favoritism. She'd stopped donating to the hospital since she'd landed her job and had urged her father to do the same. She couldn't have it look as if anything was handed to her because of her family's status.

By Thursday, she found herself at Nordstrom, tucked several floors above Michigan Avenue with a personal shopper in a private dressing suite. When she wasn't wearing scrubs around the hospital or warm pajamas around the house, Darby was a bit of a clotheshorse. Maybe it was all those years of private school uniforms, of being dressed by someone hell-bent on having her look appropriately conservative at official events, that made expressing her own style such a thrill.

She rarely dwelled on her looks, but she knew she was considered to be quite beautiful apart from her taller, size six frame. Her long hair was thick, shiny, and fell naturally in soft waves to the middle of her back. Its color, a dark reddish-brown that brightened in sunlight, contrasted eyes on the lighter side of amber that seemed to do the same. Yet it was her face—ovular with high cheekbones, and perfectly symmetrical—that imitated her mother's beauty. Darby liked looking at pictures of her mother when she was Darby's age. Everyone who had known her said it, and Darby saw it as well—the two of them could have been twins.

The navy suit she'd chosen for the grant review board was every bit as chic as you would expect from a sophisticated young doctor, but the blouse she'd chosen had a little bit of flair. The bright green border accents on the collar of the white silk garment were utterly tasteful but also a bit bold.

"Anything else, my dear?" asked Iris, her favorite stylist.

Iris had been there for as long as Darby could remember. She knew how every designer cut his clothes, knew which fashion trends to jump on from which ones to avoid, knew every garment in the store, and worked miracles to deliver anything they had to special order.

"When was the last time we looked at gowns?" Saturday's date with Michael had been at the forefront of her mind. Thinking about seeing him gave her a little thrill. Every moment she hadn't been immersed in work that week, she'd been preoccupied with thoughts of him.

"I remember you bought three," Iris began, referring to Darby's pre-season shopping spree. The woman had freakish recall. "A print by one of the new designers, the green Valentino, and something red."

Darby had worn the Valentino to Ben's wedding.

"So nothing I could wear to the Frigg Foundation Gala?"

"Not even close." Iris's response was typically blunt. "This year's theme is Gatsby, so we'll have to go with beads and sequins. I've been dressing women for it all week. Give me a minute—I may have just the thing."

Five minutes later, Iris was helping her into a stunning Monique Lhuillier. It was sheer gray chiffon underneath, yet covered in so many elaborately-embroidered silver beads that the entire dress seemed to shimmer in resplendent Art Deco style. Darby's breasts were just small enough to pull off the plunging V-neckline without seeming as if the look she was going for was sexy. The dress was cut across the bias, with a small train that mimicked the even steeper plunge in the back.

"I tried this on somebody else yesterday, but she didn't buy it," Iris said with soft sincerity as she zipped Darby up. "I'm glad she didn't—it looks much better on you."

Darby gazed at herself under fitting room light, which she suspected was deliberately flattering. It seemed to make her glow as she stood upon the platform. She watched as Iris silently fixed a bejeweled cuff bracelet around her wrist, another Art Deco piece, and pressed what looked like pale sapphire teardrop earrings into her hand. Sometimes cool colors like grays and blues were tricky to pair with Darby's warm tones, but Iris always got the hues just right.

"I'll take it all," she said, hoping that what she saw in the mirror would have the desired effect on Michael.

She hadn't heard from him again that week, not that she'd expected to, and she already liked how easy and casual it all felt. If they could really pull it off—repeat performances of sex that steamy without complications—it would be a phenomenal match.

Darby's last affair with a television producer named Felix

had ended so badly that it had been the catalyst for her to swear off dating altogether. But this thing with Michael wouldn't be *dating*. It would be moving the dreaded pressures and protocols of carrying on a relationship out of the way. It would be taking it all off at the end of the night and getting on with her real life the following morning.

CHAPTER FIVE

THE GALA

Two days later, Darby was putting in her last sapphire earring when she heard the doorbell ring. She inspected herself one last time in the stylish floor-to-ceiling mirror and smiled at what she saw. Darby adored her massive closet. It had once been a guest bedroom, but she'd converted it. Picking up the bejeweled sandals that sat in their place on one of her lighted pull-out shoe shelves, she bent to slip them on. She gave herself one final look before turning to answer the door.

Darby's cozy little brownstone suited her perfectly. It was situated in the middle of a quiet street on the Gold Coast a few blocks back from the water and walking distance to the Lincoln Park Zoo. It was a far cry from the ostentatious Evanston mansion she'd grown up in, which had been no place for a child. In place of the Fabergé eggs and Waterford crystal, Darby had chosen more practical themes. Bamboo floors and neutral creams were the base motif for every single room. Yet the lamps, rugs, pillows and other accent pieces in each room splashed teals, chartreuses and other bold colors. Comfortable furniture throughout gave her space the feel of a lounge.

Though most of the rooms felt finished, it nagged her that the space above her fireplace mantel was conspicuously empty. She saved her movie-watching for the living room, and felt it would have been a bit of a cop-out to install a TV where she slept. She glanced at the empty spot for a moment as she walked back out of her closet to descend the stairs. It had been half a minute since he had rung and she needed to answer the door.

Michael's enchanting blue eyes sparkled more brilliantly than her sapphires when she opened the heavy door to him. For a pregnant moment, he was silent. He didn't compliment her dress or kiss her hand or make any other debonair gesture. Yet, as he leaned comfortably against the frame, his eyes shadowed sultry remembrance of what had transpired the week before.

"Hi." His smile was roguish.

"Hi." They held each other's gaze for another long moment before he finally took the rest of her in.

"You'll be the belle of the ball."

"I think we'll both turn some heads." It was hard not to notice how well he wore his tuxedo. At the wedding, he'd rocked his suit pretty hard, but Michael's elegance in white tie could have rivaled Robert Redford as Gatsby himself.

"Is it too soon to bail?" Her eyes lingered on his body for a moment longer than she intended before returning to meet his gaze.

"The night is young," he rejoined, though she thought she heard a twinge of disappointment. "Besides, it's time for *your* interview."

"I should've known." She liked their game. "What am I being evaluated on?"

"Apart from making me look as unavailable as possible?"

"How could I forget? There will be cougars on the prowl. If anyone grabs your goods on my watch, I won't expect an offer."

Straight teeth peeked through an amused smile.

"I also need you to be my wing woman. Standard stuff—rescuing me from boring conversations, charming donors with deep pockets who like pretty girls, which is most of them. I'll charm the ones who like pretty boys," he added cheekily.

"Fundraising. Check." She nodded.

"It won't be as fun as the sex." He said it apologetically, as if he were afraid she would be tempted to bail on this part of the arrangement.

"I'm a politician's daughter. I can do this in my sleep," she reassured him. "And didn't you say that if the main event was boring you'd make it up to me later?"

"I did. And I will." His voice was deliciously low as he offered her his arm.

From the small table just inside her door, she grabbed her silver sequined clutch and her mother's white fur stole, and shut the door behind her. Michael ushered her to his car—a dark gray Maserati that suited him somehow—and tucked her safely inside. She hadn't noticed until after he closed her door that in place of formal shoes, he wore black and white Converse All-Stars. This detail made her smile.

She watched him discreetly for several minutes as they sped down city streets. From the reverence with which he handled his car, and the obvious enjoyment with which he drove it, she got the sense that he was not just another handsome boy with an expensive plaything—he had a gentle way of handling anything he touched, and seemed like the kind of person who treasured his possessions.

Yes, Darby realized. There was something different about

Michael. Already, she had a tender curiosity about him. She was already looking forward to spending the evening together.

"What?" When he asked, she knew she had been caught watching him.

"The way you're touching your car…I think I'm getting a bit jealous."

The corner of his lip quirked up. "I thought we said no jealousy."

"We agreed that our jobs came first, but we never actually agreed on rules," she pointed out.

"Should we?" He shifted gears and glanced over at her as they turned south onto Lake Shore Drive.

"Maybe there's only one…" she mused. "No hard feelings about competing priorities."

"Is that enough for you?"

She thought back to how inflamed she'd been at his comment about women being biologically incapable of not wanting commitment.

"Still think you're going to break my heart?" Darby teased.

"Maybe I'm worried you'll break mine." His mouth widened into an even fuller smile.

He smiled a lot. Working in medicine meant Darby was often surrounded by illness and despair. She appreciated that Michael seemed happy, albeit a bit intense.

"How about this? We promise each other that when it ends, it ends in a single word—whether that be tonight or a year from now. No awkward confrontation. No messy breakup talk. That's the shitty part anyway, right? We agree to keep it fun and simple. And, when it stops being fun, or stops being simple, it's over."

"Sounds sensible." There was hesitation in his voice.

"But?"

He seemed to think about it, as if deconstructing the idea in is mind.

"No, you're right," he said finally after he had worked out whatever was holding him back. "So what's our code word?"

"Lotus."

He looked offended. "What if we're talking about cars?"

"Skittles," she offered, her eyes falling to the red packet of candies she had noticed sitting in the cup holder on his center console.

"I use that word too much in everyday conversation."

He sounded completely serious.

"Broadway," she blurted as her eye caught a billboard for a musical.

He smiled as he looked over at her. "I love show tunes too much."

That earned him a laugh.

"Alright, smart ass—what do *you* think it should be?

He was quiet for a moment as the smile faded from his face.

"Snapdragon." His voice was quiet as he said it. She had no idea what had made him come up with that word, but she liked it.

"Snapdragon, then," she repeated, just as he stopped at a red light and looked over to meet her gaze.

Darby hadn't been lying earlier. As a senator's daughter, she had attended events like this all her life. She would not have been surprised to find her father himself lurking someplace. But they were always on the outs and she hoped not to run into him that night. Michael, too, seemed at ease in this environment. Both of them were well-acquainted with a number of partygoers, so much so that she wondered how they had never crossed paths before.

"So you fundraise for the foundation?" She asked when they had a moment to themselves back at their table. The mingling had dulled after the first two courses were served. They'd set down dessert and she was now enjoying watching Michael's lips melt into a tiny smile every time he slipped a mini fruit tart in his mouth.

"My tenure as fundraising chair ended last year, but I'm still on the Board. I have relationships with most major donors, so it's always a good idea for me to show my face."

And a beautiful face it was. At the wedding, she'd mainly seen him in dim light. But, fully-lit, he was splendid. He possessed a striking combination of undeniable masculinity and delicate beauty. His strong jaw juxtaposed full, kissable lips, a heavy brow and hooded eyes as blue as deep ocean waters. Light stubble shadowed skin that was otherwise baby-smooth—a fact she remembered from the week before.

"I didn't know you had such a tangible connection to all this, "Darby said.

"You thought I came for the hors d'oeuvres and free booze?"

"$5,000 a plate isn't free."

He fixed her with a pointed look. "Nothing in this world is free."

She noticed once again how even his most casual words never seemed off-handed; they always seemed to convey an absolute truth.

"I give to the foundation every year," she offered.

"I know you do. And not a small amount. But you save the majority of your giving for the arts. I hear they want to name a gallery after your family at The Art Institute, but you won't let them."

Something inside her hardened a bit at his comment. It must have shown on her face.

"Chicago's a small town, Darby. Everyone in philanthropy knows where the big families give."

She took a long sip of her drink, swallowing down the reminder of how little privacy she had. She didn't mind that Michael knew, but she did resent that so much of her business was spread through the grapevine, and freely shared for public consumption.

"It only seems right that I use the money my mother left me to support causes that she loved. The Art Institute was her favorite museum."

"But not one of yours, I take it. I've never seen you at any of their events."

If he knew whether or not she attended events, that had to mean he supported the museum as well.

"Actually, I love it there. It's just…been hard to go since she died."

Realization dawned in his eyes.

"I know a thing or two about that." As he said it, some of his intensity softened.

"What else do you know about me?" She was eager to change the subject and curious about what else he had heard.

"Not nearly enough."

"So you're saying you want to know more?" she flirted.

He leaned in closer, his voice lowering as he said the words.

"I told you before. I like complex things."

Before she could respond, he stood and held his hand out, beckoning her to join him for a dance. She couldn't remember the last time she had accepted an offer to dance with someone. As they swayed together, it was hard not to notice that everyone around them was watching them with interest—even more interest than Darby was accustomed to. She couldn't remember hearing his name mentioned in her Chicago society circles. But it was becoming clear that Michael was an object of attention all on his own.

"Did you recognize me? At Ben's wedding?"

"Not until you told me your name. When you did, I pieced together your connection to the senator and to the foundation, but by then I was already interested."

"I thought you said you'd given up on women..." she challenged lightly as they moved to the song.

"Given up hope on dating, yes. Stopped being attracted to fascinating women?" He shook his head. "I didn't think anything would happen between us when we first met, but I fully planned to enjoy our time together."

"How very Buddhist of you..."

"I don't take Buddhist practice literally, but I identify with its principles," he rejoined unexpectedly. "I try to be present in the moment—to enjoy what's right in front of me. Right now, I'm enjoying the smell of your hair and your breath on my cheek and the way you feel when we're dancing this close. I'm not thinking of what happened earlier today, or what will happen tomorrow."

"Be here now," Darby smiled, thinking of the name of a book she'd once read.

Trying to piece together his psychology, as she was doomed to do with nearly everyone she met, she recognized the consistencies between what he said now and the man she had met the week before. Michael had mastered the art of paying rapt attention to whatever was in front of him. It made it difficult for women to reconcile feeling so close to him in certain moments yet so unimportant to him in others. Of course his relationships had failed. It wasn't only that he didn't have time to commit—it was the confusion he must have caused.

If she was right about him, he was someone who experienced his life in a way in which he could achieve extraordinary connection and pleasure. But he had learned to do so without attachment. It explained why sex with him had felt so gratifying. Whereas most people held back parts of themselves, guarding them for a select few, Michael surrendered, giving more than expected. There was something so beautiful—so extraordinary—about it. But most people weren't ready for that. His relationships had failed because of his honesty, not in spite of it.

It also snapped the comment he'd made when they first met about how he was looking for companionship into clearer focus. It made sense that he wasn't just in it for the sex—he enjoyed people. But relationships—even friendships—came with rules; people like Michael, who defied convention, could find themselves left behind. She felt comfort in the notion that she was figuring him out. Understanding his motives helped to quiet the nagging inner voice, which cautioned her that casual sex with a stranger—even a close friend of Ben's—was risky.

He'd picked up on her wandering thoughts. "Are *you* here now?" His voice was neutral, more curious than accusatory.

"Just deconstructing your psychological profile. It comes with the territory of befriending a shrink, I'm afraid. But don't worry—I never tell people how fucked up they are unless they ask."

She enjoyed the sound of his responding laugh. They were so close now that the vibrations from his chest echoed pleasantly within her.

"I've been told how fucked up I am, believe me. My sister is a social worker. If she found out what you and I are doing, I'd never live it down."

"That brings up a good question." It was her cue to mention something that had been on her mind. "What do we tell everyone else?"

"Do we have to tell anyone else anything?" It was the first time something about him seemed naïve.

"You might find that being seen with the daughter of a controversial Senator will invite unwanted attention. It won't be as fun as the sex." She repeated Michael's phrase with the same apologetic tone he had used, worried that he hadn't considered this downside to their arrangement.

"I see them looking. We'll be in the society pages by tomorrow. It'll be the gossip pages by the end of the month." He said it more casually than she could comprehend.

"They'll want to know whether we're dating."

"If we're seen out together enough times, denying it would make no difference."

She'd been so focused on sizing up Michael and reveling in the memory of their hot sex that she'd barely thought about the rest. "Companionship" meant that this gala was the first of dozens of events she might attend with him. Privately, she'd signed up for a booty call and a hangout buddy. Publicly, it would seem as if she had a boyfriend.

She must have looked as distressed as she felt, because his dancing slowed, and he leaned in to speak discreetly into her ear.

"I like going out, Darby. I like dancing with you right now. I like treating you like a lady and feeling like a man. I'm tired of turning down invitations to parties that could be a good time if I only had someone fun to go with. I'm sick of eating alone."

He paused for a moment, and when he spoke again, regret laced his voice.

"People *will* talk. And I didn't think through what that would mean for you, being Frank Christensen's daughter. If all that comes with it is more than you signed up for, I understand. But it's your life. And pardon the unsolicited advice, but I think you should live it the way you want to."

The sensible words she'd been ready to say in defense of damage control died on her tongue. She was having a better time with him than she had ever had at any other charity gala. And she knew she'd have an even *better* time at the end of the night. That was what she'd been in it for, at first—her "give me four orgasms and get the fuck out". But hadn't she enjoyed dress shopping and having some place to go? Didn't she love dancing with him and being on his arm? Hadn't her mind drifted three or four times to what it had felt like to be carried bridal-style up those steps on that cliff? Didn't she deserve a little romance?

"I'd be home watching a movie." Her voice was weaker than it had been a minute before. She didn't know why she was admitting this to him. "If I wasn't out with you right now, I'd be at home with takeout from Boka, a bottle of wine, and I'd be watching a movie. Alone."

Upon hearing her confession, he held her more tightly, yet more softly somehow.

"This is better," she concluded quietly. In that moment, she comprehended something she realized that Michael had known implicitly: not having to be lonely was the cake. The sex was just the icing.

The song was ending and Michael leaned back to peer into her eyes, that penetrating gaze making her feel as if he could see right through her.

"I don't care what those people think. Do you?" His voice was even softer now.

The truth was, she didn't. But she had spent a long time

being conditioned to feel that she should.

"No." Her voice rang with a sincerity that felt like relief.

"Do you care about this, right here, right now, just me and you?"

Afraid of how her voice would sound if she spoke an answer, she nodded her head.

"Good. Because that's what I care about right now. I want to keep looking at you in that gorgeous dress, and hear that sharp wit of yours, and think about the sound you'll make when I bite you again in this place, right here…"

He ran a finger lightly over the column of her neck, and something in her changed. In her mind, it flashed before her in an instant, a vision of what they could give to one another. She could have him now, like this, and again later in her bed without expectations for anything more. Even if other people got the wrong impression about them, it was a small price to pay for something that would give her what she hadn't dared to let herself crave.

"That's not exactly living in the now, is it?" she asked, her voice compromised. "Unless you'll be biting me right here, in front of everybody…"

He didn't smile at her quip. Instead, a fire she recognized from the week before flashed dangerously in his eyes.

"So why don't we make the future now?"

He slid his eyes to the exit door, then back to her. Twenty minutes later, they were parking in the underground garage at Lake Front Tower.

CHAPTER SIX

THE APARTMENT

LAKE FRONT TOWER WAS AMONG THE CITY'S POSHEST HIGH-rises. It was in Streeterville—the building closest to the lake. Darby might've guessed that Michael lived in a building like this—something that looked as sleek and modern as he did. Its unique architecture was iconic, its three rounded prongs jutting outward like satellites. She had only managed to open the passenger door a crack before he'd jogged around to finish the gesture for her, holding out his hand to help her out of the car.

They hadn't said much to one another since they'd left the gala—not out loud, at least—but he hadn't stopped touching her. He had placed his hand on the scruff of her neck, massaging it gently as he led her out of the party. To an outsider, it would have looked casual. But the gentle precision with which he had caressed the spots that had undone her the week before was anything but. And the way he lifted her hand toward his lips after pulling her gently from the Maserati surprised her. Instead of kissing her fingertips, as she anticipated, he turned her arm to kiss the inside of her wrist and gave her a searing look.

The elevator ride felt maddeningly slow. Instead of pressing a button he keyed in a code with swift precision and the small television screen that displayed what floor they were on informed her that they were ascending to Penthouse West. He did all of this while keeping hold of the same hand he'd held in his since he'd helped her out of the car. Just as she was wondering distractedly whether he was left-handed, he rounded on her. He defied her expectations yet again, because the kiss she had thought was sure to come, deep and needful like the ones he'd given her the week before, never did.

Darby knew that she was beautiful, and the bold attention of men who wanted to sleep with her was nothing new. But the way Michael took her in—his eyes searching her face rather than roving her body, his fingers intertwined with hers rather than making their wicked rounds—made her feel undressed. There was a difference between knowing that a man craved your body and the feeling that some authentic part of you was utterly desired. Without words, without kisses, without pressing his body against hers, Michael had her feeling the latter.

She'd once read somewhere that sex never really started in the bedroom—that the only sex worth having started in the mind. The silence that had stretched between them in the car, and now in the elevator was a strange kind of foreplay, too intense to fight, too complicated to understand. She didn't really know Michael yet, but some strong magnetism drew tension into every inch of space between them.

Darby had long since learned to appear neutral, to perform under the prying eyes of a crowd. But however formidable her performance at the gala, she knew in that moment that Michael had seen through it. Without laying so much as a finger on the zipper of her dress, he was stripping her down. She realized then that he had been undressing her all night, that what he was doing had begun the second she'd opened her front door.

The elevator opened straight into his sprawling apartment. He kept firm hold of her hand as he led her into a large, open hall that separated an enormous kitchen on the right from a living room on the left. Adjacent hallways veering off in both directions hinted at the presence of other rooms.

Like Michael, the decor combined masculinity and style. The living room had a series of Scandinavian-looking sofas in neutral brown colors that went perfectly with his leather-bound coffee table books. The sofas encircled a large flat screen television mounted inside a recessed shelf space. The surrounding shelves were tastefully asymmetric, and filled with what looked like mementos from around the world.

One shelf held a series of elephant statues, from India, she surmised. Another held African masks that looked Masai. She recognized an evil eye charm from Turkey nestled among other art that she wasn't familiar with. Though each shelf was mismatched next to the other, it all somehow coordinated perfectly.

The pièce de résistance was a framed rendition of a colorful butterfly, with elaborately patterned wings of chartreuse and teal that reminded her of the color scheme of her own bedroom. It was exquisitely realistic, and the shimmering quality of its wings made the exact medium difficult to ascertain.

But his view made it difficult to focus on the interior décor. Darby had seen prime Chicago real estate in her day, but she didn't think she'd ever seen a vista so exquisite. The windows spanned the entire space without interruption, boasting a view of the city below that was nothing short of stunning. They had no frames or visible panes—they gave the illusion of just one long glass wall. She had expected a lake view, because Michael was a man who seemed to have the best of everything. Barely anything surprised or excited her anymore, but this scene did.

"I'm an architect. I like to look at the buildings." He seemed to read her thoughts.

He led Darby to a section of the window and leaned casually with his back up against it. He took her other hand in his, ignoring the view that was captivating her, one he'd no doubt seen a thousand times. Instead, his gaze was on her, his ability to answer her thoughts in that moment both thrilling and scaring her a bit.

She liked this feeling, of someone coming close into her space, of someone else minding her business. Growing up the way she had made her an expert at outward congeniality. But it only masked the fact that she was keeping more people than realized it at arm's length. She had spent all week trying to ignore the fact that it wasn't only the fantastic orgasms she kept remembering, but also the way that he'd held her close to him, and looked at her in-between kisses. It had gotten her to thinking. Maybe some part of her did want it all—someone to make her feel like a woman, someone to keep her in his fold.

"You're very particular." He noted her observation with a small smile.

"Precision is underrated. The beauty is always in the details."

She couldn't tell whether she had stepped closer to him or if he had pulled her in, but somehow she was pressed against him and his arms were circling her waist.

"I admire your precision. I don't think I've ever met anyone so precise." Their lips were now close enough for them to kiss. One of his hands floated up to smooth her hair, his palm following the curve of her head until it settled on her neck.

"You haven't seen the half of it." His voice was now as dark as his eyes.

"Show me."

In fifteen seconds flat, her dress was off. In thirty, she sat astride him in a modern-looking chair. In forty, a condom had been rolled on. With that first delicious stroke, they both made soft murmurs of relief. Their foreheads came together for a long moment. Sinking down onto him felt like going home to a sacred place where she belonged. It took her a moment to remember to move. When she did, she braced her hands on the back of her chair for leverage and tried to hoist herself above him, but he held her hips in place.

"Look at me," he whispered.

She did. And blurred seconds from the weekend before sharpened back into focus. The tenderness that had passed between them in vulnerable moments. The way it had felt as if he were opening so much of himself to her, even though he'd been driving her pleasure, even though he'd been the one in control.

"You're beautiful," he breathed.

He wasn't looking at her body, wasn't touching her breasts, wasn't grinding his hips to stroke her. His words held no hint of flattery. They felt like a confession, something said more for his own conscience than for hers. She exhaled a shaky breath she hadn't known she'd been holding. Was this what he needed? For some part of him to be seen? She didn't understand.

He didn't stop her the second time her hips began to move. One of his hands moved to her waist as the other rose to her shoulder. He was gripping her in a way that pressed his thumb firmly in the divot between her neck and her collarbone, a sensation that felt amazing. She let her eyes fall shut and her body do the thinking.

With a breathy grunt, he joined in, thrusting into her deliciously slowly from where he sat on the chair below, guiding them back into their rhythm. Her nipples ached from how hard they had become. This was sensory overload. Once again, he seemed acutely attuned to what her body needed and was hitting some spot that made her delirious with pleasure. The hand on her shoulder snaked up her neck, touching what she was beginning to think of as 'his spot'. She whimpered when his hand didn't stop to tease it. His fingers continued upward until the heel of his hand held the base of her skull and his fingers were threaded in her hair.

She arched her back and reared her head into his touch, hoping only to encourage his fingers to keep massaging her scalp. But his lips closed around her nipple, sucking hard before punctuating his motion with a not-so-soft bite. Darby's orgasm ripped through her so suddenly, and with so much intensity, that her desperate hands moved to Michael's biceps. She gripped so tightly that her short nails inadvertently dug into his skin.

His rhythm faltered, and the lids of his eyes dipped. His full lips whispered soft, unintelligible words. She was still fluttering around him when she felt a dull sharpness on her scalp a second before she felt the swoosh of her hair on her back. Michael had taken out the pin that was holding her loose chignon together. With her head tipped back as it was, the tips of her hair were long enough to tickle the top of her bottom. She shook her hair out, loving the way it felt that moment on her back. It was another night of firsts—another night of chasing sensations she'd never had before, another night of feeling things she'd never felt.

She could tell when he was getting close—his fingers fell from where they were still woven in her hair to grip her hips more firmly. His words were replaced by deep moans that rose in pitch with every breath. He rolled her into him over and over, completely in control now but using that control to intensify their connection. It undid her. His hands slid behind her back, his cheek now pressed to her chest as he braced them both, as if he didn't, she would fly away.

"Sorry," she murmured with genuine regret ten minutes later, still feeling lazy in the afterglow. Her finger circled four deep indentations on his tricep, caused just minutes before by her nails. They weren't bleeding, but they were beginning to look angry—they'd definitely broken through a layer of skin. Her repentant eyes met his playful ones.

"Totally worth it," he smiled.

Between them was a box of cupcakes. Apparently, Michael bought them by the half dozen. It was unexpected, just like his All-Stars and his Buddhist principles and his city view, but she was coming to learn that for every predictable thing about him, there was some random contradiction.

"What?" he asked as she watched him slide a bite of a cupcake into his mouth. "Does my sweet tooth offend you?"

"Nothing about you offends—only surprises."

"Such as?" He licked icing from his lips.

"Such as the fact that I just watched you put 2,000 calories worth of cupcake into a GQ model body." She ran a finger over his washboard abs wondering how an architect who worked all the time kept himself in such great shape.

"Mmm-hmmm, what else?"

"Like the fact that you have a waterbed." She bounced her body in a way that made the surface they were lying on move. "I don't think I've seen one of these since 1989."

"It's not the size of the ship, Darby..." He threw her a suggestive grin. She smiled at his innuendo.

"And the fact that beneath your impeccable custom-tailored suits, you wear Chuck Taylors and have this edgy, beautiful tattoo."

She had finally seen the tattoo in full light. Splayed across his back and shoulders were the wings of a bird that she was pretty sure was an owl. The bird was face down, as if Michael himself were flying and the bird stood, wings spanned, riding in flight on his shoulders.

He polished off the last bite of his cupcake and licked icing off of his finger.

"So I'm an epicure, a hedonist and a philocalist. Since when is liking beautiful things that feel good a crime?"

"Not a crime. Just a paradox. Everything about you as soon as you walk out that door seems structured and buttoned-down. But, like this…eating cupcakes naked, smiling down at me…you seem different."

"I told you, Darby. I'm not like other people. And let's be honest—neither are you."

It had come back to this again—those sapient eyes and that impossible way of knowing—now back in the forefront. Such a definitive assessment from somebody who had just met her would have usually been irritating if it hadn't rung so true.

"I like you."

The words tumbled, unbidden, from her mouth, but she meant them, and apparently some part of her wanted him to know.

"I like you too, cupcake," he said with a sincerity she was still getting used to. He held her eyes for a long moment before reaching into the pink box and picking up another one.

CHAPTER SEVEN

BACK AT THE HOSPITAL

"CHRISTENSEN!" HUCK BARKED, FROM HALFWAY down the hall. Darby cringed, but didn't look up from her iPad, which she was using to chart notes on her last patient.

Her boss was the only person who insisted upon calling her by her surname, which, given its inevitable connection to her father, she preferred to avoid. She typically went by Dr. Darby, a moniker that every other colleague of hers respected. The fact that Huck didn't irritated her, but she was used to these sorts of micro-aggressions (and much worse) from him.

She had figured out long before that he had a chip on his shoulder about her pedigree, and what he viewed as her privilege. Whereas she came from a wealthy family and had enjoyed the best things money could buy, Huck was a self-made man. He had put himself through state schools, clawed his way up the ladder and made a name for himself after he helped a drug company develop a breakthrough rescue med for opioid overdoses. He was considered to be one of the world's foremost experts on opioid addiction, and she had once felt lucky to have landed a position on his staff.

She didn't feel lucky now. Darby wasn't the only one he targeted, but he gave it to her the worst. He missed no opportunity to remind her that while she had eaten from silver spoons, he had pulled himself up from his bootstraps. He made clear his belief that every accolade she had ever received had been because of who her parents were. She might have stood up to him more if she hadn't known that he would use that against her. He had insinuated more than once in front of their superiors that her standing in the community caused her to take too much for granted.

"It seems you've done it again." He was next to her now. Unable to ignore him any longer without seeming blatantly rude, she looked up from her tablet.

"What's that?" She wondered what he would press into her about this time.

"The hospital will continue to fund your research." He looked as if he had just sucked a lemon.

"How much?" She was usually careful to be as emotionless as possible in front of him, but couldn't train the hope from her voice.

"Three hundred thousand."

It was exactly what she'd asked for.

"I agreed to what they offered," he continued. The funding board's decision wasn't anything Huck remotely had the power to approve or deny, and both of them knew it. But that wouldn't stop him from puffing up his own self-importance at Darby's expense.

"You can't let your clinical work slip, got it?" His threat made her want to knee him in the balls.

"It never has before," she nearly sang with put-on levity, though her words were absolute truth.

Darby began walking away before she gave into temptation and actually *did* knee him in the balls and made her way down to Emergency, where she'd been called in for a consult. A fourteen-year-old girl who had nearly died from whatever cocktail of drugs she'd ingested at a party the night before was finally coming to.

She didn't have to check her iPad a second time to know which room her patient lay in. She could tell from the distraught-looking parents, a white couple in their early fifties with red-rimmed, haunted-looking eyes who stood uneasily outside.

"Mr. and Mrs. Agid?" she asked, hoping she was pronouncing the name correctly. She extended a hand. "I'm Dr. Darby. Can you tell me what you know about what's going on with your daughter?"

The story they launched into was one she had heard before. Hannah had been a good kid, thriving in school until she'd fallen in with the wrong crowd. For the past six months, she had become unrecognizable—disinterested in her studies, skipping sports practices to go out with her friends. She'd never missed curfew, so, in their minds, there had been no reason to ground her. But they'd known there was something going on.

"Did you ever suspect drugs?"

"Honestly, no." Mrs. Agid looked guilty. "We thought she was just moody…going through regular teenage stuff."

"The toxicology report still hasn't come back." Darby was careful to keep her voice calm but not reassuring. Chances were, things were worse than the parents thought. Kids who just dabbled rarely overdosed. "We don't know anything conclusively, but from what I'm reading in her chart, she's most likely on an over the counter drug that's sometimes called 'Lean' or 'Syrup.'"

The parents exchanged a confused look.

"It's an opioid made from a cough syrup that contains codeine. Kids mix it with Sprite and a few other things for flavor. It tastes like a sugary cocktail, but it is highly addictive. Given Hannah's state, she may have mixed it with alcohol or other drugs.

"I don't understand how this could've happened." Mrs. Agid said shakily. Darby kept her face neutral. She had no platitudes to offer, and figured she'd better get to the examination.

"Let me see what I can find out." Darby nodded a silent goodbye as she slipped into the girl's room.

"My parents are going to kill me," Hannah offered in a raspy voice, skipping introductions altogether. Before she had spoken, Darby had wondered whether the girl was even awake. This particular drug had a mellowing effect, and it took a long time to fully break out of it. A sheen of sweat coated her skin, confirmation that the withdrawal was underway.

"You don't need them for that." She said without an iota of humor. "You nearly did that yourself."

Hannah said nothing in response.

"We could waste time waiting for the toxicology report, which will tell me everything I need to know, or we could save time and have you tell me exactly what you remember."

Twenty minutes later, Darby emerged from the room having heard yet another familiar story. Peer pressure. Some guy Hannah liked. And the next thing the teen knew, she had a thirty dollar a day habit that she'd been quietly nursing for months. Like other young girls her age, Hannah didn't seem to appreciate the seriousness of her problem. She figured that she'd be grounded until she was old enough to vote, which was probably true, and that all the fun would stop. She viewed herself only as a teenager in trouble with her parents. She had no idea how wrong she was.

Steering the Agids to one of the small consultation rooms just outside of the ER, Darby sat them down for a talk. "I know it might be a stretch to think of your daughter this way, but, physiologically speaking, she is an addict. She will go through withdrawal. She will crave the drug she was on. And, because she can't have it, she will be attracted to other addictive behaviors. I know that, right now, the drug seems like the problem, but drugs are always a symptom of other problems. Her addiction, and the problems that fed her addiction, won't simply end once the chemical is out of her system. Her life will need other changes as well."

When he finally chimed in, Mr. Agid's voice was angry and louder than it needed to be. That was usually how the dads reacted in situations like this. "What kind of other problems could she have? She wants for nothing. Three months ago, she was thriving. She's a good kid."

Darby kept her composure.

"Even in homes in which parenting is strong, teenagers can struggle. It's common for girls Hannah's age to have body-image issues, feel pressure to perform socially as well as sexually, and prioritize peer relationships above everything else. Establishing social status is a natural part of child development, but kids today often lack certain social skills that were common in your generation. At the same time, they're thrown into adult situations from a very young age."

Mr. Agid still looked angry. Mrs. Agid simply looked tired. Darby suggested they join a parent support group and recommended a few other resources before she bade them goodbye.

By the time she walked off her shift, Darby felt as if she had been on duty for much longer than twelve hours. Hannah had taken a turn for the worse and was in critical condition. Her body wasn't processing the drugs and alcohol out of her system as quickly as it needed to in order for her to recover well.

Darby had been stoic when delivering news to the Agids, but the parallel emotions of anger and sadness, not to mention the worry, always ate her up inside. It was hard to explain to people how the emotional drain of her job took a physical toll. She put on a brave face—to be strong for her patient's loved ones, and to be seen as the consummate professional. But spending so much of her day tamping down her emotions came at a price.

At home, she took a long, hot shower, and slipped into flannel pajamas that engulfed her in pleasant warmth. She fed herself and her beloved hermit crab, Consuela, and settled into bed with her Kindle. She wasn't even two pages into her book before a Facebook alert slid across her iPad's screen. *Michael Blaine is online*, it read. She found it hard to ignore, no matter how good her book was.

Burning the midnight oil?

Immediately, she saw that he was writing back.

Something like that...I'm still in the office. You?

Just left. Need to sleep, but I'm too keyed up.

I know the feeling, he commiserated.

My patient might die, she admitted.

My building might fall down. Literally.

For some reason, this made her laugh.

So what are you going to do to fix it?

I don't know. What about you? How are you going to fix your patient?

I don't know.

We suck.

You're right. Let's self-medicate.

...says the doctor who works with addicts. ::head shake::

She smiled.

Right now? He texted back immediately.

Too tired. Tomorrow night?

Good timing. I'm out on the red eye at midnight.

I'm not off until seven o'clock. How about eight o'clock at my place?

Perfect.

CHAPTER EIGHT

THE BOOTY CALL

AT SEVEN FIFTY-NINE THE NEXT NIGHT, DARBY'S doorbell rang. She found Michael dressed much differently than she had ever seen him. His asymmetric black military jacket, black textured pants and black ankle boots held hints of steampunk, and he still looked like he'd stepped out of the pages of a magazine. He smelled faintly of cinnamon gum and of some increasingly familiar designer soap that, by then, she associated with him. He carried both a duffel and a garment bag, a reminder that he'd be headed to the airport from there.

Darby was also freshly showered, but she hadn't bothered to get fully dressed. Instead she wore a silk robe and a mauve bra and panty set that she hoped would flatter her. Though its coloring was understated, it had detailed silk lacing reminiscent of corset binding that formed patterns above the lace. She had noticed the way Michael's eyes had flashed the weekend before when he'd taken stock of the lace panties and gartered stockings she wore beneath her evening gown. She planned to find out tonight whether it had been a fluke or a fetish.

Wordlessly, she relieved him of his bags and peeled his jacket off of his shoulders, placing them carefully on her entryway chair. She came in close to stare up into his hypnotic eyes. This was only their third meeting, yet she was coming to realize that every time she was with him she felt instantly bewitched.

"Hi."

With her body already craving his, her gaze fell involuntarily to his lips. She thought about his mouth—how skilled it was—and how dearly she hoped to avail herself of its talents. He didn't smile as his eyes surveyed her briefly before flicking back up to hers.

"Hi."

She felt breathless, but tried not to appear so.

"Do you want a tour?" She didn't quite know where to start.

"Do you want to give me one?" She didn't miss the amusement in his voice. But she was still enthralled with his lips.

"I don't know. This is my first straight-up booty call."

The corner of his mouth quirked upward.

"You can try it. But I if I get distracted, I make no guarantees I'll be able to finish."

"You know I always let you finish." She smirked as she turned and began walking. It took a moment before she heard his steps follow hers.

Just beyond the entryway of her house was a small rotunda, with rooms opening off of it like spacious satellites. She had a formal dining room on the far right and a modern kitchen on the same side; her office and a winding staircase were off to the left; the largest opening from her rotunda went to a living room straight ahead.

"This is the kitchen, which is not clean because I'm a tidy person, but because I'm bad at keeping up with grocery shopping and I'm usually too tired to cook."

"But you bake…"

She looked back to see him eyeing her row of cookbooks, which mostly revolved around desserts.

Again with the details.

She started to walk into the living room, but turned when she heard the sound of a cabinet door closing. To her stunned surprise, Michael was searching the cabinets next to her stove, one by one.

"Looking for something?" She stared in disbelief.

When he rose back to full height, his hand held a spring form pan.

"You make cheesecake?" He stared right back without an iota of shame.

"Flourless chocolate cake," Darby said, remembering his fixation with sweets.

He smiled conspiratorially and launched into an interrogation about the other sorts of things she liked to make. Once they established her full range of baking proficiency—discussed her amazing talent for cakes, and her utter uselessness with cookies and pies, Michael observed that she avoided things that involved dough. Darby had never thought about it that way, never noticed that her strengths and weaknesses had a pattern, but he was right. He was *always* right. Apart from patients with diagnosed psychiatric disorders, Michael was one of the strangest men she had ever met.

They made their way into her living room, where Michael crouched to study Consuela's cage with interest.

"'What's a nice girl like me doing without a drink in her hand?'" Michael read the words painted on the bottom of Consuela's water bowl.

"A hermit crab's home can't have a little panache?"

"These look fancy." He was referring to the various shells that were the right size for Consuela to live in, which were distributed across her habitat.

"A girl's gotta have something nice to wear."

This made him smile, though he didn't look back at Darby, only continued to admire the contents of the cage. "Impressive," he murmured, before rising back up.

Next, he made his way to the shelves that held her DVDs, a format that may have seemed outdated to some, but a collection she'd been building since high school nonetheless. She inspected Michael as he inspected her DVDs. He ran his finger over titles for what seemed like minutes with what appeared to be growing approval on his face.

"You're a cinephile," she observed, because nobody who wasn't would spend so much time at this.

"In theory. I haven't been to the movies in ages."

"I go every week."

He looked at her with admiration in his eyes.

"What's your favorite?"

"*Before Sunrise.*" Darby barely needed to think in order to recite this indelible fact. She wondered whether he knew the film. It had a devoted cult following, but couldn't be considered mainstream.

"What did you think of *Before Midnight*?" So he *was* familiar with the series. The films were extraordinary in that they had taken nearly 20 years to finish the trilogy. *Before Sunrise* had been released in 1995, and its sequel, *Before Sunset* had come out in 2004. The final film, *Before Midnight* had come out in 2013.

"I couldn't bring myself to watch it." It was the first time she had admitted this out loud. "I'm sure it will be genius, but I didn't want to see it end."

She liked the way he smiled at her then.

"What's your second favorite movie?" It was her turn to smile.

"*Heathers*," she replied, again without having to think.

She saw his face change into something different, and she got just a little wet when he began to recite a line from the movie.

"Heather says: real life sucks losers dry. If you want to fuck with the eagles, you gotta learn to fly. I asked her: so you make people fly? She said 'Yes'. I said—"

"You're beautiful."

For a pregnant moment, Darby wondered whether she'd had completely imagined this man whose performance in bed was the stuff of legends, and who seemed to connect with everything about her. She had never questioned her own sanity, but there was a first time for everything.

Drawn away from her thoughts by the familiar heat in his eyes, her body had a nearly Pavlovian reaction. Apparently, trading lines from '80s movies got him hard. She flashed with her own heat and, suddenly, her throat felt dry.

"We're not going to make it upstairs, are we?"

He shook his head slowly, and said, "You're wearing too many clothes."

His pants were fitted enough to show the beginnings of an erection. By the time he had pulled off his V-neck, she was halfway to him. He was throwing the shirt aside as she tugged the tongue of his belt loose, slower than she needed to as she admired his physique. Once his fly was open, she didn't push his pants down over his hips, but instead dipped her left hand deep inside. His breath faltered and he angled his hips toward her, either to give her better access within the tight space of his pants or seek more friction.

They were standing in the middle of her living room floor, but Darby needed him against something. She walked him slowly, and a little forcefully, backward and out of the room. He was pliant to her silent demands, and she got the sense that he liked the fact that she was taking charge. Up until then, he had been making good on his promise to deliver an astounding number of orgasms, a fact that meant the few times they'd been together he had been very focused on her. Still, there was something Darby had been wanting to do.

Pressing him more roughly than necessary against the wall in her rotunda, she removed her hand from his pants and ground her lower body against his. He gasped a bit, grinding back, moving his fingers on her hips until he found her silken robe's sash, bending to kiss her as he began to push the robe off her shoulders. He did notice the bra and panty set she wore underneath the robe, and he cursed under his breath when he saw them.

Oh, yeah, Darby thought. *Definitely a fetish.*

Darby turned her cheek before his next kiss could land. She shook her head as she looked into Michael's confused eyes before shifting her own to his erection. "Not you. Him."

Not bothering to wait for his reaction, she reached down to push his pants down his hips. He shook them off, letting them join her discarded robe on the floor. She sank to her knees and helped him out of his socks, because socks on during any kind of sex was just wrong. And she ran her nose along his thick, beautiful length before grabbing him at the base and laving him thickly with her tongue.

"Fuck." She didn't think his strained whisper had been one she was meant to hear.

He was big, and he knew it, and he stood still enough to give her complete control. She took him into her mouth, sliding

wetted lips down his shaft and suck him in deeply, as much of
him as she could. She knew by then how he liked to savor it, to
torture himself slowly with every gratifying sensation. So she
made sure her ministrations were exact and that her strokes
and sucks were more slow than fast.

Darby wasn't just doing this for him, though she'd been
told she was quite good at it. Fellatio was one of her favorite
things to do in bed. The feeling of him filling up her mouth to
the back of her throat, his moans when she scraped her teeth
against his sensitive head, even the way he smelled were making her wonderfully wet.

But she wanted more. So when she sensed he was close,
she showed him how she liked it. She slid her hand up to find
his, where it was splayed against the wall and pulled her mouth
off of him long enough to place his fingers on the back of her
head and look up at him to voice her quiet demand.

"Fuck my mouth, Michael."

His cock twitched a second after the words were said, and
she knew for sure at that moment he got off on her bossing
him around. She dove back in then, catching the head of his
cock in her mouth, yet refusing to resume her motions until he
began. He cursed again as he started to oblige her, beginning
tentatively, but emboldening himself with her every approving
moan. Soon he was thrusting harder and faster than she could
have done on her own but still not hard and fast enough.

"More." The plea was whispered when she pulled off of him
for a single stroke before going right back in. He was moaning
now, louder, and did as she said, penetrating her more quickly
and deeply. She loved this feeling too, of giving up this piece of
her control to give him his, and she itched to be touched for as
turned on as she was.

His fingers threaded in her hair in a way that gave him

better leverage, better precision that she suspected had both of them nearly undone. Wanting to give him even more, she maneuvered her free hand so that the pads of her fingers could graze his balls. It set him off.

"I'm gonna come." His voice was thick with warning and he tugged at her hair a bit to pull her off.

But that wasn't what she wanted. She removed his hand from her hair then, replacing it back on the wall as she resumed setting the pace. Her hand returned to stroking him while she sucked and he nearly roared when he came, shooting into her mouth. She let him fall from her lips slowly after he'd finished, and as he had done each time for her, she stroked his legs tenderly as she let him come down.

He was still out of breath when his strong arms lifted her up, and brought her to her feet. He kissed her deeply, and when he pulled away he murmured, "If I didn't have a plane to catch, I'd fuck you all night."

Yet, apparently, Michael's idea of a pre-flight quickie was to spend the next hour with various parts of himself lodged deeply inside her. They didn't make it to her bedroom that night. But he did splay her out on her staircase and bury his mouth and his fingers between her legs. She was still pulsing with pleasure after he'd made her come that way when he pulled her panties off but left her bra on. A minute later, he had her bent over the sofa, one hand on her hip as the other gripped her shoulder, fucking her slowly but thoroughly, and God, so hard. She'd never had anything remotely like this before, not with anyone. Sex hadn't ever been this good.

Afterward, she felt dazed as she leaned against the wall, first hearing the water run as he cleaned himself up in the powder room, then watching him collect his clothes and redress to magazine-perfection. He even found her discarded robe, slid it back onto her shoulders, and gently tied its sash. He picked up his phone, his fingers moving swiftly and she surmised that he was calling an Uber. When he pocketed his phone, he turned his full attention back to her.

Coming to stand in front of her, he cupped her face in his hands, looking between her eyes before kissing her deeply. And not for a minute, either. For a good long time.

"To be continued. I'm back in a week."

CHAPTER NINE

THE DEATH STAR

GET IT TOGETHER, GIRL.

Darby tossed her phone down on her desk and swiveled in her chair until her back was to the offending device. Out her window, the sun shone brightly—a rarity for a fall day in Chicago—and the light dress of the people walking on the streets below confirmed that it was warm. It was the first time in a month that she had time to take a real lunch hour and she should have been outside on a walk.

But she wasn't outside. To her horror, she was holed up in her office, preoccupied with thoughts of why Michael hadn't called. She hated herself for it a little bit more each time she checked her phone.

"I'll be back in a week." That was what he had said. Today was day nine. And it bothered her that he hadn't called. She didn't know what was worse: the fact that she hadn't heard from him, or the discovery of her backwards expectation that he should be the pursuer. The rational part of her reminded herself that he'd initiated everything so far. Maybe it was her turn to step forward. Maybe he was somewhere waiting for her to call.

But even if he called that second and they fucked that night, this line of thinking hinted at bigger problems. He'd gotten under her skin in a way that didn't feel casual at all. Wondering where the other person was, what they were doing, and when you got to see them again was something dating people did. She wasn't quite there yet, but she had begun to crave him, which meant that she'd come to care about his whereabouts more than she would have liked.

It troubled her deeply. How could somebody she had just met, who meant so little to her in the grand scheme of things, make her feel that their connection was everything? The way he looked at her, touched her, fucked her…in those moments, he felt like someone she couldn't live without. She wanted to believe that she could adopt an attitude as laissez-faire as his— of living in the moment—but she found herself caught up in old beliefs. She thought about Dave. She didn't want to be any-body's girlfriend, but it seemed she still didn't know how not to act like one.

She was roused from her thoughts by the buzz of her phone. The accompanying ringtone—the *Death Star Theme* from *Star Wars*—signaled that it wasn't Michael. It would have been pointless to ignore the call, so she figured she'd better get it—whatever it was—over with.

"Senator," she answered with trained cordiality.

"Dad would be fine too, Darby." Frank Christensen sounded as petulant as ever.

"To what do I owe this call?" She kept to her formal tone, already mining her brain for excuses to get off the phone.

"Can't a father call his daughter just to see how she's doing?"

"Yes, a *father* could," she agreed, emphasizing the third

word. "But that's not like you, so why don't you tell me what you want?"

He didn't speak for a moment, and Darby was sure he was weighing whether to continue the ruse or to drop false pretenses. Ever the politician, he chose the former.

"Honey. I want to see you, and I thought it might be nice for you to come to the Silberstein's son Jonah's wedding in February. Did you get the invitation?"

"I haven't seen any of them in, like, ten years."

"It would be nice to reconnect." He sounded optimistic. "You and Jonah played together as kids."

Darby rolled her eyes. The only time her father wanted her to attend an event was when he was desperate to keep up appearances. It was good business for a senator to show off his wholesome family, and she was all the family he had left. But Frank Christensen was the most depraved man Darby had ever known, and given the motley crew of politicians, pimps and drug dealers she'd come across over the years, that was saying a lot.

"I'm busy that night."

"With plans that are better than attending one of the most important weddings of the year?"

"I have to wash my hair."

The enthusiasm left his voice. "You knew this was part of the deal. There are big things coming and we need to saddle up."

Her heart beat a little more quickly at that. "Big things" for her father always meant running for another office, or an appointment to a major post. Any new office would come with a vetting, and any elected office would come with opposition research on top of that.

"Define *big things*."

"They're talking about putting me in the White House, honey."

He didn't even have the decency to sound regretful about what it would mean for her. On top of every other reason she had to hate him, he had always been unapologetic about invasions of her privacy.

"You can't win," she said bluntly. "You'd have to get through Prescott and Sanderson, and neither of them—"

"Prescott's out of the game," Frank interrupted. "And Sanderson has roadblocks that I am uniquely positioned to remove. He'll make me his VP. I'll be on the ticket."

Darby wondered what scandal had befallen Prescott, the Texas governor, who had been groomed for the past year to become the Republican nominee. She hadn't seen anything on the news, but she knew how these things went. There was a good chance the world would never find out.

She set her phone down and put it on speaker so that both hands would be free to rub her tired eyes.

"Three events…I told you I'd give you three events a year. This is number two."

"So you'll come?"

"Choose wisely. That number won't change even if you run," she continued more sternly.

"That's not an answer, honey."

"I'll come. Just don't lay it on too thick." He had a tendency to go overboard on the happy family façade.

She hung up without saying goodbye.

Darby spent the rest of the day with a different complicated man on her mind. Unlike Michael, she knew her father too well and understood exactly how she felt about him. 'Hate' was a strong word, but it applied. She wasn't keeping up appearances for him—she was doing it for her. The less interested the press was in possible discord between them, the less unwanted attention.

When she got home that night, she kicked off her clogs in the mud room inside the garage door and shuffled into her office in nothing but her socks. It took her a minute to rifle through her mail and locate the RSVP card she had planned to return with her regrets. Instead, she pulled out her phone and took a picture. Apparently, the threat of facing her father alone was all she needed to make the next move.

Beef, fish, or vegetarian?

Calling up her chat history, she texted the photo to Michael. She was being a bit flip, her casual tone conflicting with her hope that he would be available and would agree to attend. She was relieved to have an overture that didn't make her sound desperate to see him.

Waking some hours later to short buzzing sounds close to her head, her hand groped her nightstand for her phone.

Sorry. Business trip was extended. I'm in London now. Just finding time to respond. Sure I'll come. Who's getting married?

An old family friend. My father very much wants me to make an appearance.

You sound thrilled.

Oh, I am.

Do you really go to the movies every week?

Wow, that was a non-sequitur.

Are you sure you're not a lawyer? You're good at dodging questions.

Fine, I go to the movies once a week. I buy myself a ticket to the matinee, order a bag of small popcorn with butter and smuggle in a flask.

He didn't answer for a minute.

Invite me sometime.

For real?

::eyeroll::

She laughed out loud and was embarrassed by her giddiness at finally hearing from him.

Alright, I will.

You'd better. Have a good day, cupcake.

She smiled at his term of endearment.

Have a good night.

CHAPTER TEN

CASABLANCA

S HE DIDN'T ASK HIM TO THE MOVIES THE NEXT TIME SHE
went, which was just one day after they had texted. She
doubted he was back in town and, besides, she didn't know
how she felt about inviting him into her routine. She tended
toward independent films, which could be more serious than
whatever Hollywood was offering. She usually ended up crying
into her Kleenex by the end of the movie, and she didn't think
Michael needed to see her like that. But she did invite him to
the one she was seeing a week later.

*They're screening Casablanca at the Siskel Center. I'm head-
ed there after work. Want to join?*

Casablanca seemed safe enough—touching, yes, but not
quite a tearjerker.

What time?

Eight o'clock. Will you still be working?

No, I think I can make it. Save me a seat.

At quarter past eight, toward the end of the previews, a
body settled in next to hers. She noticed two things immediately. The first was the way he smelled. It felt as if she had

sensed him through her nose before he actually sat down. She doubted he had stopped at home to shower, but his scent still wafted off of him like a second skin. The next thing she noticed was the enormous tub of popcorn in his hand. She surveyed it with interest before handing him the flask.

"Are you going to feed a small nation?"

He eyed her tiny bag.

"Are you going to feed a small child?"

She reached off to her side and produced a king size pack of Reese's Peanut Butter Cups.

"I was going to offer you one of these, but now I'm not sure."

"I'll shut up."

Yeah, he was definitely interested in her peanut butter cups. Though she paid moderate attention to the beginning of the movie, she noticed him looking at her candy five times. She ate the first three, slowly, painfully. As she picked up the fourth, she flicked her eyes to him. He was nearly pouting. She shook her head, and held it out in front of him.

"Your sweet tooth is embarrassing. I hope you know that."

He leaned in and kissed her on her neck, in a way that wholly distracted her. It was the first physical contact they'd had in more than two weeks.

"Indulging in pleasurable things is not a crime, Darby." She thought she heard him sigh softly when he slipped the peanut butter cup into his mouth.

It was Darby who sighed softly when the movie ended. It had always been one of her favorites. When she looked over at him, ready to get out of her seat, he was smiling down at her.

"You're cute when you're starry-eyed." He wasn't shy about sharing his observation. "And when you blush." Darby couldn't help it.

"Mock me all you want. I live my vicarious love affairs in style."

"Fair enough." He took her haughty retort in stride. "*Before Sunrise* is your favorite movie after all...though I think you have a dark side. You love *Heathers*. And I saw the entire 'Twin Peaks' box set on your shelf."

"Dark? Yes, but maudlin too. If you had analyzed my movie collection a bit more closely, you would have also found *The English Patient* and *Out of Africa*. I guess you could say I'm intrigued by characters who want what they can't have."

He studied her but didn't respond. She could tell he was really thinking about this.

Three minutes later, they were outside the theater, the brisk air signaling that Chicago winter would soon begin. Chicago winter, unfortunately, imposed its chill as early as October. People who didn't know the city thought that its reputation for extreme cold came from it being, literally, a windy city. More accurately, the winter was simply long. That late summer night on the beach was the last truly warm one she had known. The cool air caused her to think of how things would look a month from then. Fewer boats in the marina. Michigan Avenue lightly sprinkled with its first snow.

"You haven't told me what *your* favorite movie is." His hand was warm in hers and she liked the feeling. "And if you say *Fight Club*, I might have to say the word that rhymes with 'slap wagon.'"

He laughed. "You would give up all this..." he said, motioning to himself, "...if my favorite movie were cliché?"

"I have high expectations of you, Michael—remember, we're not like other people."

He looked tickled that she had used his words.

"It's a three-way tie," he said finally. "Among *Harry Potter*,

The Shawshank Redemption and *Talk to Her."*

"Pedro Almodóvar..." she said, "I love him."

Michael looked at her.

"I know." Clearly he'd seen Almodóvar titles in her collection.

"So what's the common thread?" she asked. "My movies star characters who want what they can't have, or who can't shake people they wish they didn't want. Yours, on the other hand—"

"Have characters who value loyalty," he finished for her. "And justice, and maybe just a little revenge."

They continued walking, to where she didn't know, but she thought about this for a minute.

"So, you consider yourself loyal." It was more a statement than a question.

"Loyalty is underrated. My inner circle is small, but there's not much I wouldn't do for the people I love."

Darby felt something akin to longing in that moment. Loyalty was the one thing that the people who should have been closest to her had always lacked. It made her think of her father.

"I need more friends like you."

At that, he kissed the top of her head and tightened his grip on her hand. They continued walking and ended up at his place that night, to do what they did best.

CHAPTER ELEVEN

LABOR AND DELIVERY

STEPPING OUT OF THE ELEVATOR ON THE FOURTH FLOOR, Darby made her way to the staff lounge in Labor and Delivery. The ER was dead, as was the Psych floor, so she had time to kill in one of her favorite places. Unlike the staff lounge in the Psych ward, a barren wasteland of a water cooler and a coffee pot with muddy contents that were always poorly made, overheated and stale, the lounge in Labor and Delivery always had a cornucopia of good things: half-eaten cakes with blue and pink icing, and savory meals provided by grateful parents wishing to thank the staff who had ushered their babies into the world.

Darby's bad habit of forgetting to eat and her disdain for cafeteria food meant that she made her way up there whenever she got the chance. It wasn't uncommon for the new nurses and aides to think that Darby was herself an OB and, once upon a time, that had been her plan. A few times when OB had been understaffed, and quite against hospital rules, she'd been recruited to assist in a birth. It made her fleetingly regret having specialized in psychiatry. Cradling newborns every day was an enviable reward.

Upon entering the lounge, she immediately spotted her friend Anne leaning against the counter closest to the coffee machine. The heavyset nurse was drinking greedily from a comically large mug that read "The blood of Christ. The cup of salvation." and pictured a chalice embossed with a coffee bean.

Darby shared Anne's sardonic sense of humor, and between the two of them they had an impressive collection of what they lovingly referred to as 'sarcastica'. Just as Darby had bought Anne the coffee mug she held, so also had Anne bought the one in Darby's hand. It read 'She was one cocktail away from proving his mother right.' Anne Taintor was pretty much their idol.

"Someone brought in sushi." Anne offered between gulps, already knowing Darby's intentions and also knowing that her friend loved sushi. "That shit goes straight to my hips, but knowing you, you'd eat the whole thing and not gain a pound."

Darby made her way to the refrigerator. "You just get here?" she asked. The Labor and Delivery shifts were on different timing from hers.

"Ten hours in." Anne said it softly. "But one of my moms is having trouble, so I'll probably stay late."

"Is she going to be alright?" Anne was one of the most fiercely caring people she'd ever met. She was irreverent and had a wicked sense of humor, and they were alike in that her bluntness rubbed some people the wrong way. Still, Darby had never met a single person who cared so much about her patients. If Darby ever wanted kids, and if it were possible for her to have them, she'd want Anne in the room.

"Maybe." It confirmed something subtle that Darby had thought she'd seen in her face. "Tell me something good," Anne diverted before Darby could find comforting words. "Did you stick an apple in Huck's mouth and roast him slowly over an open fire? Did you meet a tall, dark stranger and are having monkey hot sex?"

Now it was Darby who must have given something away, she immediately knew when she saw Anne's eyes widen.

"Are you *seeing* someone?"

Darby didn't answer, not because she wouldn't have confided in her friend, but because she realized she didn't know the answer. Shoving a section of shrimp tempura roll into her mouth in order to buy herself some chewing time seemed like a good idea.

"Seeing may be too strong a word."

"Are you *fucking* someone?"

Darby weaved her head from side to side, in the universal gesture for "maybe", as she devoured another piece of sushi.

"A little bit of both."

Anne stared at her unforgivingly.

"Yeah. You're gonna have to elaborate."

"So, there *is* a guy...and we *are* fucking...but we also go out together sometimes."

"The rest of us call that dating," Anne said slowly, as if Darby were in kindergarten.

Darby really needed to get it together, or else she would be dangerously full of sushi by the time she returned to her floor.

"Actually, it's more like...an arrangement."

"It's not Prince William, is it?" Anne lowered her voice even though they were alone. That was what Anne liked to call Rich. She'd been candidly instructing Darby to 'hit that' for years.

"What? No. It's not like that with us. Besides, Rich is married—remember?"

"Not for long." Anne cast her a knowing look. "I heard

they're getting a divorce."

Darby stopped chewing and spoke around a mouthful of avocado roll. "No shit..." She and Rich saw each other all the time. She wondered why he hadn't said anything.

"Well if it's not him, who is it?" Anne didn't miss a beat.

"Just a guy. No one from the hospital. I met him at a wedding, one thing led to another, and..."

"And you made a new friend with benefits."

Darby weaved her head indecisively yet again.

"Something like that."

"You know that men and women can't just be friends. Someone always grows feelings."

Darby shook her head. "Not us. We made a deal. As soon as things get complicated, we break it off—no questions, no strings."

Her friend continued to give her a skeptical look.

"Don't give me that look—have I ever gotten attached to a guy in the time you've known me?" Anne didn't need to answer. "That's what I thought. I don't know why people act like having a fuck buddy is weird. What's weirder is the idea that two adults can't figure out a relationship that works uniquely for them. Look at Oprah and Stedman—nobody understands *their* relationship but they've been together for, like, 20 years."

"So you're in a relationship with this guy?"

Darby felt caught.

"Yes," she decided finally. The moment she acknowledged it to Anne was the same moment in which she acknowledged it to herself. "But it's not what you think," she cautioned. "We're not *together*, together. We serve a purpose to one another. He's sick of eating alone. I'm sick of watching movies at home with my hermit crab."

Though Anne still looked wary, the expression on her face

softened a little. "And you're sure that's enough?" she asked carefully.

"I like him. And I like fucking him. But I've got too much of my own shit going on to have time for anything else."

"So, what's he like?"

Darby smiled as she began to dish about him.

"He's an architect. Hotter than all get-out—like, Calvin Klein model hot, and he dresses like a model, too. He's a total pro in bed. The sex is almost…spiritual."

Anne sat next to Darby at the table, placed her elbow down and propped her chin up on the heel of her hand. Darby was thankful her friend didn't mention her blush.

"He's really smart. Mysterious, but not in a creepy way. A really good guy, but ambitious like me."

"You're right—that's not the kind of guy girls fall in love with." Anne smiled, the sarcasm in her voice joking and light.

"It's not like that. We know that our careers come first. We understand each other."

"Sounds like you have it all figured out." Anne's voice was some mix of admiration and skepticism. "You know I'm going to live this vicariously through you, right?"

"Still not dating, I take it?" Darby asked sympathetically. She knew Anne was having trouble bouncing back after a rough break-up with her girlfriend of five years.

"Worse than that. Susan's getting married," Anne said bitterly, speaking of her ex.

"Ouch." Darby winced.

Darby listened sympathetically to Anne, letting her vent about her shitty ex, about the entire shitty situation. As she made her way back to her own floor some minutes later, she felt relieved to have told someone about Michael.

PART II

DATING

CHAPTER TWELVE

YELENA

*G*T *Prime tonight?*

Michael's text came in as Darby walked toward the nurse's station. She'd only been on her shift for four hours and already her feet hurt and she was starving. But the nursing staff was changing over and she needed to be briefed on the status of her patients before foraging for her lunch. If she was lucky there would still be Fritos left in the vending machines by the time she could steal a moment.

If you can get a reservation.

She'd heard amazing things about that restaurant. She'd also heard there was a month-long wait.

I can do all kinds of things.

A flush came over her body as she remembered he could.

Let's do it. I'm starving.

I meant for dinner.

I know.

Why are you starving?

Because I haven't had lunch.

So grab something.

No time.

You have to eat.

I'll find something to munch on.

She pocketed her phone as she reached the nurse's station.

"Hey Darby," Kathy greeted her sweetly. The long-haired blonde was one of the more senior nurses on Darby's service and she was great at her job. Darby loved working with Kathy, not only because she never had to worry about mistakes, but because she loved their chats. Kathy had two grown sons of her own, and reminded Darby a little of her own mother. Kathy had been on pins and needles for days waiting for her grandson to be born.

"Hey, Kath," Darby replied with a warm look. She'd barely seen her all shift. "Do we have a baby yet?"

Kathy pursed her lips and shook her head.

"Joey told me that if I didn't stop texting every half hour, he's gonna send Jase to take my phone."

Jason was her other son. Darby feigned offense at the news.

"You're a grandmother. It's your sacred right."

"That's what I said," Kathy agreed.

"I expect pictures," Darby said with a smile. She then shifted reluctantly back into work mode. "So what do I need to know?"

Her friend launched into a full but efficient briefing. All of Darby's patients had been given their meds. The two who were scheduled for discharge had just gone, and another who wasn't scheduled to leave had checked himself out. One of the families wanted to talk to her about their son's drug regimen. Radiology was backed up, which meant she still didn't have some test results she needed.

Darby frowned at this news. She'd been in the ER for the past three hours. The test results should have made their way to psych in no more than one.

"I'll call them," Darby assured Kathy. They shared a dislike for how cavalier the labs could be about ignoring the nurses' requests. The labs only paid attention when an attending called, which just made it a bigger hassle for everyone.

"There's one more thing," Kathy said. "One of Dr. Skubic's patients is asking for you."

Dr. Yelena Skubic was Darby's peer, another psychopharmacologist with slightly more tenure. Not that Yelena acted like a peer—she was first in line to replace Huck and made sure everybody knew it.

"Who is it?" It wasn't uncommon for patients to show up again and again. Addiction recovery was a marathon, not a sprint.

Before Kathy could answer, Darby heard her name spoken urgently by somebody down the hall.

"No…what I would really like right now is to speak to Dr. Darby," a firm voice said.

Darby held up a finger to Kathy, asking her to wait a minute while she tracked down the speaker. She grabbed her iPad and rounded the corner in the direction the conversation was coming from.

Darby immediately recognized Leslie Fields. She stood with her arms crossed, her face blotchy, and her eyes filled with desperation. Her younger sister Charlene was addicted to meth.

Yelena was trying to reason with her. "Dr. Christensen isn't here. Right now, I'm Charlene's doctor—I can answer any questions you have about your sister's condition."

For some reason, Leslie looked up at that moment, relief washing over her face the second she laid eyes on Darby. Briefly, she glared back at Yelena, recognizing her lie. In seconds, she and Darby were face-to-face.

They greeted one another with a familiar hug. Her sister had come in three times on the brink of death from overdoses. Darby had held this woman as she cried on more than one occasion.

"What's going on, Les?" she asked. "How's Charlie?"

Yelena's lips pressed together.

"Something's wrong. Her detox isn't going the way it should." Leslie looked terrified. Darby knew she'd been through this enough times to know the difference between what to expect and when to know something wasn't right.

"Why don't I look in on her?" Darby asked soothingly. She knew it would earn her Yelena's resentment, but she trusted Leslie's judgment. The way she saw it, addressing Leslie's concerns was part of managing Charlie's care.

"Can you let Dr. Skubic brief me?" Darby's voice was gentle. "Right now, she's the best source of information."

Leslie nodded, fidgeting with her necklace nervously. "Why don't you go grab something from the cafeteria?" Both women knew it was code for 'Get lost for a while and let me handle it'.

Darby walked toward Yelena, ignoring her icy scowl. She had never been as cruel as Huck, but she seemed just as hellbent on keeping Darby in her place. Those two were made of the same ugly. It was no surprise that Huck had chosen her to succeed him.

She wasn't a beautiful woman, though she had a certain old-world charm. Her long brown hair fell over her shoulder in disorganized waves, her smart glasses complemented her face, and her short stature might have been considered by some to be cute. In fact, she might even have been considered pretty if her personality hadn't been so black.

Brushing past her, Darby walked purposefully into Charlie's room.

"When did she get here?" she asked, trying to keep it professional.

"Respectfully, Dr. Christensen, this is my patient—and I don't need a consult."

Meaning to disarm her, Darby softened her stance and thought of words designed to put her at ease.

"I know you don't. But her sister has asked for one."

"Yet, she remains my patient." Yelena's voice held more conviction now. "And it would be most helpful to the situation if you deferred to me."

"My patient load isn't that heavy today." Darby was a smooth liar when she needed to be. "All Leslie wants is a second opinion. I'll give her one. It will corroborate yours, and then I'll be out of your hair."

The other doctor pinned her with another hateful glare. Now Darby was losing her patience.

"She has a right to a second opinion." Abandoning her soft approach, she went for intimidation. "When did she get here?" Darby repeated with staccato intonation as she pulled up Charlie's chart on her iPad.

"The middle of the night," Yelena said grudgingly. "She came in with heart irregularities, so we treated her for arrhythmia, and now we're using saline to flush her system."

"Did you do a tox screen?"

"I didn't need to. She's a known meth addict."

Darby looked up at her then.

"She could be poly," Darby said flatly.

"She's been in here ten times. Every single time it's been meth."

Darby had been casting intermittent glances at Charlie as

she went through her checklist of symptoms, but now she took a closer look.

"Does she *look* like someone who is detoxing from meth?" Darby knew her tone was accusatory, but she couldn't help it. Yelena's negligence could cost Charlie her life.

Yelena's nostrils flared.

"We need a tox screen." Darby moved to leave the room, to collect the phlebotomy supplies from the closet in the hall, when Yelena grabbed her arm.

"There's no reason for you to get involved."

Darby shrugged her arm away.

"If you're right, you have nothing to be afraid of."

After taking the blood sample, Darby walked it up to the lab herself. She got her friend Sid to do her a favor and process them on the spot. During the short wait, she reflected that it was unwise to show up the woman who would probably become her boss, but she couldn't let disregard for safety protocols slide. She'd rather have a pissed off boss to worry about than a dead patient on her conscience.

The results came back quickly and they were exactly as she had feared. Charlie hadn't overdosed on meth the previous night—she'd overdosed on OxyContin. By the time Darby returned to Charlie's room, Leslie was at her bedside. Both women looked worse than when Darby had seen them just an hour before.

"I figured out the problem," Darby said calmly. "Now I need you to leave the room. I promise, I'll take care of her."

Leslie looked alarmed, but did as Darby asked. When she was gone, Darby fished a vial of Naloxone, the rescue med for an OxyContin overdose, out of her pocket. She administered a hefty initial dose and set the machine to meter out smaller doses over the next few hours.

Just as she was finishing up, Yelena reappeared. Darby could barely look at her.

"What are you doing?"

Darby rounded on her.

"It was Oxy."

Yelena's face grew pale.

"Your lazy treatment approach nearly killed her. I've administered Naloxone."

Darby ripped off her gloves and threw them in a nearby trash can. Yelena looked sick.

"You're welcome." Darby said it spitefully as she headed for the door.

She was shaking as she emerged into the hallway. It was a struggle to keep her calm as she briefed Leslie on the situation. She wanted to be honest, but knew she couldn't be too candid—she had to insulate the hospital from liability even if it had been their mistake.

She returned to her own floor feeling weak. Her plan was to lie down on the couch in her office until she collected herself, then return to her patients. But she was surprised to see a strange man standing in front of her office door.

"Darby?"

A strange man who knew her name, apparently. He was a bit taller than she was, slightly heavyset, and appeared to be in his late twenties. His voice was unexpectedly high-pitched and absurdly bubbly. She wasn't used to seeing strangers in this area of the hospital, let alone strangers who called her by her first name.

"Uh…yes?"

He held out his right hand. His left hand held a plain white paper shopping bag.

"So great to meet you! I'm Andrew," he chirped, drawing

out the 'w' sound in his name.

He smiled at Darby for an awkwardly long time, as if she should know who he was.

"Michael's assistant?" It sounded like a question, even though it was an explanation. Michael had mentioned his assistant before, but had never called him by name. "He wanted me to bring you lunch."

She blinked in surprise.

"How long have you been waiting here?"

"Not too long," he replied vaguely. She suspected this was a lie.

"Here you go! Enjoy!"

He held out the bag. She took it.

"And so nice to meet you. Michael says the nicest things about you."

He does?

"Wow. Thank you. And please thank Michael for me," she managed.

"I will!" Andrew's enthusiasm was bottomless. "He lands in five minutes," he confirmed after looking at his watch.

Michael had orchestrated all of this from a plane? He'd been texting her just an hour before. Before she could express further surprise, Andrew was gone.

CHAPTER THIRTEEN

GT PRIME

SIX WEEKS HAD PASSED SINCE SHE AND MICHAEL HAD struck up their arrangement, and they had settled into a rhythm. They worked out the logistics of their meetings in between flirtatious texts. Neither had been joking about their punishing work schedules. Darby's shifts could be erratic, depending on her patient load at the hospital. If one of her charges was in crisis, she had to stay late. It meant she flaked on plans sometimes. But true to his word, Michael never gave her shit about prioritizing work, no matter how late she was or how many times she cancelled.

"The cold flatters you." Michael smiled, smoothing the backs of his warm fingers over her rosy cheeks. He'd been waiting at the bar at GT Prime for twenty minutes. Even when she looked like an underslept hag, he always found a kind thing to say.

Unwrapping her cream-colored cashmere scarf from around her shoulders, his fingers grazed that spot on her neck. It was the first of many small gestures that would ground her. Kissing her cheek hello, he extended the pressing of his soft lips a moment longer than he needed to. She shivered from his fingertips on her neck again as he swept her hair over one shoulder before slipping her white woolen trench down her arms.

GT Prime was the latest eatery by a restaurant group that had won Darby over with its first two offerings. The decor had a cavernous feeling to it, despite its two-stories and the unlikely combination of exposed concrete and reclaimed wood. Eclectic accents such as fur-lined bar chairs and lighting that was slightly reminiscent of playing jacks fit together so tastefully that even in her tired state, Darby felt like she was dripping with style.

Michael had disappeared to the coat room after coaxing her onto the high-back bar stool he'd been sitting on when she arrived. She was glad they had a spot at the end of the bar closest to the open kitchen, where she could feel the warmth of the grilling ovens with their open flames. Taking a long, relieved sip of something with rosemary and plenty of gin, Darby began to relax. It felt good to be off her feet, to be among people whose focus was having a good time. With the weather getting colder, she was craving comfort food and a large glass of red wine.

They had been eating together more and more. Between their acrobatic sex, the fact that they both forgot to eat when work got crazy, and a general aversion to cooking after a long day, one or both of them was always starving. When Michael returned, she had just set the nearly-empty drink down on the bar. He plucked it up and took the last sip before motioning to the bartender for the check. He looked down at her, sweeping his eyes over her face, smiling gently as if he were happy to see her. She wanted to lean in to him, to feel his touch again.

"Thank you for lunch," she said, ignoring her impulse. She had to remind herself that they were in public.

The bartender arrived with a receipt, and she watched him pen what looked more like an elegant insignia than a written-out name. Though the "M" and the "B" of Michael Blaine were discernible, the whole thing was very artistic.

Even his signature is beautiful, she thought. She didn't know why she hadn't noticed it before.

"You're welcome." He touched her neck softly once again before helping her out of her chair. This was almost as good as the sex—the way the forces of their magnetic fields pulled them together at the same time they kept them apart.

After they had moved from the bar to a table, she perused the menu hungrily. She was about to ask Michael what he would order when a buxom waitress approached, looking only at him. The waitress leaned over—unnecessary since the restaurant was full, but not loud—and spoke directly to Michael.

"Can I help you choose a wine?"

Michael kept his eyes on the menu for a moment before flicking his eyes straight up to hers, ignoring her ample breasts, despite her obvious display.

"My girlfriend knows what I like," he said smoothly, the corner of his mouth crooking upward in a knowing smile. "I think you'd better ask her."

The waitress' face soured as she turned to Darby.

"Do you have the Bodega Catena Zapata Malbec?" Darby asked, not bothering with the menu.

The waitress nodded curtly.

"We'll take that," Darby said dismissively, shifting her eyes back to Michael.

"Good choice," he returned, smiling conspiratorially and keeping his eyes on her.

It wasn't the first time Michael had thwarted the attempts of a blatant, hopeful flirtation, though Darby felt disconcerted by how often women did it right in front of her. She didn't blame Michael for playing up their relationship when he needed to, either. If she were his real girlfriend, she might be annoyed, and if she were the insecure type of girlfriend, she might even feel threatened. But for now, she was just a clever decoy.

She could tell he didn't like this kind of attention. Witnessing him have to deal with so many unwanted advances from strangers showed Darby they were more alike than she'd originally thought. Both of them were targets for the shallowest of reasons.

"I'm sitting right here", Darby mouthed, shaking her head in disbelief.

"Shameless hussy," Michael whispered. Darby stifled a laugh. The waitress was still within earshot, and had glared at them at least once.

She couldn't help but think about her exes and compare Michael's behavior to theirs. None of them had a wandering eye—Darby never would have put up with that—but none of them had ever set boundaries like Michael did either. Most guys relished female attention no matter how often they received it. But when it was objectifying, and cheap, not to mention rude for being delivered in front of a date, Michael let them know the score every time. She had heard of men like this, but never really believed they existed. If even only a little, Michael was restoring her faith in men.

"So what's the psych ward like?" Michael asked after the wine had been poured. The question startled her a bit. They'd been seeing each other for nearly two months. How was it that they'd managed not to talk about their jobs?

"Either totally quiet, or totally insane," she admitted.

He raised an eyebrow at her choice of words. She shook her head and tried not to indulge him with a smile.

"It's not designed for patients to stay long-term. It's usually a family member who brings in a relative when they can't handle a psychotic episode alone. We stabilize the patients and then work with the families around longer-term strategies."

He hadn't tuned out yet. In fact, he was looking at her expectantly, so she continued.

"I get a fair number of patients from the ER—mostly overdoses or people who need to be on suicide watch. I also get calls for consults in other parts of the hospital. And when I'm not dealing with whatever walks through the door, I do my research."

"What's your research about?"

"Do you seriously want to know? Isn't this boring?"

"I'd rather find out sooner than later whether your research involves overachieving professional men who solicit brilliant women to become their companions."

They both smiled.

"Try permanent changes in the brain among people who are addicted to opioids."

"So you're trying to prove that opioids cause permanent changes in the brain?"

She shook her head.

"That's already been proven—I'm looking for patterns in the changes that do occur so that we can learn how to treat opioid addiction more effectively."

"Will your research lead to the development of a drug?"

"Maybe," she continued. He already knew that her specialty was psychopharmacology, a subspecialty of psychiatry that deals with prescribing medication for psychiatric disease.

"Right now, we treat opioid addiction by getting addicts off the drug, often by giving them substitute drugs like methadone. It's an old way of thinking. The logic is that if you wean people off of the drug itself, they'll be able to progress from physiological dependence to psychological dependence. And once it's out of their system, we treat the psychology. The problem is, psychological approaches to managing opioid addiction aren't working. The recidivism rate for opioids is higher than for any other drug class, which suggests that we may be wrong about our ability to eliminate the physiological addiction. Opioid addiction might need a new treatment model—different from what we use for other drugs. If we understood brain changes related to opioids more specifically, we would be in a better position to understand the best courses of treatment."

"Wow," he said simply. "How close are you?"

"Not as close as I want to be," she said, and it felt vulnerable for her to admit. "My boss isn't exactly on board."

She didn't mention how she wasn't making nearly as much progress as she had hoped, mainly because Huck was giving her loads of busy work. Darby suspected that this maneuver was specifically designed to keep her away from her research.

"I can prove persistent and specific changes within the brain that are different from previous observations but nothing that offers a clear path to treatment. But, they just gave me three hundred grand, which will buy me another six months."

He put down his glass and leaned toward her.

"That's really important work. I'm not surprised that you're doing something great, but I'm still impressed."

"I'm impressive." She shrugged.

"Yes, you are," he said, his voice a bit lower.

He's not flirting with you for real, she had to remind herself. She'd had to remind herself of that a lot, lately.

"What's your work like?" she asked, genuinely interested as well. "Like, what do you do every day?"

"It depends on where we are in the project life cycle," he

replied. "When we're in design phase, I spend a lot of time drafting at home or in my office. It's creative work and it's fairly solitary."

She nodded, sitting back in her chair and taking a long sip of wine.

"Once I have concepts to show, it's a lot of internal meetings to decide which ideas we'll show to clients, what changes we need to make. When plans get approved, projects go into planning and I'm minimally involved unless questions come up that would impact the build."

"So, why architecture instead of art?" she asked, voicing a question she'd had for a while. "Was art just too impractical?"

"Not exactly...growing up, we didn't have a lot of money. My dad was out of the picture. My mom was the head housekeeper for this family in Glencoe. She worked for them since before I was born until the day she died. When I was a kid, she would have to take me to work when there was nobody else to watch me. We'd be driving through all those nice neighborhoods, and she would point out the houses she liked. She knew the Victorian Gothic from the Italianate, the Georgians from the Tudors. She loved the Mansard roofs, and I loved to draw. Soon I was drawing the kinds of houses I saw. It became kind of a game—I would show her my drawings, and she would tell me what she liked about them."

As he told the story, he intermittently looked between Darby and a place that seemed worlds away. She wondered how many people he had ever told this story to.

"One day—I'll never forget it—I was in our kitchen, just sketching whatever was in my brain. She had a pot in her hand, but she put it down on the table when she saw what I was drawing. She gave me this look, this smile, and she said, in a voice I'd never heard before, 'That's my house, Michael. Will you build it for me one day?' But she got so distracted by the picture that she forgot about the pot and it made a big heat stain on the wood. Each time I saw the stain, I remembered her face that day."

Even in low light, she could see the subtle shining of his eyes.

"When did she die?" Darby asked softly, not shying away from the topic. She knew it was so much worse when somebody mumbled an 'I'm sorry for your loss," rather than giving you the chance to remember the person you loved.

"When I was twenty-one." He looked back at her with a sad smile. "She didn't live long enough to see me build it, but she lived long enough to see the plans."

He reached into his pocket, pressed a button on his phone, and handed it to her. His screen saver was an architect's color drawing of a beautiful house, landscaping and all, with a woman's name written on the bottom.

"Tara."

Darby's own eyes were wet with tears.

"It's beautiful." She didn't relinquish his phone, but pressed the side button so she could look at the drawing again after the screen went dark.

"Will you build it?" Her voice was hopeful.

"I'll live in it one day. It's all part of the master plan. My mom is why I'm so involved with The Frigg Foundation."

She tore her eyes away from the phone and finally met his gaze.

"Breast cancer?" The sad story finally came together. "My grandmother too," she said. A silent understanding passed between them as she gently handed him back his phone.

"Have you always wanted to be a psychiatrist, since you were a kid?" he changed the subject. "I can picture a 5-year old version of you psychoanalyzing your teddy bears."

"Actually, no," she admitted. "Growing up, I always wanted to be a writer. I loved stories—I still do. I spent a lot of time surrounded by people, but alone, you know? Always on the campaign trail, nobody my age to play with. I took my journal with me everywhere."

"What happened?" His voice was deep and soft. His eyes were clear and curious.

"Apart from the fact that I was presented with a very short list of acceptable professions as a requirement if I wanted my father to pay for school?"

Michael raised his eyebrows.

"Yeah, my dad is like that." He subtly shook his head in disapproval.

"It was the year I had to pick a specialty when my mother overdosed on pills. I was angry. And confused. And on a crusade to rid the world of the pain suffered by addicts and their families. So I chose psychopharmacology—"

"—so you could save people like your mother," Michael accurately concluded.

She nodded confirmation.

"What was she like, your mother?" he asked in a soothing tone.

"She was beautiful. We loved each other a lot. It sounds stupid, but even though she went down a bad path with pills and alcohol, she was the sanest person in my family."

She hesitated before asking her next question. Michael was thirty-one, and had been without his mother for more than ten years. Yet, for Darby, it had barely been four and in many ways, her pain felt fresh.

"Does it get easier?" She barely looked at him as she said the words, still feeling emotional from their exchange.

From across the table, she felt his larger hand cover hers. Her instinct was to turn her palm up and take his hand. Michael's comfort felt good.

"It changes, for sure. But, easier? No. I don't think so." His thumbs stroked her knuckles.

"Do you want to see a picture?" Darby sniffed.

"Yes," he said without hesitation.

Reluctantly, Darby freed the hand Michael was holding in order to recover her phone. She clicked to reveal her own screen saver, handing it to Michael. His face brightened.

"She *was* beautiful…" His eyes were fixed on the image of the two of them and he smiled. "And she had your energy. I can see it."

And then she really did want to cry. Because it was true.

"What would she think?" Michael asked. "If she knew what you were doing with your life?"

Darby laughed through unshed tears. Nobody had ever asked her that. "She'd tell me to be a writer. What would *your* mom say if she could see you now?"

Now it was Michael's turn to smile. "She'd tell me to quit dicking around with skyscrapers and build her fucking house."

Darby laughed harder as Michael handed back her phone.

"My mom was always bugging me to settle down. She wanted me to meet a nice girl, start a family, not get caught up in my job…pretty much the opposite of what I'm doing now. I think she had a lot of guilt around us growing up without a dad. Her highest hope for us was that we would create the families we never had."

Darby understood.

"My mom always wanted me to be my own woman," Darby offered then. "She was kind of…trapped in this awful marriage. She'd been raised to find a good husband and be a good wife, but that life suffocated her. She wanted it to be different for me. She really saw me, you know? It was a big fight when my mom told my dad she would pay for me to go to whatever school I wanted to go to. She went to bat for me. But Frank Christensen always wins…"

Now it was Darby who must've been a million miles away, because when she looked back at Michael, she felt as if he had been studying her for a long time.

"What does that mean?"

"Having status like his does more than just open doors—it closes them, too." She'd only ever told this to Ben. "Two weeks after I got my acceptance letter from Oberlin, I got a second letter rescinding the offer."

The look on Michael's face was a broad spectrum of shock, anger, sadness, and pity.

"I hope you don't take this the wrong way…" he began, "… but, at this wedding we're going to, do you need me to pretend to like your father? Because you're making him sound like a total jerk."

She cast her eyes to the side, uttering bitterly, "You don't know the half of it."

Her mind went someplace else for a moment, to a single memory that was better-left in the past. When the sound of his voice pulled her back, he had a strange look on his face.

"Are you're sure you want to go to this thing?" He asked it with caution.

"We'll make an appearance," she muttered. "But believe me, we're not staying for long."

CHAPTER FOURTEEN

RESTLESS

DARBY SHIVERED FROM WHERE SHE STOOD IN THE doorway, colder from her own unwelcome thoughts than she was from the temperature in her room. The clock on the nightstand told her it was 3:00AM. That was about two-and-a-half hours longer than she'd planned on letting Michael stay. It was her own fault for falling asleep—she hadn't meant to drift off after their vigorous sex, and she imagined that he hadn't either. He slept deeply, wholly unaware of how his presence at that hour, under those circumstances, unraveled her.

She hated herself for standing there, cold and numb in her own house when she could have been cozy and sleeping next to the gorgeous man in her bed. After all, Michael wasn't going to hack into her computer searching for state secrets as she slept. He wasn't going to make a tawdry sex tape of the two of them together to blackmail Frank Christensen. He wasn't going to get attached and make himself comfortable like Felix had.

Why can't I just be normal?

The thought repeated itself in her head. It was the question that had caused her so much fruitless agony over the years.

Granted, she knew her trust issues weren't pathological—they made sense, given all she'd been through. Thanks to her father's politics, Darby had been stalked twice. An apartment she'd lived in had been bugged. There had been a kidnapping attempt when she was a teenager, and a long list of death threats.

There were other things. Her parents' marriage had been a train wreck. Her friendships growing up had been a sham. She'd learned the hard way that people who tried to get close to her were often more interested in currying favor with her family than they were with her. Being the daughter of Frank Christensen meant that a normal life wasn't possible. Acting normal would be pretending.

Yet Darby still felt more normal than she had in years. She finally felt in control of her own life and comfortable in her own skin. After all that had happened to her as a kid, it was a small miracle that she functioned as well as she did. Things that came easily to other people—like having friends, and holding down a job, and maintaining any semblance of a relationship—were things that Darby had earned. She didn't like moments like this—moments that cast a shadow over the many battles she'd fought, and won.

It was no coincidence that she had been drawn to psychiatry. Darby wasn't too dense to realize that some part of her had wanted to confront her issues. Growing up in the shadow of an important man—a bad man—had screwed her up. But she thought she'd come farther than this. She liked Michael. She was already trusting him with so much. This arrangement had been a big step for her. It had been more than three months and he had never done anything to break her confidence. Yet, there she stood against her doorjamb, paranoid about letting him stay over.

Completely restless and no closer to peace, she grabbed her phone off of the bedside table and walked down to the kitchen. She needed something—anything—to relax her. Filling the kettle and putting it on the stove, she rummaged in her cabinet for tea before setting about finding her favorite mug. She dropped a bag of chamomile inside and poured boiling water over it after her kettle had whistled.

Sitting on a bar stool with her tea in one hand, she finally tapped the screen of her phone. Three texts had come through from Anne while she'd been upstairs.

Drink?

I'm off in half an hour.

Then, *Where the hell are you?*

With practiced ease and a single thumb, Darby texted back, knowing that if Anne hadn't gotten off of work more than a few hours before, she might still be awake.

Sorry. I'm home. Michael's over. I didn't hear the phone.

Dancing dots appeared on her screen moments later as Anne tapped her reply, proof that her friend was awake.

What the fuck are you doing texting me instead of getting some more of that?

Darby had to smile. Although Anne hadn't met Michael, she had seen pictures of the two of them together when they'd shown up on Page Six.

Can't sleep. Making myself some tea.

A ringtone version of *Seven Nation Army* began playing on Darby's phone seconds after her text message had been delivered. Anne was calling her.

"Don't bullshit me," Anne accused. "You've been working crazy hours. Why aren't you asleep?"

Darby sighed. She wanted to tell Anne everything, and knew she could trust her friend. But she didn't want to reveal her constant state of confusion, and Anne was the kind of friend who wouldn't let her beat around the bush. Sharing this with her would corner Darby into admitting her fears. She barely wanted to admit to herself, let alone anyone else, how hard it was for her to let people in, how much trouble she had understanding why people liked her.

It was easier with friends from the hospital. They'd been in the trenches together, seen each other through moments when they had to be strong for sick and dying patients. They kept each other going through grueling double shifts. They gave each other pep talks after dealing with difficult families. But outside of work, things were different. Michael was different. And while she understood why he loved their white-hot sex, she didn't get why he invited himself to the movies with her, why he grilled her about details of her life and bought her lunch. Yes, he was lonely and craved companionship. But, why was he drawn to *her*? Why was he sleeping in her bed when he could have his pick?

"I'm not used to sleeping with someone else."

"Does he fart in his sleep? I'll bet that from his pretty ass, they don't even stink…"

"His pretty ass? Don't you like girls?"

"I'm gay, sweetie. Not blind. Why aren't you next to that man?"

Darby took a long sip of her tea, wracking her brain over how to ask for Anne's advice without starting a big conversation about it all.

"You know I like having my own space," Darby hedged.

"I know you're missing the best part," Anne countered. "Wanna trade places? You can come over and cuddle with Mr. Bigglesworth."

Mr. Bigglesworth was Anne's ironically fluffy cat.

"I know," Darby groaned. "You're right. I should let myself enjoy it."

"I'm hanging up now." Anne sounded satisfied as she said it. "Now, stop overthinking things, and *go to bed*."

Several hours later, Darby awoke to Michael's body pressed up close behind her. She had heeded Anne's advice. Slipping into bed next to Michael had felt nice. In his sleep, he had sensed her presence and before she drifted off, they were back in each other's arms.

"Keep grinding me like that and I'm gonna have to fuck you." Michael's deep voice, raspy with sleep, stirred her in private places as his breath fanned out over her cheek.

Involuntarily, she flexed her back, creating more friction between her ass and his erection. She had no idea how long she'd been doing that, but the wetness between her legs and her erect nipples told her it had been long enough. She must have been rubbing against him in her sleep. It wasn't the first time she'd gravitated toward him like that.

"Do you need an engraved invitation?" She ground back against him again, this time reaching her hand down to meet his, and sliding it up to cup her breast. He bit a delicious spot on the back of her neck as he squeezed, causing her to gasp at the sensation. His other hand reached downward, sliding her panties aside.

"It only seemed right to wait 'till you woke up."

He pushed into her in one swift move, just as she reached her arm around, desperately gripping the back of his head. And she was glad she did—he drove into her hard, her whole body jolting with every thrust. In seconds, she was breathless with pleasure.

"I think I'm awake now," she managed.

He let out a little moan as she pushed back with more

vigor, meeting him with every stroke. Though he was fucking her hard, his movements were slow and deliberate. In this position, with him behind her, he was hitting her so deep it almost hurt, yet he seemed to know her limits. He was fucking her so good—gently enough not to really hurt her, but rough enough to make it so, so hot.

Five amazing minutes later, her pussy was still twitching from the orgasm she'd had from their little display. He'd pulled out at the last second, and had just finished cleaning her up. Waiting for him to clean himself up, she lounged on the bed with her eyes closed, anxious for him to get back in. Instead, she felt a dip on her side of the bed and opened her eyes to see him. Not only was he not getting back into bed, he was fully dressed.

"I'm gonna head out."

She sat up a little, her mind registering not only her disappointment but also the irony of that sentiment. Just four hours before, she'd been the one close to kicking him out.

"The morning sex was nice." Eager to make the moment less awkward, she said it with a smile.

"Morning sex is always nice," he laughed. "We're gonna have to do that more often."

She envied the casual way in which he made the suggestion. When she heard the dull thud of the front door closing behind him, she felt as mixed up as the night before. She felt once again in control of herself now that he was gone, but somehow she missed him already.

Though Darby had her own office in the hospital's administrative building, she spent most of her time away from patients in her research lab, which had work tables, refrigerators, a large supply closet, computers and other specialized machines. When Rich strolled in, she had already been there for an hour. She sat on a lab stool, a neat row of petri dishes and a timer set in front of her, as she waited for the solutions to react.

Darby liked bumping into Rich at the lab—they sometimes scheduled formal meetings there to tackle results they needed to look at together, but more often they worked independently. Given recent events with Huck and Yelena, who both seemed to have deepened their grudge against her, it was nice to know she still had a friend.

Darby was measuring the presence of a certain chemical in the brains of opiate-addicted cadavers against its presence in the brains of cadavers who had no history with opioids. It was the fifth on a long list of chemical properties she was looking to isolate. She had plans to test twenty more.

"You've been smiling a lot lately," Rich observed and she realized she'd been caught laughing at something Michael had texted. She finished tapping out her reply before putting the device down and focusing her attention on Rich.

"New boyfriend?" he asked.

"No, just a friend," she answered vaguely. "You know I don't really date." She knew that if she admitted she was seeing somebody, Rich would insist on having her bring him around. Anne was already begging to meet Michael in person, and Darby didn't need them teaming up against her.

"I can't blame you for that…" he said stoically. He had finally revealed to her that he was getting a divorce, confirming the rumor that Anne had heard. Rich didn't seem to be taking things well.

"I take it going through a divorce is every bit as awful as it's cracked up to be?" she cringed a bit as she asked.

He flopped heavily into his chair.

"She's turned into a completely different person."

"You still haven't told me what happened," Darby pointed out gently.

"It was my fault, really. I fell out of love with her. When she insisted that we actively try for kids, I came clean. But she's bloody angry. I never cheated. Never lied. When it was time to tell her the truth, I did the right thing. I told her she could have anything she wanted in the divorce. But she's made it quite hard."

Darby tried to keep her cool. Rich may have been her friend, but he was yet another man in her life who rationalized his selfish behavior. She hated this man-logic, this comfort in playing the victim when it was he who had done wrong. Darby neutralized her facial features and spoke in her soft but stern therapy voice.

"It sounds like Lindsay feels out of control. *You* decided that you didn't want kids anymore. *You* decided the marriage was over. *You* moved out. And now she probably feels like you're trying to dictate the divorce by setting the terms. Why don't you let her be in charge a little? It might soften the blow."

He put his head in his hands and rubbed at his eyes with the backs of his fingers. She realized then how tired he looked.

"I just want it to be over," he said definitively before lowering his voice. "But you're probably right."

Her timer went off as he said his last words. She cast him a sympathetic glance as she went to her microscope. A silence settled into the room as she looked at her specimens and recorded her results.

"You'd tell me, wouldn't you…if you were seeing someone?" he asked a minute later and she was surprised he brought it up again.

"I'd tell you if it was serious," she said, one eye squinting to see through the viewing column of her scope.

"So you're open to meeting Mr. Right, then," he prodded, sounding anxious enough to make her lift her head and turn around to regard him.

"Don't worry about me, Rich," she said, smiling at his concern. "I'm not lonely. One day maybe I'll meet the right guy at the right time, but for now, my work is more than enough."

Like everyone else in her life, he didn't look convinced.

"Promise me you'll at least be open to it," he pressed. "Lindsay and I were very happy once."

Look how well that turned out, some part of her felt like saying. But Rich was hurting and she didn't want to make things worse.

"Everyone has a different ideal. Falling in love and living happily ever after is yours. My ideal isn't wrong—it's just different."

His intensity didn't soften at her appeasing words. If anything, he studied her harder.

"What *is* your ideal?"

"Companionship," she said simply. She was surprised by how slippery Michael's words felt rolling off her tongue, and how genuine and true they had become for her.

"And you have that?"

It was her turn to scrutinize him. Something about this didn't seem casual.

"What's with all the questions?"

"You said you weren't seeing anybody."

"I wasn't asking for an interrogation. I was asking how you were dealing with the divorce," she retorted somewhat tartly.

"A divorce I just poured my heart out to you about," he challenged.

"I pour my heart out to you about my asshole boss on a

daily basis."

"It's not the same thing."

Darby ran her hands through her hair. He looked at her for a long moment, through eyes that held emotions she did not understand. She looked away when he dipped his chin toward his chest and palmed the back of his neck.

"You know everything about the most important thing in my life," she pointed out.

"Your work."

"Yes, my work. And I'm not ashamed that it's my priority."

"Maybe you should be."

His voice was soft but his words weren't kind. The fabric of her compassion was becoming threadbare. She was going to have to break it down for him.

"Rich. I don't need this job. I don't need to work another day in my life if I don't want to. I'm here because I choose to be. Even though my boss hates me. Even though patients die. Even though one of my best friends doesn't trust me to make my own choices."

At last, he looked repentant.

"I've spent the majority of my life under my father's thumb. The last thing I will ever need is more people telling me what to do. So promise me that we are *never* having this conversation again."

He nodded. "Forgive me. I'm...not myself."

She wasn't sure she believed him. But she was glad to bring the conversation to a close.

Bored from a slow night at work and too tired to focus on her research, Darby mindlessly checked apps on her phone in between consults. She had a bit of a routine—first she cycled through her e-mail, then her Instagram and Facebook. If she was desperate, she browsed Vine, and when she could barely stand from fatigue, she might default to Candy Crush.

At the moment, watching *Tasty* videos on Facebook was not only making her depressed about her lack of cooking prowess—it was also making her hungry, which was not a good thing given her limited choices. She was about to abandon the app altogether when something new popped into her feed. Ben and Tami posted a happy picture of themselves at what looked like a fancy restaurant, announcing that, as of today, they'd been married for four months.

Four months.

Had it been so long since she and Michael had begun sleeping together? It didn't feel like that much time had passed, yet it simultaneously felt as if they'd known each other for much longer. Between his frequent business trips and her odd work schedule, they barely saw each other more than once a week, but when they were together, it counted.

On impulse, she pressed the "Share" button and private messaged Ben's status to Michael. A minute later, her phone was ringing in her hand.

"So today's our four-month fuck-aversary?"

She laughed, a bit of her energy returning.

"I guess it is."

"I should've bought you flowers."

"Flowers are for boring boyfriends. You can do better than that…"

"Are you doubting my creativity?" His voice became low and her nipples tightened at the thought of how creatively he'd made her come the night before.

"Not that…" she drew out, allowing her own voice to lower. "Never that."

"How soon can you get out of work?" he asked.

"I'm still stranded 'till ten. I thought you had to work late, too."

"Suddenly I'm having trouble concentrating."

An hour and thirty-eight minutes later, the elevator doors to his penthouse were opening and he was on top of her the second she stepped out. Sliding his hand behind her neck, he pulled their bodies flush and invaded her mouth with a ravenous kiss. She heard the thud of the large purse she'd packed with clothes for the next day hit the floor. Sliding her hands around his waist, she began to untuck his shirt. He moaned as she kissed him and pulled at her bottom lip with his teeth as her cool hands met the hot skin of his back.

She felt his hands tugging at her oversized lapels. He realized right away that she wasn't wearing her usual coat. Pulling back, he looked down and took in her appearance more fully.

"What's this?" he asked, eyeing the shimmery black trench coat he'd never seen before.

She silently congratulated herself for stopping at her house before coming to Michael's. "My fuck-aversary coat."

His eyes traveled lower, slowing as they moved to take in her sheer black panty hose and tall heels.

"What's underneath it?" His hand was reaching down. A moment later, his open palm was running up her nearly-nude thigh.

She moved her own hand to the sash of the coat and pulled slowly until the tie released.

"Not much."

Well aware of his lingerie fetish, she'd been building a small collection. If he ever raided her office, he would find catalogs for Rigby & Peller, La Perla and Agent Provocateur. His eyes flicked up to hers, dark realization dawning.

"You are in so much trouble," he growled.

Darby shifted her weight in a way that allowed her to rub her legs together at their apex. The silk of her tiny panties was no match for the wetness that was building there.

"What am I being punished for?"

There was no playfulness in his eyes when he looked at her then.

"For making my body crave yours every second of every day."

His words knocked the wind out of her.

"For giving me mental images of you in lingerie that make me hard for you every night I'm gone," he continued.

Darby's heart thundered so hard in her chest that her breath became shaky. He had looked at her like this before, with wild desperation. But now he'd confessed it out loud. She owned some part of him. But she couldn't return with words that every cell in her body knew were true.

You're the best I've ever had.

I dream of you.

You own some part of me, and I hate myself for letting you.

"Give me what I deserve," she whispered.

She had hoped her punishment would begin with a good hard fuck against the glass wall of his living room. Maybe another one in the hallway en route to his bedroom, and even more once they reached his bed. There was something she loved about waking up in the morning and following their trail of discarded clothes. But he had different plans for her. They involved teasing her for what felt like hours without letting her come.

They did leave a trail of clothing as they made their way to his bed—her coat draped against the back of his sofa, her panties in the hallway, her shoes at the threshold of his bedroom door. He had lifted her high up against his panoramic windows, her thighs on his shoulders as he buried his mouth in her pussy. When she'd begged him to let her come, he'd eased her down gently, first onto her feet, then onto her knees as he'd fucked her mouth instead. On the way to his bedroom, they had kissed as she tore his clothes off, and tried to take off her own, but he'd made sure she kept her bra, garters, and panty hose on.

As she lay on his bed, she felt desperate. What he was doing to her was sweet agony, and she was aching to come. His long middle finger was inside her and his eyes were affixed on hers. They both knew how firmly he was holding her in limbo, how with one hard stroke of his finger or smart flick of his tongue, she would go off.

"You have an iron will," she'd taunted in a strangled voice.

"I have a photographic memory," he whispered, stroking her at a pace that was painfully slow.

"Is this how you want to remember me?" she panted.

His finger had gone in to the hilt, and was now withdrawing in another measured stroke.

"No," he'd said, his finger exiting her completely, not breaking contact, but sliding lower. So easily, it slid into her other entrance, the pad of his finger pressing firmly on some other glorious spot.

"I want to remember you like this," he said simply, breaking their gaze to sharply suck her clit.

She fell, completely, apart.

CHAPTER FIFTEEN

FELIX

MEET ME AT MY APARTMENT.

They hadn't seen each other in six days—she wasn't even sure where he'd been that time. When he'd texted two hours before saying he'd taken an earlier flight, she'd gladly obeyed his command.

She was surprised to find him in the lobby of his building when she arrived. His muscular chest and arms looked amazing beneath the dark gray Henley he wore. He stood barefoot in an old pair of jeans that reached the floor and something told her he was fresh from the shower. Before he saw her, she watched him hold court at the reception desk. They were all laughing—Javier the doorman, Jim the security guard behind the desk, and the delivery man who had just handed over a large paper-in-plastic bag. But it was Michael's smile that lit up the room, Michael who had everyone feeling good. He would've made a great politician.

She recognized the second that he spotted her. His smile widened. His eyes brightened as he took her in. She thought she would melt from how he made her feel.

"You're right on time," he said as she approached, nodding his thanks at the delivery man and shifting the bag of takeout into his other hand so that he could hold hers. He kissed her cheek in the friendly manner they reserved for public greetings. He would wait until they were in his apartment to kiss her for real.

"Prying eyes," he'd clarified once as they'd ridden the elevator and he'd shifted his gaze up to the iridescent black sphere that she recognized as a camera.

But once the elevator doors closed behind them and they walked into his space, he hastily dropped the bag on his kitchen counter. Still holding her hand, he pulled her body toward his and devoured her mouth in a hungry kiss. She could feel it already—the familiar magic that happened when they were together. At that moment, it was just a kiss, but she knew how it would manifest next, knew how she would feel it in the desperate way he touched her, how she would see it in the way he looked at her when he moved inside her. Touching Michael always felt like touching the divine.

When her stomach growled again, he pulled away from her reluctantly and kissed the tip of her nose lightly. Turning away, he dug into the bags to extract the food and began making each of them a plate. Her eyes wandered to the television, which she had just noticed was on. It was the news—they were running a story about her father. Not wanting to sour a nice moment with thoughts of him, she searched for the remote.

"You look nothing like him," Michael commented lightly as he spooned green curry tofu onto their plates.

Darby had been told this all her life. Frank Christensen had a polished movie star look to him—smooth dark hair that was always perfectly coiffured, a smile that tempered cockiness with charm, and blue eyes that foreshadowed mischief. Being compared to a man as striking as her father would have normally been taken as flattery. But for Darby, being told that she was not like Frank Christensen was always the better compliment.

"I am my mother's daughter…in more ways than one," she agreed. Not seeing the remote, she considered walking to the television and turning it off the old fashioned way. Her father's voice always sounded grating to her.

"I take it you don't share his politics?" Michael asked.

"We disagree on every issue."

"Did your mother disagree too?"

"Their fights were legendary." Darby didn't want to elaborate. "How about you?" she asked, shifting her focus back to Michael.

He stopped what he was doing and pinned her with a remorseless look. "Every time he's run, I've voted for the other guy."

You and me both, she thought. Forgetting the remote for a minute, her face broke into a wide smile.

Later, after they'd eaten and made good use of his bed, the soft vibration of her phone against the bedside table began a split second before the ringtone. As she recognized the guitar intro to *We Are Never Getting Back Together*, Darby untangled herself reluctantly from the peaceful cocoon of Michael's waterbed, resplendent with its 800-thread count sheets, to press the red button that would let her decline the call. Twisting back toward the bed, she again wrapped herself in the blissful afterglow of their rendezvous. Sinking in made her feel like she was being enveloped in a warm hug.

Michael's footsteps on the bamboo floors could barely be heard as he returned from the inner chamber of his master bath. She had learned to expect the warm washcloth tenderly pressed between her legs. When he was done, he tossed the washcloth on the floor, straightened the disheveled covers and tucked her back into bed. Being cared for like this was splendid and she loved it more than she ever planned to let on.

Her eyes were trained on Michael. There was a clear line of vision through his enormous dressing suite. Michael even made washing up look sexy. God, his body was beautiful. She was becoming obsessed with his arms—his biceps and triceps were like steel. She especially liked the visual of his corded forearms and long fingers as they did simple things like swipe the screen of his cell phone or make coffee in the kitchen. He hadn't called her out on her staring, and she was glad because she couldn't help it. Clothed or unclothed, the man was gorgeous.

After climbing back in bed, he shimmied close to the middle and tucked his arm underneath her head, pulling her to his side. He was a master cuddler, a fact she had learned from hours of pillow talk. And he'd held to their agreement—to at least six orgasms every time they were together. That commitment meant they had plenty of down time in between rounds. Sometimes they snoozed, but mostly they snuggled, snacked, and talked. She tried not to dwell on how much she was getting used to it.

"The sushi today was so good," she murmured, drawing out the "o".

"You love sushi." He said it as if it explained why he had started to have lunch delivered to her regularly. Any time Michael even *suspected* Darby was too busy to eat, Andrew showed up at her office with a brown bag and an effervescent smile

"Thank you," she murmured against his chest, sniffing him discreetly as she always did.

"How many 'you're welcomes' do you need to hear before you stop thanking me?"

She felt a bit embarrassed. She had thanked him three times that day—once after Andrew dropped off the bag, then after she'd eaten because, holy shit, that shrimp tempura roll had been good. And again just now. She had thanked him profusely each time he had done something like that. Eating lunch every day was making a big difference. She had more energy, felt less irritable, and made better snack and dinner choices because she wasn't so ravenously hungry. Plus, he always ordered from the best places. They worked in more or less the same neighborhood, but Michael—or, rather, Andrew—knew his way around the local restaurants better than Darby did.

"It's just…really nice."

As the last word left her mouth, her phone began vibrating again with the same ring tone she had heard a few minutes before. This time she really didn't want to get up to turn it off. Still, if he'd called twice already, he would probably keep on calling.

Fucking Felix.

Rolling over, this time she didn't merely decline the call—she turned off her ringer altogether. She set her cheek back down on Michael's chest, and his hand returned to stroking her hair.

"I take it he didn't get the memo?"

Crap. He heard both calls.

"You know, the one where you told him that you are never, ever, ever getting back together." He said it in a girly voice.

"I wouldn't have pegged you for a Taylor Swift fan."

He pulled back a little bit and looked straight down at her. "I wouldn't have pegged *you* for one."

Fair enough.

She put her head back on his chest. "He's holding out hope," she explained.

Michael didn't say anything, but his silence was heavy with expectation. He had a way of coaxing out all the stories that she didn't want to tell. Sometimes Darby thought that, between the two of them, Michael would have made for a better shrink.

"He thinks things between us could work if we reimagined them."

"Could they?"

"Oh, wow—we're gonna do *this*?" she hedged.

"Avoid questions? I don't know. You tell me."

It was always like this with them. No small talk or shallow conversation. Like that first night, nothing was out of bounds, no topic too heavy when covered in witty repartee.

"*Felix...*" she began, emphasizing the name of her ex-boyfriend, "is a cable network executive. He spends a lot of time in New York and LA."

"Is that why you broke up?"

"Let's just say we had misaligned expectations."

"Did he cheat on you?"

Michael sounded mildly irritated by the possibility, but it was hard to tell. His guess was so far away from the truth that Darby let out a small laugh.

"Worse. He wanted to get married. I didn't."

She waited for Michael to express shock of some kind, or at least to question her decision. That was what every other person did when they got wind of the proposal.

"Well aren't you going to ask why?" she baited, irritated with herself for even caring whether he was interested.

"I don't need to ask why. It's obvious that *Felix* wasn't taking care of you."

She didn't miss how Michael emphasized her ex's name sarcastically.

The next thing she knew, she was sitting upright, staring at him expectantly. "How could you possibly know that?"

"Because you thank me three times every time I buy you a sandwich."

When he put it like that, it sounded a bit depressing.

"I think you're overthinking my gratitude for your having bought me lunch."

"Am I?"

He was entirely too observant.

"You know that you're more of a gentleman than monarchs I've met, right? Your chivalry is uncommonly refined."

It was true. Despite her high-society upbringing, Darby was hard-pressed to recall a single person as genteel as Michael. Michael, meanwhile, had grown up on the South Side, where his life had surely involved none of these absurd civilities. And yet, he had shown her more refined attention to her needs in the short time they'd been fucking than Felix had during their entire relationship.

"And your standards are lower than they should be," he retorted. "You're the last woman I know who should settle."

Don't settle, Darby.

Those were the words her mother had spoken to her over and over again, the one piece of advice she had consistently dispensed. The unspoken confession said everything—that she'd married the wrong man, that in choosing Frank Christensen, she had made a terrible mistake.

"I didn't settle. I told him no."

Michael quieted, ostensibly satisfied with this response. But before Darby could relax, he spoke again.

"There are only three kinds of guys who call, Darby. The kind who are actively dating you, the kind who think they have a shot at dating you, and the stalker kind."

"Oh, yeah? What does that make you?"

He ignored her. "How long has it been since you broke up?"

"Almost a year." Darby cringed.

Michael sat up even more, further disrupting her previously comfortable position.

"How often?"

She sat up, too. This was not how she had wanted to spend their time.

"A few times a month."

Michael was starting to look pissed.

"Stalking is serious shit, Darby. Do you think that just because you're a psychiatrist you can handle your own situation?"

"He's not stalking me. He thinks he has a shot, and I understand why."

When Michael looked at her impatiently, she relented and began to tell the story.

"So out of the blue, Felix proposed to me…and, practically in the same breath, tried to sell me on having kids. It turned into a huge fight. He pinned me down about exactly why I didn't want kids. I admitted some things I'd never told him, which pissed him off more and made the fight worse. It got so ugly, I broke up with him on the spot.

"It didn't take him long to figure out that he'd gone about everything all wrong," she continued. "He shouldn't have sprung it on me like that. He thought he'd just messed that one thing up and that if we could press rewind and have that same conversation differently, we could get everything on the right track."

"But that's not what you thought."

She shook her head.

"Him proposing was the wake-up call I needed to realize we were in two different relationships. He was…"

She hesitated, because it was uncomfortable to say.

"...deeply in love with me. More than I realized. The proposal was a surprise. It proved how little we understood each other. He didn't know how lukewarm I was about marriage... about him, really. He didn't know I—"

I was too fucked-up to get close to someone, she almost let slip out.

"—didn't want kids. I had to break up with him."

She watched Michael's face as he absorbed the story and waited for him to ask her again why Felix was still calling after a year. But he went in a different direction.

"So you just walked away? Maybe you didn't want to marry him, but weren't you at least a little in love with the guy?"

Michael picked up on everything.

"I really, really liked him."

And he gave her that look again, that look that said he could see right through her, the look that, in moments like these, scared her to her core. Because she wasn't lying, but she wasn't telling the whole truth and she wondered whether Michael really saw *that* part of her.

"Tell me why he's still calling you." This time, his demand was softer than before.

"He rarely does anymore. And rarely on purpose. It's midnight in New York right now. He's probably drunk dialing." And her voice held her compassion. "He really is getting over me. Just...every once in a while, he has a bad day."

Michael still seemed wary. Instead of speaking, he pulled open the drawer of his bedside table and pulled out two pixy sticks. He opened both of the candies before pulling Darby back into his arms and rearranging their bodies so they were once again reclining on his bed.

"Do you want me to have a little talk with him?" he asked

finally, breaking their silence after he had poured the flavored sugar into his mouth.

"Is that a euphemism, Vito Corleone? Are you going to make him an offer he can't refuse?"

"Guys know what to say to one another in these situations," he said. "You think I've never had to talk a guy down from chasing a woman he couldn't have? Besides, any call he gets from a guy he doesn't know telling him to back off of his ex is gonna be a pretty clear warning."

She'd never thought of it like that. Felix was getting better about not calling her, but what she hadn't admitted to Michael was that some part of her was concerned. On the very rare occasion when she picked up the phone, Felix sounded unhappy, and very much still in love.

"Alright. The next time you hear that ringtone, have at it."

She would be curious to eavesdrop on what she guessed would be an insightful conversation. Michael held her tighter in response and she snuggled back into him, finally tipping back the straw full of sugar and pouring it in her mouth. A moment later, he spoke again.

"Hey...you wanna watch *The Godfather* later?"

It made her laugh.

"Yeah. I do."

He kissed her hair.

CHAPTER SIXTEEN

YOU'RE SO VAIN

"SHIT."

Darby bristled at hearing the staccato bass guitar opening of *You're So Vain* by Carly Simon from beyond the door of her research lab's supply closet, her makeshift dressing room when she had somewhere to go after work. She'd been using it a lot lately. In the past month, she'd been to more bars, restaurants and night spots with Michael than she'd visited in the previous six months combined. After Felix, swearing off dating and avoiding social events had turned her into somewhat of a recluse. But she liked going out with Michael. He seemed to know every nook and cranny of Chicago and spending time with him gave her the sense of discovering her own city again.

The most amazing meal they'd shared had been at a tiny place in Little India. An older man sat near the front of the festively decorated dining room playing mesmerizing music on his sitar; the meal had cost them less than $45, including beer. The following night they'd done the tasting menu at TRU, a $700 affair that was walking distance from his house.

She loved all of it—loved the way he took her out, and loved the way he fucked her, loved that things between them felt natural and easy. When he was gone, some part of her missed him, but some part of her liked having her space. He was back in town now. For once, she was on track to be early—in half an hour they were slated to meet at the Four Seasons for drinks.

But Huck calling her on the phone now was standing in the way of her enjoyment of the cozy little bar, creating distance between Darby and her dirty martini with blue cheese olives. Still only half-dressed, she threw open the closet door and rushed to the phone, not wanting to miss Huck's call. God forbid she fail to be on duty five minutes before the end of her shift.

"Dr. Christensen," she answered, as if she didn't know exactly who it was.

"The results from the clinical refresher are in. I need to see you in my office. Now."

"On my way," she said, but before she'd even finished her sentence, he had already hung up.

Charming.

Darby threw the phone back on the lab table and buttoned her jeans as she returned to the supply closet. She pulled on black boots and a sheer black cowl turtleneck before flipping and rearranging her hair. God only knew what Huck wanted now.

"We've got a problem."

Huck's bald head, which she'd always thought he'd shaven completely in order to look younger in the face of actual balding, made him look like a diminutive version of Lex Luthor. She sat down in the guest chair and picked up the folder he had slid across the desk. Inside was a printout of her scores from the test she'd taken the week before. She couldn't believe her eyes.

"This can't be right."

The scores indicated that she had failed, and failed badly. She was licensed and board certified, but the hospital required all physicians to demonstrate that their specialty knowledge was still current. Quarterly testing was routine. The test had been administered to every doctor in her department. She remembered the day she'd taken it the week before. Huck himself had been the proctor.

"There's been a mix-up." She looked at him defiantly.

"The scores don't lie, Dr. Christensen."

"Except this *isn't* my score," she seethed. "I'll retake the test."

"That's against protocol. Tests are administered no more frequently than every three months. I'll have to suspend you from clinical work pending Board review."

Darby stood up.

"My scores have been in the 97th percentile every other time I've taken it," she protested. "Would you have the hospital incur the cost of backfilling my shifts with temps over an obvious mix up?"

He paled a bit at that. "Rules are rules."

"And who will take my shifts for the rest of the week?"

He rose, grabbing his coat and giving her a withering look.

"It's not your job to worry about the schedule. Be available tomorrow to Dr. Skubic for any transition work."

Five minutes later, Darby was barging into Dr. Chandrashekar's office. Three of those minutes had been spent collecting herself in the bathroom. Still too angry to speak, she threw the folder down on her mentor's desk.

Chandy, as she called the older woman, wasn't merely a mentor—she was a longtime ally to Darby. She'd overseen Darby's residency years before and they shared a deep respect for one another. Chandy was someone who had seen her work and could speak to her knowledge and skill—someone who could vouch for her.

Although Darby had been subtle about it, she had shared her concerns about Huck's treatment with Chandy a few times. No stranger to common troubles of women in male-dominated fields, Chandy had subtly indicated that she understood. She had once been Chief of Staff to the entire hospital and had faced her own challenges on her way to the top. She was highly respected, but semi-retired. Best of all, she outranked Huck.

"This doesn't look right," Chandy murmured, confirming what Darby already knew.

"Huck wants to suspend me."

"Tell him it's a mistake."

Darby pinned Chandy with a pointed look. "I did."

Chandy looked at her watch. "How long do you need to retake it?"

"Last week, I finished it in half the time."

The older woman nodded. "Let's go." Together, they went one floor up, to the training suite.

Chandy made quick work of pulling up the computer-generated test, which randomized questions to each user. It wouldn't be identical to the test that Darby had taken before, so a good score would be a strong indicator that she knew the material. Darby sent a quick text to Michael, letting him know she would be late.

As she retook the test, she double-checked her answer to every question, not wanting to make a single mistake. Since the test was multiple choice, her scores could be instantly tallied.

"You got 100%," Chandy said less than a minute after Darby had submitted her last answer.

Darby felt more anger than relief, but suppressed it. She

appreciated the fact that Chandy had dropped everything to help her.

"Thanks for letting me retake it. It's better I do it the same day I found out about my scores. It will take care of speculation that I had to cram to pass it."

"With your record, there should be no speculation," Chandy said the same moment that the printer roared to life. "Though these new scores will make any conversation about it pretty short. The only one who needs to be called out here is Dr. Huck," she finished bluntly.

Darby voiced the question that had been in the back of her mind since this had begun.

"What do you think happened?"

Chandy handed her a copy of the results and gave Darby no less than what she wanted—an honest opinion.

"A bad score didn't find its own way into the system. I think someone else failed the test."

Order me two.

It was the text Darby sent to Michael seconds after she had tucked herself into a cab. She probably needed a walk, to clear her mind, but she needed a drink more, and didn't like that she was already late.

Michael rose to greet her when she arrived at the bar, taking her hand briefly and pressing an innocuous kiss to her cheek. This bar, with its dark woods and rich fabrics, was familiar and comforting, and recalled what a hotel bar may have looked like a century before. He had chosen an out-of-the-way table, and sat in a chair that had him facing the room while hers would face the wall. She was grateful for his constant mindfulness of maintaining her anonymity. She didn't want to be recognized—especially that night.

"Thanks," she said as he pushed one of the two large martinis toward her—a Belvedere dirtied by olive juice with a skewer of olives filled with blue cheese. She took a long gulp before setting the glass back down.

"Easy, tiger."

She picked up the skewer and pulled an olive into her mouth. "You have no idea the day I've had."

He set down what looked like scotch. "Tell me."

She could hardly say it. Anger still hummed through her body. The accusation that was forming in her mind was too scathing to say out loud.

"My boss is sabotaging me." It felt big to admit. Darby had complained about Huck being a colossal jerk, but she'd downplayed parts of it to Michael. "I don't have proof but I think he's actively trying to destroy my career."

Michael frowned. "Tell me what he did."

"Today he suspended me from practicing after I failed a test that he proctored. It's a skills refresher everyone has to take once a quarter. I've passed it with flying colors at least ten times."

"You think he tampered with the results."

I know he did, she thought to herself. She was afraid that saying it out loud would make her seem paranoid.

"I'm sure it could have been a computer glitch or some other error," she admitted. "I didn't speculate on what went wrong, but I offered to retake the test."

"Which is why you were late." She nodded. She had vaguely explained that she had to sit for an exam in her text.

"I got a perfect score."

"What did he say?"

"He doesn't know yet. When he refused to sit with me for

a retake, I got my former advisor to administer it on my behalf. She outranks him, so she'll fix it. I'll be reinstated by tomorrow, but…"

"But your boss just tried to bench you. And going over his head will only make things worse."

She nodded. Medicine and architecture couldn't have been more different, but workplace politics were something they both understood. By then her first drink was nearly gone and the alcohol had done nothing to make her less emotional. Michael was right. She should probably slow down if she wanted to avoid becoming a sobbing mess.

"You know you have to report him, right?"

"Who am I gonna tell? My boss?"

"That's exactly the logic he's hoping you'll adopt," Michael said bluntly. "It's classic bully behavior. He's banking on the assumption that his intimidation will be so effective that you won't tell."

The truth of his words stung her. She pushed aside thoughts of other bullies, of others who had gotten the best of her before. Maybe later she would return to thinking about what had made her such a target for manipulative men.

"I'm not saying you *are* weaker," Michael followed up when she didn't respond. "I'm asking why you're playing the shrinking violet."

She looked up at him sharply.

"Is that how you see me?"

"You know better than that."

She looked away again, feeling irrationally betrayed.

"I know I'm not weak."

"So fight back."

"By doing what? I can't prove any of this."

Michael shrugged. "I don't know. But you have to play

dirty. Beat him at his own game."

That phrase was one that her father used. She didn't like it coming from Michael's lips. Darby had spent what felt like a lifetime watching people fight dirty with dirty. She'd vowed to be the opposite—to never let herself play that game.

"That's not how I like to operate."

He finally picked his drink back up and took a long sip. She appreciated the he wasn't pushing her, but she could tell he had more to say.

"When people show you who they are, believe them," Michael finally said.

She recognized the quote as Maya Angelou.

"What he did is unscrupulous and reckless. It's an indication of how far he's willing to go. He's not done with you."

She groaned a little. "Let's talk about something else."

"Fine...I have a surprise for you," he said after setting his drink down, his face transforming until a small smile showed through.

"For me?" Her spirits brightened a little. "What is it?"

He opened the flap of his messenger bag and pulled out a DVD case.

"*Julieta*," Darby said in English pronunciation.

"*Julieta*," Michael corrected, sounding the 'J' as an 'H'. "It's the new Almodóvar flick. When I was in Europe, I scored us a copy."

"For real?" She gaped at him. "This hasn't even opened in the U.S."

He shrugged, and she knew that even if she asked more directly, he wouldn't answer her silent question.

"We can watch it tonight, right?"

He nodded. "Let's go to your place. Your couch is comfier than mine."

Ninety minutes later, she was tucked into his arms as they lay on her sofa engrossed in the movie. She hadn't thought of this—of the certainty that any Almodovar film would make her cry. That she would have to cry in front of Michael.

She'd come close before, when they had watched *Forrest Gump* together. She had remembered it as a benign enough movie, but she'd forgotten about the part when Jenny died. Since then, she'd been more careful about avoiding movies that would turn her into a sobbing mess. She'd held back during *Forrest Gump*, but she couldn't hold back right now.

His arms tightened around her at her first sniffle, causing her to abandon all hope that there was any fooling him. But it changed into something more. Those first tears opened the floodgates, and it wasn't about the movie anymore. It was about her shitty day and the growing fear that this was only the beginning of a huge war at work.

When Michael shifted, she began to sit up, swiping her tears with the back of her hands. An apology was on her lips. But before she could form the words she felt her body being shifted. She bit her lip as he pulled her into his chest and tucked her head under his chin.

"Let it out," he whispered, kissing the crown of her head.

And she did. She was too tired to fight the unwelcome emotions and for those few moments spent in his arms, she gave in to thoughts about everything she feared. Just when she thought she was past it, he kissed her hair again, held her just a bit tighter and whispered "It's okay" in her ear. It set her off again. She hadn't been comforted like this in years and she'd been too stubborn to admit that she needed it.

"I'm sorry," she said finally.

"You're having a really tough time."

"This wasn't part of the deal."

"Don't do that." An edge crept into his voice and he pulled back to look down at her. "Don't treat me like some creep who just fucks you. I'm your friend."

"I know you are," she whispered. "I just…hate being like this."

"Why don't you let me help?"

"What would you do?"

"Find out why he's doing this. Something doesn't add up."

"How would you find out?"

"I could always hire a private investigator."

Her jaw tightened at the suggestion.

"That seems a little extreme…"

"Falsifying test results to get someone out of the way sounds a little extreme, too."

She put her head back on her chest and nuzzled in. He kissed her hair again.

"Not yet, okay?"

CHAPTER SEVENTEEN

CHAMPAGNE AND BIRTH CONTROL

B Y THE NEXT DAY, THE TEMPORARY CRISIS AT WORK HAD blown over, but things had worsened between Darby and Huck. She didn't know for sure what had happened with the Board, but when she'd checked her phone the next morning, she'd had a text from Chandy letting her know she could come to work. She'd awakened on the sofa that morning, still wrapped in Michael's arms. It was the first sexless night they'd spent together. She wondered whether it would have turned out the same—with them falling asleep watching movies like normal couples did—if she hadn't been in such a fragile state.

But now, work was over. They had reconvened at his place and he was serving her champagne. She'd had a predictably bad day at the hospital, and she could tell he was trying to take her mind off of her problems. As they sat up against the upholstered headboard of his bed, the sheets only half-covering their naked bodies, they talked casually about the strange fetishes of people they'd each been with before.

Darby remembered a different Michael, a six-foot-five hulk-ing Adonis from her sophomore year French class in college, who had harbored a deep obsession with her feet. Her Freshman year roommate—a girl named Ariel—had a tongue piercing that had brought Darby hours of pleasure. After sharing her own same-sex experience, she asked Michael something she had been wondering.

"You've been with guys, right?"

He smiled through a playful frown. "Let me guess…the ass play gave me away."

"Maybe," she shrugged, stifling a laugh.

"The first time I got my heart broken was by a guy," Michael admitted easily. "He wasn't the first guy I was ever attracted to, but he was the first one who was ever attracted to me," Michael continued.

"Doubtful," she muttered and he kicked her gently under the covers, which made her smile.

"Everything we did together was new to me…you know? He made me feel things I never felt before. He would fuck me to within an inch of my sanity and whisper filthy things in my ear while he was doing it. He owned me. And I loved it."

The smile disappeared from her face. "That is hot," she whispered, almost reverently.

He slid a wicked finger beneath the covers, reaching between her legs, presumably to confirm his suspicions.

"You minx," he accused, with a smile as wicked as his fingers. "I've heard of this—women who like thinking about two guys together."

She leaned her hips in toward his fingers, increasing the friction.

"So what?" she countered. "Guys love to watch two girls together—it's the same thing."

"Tell me what's hot about it," he demanded, slipping the long finger of one hand inside her as he set the champagne flute down with the other.

"I don't know…" she said, somewhat breathlessly, clearly affected by his ministrations. "One beautiful man is hot. Two beautiful men is hotter."

"Have you ever actually seen it in action?"

She set her own champagne flute down, angling herself still closer to him.

"Is that an offer?"

She kissed him deeply.

"Hell, no," he replied when they came up for air, positioning himself over her and fixing her with his eyes. "And risk you getting distracted by some other dude who fucks you better than me?"

"Nobody fucks me better than you."

He entered her sharply, and she half-gasped. He wouldn't last for long, but then, neither would she. She bit back words, about how it felt to come around him while she was riding his cock, about how she had never even come close to feeling so good with anyone else. Moments later, her teeth sank down hard on his shoulder as she climaxed, the last straw before he growled his own satisfaction. It had been months, but with Michael, the pleasure never wore off.

"Hey, Darby," Andrew chirped, picking up on the second ring. Michael had vowed that he would be attentive to her texts and calls, no matter what time of day, no matter where he was in the world. Though he'd made good on that promise, she refused to wake him in the middle of the night to coordinate schedules. Whenever it made sense, she just called Andrew.

Something about having to work through Michael's assistant to get through to him made her mildly uncomfortable. There were things about Michael—little things like this—that made her think of her father. But today, she wasn't trying to reach Michael—it was Michael who was trying to reach her.

In the message Michael had left her, he'd told her explicitly that he'd instructed Andrew to pull him out of whatever he was doing to take her call.

"Let me get him for you, sweetie," Andrew chirped without her even explicitly asking.

With all the lunch deliveries and other indulgences orchestrated by Michael, Andrew and Darby had become fast friends. When he'd texted her his contact card to add to her phone, she'd been tickled to find that it held a picture of him in huge bedazzled sunglasses, a gold lamé jacket, and a brilliant smile as he posed with his tiny dog. The image came up every time he called her and on more than one occasion, that photo alone had turned around a bad day. His ringtone was *Sexy and I Know It* by LMFAO. It had been the easiest ringtone decision she had ever made.

"Hey," Michael's much deeper voice came in, faster than she'd expected.

"Hey," she said, curiosity lacing her voice. No call between them had ever been urgent. "Everything okay?"

She heard him sit down and exhaled a bit of a sigh.

"I think I forgot something last night."

He sounded uneasy, but the mere mention of the night before caused her lips to melt into a smile.

"Really? Cause I thought you were pretty thorough," she said, her voice lowering as she remembered how good he had felt. With them both having to work that next day, neither had planned on an all-night fuck session. Months into their arrangement, they had never tried a sixty-nine and she didn't quite know how they had found themselves in that position the night before. Yet the sixty-nine had gone so much farther than being foreplay, and been so sublime, that they had fucked until dawn.

"Protection," he said gravely.

His words snapped her out of her very welcome memories.

"Oh," she said a bit sourly. "Do we need to have the talk?"

"How does your lunch look?"

"Open."

"Sushi?"

"No. Come to my office."

At 11:59, she heard a knock on her door.

"Come in," she called, rising from behind her desk and motioning to her sofa. She had planned on napping there during lunch, but this was a talk they needed to have. She slipped into doctor mode and started to talk.

"I'm not worried about pregnancy. Birth control is covered. Hospital workers are tested monthly for all kinds of things given our exposure to bodily fluids, so I know I'm clean from STDs. And I'm not sleeping with anybody but you, let alone without a condom."

He'd looked relieved the second she'd clarified the pregnancy risk. Upon that, the air in the room had changed.

"I had my physical last month. And I haven't slept with anybody but you," he echoed.

"Then we have nothing to worry about."

He looked at something on her desk before setting his intense gaze back on her.

"You know that I respect you, right?"

"I do."

"And that I would never betray any agreement we made."

"I know that."

"But we never agreed to be exclusive."

His words hung heavy between them.

"And you're afraid that if we do, I'll fall in love with you."

He groaned. "I'm sorry I ever said that. It makes me sound like an egotistical jerk."

She nudged him playfully. "I get why all the girls fall in love with you, Michael. You're kind of amazing," she admitted in a joking-not-joking kind of way. "But you're a pretty amazing fuck buddy, too. I'd be pretty stupid to jeopardize that."

It took him a moment to build up what he had to say.

"Last night was hot," he said finally. "I wouldn't mind another night like that."

Darby felt a flush in her body and a tingle up the column of her neck.

"Neither would I," she said quietly.

He reached out and took her hands.

"But I don't want to complicate things."

He searched her eyes.

"Neither do I."

His studied her carefully.

"I'm not gonna sleep with anyone other than you, cupcake. I know it's temporary, but for as long as it lasts, I'm in."

Her heart sped up at his words. It was the strangest declaration of commitment she'd ever imagined. But for them, it was perfect.

"Ditto." She watched him as her words sank in. "If that changes, I'll tell you upfront. Things will only get complicated if we stop being honest with each other."

They continued to look at one another intensely.

"A wise woman once told me that the most successful relationships are the ones that define themselves." She was surprised to hear him echoing her own words from that first night on the beach.

"Wise words indeed," she said. By then, they were gravitating toward each other for a kiss.

His tongue was just beginning to massage hers in the most delicious way when her phone rang with the least welcome ringtone of all. It was *You're So Vain*.

Michael pulled away and raised an eyebrow. "Who's that one for?"

By then, he was well aware of her obsession with personalized ringtones.

"Huck." She said his name as sourly as ever. "He prob'ly thinks this song is about him."

She leaned back in to resume their kissing, but he gave her a chaste peck after chuckling a bit at her pun.

"He's also your boss."

She scowled at Michael and picked up the phone.

"Dr. Christensen," she answered formally.

"Do you want to tell me why you spent $45,000 of the hospital's money on a microscope that we already own?" he practically shouted. She held the phone away from her ear.

She tensed immediately, shaking her head as she held Michael's eye. His brow furrowed as he listened.

"I assume you're talking about the Zeiss?" she asked, referring to the brand name of the molecular scope she had purchased for the current phase of her research.

She put the phone on speaker and made her way over to her desk. She needed two hands to log onto her computer. In the meantime, Huck continued his rant.

"Yes, I'm talking about the Zeiss. The one this department already owns. I know money means nothing to somebody of your means, but carelessness with hospital funds is wasteful and unacceptable."

She cast a quick glance at Michael, who was beginning to look upset. She cheered internally at his protectiveness.

"Actually," she retorted, keeping her voice as even as possible, "we discussed this back in June. I asked whether I could have the scope transferred from your research lab to mine or to gain limited access to your lab in order to use it and you declined my request."

"I would never decline a request to share an expensive piece of equipment, Dr. Christensen. Money doesn't grow on trees." He said it indignantly.

But Darby had searched her e-mail quickly.

"Actually, I've found the e-mail exchange in which we discussed this issue specifically. Shall I forward it to you? Your instructions to have me order my own are stated clearly."

She was already typing in Huck's e-mail address as well as that of the financial controller for her department. She clicked out a brief note.

Per your inquiry about my approval to order a second Zeiss microscope, please refer to the below exchange. Thank You, —Dr. Christensen.

She pressed send, and waited a pregnant moment to ask, "Did you receive it?"

"Hang on, please," he groused testily, "I'm reading."

So she gave him a moment. Michael shook his head slowly, looking pissed.

"Don't do anything like this again," Huck growled, before hanging up the phone.

Before she had even pressed the "end" button on her own phone, Michael had risen from her sofa and pulled her into a hug.

"I don't like that guy."

"Me either."

"Have you figured out how you're going to stand up to him yet?"

"No."

CHAPTER EIGHTEEN

THE MUSEUM

MICHAEL HAD TOLD DARBY THAT HE WOULD MEET her outside the hospital to pick her up. What he hadn't said was that he'd be leaning against his Maserati, which he'd parked illegally right in front of the exit. Darby's first reaction was to laugh, then to hide her face in her hands as she walked through the sliding automatic doors. Until then, she'd only seen the Maserati parked on her own quiet street, or coming out of valet parking. She supposed, with a car like that, he was used to parking anywhere he wanted. Besides, any ticket he couldn't charm his way out of, he could afford to pay. The car drew a lot of attention in this setting.

So did Michael. On any given day, he could have stood alone, hiding behind a tree wearing a burlap sack, and he still would have caught the attention of everyone who passed. But in a fur trim shearling parka, sporting $1,200 sunglasses, leaning against a $160,000 car, he looked like a million bucks. Since everyone was looking with interest at him, and he was looking with interest at her, Darby knew she'd have a lot of explaining to do the next day.

"Really?" She failed at sounding more stern than amused as she asked the question, her hands in the pocket of her own fur trim parka as she approached. "I thought we were going to dinner in the loop—that's, like, a six dollar Uber drive away."

He pulled what looked like a blow pop out of his mouth. *Holy hell.*

"I missed her," he shrugged unapologetically, the smile that had come to his lips when he'd caught sight of Darby widening a bit. "Ten days away from Starla is ten days too long."

She chuckled, happy to see him, because ten days had felt long to her, too.

"*Starla* is the name of a diner waitress."

"*Starla* has a 4.7 liter v8 and 460 horsepower."

"*Starla* gets twelve miles to the gallon."

"Thirteen. Don't be rude."

"You gonna let me in, or what?"

"It depends. You gonna stop talking smack?"

She raised two fingers to her mouth in a pincer grip and drew them from one corner to the other, in the universal sign for zipping her lips shut.

"Alright, then," he said smugly. Taking her bag from her shoulder, he opened the passenger door and held her hand as she stepped in.

For all the marathon kissing sessions they had in private, they had still never kissed in public. Darby noticed that in moments that might have merited a kiss, he touched her neck and looked in her eyes instead. They had their own private language now, which she supposed was bound to happen between two people who had cultivated such an intense connection with one another's bodies. The more important things they said were rarely spoken out loud.

"*You* look fresh for someone who just got off a plane," she observed during their short drive.

"That's because I didn't just get off of the plane. I landed this morning and slept all day," he admitted. "I needed it. I wanted to preserve my energy for tonight."

His comment caused her mind to wander to all she'd been missing while he was gone. She would've preferred to take him home then, to lose herself in that kiss she'd been craving, to beg him to fuck her all night, but he'd been adamant about having an early dinner out. After crossing the river, he took them north on Michigan, but instead of turning in toward the loop, he stayed on Millennium Park. When they passed by the front of the Art Institute before turning onto a side street and into what appeared to be a private underground garage, realization dawned.

"Is there an event here tonight?" she asked, her mouth suddenly dry. She remembered telling Michael that she hadn't been there since her mother's death. She knew he hadn't forgotten. He was like an elephant.

"No," Michael said. "The museum's closed."

He pressed the button on the intercom and before he had a chance to speak, the chain-link gate lifted to let the car in. She didn't say anything more—not as they parked, not as Michael ushered her out of the car and slid her coat off of her shoulders, and not as they took the elevator to the main floor. The dimly lit interior and the sole security guard who greeted them inside confirmed what she had begun to suspect.

"It's all yours, Mr. Blaine…Ms. Christensen." Butterflies stormed Darby's stomach as Michael thanked the guard. A moment too late, she realized how rude it had been of her not to do the same. But she had felt paralyzed.

"Where to first?" Michael asked casually, her hand still in his. His gaze was soft and knowing.

She swallowed to find her voice. "The Impressionists?"

"I thought you might say that." He smiled.

It was overwhelming—the feeling of being back in this place, and even more overwhelming to have been brought there by Michael. She felt almost out of her body as he ushered her up the elaborate four-way staircase, turning them left, and then right, until they met the grand glass doors of the Pritzker Galleries. Although she had navigated to this section at least one hundred times, at that moment, Michael's solid hand at her back felt essential.

The closer they got to the exhibit, any thoughts of Michael fell away as Darby was consumed by nostalgia. As a child, she had never been taken to children's museums, but she knew every nook and cranny of this place. She knew how to navigate the labyrinthine exhibits without getting lost, knew every shortcut that would take her swiftly from one wing of the museum to the next. Every staff member and security guard had once known her too. It had been a playground of sorts—when not directly at her mother's side, she had explored on her own. They had stopped going so frequently when she was shipped off to boarding school at age twelve, but during most of her school breaks, she and her mother had gone there together.

As they reached the beginning of the exhibit, tears sprang to her eyes. Darby had her own favorites, but her mother had truly loved this impressive collection—the Van Goghs and Cezannes and Gauguins and Seurats. Letting Michael's hand go, she strode forward, outpacing him, as she stepped into her forgotten world. She drank in painting after familiar painting—the Renoir of the little red-haired boy sewing and the many renditions of water lilies in the Monet room. Time played tricks on her. It wasn't just the familiarity of the paintings themselves that got to her—it was the smell of this place.

It felt like a part of her.

How have I stayed away from here for so long?

She didn't know how long it took for her to remember Michael's presence. It must have been a while, because she found herself near the end of the exhibit before she thought to turn to him. He appeared slightly blurry to her through the tears that brimmed in her eyes, but she could see his apprehension.

"If it's too much—"

"It's perfect," she interrupted.

For a long moment, his eyes didn't leave hers.

"I thought it might be easier if you had it all to yourself."

The next blink of her eyes caused the brimming tears to fall.

"Thank you," she choked.

She held out her hand, still feeling overwhelmed but needing to bridge the space between them. She watched him extend his own, watched his eyes lower and take in the sight of their hands held together—not palm to palm, but fingers intertwined, thumbs wrapped around one another's. Stepping closer to her, he used the thumb of his free hand to wipe away her tears.

From there, he took her lead once more, this time walking by her side. She turned to go back through the exhibit. The minutes felt infinite as she flowed in and out of memories, remaining silent about some but speaking others aloud.

"These were what made me want to visit Paris," she murmured as they looked at a Pissarro together. "And these, too," she said, turning toward the middle of the room to look between two Rodins.

"This one always scared the hell out of me," she remarked as they walked by a Lautrec called *Moulin Rouge*. She and Michael shared a smile.

When they arrived once again at Seurat's iconic *Sunday on La Grande Jatte* she stopped.

"I always imagined that was us in this painting—me and my mom."

Darby stared at the little girl in the white dress and hat and the mother dressed in soft reds who stood next to her with a matching parasol. The people in the painting were faceless, making their body posture important to interpreting mood. The mother and daughter, who stood at the very center of the painting stood somberly, staring forward, amid an otherwise light hearted scene.

"It was like staring into a mirror," she continued thoughtfully. "It wasn't like I was an unhappy kid…but I wasn't like that other girl either," she said, referring to the other young girl in the painting. "I wasn't like the one who's running around."

"I've never thought the girl in white looked unhappy," Michael said gently. "She's the most important person in the painting. She'd looking straight at us, the viewers. Everyone else is distracted, or self-absorbed, but she's the only one who's paying attention. She's the only one who knows something."

She turned to him then, wondering for the very first time where he fit into all of this. She already thought the world of Michael, but this moment—right now—made her want to know him better. It made her feel that she had underestimated him.

After they had gone all around and back through the exhibit a third time, the breath she took as they reached the passageway to the modern wing cleansed something inside her. She turned back to Michael, moving close enough to clutch the lapels on his jacket. Her eyes bore into his a moment before she kissed him.

Their kiss held every emotion—gratitude, awe, and

longing. It was not the kiss she had envisioned all week, not the one she had thought would happen in the privacy of one of their houses, not the gateway kiss to their soul-deep sex. His hands floated upward to cup her face and she could tell something had awakened inside him. His kiss held that unfathomable intensity she had once felt before but didn't yet understand. He was barely pressed against her—it was only his thumbs gently stroking her cheeks as his lips gently devoured hers. Yet she felt thoroughly enveloped in his warmth, every bit as much as she would if she were tightly ensconced in his arms.

"What next?" he asked softly, his thumbs still on her cheeks a long moment after they had pulled apart.

"What do *you* want to see?"

He shook his head. "I come here all the time. Tonight is for you, cupcake."

So they continued, with her leading him with perfect memory around the museum, to the medieval coats of armor, and American folk art, and the contemporary wing. She stopped to admire the sole Liechtenstein.

"I've always wanted one of his," she murmured.

"Have you ever studied him?"

"Not formally," she admitted.

"There have been some fairly detailed psychological assessments of his work. In real life, his relationships with women were very dark."

Just when she'd thought there could be no more surprises, they entered the Warhol room. In place of the large bench that normally sat in the middle was a dinner table set for two.

"Michael, this is—"

The most thoughtful, romantic, gesture that anybody has ever made for me.

"Something I thought you might like, so I arranged it."

She spun around slowly, taking in all of the paintings—the self-portrait of the artist, the bright-colored Elizabeth Taylor, the repeating black and white of Jackie Onassis. That one had always struck a chord in her—the politician's perfect wife.

He pulled out her chair and let her sit, pushing her back in and unfolding her napkin to place it on her lap. She was still having trouble comprehending that he'd done all this for her, but she knew he'd brush off any further gratitude. So she asked something that had been rolling around in her mind since the second he'd said it.

"You come here all the time?"

A waiter appeared at their table, seemingly out of nowhere, and set two plates in front of them before pouring from the champagne bottle that had been chilling on ice. The plates boasted an assortment of well-crafted canapés. Michael had really outdone himself this time. When they were alone again, he spoke.

"I kind of grew up here, too. When I was younger, art was the only thing I cared about. As soon as I was old enough to take the train by myself, I would ride all over the city, finding people and cityscapes, and objects that looked interesting to me. I spent hours and hours just drawing. I'd lose track of time…come home late for dinner—it worried my mother sick."

He smiled at the memory.

"I also hit the museums, wanting to study all the greats. But also to find my own style, figure out who I was as an artist. I spent hours here, seeing whether I could imitate certain artistic styles and sketching other things I saw—mostly people."

As she followed his story, she tried to imagine a teenage version of him sitting on these benches and wandering these halls. She couldn't help but wonder whether teenage Michael and teenage Darby had ever locked eyes.

"Do you still come here to sketch?"

He shook his head, his long fingers playing with the base of the champagne flute.

"I like to come when it's quiet and look at the art."

She looked around.

"This is pretty quiet."

One corner of his mouth crooked upward.

"I didn't mean I come after hours. I usually come about an hour before closing. This, right now, is just for you."

A lump formed in her throat as she swallowed back every word their agreement would forbid her to say. They spent the rest of their evening discussing their favorite art.

CHAPTER NINETEEN

CUPCAKE

S*TUCK AT WORK. WANT TO WAIT FOR ME AT MY PLACE? I can order dinner and meet you in about two hours. Sorry. You know I hate to be late. It's been a shit day.*

Michael did hate to be late, she had noticed. His punctuality on a good day was actually kind of freakish. Lately there had been more bad days than usual, for both of them. Michael had been called out of town a couple of times at the last minute, and with Huck berating Darby even more than usual, she'd been cancelling on account of work a lot more often than Michael. Huck had been punishing her with the least interesting and most time-consuming patient cases and forcing her to follow tedious administrative protocols that he wasn't asking of anyone else. She had even begun to suspect that he was sabotaging her ability to work fluidly with Rich, whose schedule decreasingly overlapped with hers.

She found herself looking more and more forward to her time with Michael, and was grateful of how forgiving they were to each other. Besides, she didn't mind waiting. A bit of downtime would be welcome before becoming wrapped up in his intensity.

No problem. Don't worry about food. I'll stop at Whole Foods on the way.

Thanks. You still have the elevator code, right? he asked, referring to the fact that, in lieu of a key, one could use the security code to enter his penthouse.

32729, she texted back from memory.

It wasn't until she got to the store that she realized how hungry she was. She had originally planned to grab something for both of them from the hot food bar, but found herself walking down each of the aisles grabbing random items that caught her interest—Humboldt Fog cheese, shelled pistachios, a baguette, a bottle of Sauvignon Blanc, and cold sesame noodles. She was en route to the cash register when she spied a serious-looking cupcake tin in the aisle full of other baking things. She spent another few minutes plucking her favorite flour, sugar, and baking chocolate from the aisle that she was in, and circling back to the dairy section for the butter she liked, and some eggs.

Forty minutes later, she was humming softly to a playlist that Michael's stereo system was blaring all over his house via the Bluetooth on her phone. She whipped up the batter expertly, not needing a recipe. The butter needed to soften more before she made the icing, so she took a shower, glad for quiet moments in Michael's apartment.

Since that first time he'd invited her to veg out in his apartment all day, he'd been cavalier about having her arrive before him, and letting her stay after he left. He'd always been cool about that kind of thing. Ever since she'd come to appreciate the sleepovers, there had been no walks of shame, no sneaking out in the middle of the night. Each of them was tired and most nights they were together, whoever's house they were at, the other one made themselves comfortable. She'd used his washing machine to freshen her scrubs—he kept dry cleaning at her house. It didn't quite feel as if they were domestic—only practical about such things.

Yes, she knew she liked his apartment, with its spectacular views, stylish design, and his impressive movie collection. Michael was a total hedonist, and his apartment was filled with so many creature comforts that being there felt luxurious. His rainfall shower, his zero gravity chairs, even his fancy Japanese toilet. Darby had reflected more than once that she wouldn't mind having one of those. He knew that she loved his shower, and the heated floors in his bathroom, but he did not know how much she loved his closet.

It was so Michael—so neat and organized, so shamelessly indulgent, and so unapologetically fashionable. She liked to run her fingers over his rows of tailored shirts, open the drawers that held his smartly-rolled silken ties, and peruse his eclectic collection of shoes. She liked how his closet revealed so much about him—how the high-top Vans with a Nintendo controller pattern sat right above a pair of custom-cobbled Berlutis, and how a drawer filled with undershirts made of sea island cotton was right next to one filled with t-shirts he must've had for fifteen years.

Smelling, more than needing to look at a clock to know that her cupcakes were nearly ready, she opened the old t-shirt drawer and put on the soft gray cotton one that read *Tufts Crew*. She smiled as she put it on. He'd only worn it once, but somehow she knew it was his favorite. Next, she slipped on a clean pair of simple white French-cut briefs—her preferred style of underwear—which she had brought in her purse.

While her cupcakes cooled, she cut a third of her baguette and spread her Humboldt Fog across the small surfaces, crushing the pistachios with the hard handle of the knife on the cutting board. The Sauvignon Blanc had been long-since opened, and she poured herself another glass. She stood at the counter, sprinkling the nuts on top of the cheese before devouring each piece and sipping her wine in-between bites. When she was finished, she used Michael's Kitchen Aid to fold her butter, sugar, vanilla, lemon zest and other ingredients in to make the frosting. She sang along softly to her playlist as she turned her cupcakes out of the tin, icing all twelve skillfully and placing them neatly on a large tinted glass platter she had found.

Keeping to tradition, she took the spatula she had used to apply the frosting and scraped the dregs of it from the mixing bowl. She turned her hip in such a way that allowed her to focus beyond the space of his open kitchen, toward the windows she loved so much and the city view below, toward the butterfly painting she loved. Slowly licking the frosting from the stainless steel spatula, she smiled from the nostalgia of its taste. Her belly was full, her skin was clean, and the wine had her feeling relaxed. Content moments such as these were rare.

She saw Michael out of the corner of her eye a split second before she felt him at her back. A second later, she realized that he was already very, very hard. He ground into her and slid his hand down until his fingers and the heel of his hand were low enough to cup her sex through her simple underwear. He stayed there for a minute, giving her time to melt into him, giving them time to breathe together.

She set down the spatula and her energy changed. As always, his hold on her felt just short of forceful, not as if he were constraining her, but as if it were imperative to him that she be very close. She tilted her head away from his lips, exposing her neck to him. He waited until he had pushed the crotch of her underwear aside, and slid a knowing finger through her slit to open her, before he gave her what she wanted. Raking his teeth across her neck teasingly before nipping her with precision caused Darby to bite her lip and smile with satisfaction. He paused to palm her lower cheeks before deft fingers played at the waistband of her underwear long enough to send them straight down. The unbuckling of his belt was music to her ears.

No sooner did he turn her to face him than did she hop up to wrap her legs around him, crossing her ankles behind his back. He supported her weight easily and he already had one hand on his cock while the other guided her hips. He pushed inside her in one languid move, sighing into her upturned jaw in what sounded like relief as he sank all the way in. Yes, she realized, he was granite-hard and balls deep and his girth made it so that he was already teasing her most delicious parts.

He braced one hand against the counter while his opposite forearm created a seat beneath her bottom. The heel of Darby's one hand reached back to find purchase on the counter, helping to keep her upright, as her opposite arm circled his neck. He pumped inside her then, in that slow but desperate rhythm her body called for but that only he had ever understood.

He moved his mouth to kiss her hungrily, and she realized after a moment that he wasn't so much kissing her as sucking the remnants of sugary icing off her lips. It was his defining quality—his ability to find pleasure in the details—and to commit himself to experiencing it completely. She could see it in the way he dressed himself in the morning, the way he gravity-dripped his perfect cup of coffee, the way he bathed with that fragrant soap in his shower. And she certainly felt it in the way he fucked her, in the way his body responded to her every tiny sound and approving movement, in the abandon with which he surrendered himself to everything he wanted and everything she was willing to give.

The thought unraveled her and she cried out in anticipation of her own orgasm, gasping for breath at the sensation of her walls pulsing around him. She knew he would be soon to follow, and she waited for it, still so sensitive and wanting. She wanted to hear the moment he came undone, to feel him throb inside her—she relished it every single time. And, when he did, it was glorious. The sounds he made were a hybrid of short grunts and desperate moans. As her hand moved from where it sat on his shirt to cup the nape of his neck, she felt his light shimmer of sweat and had the impulse to lick him.

After he had finished, he held her there for a long moment, catching his breath as he softened inside her, but not letting go. Finally, he set her down, slipped out of her, and fixed his eyes to look at her as he gently massaged her hips, presumably to prevent them from cramping. His pants were still around his ankles and his shirt was rumpled, but intact. She still wore his t-shirt and her lips felt swollen from his lust-filled sucks.

"I didn't hear you come in," she said, still breathless.

"I have feline stealth and grace," he replied, which made her smile.

"I baked," she offered needlessly. "I wasn't sure what you liked, but I figured, everyone likes cupcakes, right?"

"Good guess," he smiled knowingly, her wit familiar to him by then.

"Get changed. I'll pour you a glass of milk."

CHAPTER TWENTY

JET LAG SUNRISE

ROM WHERE DARBY WAS SITTING, SHE COULD SEE HINTS of the sunrise coming up over the horizon. The window pane felt cool against her warm temple. She'd pulled on one of Michael's t-shirts—she preferred the older ones, which were pleasantly soft.

She usually loved sleeping at Michael's place, and whenever he was away, she secretly craved the gentle rocking of his waterbed. But that morning she was wide awake and feeling restless. She simply had too much on her mind. Things moved so fast in her everyday life that she rarely stopped to take stock. But her personal life had gotten so much better while her work life had gotten so much worse that she could no longer ignore the reversal.

She had changed. Everyone who knew her saw it. Proof came in the form of tiny observations. *You're smiling more*, they told her. *You look well-rested*, they said. And Anne, being Anne, picked up on even more. *Looks like Michael's back in town*, she'd say sometimes, and she was always right when she did. Somehow, whenever Michael was around, Darby had it written all over her.

But apart from those moments, when she wasn't thinking about all the fun she was having with Michael, she was hiding behind a veneer. Her future at the hospital was still uncertain. She still went in to work every day, ready to help addicts and their families navigate precarious circumstances. She still believed in her research and felt that a breakthrough was within reach. But Huck was her boss. And, no matter her merit, her career couldn't be what she wanted, let alone thrive, without his support.

The worst part about it was that she couldn't figure out how to appease him. Darby had never won any popularity contests, but she was the consummate professional and among those whose friendship she didn't have, she had always been shown courtesy. She knew her fiery personality and straight talk weren't for everyone, but when she spoke, she spoke the truth, and that fact earned her most people's respect.

Darby knew that she had competitors, that other doctors at the hospital coveted the same funds she did, vied for the same promotions, and aspired to the same status. She'd long since learned to coddle those who viewed her as a threat, and had her ways of standing down to disarm them. But Huck could not be disarmed. He'd racked the slide on his shotgun. And it was pointed straight at her.

There was also the matter of her father. She hadn't spoken to him again directly, but she'd been through enough election cycles to know how to interpret the political landscape. His predictions about Governors Prescott and Sanderson had come true. Prescott had fallen from grace two months before at the Republican National Convention when humiliating pictures of him and a male prostitute were discovered. Sanderson was centrist enough to capture the attention of critical swing voters, but he would need someone as far right as Frank to mobilize the extreme right.

"I'm on Sydney time. What's your excuse?" came Michael's voice, deep from sleep and a little bit hoarse.

She hadn't heard him come in, but it wasn't the first time his sudden appearance had surprised her. The man moved like a cat. They'd met at his apartment the night before and shared a steamy reunion after another one of Michael's business trips.

She didn't know how much more she should tell him. She knew that she could trust him, but she was beginning to fear that the weight of her real life was too much for their fragile arrangement to bear. She already depended on Michael more than she should.

"Work stuff."

He didn't press her. But he did retreat to the kitchen, and placed a steaming cup of hot chocolate by her feet several minutes later. She was halfway through the creamy beverage when he emerged, striking as always in sleek pants and a button-down shirt. She realized she probably ought to leave, so she stood to get up, setting her cup on the counter and wracking her brain to remember where her clothes may have fallen in their haste to get their hands on one another the night before. He stood by the same counter, and she put a hand on his stomach before standing on her toes to kiss his jaw. Her own cocoa-scented morning breath discouraged her from kissing him on the lips like she would have preferred.

Her hand began to slide off of his stomach, but didn't make it past his hip bone before his own hand stopped her from walking away. She looked back at him.

"Go back to bed. Fire up the Jacuzzi if you want. Stay here and watch movies all day."

She started to say no but stopped herself, realizing how

stupid it would be to turn down his offer. What she wanted right then *was* to stay in her ivory tower, to avoid returning to a house that would surround her with her things and her problems. She wanted to keep staring out at the city. She wanted space to think. Minutes after he kissed her goodbye, she climbed back into the warm comfort of his bed, staring out at the skyline before drifting into a deep, Michael-scented sleep.

CHAPTER TWENTY-ONE

BEN

WHEN DARBY'S VIBRATING PHONE SIGNALED THAT A text was coming in, she was sure it would be from Ben. They were scheduled to meet for dinner that night, as he was in Chicago for a couple of days. Ben's tardiness was a peculiar but lovable trait—the man was a stickler for punctuality, and though he was never on time, he was never more than seven minutes late.

But the text was from Michael.

My problems with the zoning board have miraculously disappeared.

Imagine that.

She could see him writing back immediately.

You wouldn't happen to know anything about that, would you?

She smiled.

Today must be your lucky day. You should buy a lottery ticket.

The truth was, when she'd found out that Michael's firm was running into major delays in breaking ground on a building downtown, she had quickly offered to help. Chicago being one of the oldest, most corrupt cities in the country meant that getting things done was rarely straightforward, let alone for major construction projects like the kind Michael worked on. But Darby knew some of the most influential people in the city from the years when her father had been the mayor. She'd known just who to call to cut Michael's red tape. Without a second thought, she'd done it. She replaced her phone in her pocket at the exact moment that she saw Ben approach.

Ben had grown into exactly the man she'd expected him to when she had known him in boarding school, yet she would never voice as much out loud. Where looks were concerned, he was turning into a carbon copy of his father. He had the same sandy-colored hair as the older man, the same aquiline nose, the same proud stature and effortlessly lean build. Despite living in New York, his perpetual Floridian tan spoke of his life of relative leisure, and his ubiquitous, relaxed manner made him look as if he'd just stepped off of the links. Ben was a breath of summer, a warm ray of light wherever he went.

Unlike Darby, who had abandoned her teenage dreams of becoming a writer, Ben had ultimately defied his father, and done well for himself as an editor at *Vanity Fair*. She envied him that sometimes. What might her own life have been like without the interference of her father?

"How long are you in town?" she asked after she had asked him about Tami and newlywed life.

"Got in yesterday, leaving tomorrow…you know the routine," he said. "My meetings were today but last night I had dinner with one of my college buddies. You've met Michael, my roommate from Tufts, haven't you?"

Darby was mid-sip on her drink, and kept her lips on the sugar-rimmed cocktail glass of her sidecar for a few moments longer than was necessary. When she had asked to see Michael the night before, he had told her he had plans, but she'd have thought he might mention those plans were with Ben. It wasn't the first time Michael had been vague about times he couldn't see her on nights when he was in town. It bothered her, but she knew she had no right to feel that way, let alone to ask.

"Actually, he and I met at your wedding. We hang out sometimes. We're kind of seeing each other." She studied Ben, for clues as to what he might know. Something tugged in her at witnessing the surprise that flashed in Ben's eyes. Why hadn't Michael mentioned that detail the night before?

"No shit, I thought you two had met before," Ben said, seeming to search his brain for a long moment to recall an introduction. "I'm not surprised you hit it off. He's a good guy, right?" he said finally, not waiting for an answer. "Really going places. My buddy told me he's on the short list for *Top 40 Under 40*."

"As in, Forbes?" The surprise was evident in her voice.

"I know, right? That guy's seriously impressive. Back in school, we all knew he was going to do well, but he's been crazy successful," Jon said, drawing out the 'a' in 'crazy'. "He was at Tufts a few weeks back, to accept the young alumnus award. He's the youngest person to even be nominated. He's always on TV and in magazines and shit. I just saw a feature of him in *Philanthropy Digest*—last month alone, he raised $15 million for his youth arts foundation. He's pretty modest, so I'm not surprised he's never mentioned anything but, I mean it, Google him."

Darby barely knew what to say. The idea of checking him out had never occurred to her, partially because she hadn't grown up in the generation in which you Google the people you're seeing, but also because doing that had always seemed a little creepy. As a matter of principle, she wanted nothing to do with Googling Michael. As a matter of wanting to know things that apparently thousands of people knew about the man she was sleeping with, she wanted everything to do with it.

"I hear you're pretty impressive, too," Ben continued with a knowing smile. "How's your research going?" he asked with what she knew was more than casual interest.

Ben was a connector. He knew everyone, which meant he knew everything, even information about her otherwise specialized career. Theirs was a small, high society crowd—the boarding school brats, Ivy Leaguers, and global elites all knew one another—so Ben's observation came as no surprise.

"It's all fucked up," she felt perfectly comfortable, even relieved, to admit. "The project itself is bearing fruit, but I'm in a serious war with my boss. I won't bore you with the details, but he's got it in for me lately, more than usual. And I have no idea why."

Ben shook his head.

"Darbs, what are you still doing there? Northwestern needs *you* more than you need them. And don't tell me it's because your research is there. You could easily pick up where you left off someplace else."

It was a legitimate question, one she'd been thinking about more and more. Though the situation with Huck was troubling, in some respects, Darby was in a different position than she had been even six months before. It may have looked strange if she had left Northwestern earlier in her tenure, but she had now been there more than a respectable amount of time. If anything, moving on to a new place would be better for her career by signaling that she was upwardly mobile and in high demand.

And Darby was reaching her limit with all of Huck's hazing; she'd been getting more and more calls from hospitals looking to poach her. Despite Huck's best efforts to submarine her, word of her research was spreading to major institutions. She was slated for four speaking engagements over the next several months, two of them international, and had been asked to write papers about her preliminary findings for two pre-eminent medical journals. Ben was absolutely right. She had options.

"I know...you're right," she sighed. "It's time to move on. I've been so stressed out about surviving that I haven't been thinking strategically. There are a few places on my wish list—places that would have been a stretch a year ago but that might consider me now. I've been getting calls. Maybe it's time I start taking them seriously."

"Ya think?" Ben asked, his sarcastic look matching his tone. "So where would you go?"

"I'm not sure..." she mused, taking another sip of her drink.

"Well, start thinking about it quick," he said. "If you're gonna leave, you're in the strongest position to do it now. Anyone interested in you is going to want to take credit for the big breakthrough. What's the problem? Is it Michael? Is this thing between the two of you serious?"

She was used to Ben's candor. They'd always given each other a lot of love, but, between them, brutal honesty was always preferred.

"It's kind of like it was with you and me," she said just as bluntly. "We each had our own paths to walk. We knew that as soon as college rolled around, it would come to an end. It's the same with Michael. It'll last as long as it lasts, but with what our jobs are like, we know it won't last for long. We've been totally open about it."

"You and I were in love, Darby."

She let that sink in.

He looked at her in a way that looked like he was about to

say something serious. "When we broke up, it was easier for you to walk away than it was for me. I've always envied you that."

He'd never said as much out loud. She hadn't even known that he'd thought it.

"It wasn't easy for me, Benji."

"I know," he shrugged. "But I think it was harder for me."

She had nothing to say to that.

"Is Michael in love with you?" he asked openly. "Because you're easy to fall in love with."

Ben had always complimented her generously, but for some reason, this also took her by surprise.

"Not even close," she replied, after missing just one beat.

"Don't be so sure," he said. "Michael is a complex person. He doesn't wear his heart on his sleeve. And he doesn't date just anybody. If he's seeing you, he has feelings for you."

She didn't dare to mention their agreement. It didn't seem right to broadcast their business.

"Trust me—it's not like that. We're just having fun together."

"Alright," he surrendered, "but if it turns into something more, give it a chance. It's not every day the right person comes along. When it happens, don't take it for granted," he said, echoing Rich's words.

But she couldn't let herself think that way. Chances were, she'd be somewhere else six months from then. And, with Michael's punishing travel schedule, their meetings were sporadic at best. She wasn't blind. In another lifetime, another situation, there was no question that she'd want something different with Michael. But for now, she knew, she had to stick to the plan.

CHAPTER TWENTY-TWO

CRYING

THE WINTER AIR WAS FREEZING COLD ON DARBY'S SKIN AS she stood in the ambulance bay, but the adrenaline made it easy to ignore. She didn't have to wait long. She'd been out there for less than a minute when she saw the flashing lights and the vehicle with the words *Chicago Fire Department* written on the side come barreling around the corner. The driver performed a well-practiced three-point turn in order to back it up.

The doors began to open before it came to a full stop. One EMT was spread eagle on the gurney performing chest compressions on the patient. Darby recognized a second tech as he began to speak.

"Unidentified female in her late twenties. Suspected overdose, and evidence of freebasing on the scene. Track marks on her arm, but they don't look fresh."

"Who called it in?" she asked the EMT performing chest compressions. He paused just long enough to get the patient off of the truck, helping to lower the gurney. Darby looked down, wanting to see her face, needing to know whether she knew the patient.

Many of the overdoses that came into the ER—too many—were people she had seen before. She recognized Allison immediately—she'd been in more times than Darby could count. Allison had three kids who'd been in foster care for more than a year by then. One time, her eldest son had been the one to call it in. She remembered the day CPS had taken all three of them away.

Shit.

"The boyfriend, we think," the EMT continued as they walked. She helped him wheel Allison into one of the more private rooms the ER reserved for critical condition triage. "He wasn't at the scene when we arrived," the EMT said flatly, giving Darby a knowing look.

"No." Darby said emotionlessly. "It was probably her husband."

She helped hook up the monitors but barely needed to ask the next question to find out what she could already see. Allison's lips were blue and her skin was gray. She'd clearly been down for a while.

"How long?"

The EMT looked at his watch.

"Six and a half minutes since we found her. No heartbeat at the scene."

She nodded. They'd done what they were supposed to do, which was to start CPR until they reached the hospital. Only at the hospital or by a coroner on the scene could a patient be pronounced dead, and everybody had to follow the procedure, no matter how futile the process was. Darby pulled out a pen light and lifted Allison's eyelids. By then an ER nurse named Lucy had joined them and stood on the sidelines, charting.

"Pupils are non-reactive," Darby said aloud. "Monitors

show no heartbeat. Stop compressions." She felt for a pulse, looked for movement and listened for breath sounds. She found none.

"Time of death..." Her eyes flicked up to the wall clock. "12:39PM."

The room got quiet. Darby stared down at Allison's face and remembered the faces of her children. The EMT who had been performing CPR for six and a half minutes caught his breath. The machines continued to hum.

"The patient's name is Allison Handler," she said, her eyes finally swinging to Lucy. "Call CPS, and the police. If her husband doesn't turn up, they'll need to track him down."

She stripped off her gloves and threw them into the trash bin without looking, as she had a hundred times before. It wasn't until she got back to her office that she let herself cry.

It didn't escape Darby that from a mental health perspective, her career choice had been unwise. Sub-specializing in psychopharmacology placed her in a position to help addicts. It also placed her in a position to relive the trauma of her own mother's death on at least a weekly basis. Losing any patient was hard, but losing a mother with kids messed her up every single time. The younger the kids, the worse it destroyed her. Allison's youngest was still in diapers.

"Hello?" she answered her phone when it rang, so out of her own mind that it didn't occur to her not to. She hadn't even looked at the caller ID.

"Darby. What's wrong?" came Michael's alarmed voice.

"Nothing." They both knew it was a lie. But a sure way to set herself off again would be to actually talk about it. "What's up?"

"Nothing that can't wait." He sounded annoyed. "I asked you what's wrong."

"It's nothing."

"I'm not an idiot."

"Michael, it's nothing. I'll be fine."

"Have it your way."

And then he hung up. She stared at the phone in abject surprise for half a minute—he'd never done anything nearly so rude. Then she dissolved back into tears at the realization that she had just alienated one of the only people who gave her respite. She reached across her desk to grab a Kleenex, because things were starting to get messy. When she pulled one out of the box only to find it crumpled in a way that told her it was the last one, she only cried harder. Some time later—she didn't know how long—a loud knock sounded at her door.

"Come back later, please," she called loudly and in a nor-mal-enough voice, sniffling quietly a second after she'd spoken.

"Open the door."

Her crying stopped that second. That was Michael's voice. And since she knew he wouldn't take no for an answer, she opened the door as he requested. He let himself in and closed the door behind him quickly, surveying her the entire time. He seemed to be looking for evidence of some kind, and finding none, he asked.

"*What. Happened?*"

"I can't believe you came here."

He closed his blazing eyes in frustration, and she could see it was costing him effort not to lose his patience.

"Darby…" His tone was warning.

"I lost a patient," she said miserably and felt a fresh round of tears threaten.

"But you're not hurt?"

She shook her head, and only then did he look relieved.

"You can't do that," he commanded, and not gently. "You

can't let me think something has happened to you and not tell me you're okay."

"I told you I'd be okay," she protested weakly. She bit her lip and sniffled, but it was no use. Seconds later, she sobbed into her hands.

Through her tears, she heard him curse under his breath, and then he brushed her hands away from her face and pulled her into his arms. This, of course, only made her cry harder which only made him hold her tighter.

"It's okay," he whispered once, then twice, before her sobs quieted.

Finally, she pulled back, sniffling. He reached into his pocket and placed a handkerchief in her hand. Her eyes flipped up to his.

"You carry a handkerchief?"

He didn't answer, but his eyes softened even more. She lifted it to dab at her eyes and noted, even through her stuffed up nose, that it smelled like him.

He's never getting this back.

"Things between us aren't supposed to be complicated." She whispered.

This made him sigh.

"We've had this conversation," he reminded her gently.

She put her head back on his shoulder, letting him hold her again until she calmed down completely.

"What were you calling about anyway?"

"To ask you out to lunch." He kissed her forehead.

"Can we get sushi?" she asked.

"We can get anything you want."

CHAPTER TWENTY-THREE

DRINKS WITH ANNE AND RICH

"You're dressed a little too nice for this place," Darby observed as she breezed into the research lab to pick up her stuff. Unlike Darby, who was dressed in their standard lab coat and scrubs, Rich wore what looked to be a very nice suit.

Darby shrugged out of her lab coat and slipped into the supply room, where she had stashed some clothes for after work.

"Headed out to an important meeting?" she asked loudly enough for him to hear. She'd kicked off her clogs and peeled off her scrubs, but he still hadn't said a word. Peeking only her head out, since she was down to her bra and underwear, she looked to see what was the matter.

Rich wasn't just sitting in his chair; he was staring dejectedly at a manila folder that sat upon the desk.

"Hey...are you okay?" she asked, starting to become concerned. She wondered if he even heard her.

"Not headed anywhere..." he explained, still staring at the folder. "Coming from the attorney's office actually."

He looked up at her then.

"We signed the papers today," he said. "Lindsay and I are officially divorced."

She cast him a sympathetic look, the best she could do given her current state of undress, then disappeared back into the supply room to finish dressing. She pulled on her dark skinny jeans and stylish brown boots, and slipped a pretty silk green blouse over her head. When she emerged, he hadn't moved.

"What are you doing tonight?" she asked, already knowing the answer.

"Going home to my shitty little flat. Getting pissed. Regretting my life choices," he said miserably.

"No you're not," she said, taking his hand and pulling him up out of his chair. "You're coming to the bar and getting drunk with me and Anne."

Half an hour later, he was, indeed on his way to getting drunk. Darby and Anne were barely halfway through their first drinks, and he was ordering his third. She couldn't blame him. Today would surely rank as one of the worst days of his life. Love was a messy business. Sometimes getting shit-faced was the only thing left to do.

"I was so sure about everything," he lamented, as close to crying as she had ever seen him. "Until I walked into the room. I went through with it…obviously, but—" he sighed heavily. "I think I might have made a huge mistake."

"Maybe you did," Anne murmured darkly, and Darby shot her a look. Her friend was still bitter over her own girl-friend leaving her even though by then it had been months.

"It's not supposed to feel good," Darby said, turning her attention back to Rich. "Breakups never do. And since you were married, this will probably be the biggest breakup of your life. If you didn't feel ambiguous about it, that would be even worse. It would mean you never should have been together to begin with."

He ran his fingers through his hair, still looking distraught. He seemed relieved when the waiter arrived then and set another beer in front of him. He took a huge gulp, and trained his eyes back on Darby.

"Why aren't you married, Darbs?" he asked so bluntly that she knew he must already be drunk.

"Marriage isn't for everyone," she said simply, prepared to repeat the speech she'd already given him, if needed. "It's just not a priority for me."

"But don't you want someone to love you? To take care of you?" he implored.

"I have friends for that," she replied simply.

"That's not the kind of love I'm talking about," he said seriously.

"I have friends for that, too," she revealed, taking a long sip of her sidecar.

When she looked back up at him, she saw that his eyes had widened. "I knew it," he nearly accused.

She threw up her hands then. "Fine...you caught me," she said. "I have amazing sex with someone who will never be my boyfriend or my husband. You say it like it's something dirty but there's nothing wrong with it. If you want to know the truth, it's the best relationship I've ever been in."

It was true. And she'd known it for a while.

"Except it's not a relationship," Rich countered. Anne watched their verbal volley with interest.

"All a relationship is, is two consenting adults who have agreed on the rules," Darby returned easily. "The rules aren't the same for everyone. And why should they be?"

She didn't mention that her relationship was turning out better than both Anne's or Rich's had. While they had hung their hopes on forever, she had always known that her relationship with Michael would come to an end.

"But isn't it empty?" Rich asked, a bit sadly. "Sex isn't love."

She shook her head in agreement.

"No," she admitted. "It isn't. But sex doesn't have to be empty. It can be rich and wonderful. It can fulfill deep needs and serve a purpose in your life without being tied to how long you plan to be together, and under what circumstances."

She thought of *Before Sunrise* then, of the one-night stand that never stood a chance to become a real relationship, but that still meant something important to the characters who lived it.

"Sex can give love, even if that love doesn't culminate in a traditional relationship," she continued. "The act of long-term commitment isn't the important part—the love is," she finished softly.

By then, both Anne and Rich were looking at her, taking in what she realized must sound like a passionate plea for understanding. It was also her first out loud confession that whatever she was caught up in was more than just sex. And it made her heartbeat quicken.

"What happens when it ends?" Anne wanted to know then, talking outside the realm of what Rich knew.

"I walk away," she said, looking at her friend in earnest, "and feel gratitude for having had something so good."

Anne nodded, the look in her eyes changing, and in that moment, Darby knew that her friend finally got it. Just because she and Michael meant something to one another didn't mean that what they had was meant to last.

"I envy you," Anne said softly, when Rich's three beers had finally caught up to his bladder. When she said it, his retreating form was headed to the bathroom. "Do I ever get to meet this guy?"

Darby smiled wanly and nodded. "Soon."

CHAPTER TWENTY-FOUR

PERFORMANCE REVIEW

DARBY SAT ON HER BED DUMBLY. SHE HADN'T MOVED since she got home. She was still shocked by the events that had transpired at work. Today had been her performance review. Only once before in her career had Darby ever received a bad rating from her boss, but this report from Huck was worse than bad—it was scathing.

She hadn't expected Huck to be charitable in his assessment of her. He rarely took proactive opportunities to praise her, but her research work was promising and she had always excelled in clinical care. Everybody knew it and Huck wasn't known for saying anything different in his reviews. But there was a first time for everything. The review had been so bad that he'd given her an official warning, which was considered by HR to be the first step in transitioning employees out, fancy talk for getting fired.

She didn't—couldn't—dwell on the sheer injustice of it all. If she focused on how much of her heart she poured into her work, and how much it hurt not to have that remotely recognized, she'd start to cry again. A terrible review had never factored into her plans. It would raise eyebrows in the executive suite, could ruin her research funding and could submarine her if she decided to pursue a position someplace else, something she'd only just begun to consider.

To make matters worse, Huck wasn't up for promotion for another three months, which meant he would have input around her mid-year performance review. Her research fellowship was up for additional funding review in April. By then, she could be fired. Getting fired by Huck would be disastrous—it would send a signal that one of the most respected psychopharmacologists in the world didn't think she was up to standard. It would cancel her research funding. Professionally, it would leave her with absolutely nothing.

The doorbell roused her from her thoughts, and as she became aware of her surroundings again, she realized that it was already dark outside. Having no idea who could be at the door, but hearing it ring a second time, she moved to descend the stairs and answer.

"Michael..." she breathed, closing her eyes and wiping her hand over her face shamefully. "I'm so sorry. I completely forgot."

She shook her head, moving aside to let him in. She had forgotten that they had plans to hang out before he headed out of town the next day.

"Just give me ten minutes to take a shower, alright? I'm dirty from my shift, but it would be good to blow off some steam."

He pushed inside and closed the door, looking stern as he spoke his next words.

"I don't have sex with people who are too upset to remember plans with me. But I'm not leaving either, not until you tell me what's wrong."

She sniffled. She found it endearing that he was refusing to sleep with her. As she thought more about it, she realized he was right. Angry sex was a bad idea.

"Huck threw me under the bus in my performance review," she said miserably, moving aside so that Michael could come in farther.

The frown remained on his face. Over the past few months, he had said more than a few things to remind Darby that he had a sister and a niece. He'd been raised by a single mother, understood a fair bit about what girls went through, and had no respect for people who mistreated women.

"When was the last time you ate?" he asked.

She thought for a minute but honestly couldn't remember. He set down his messenger bag and hung his jacket in the front closet, by then completely at ease in her house.

"I'm making you dinner," he said. "And while I do, I want you to tell me everything."

So she did. Not just starting with the performance review that day, she told him about how it had been with Huck from the beginning. She gave him examples of ways in which Huck had treated her differently, how he'd worked to discredit her in subtle and subversive ways, but how this—which could be considered nothing less than a blatant attack on her—had been unprecedented.

As she spoke, he moved around her kitchen easily. She hadn't been grocery shopping in a while, but somehow Michael assembled ingredients from her cabinet and her freezer into a meal far superior to anything that she had ever cooked. By the time she'd finished venting, he had defrosted chicken from the freezer, cut, breaded and butter-sautéed it and whipped up a sauce using lemon juice from her refrigerator and capers he'd found in her cabinets. While the chicken finished cooking in the oven, he defrosted some frozen dinner rolls she had lying around and used fresh garlic and dried herbs to make special butter. Darby had a double oven that she'd never used, but for the first time she saw how it might be useful. Michael used the second one to brown the tops of what smelled as if it would be very tasty garlic bread.

All the while, she had been sitting on a barstool in her kitchen, sipping a glass of wine she knew she could only nurse slowly given her empty stomach, but one that felt good to drink all the same. Michael touched his own wine for the first time only after he had set two steaming plates down before them. He had rolled up his sleeves to cook, and he hadn't gotten a drop of oil or speck of flour on him as he'd made their amazing meal.

"Eat, please," he said gently, but with a bit of urgency in his voice. He didn't like it when she went hours without having something in her stomach, even though he did the same thing.

"This is amazing," she said around the first bite, and it really was. When Darby looked inside her cabinets, she saw a whole lot of nothing to eat. When Michael looked inside her cabinets, apparently he knew how to make magic. "Thank you."

"You're welcome," he said smiling a bit, pausing to acknowledge her appreciation before getting back to business. He took a sip of his wine but left his food untouched as he looked back at her with serious eyes.

"I wasn't kidding about the private investigator."

She took another bite, chewing slowly.

"I know you weren't."

"It's time you fight back. He's trying to ruin your career."

She knew Michael was right.

"But, why?" Tears stung her eyes. The injustice of it all was still fresh.

"Why doesn't matter. All we're looking for is something we can use as leverage to get him to back off."

"It's more complicated than that. Even if we find something on him, what am I going to do? Blackmail him? Walk into HR with some sort of dossier?"

"No." His voice was calm. "You're going to stay as far away from it as possible and let me do it. The less you're involved, the better."

She went quiet, not liking this idea at all.

"What you *will* do is cover your ass. Build allies. Go through the proper channels. How's the rest of your HR file?"

Darby thought about it.

"Well, I never get patient complaints. All the people who are closest to my work only have good things to say about me."

"Alright…how were your earlier performance reviews from him?"

"Not glowing, but positive."

"Good," Michael said approvingly. "You can use that. If he's never had a bad thing to say about you before and no one else has either, it will make the current performance review look suspicious. Do you have any other enemies?"

She shrugged. "Kind of. There are some people who don't like the fact that I keep beating them out for grant money."

"Is Huck friends with any of them?"

"Come to think of it…yes," Darby admitted with a sinking feeling, thinking of Yelena. She couldn't believe she had never made the connection before.

"I have a friend who works in the HR field who I can call tomorrow. I'll see what general advice she can give me. In the meantime, play dumb. Convince Huck that you're crushed and eager to get back into his good graces. You've worked too hard to let him ruin your career. Don't worry. I'll help you."

She was starting to feel better about things. Her reply felt inadequate but she'd say it anyway.

"Thanks."

That night, he held her as they watched *Before Sunset* on her couch. He knew that movie always made her feel better. After it had finished, he took her upstairs and tucked her under the covers. He murmured something about cleaning her kitchen, and smelled freshly-showered some time later when he slipped in next to her into bed.

When she woke the next morning, he was gone. But when she arrived in her kitchen, she saw that he'd left a note next to her coffee machine.

I've got you, it read in his elegant scrawl.

Darby took Michael's advice and began to build her case against Huck. Michael's friend had referred her to a worker's rights attorney, who had given her a specific list of documentation he wanted her to gather. By the time a week had passed, she had downloaded four years' worth of positive performance reviews, the results of the annual 360-degree review feedback solicited from peers (which were all glowing) and all of her grant proposals, which included letters of recommendation.

After learning that she could quietly work a few HR channels without getting on Huck's radar, she asked for her patient feedback file, which included both positive and negative feedback from individual patient cases. The few negative patient reviews were earlier in her tenure, when she'd been less experienced, and she was pleased to see that all reviews from the past two years had been positive. She was buoyed by the HR rep's offhand comment that patients rarely left positive reviews. It would be a feather in her cap to show a strong track record.

It turned out that the hospital had a policy of allowing employees who feared retaliation from another employee to file a special complaint. Darby took the opportunity—the special complaint would be considered if he ever attempted serious action against her.

Beyond just covering her ass, she'd taken Ben's advice to heart and was looking at other roles. She'd updated her resume, was returning calls, and was quietly letting people in her network know that she might be ready for a move. At absolute least, she had to hedge against whatever Huck would do.

The idea of leaving Chicago wouldn't be as easy as she'd once thought—she'd made it her home, and not just because it was where she'd been born. Five years before, she'd had offers in other cities. At the time, her mother had still been dealing with her addiction, which had made Darby's decision to return to Chicago easy. But in the years since, she'd built a cozy life. She loved her house, loved her rituals of seeing movies and going shopping in her free time, loved what she had with Michael. Moving from place to place was something she'd always anticipated, but starting over in a new city at 32 wasn't the same thing as starting over at 20.

Michael commiserated with her. When he was in town, he came around more often, or had her over to his place, cooking her dinner, massaging her tired feet. He never complained about seeing less of her, even though she was working longer hours. Working harder was her insurance policy against any possible complaints. She treated her patients and conducted her research to the same standard of quality she always had (maybe even a higher one), and stayed late to cross every "t" and dot every "i"—unwilling to allow any move she made to be viewed as a mistake.

Although she was tired, she was trying to hold onto her

new routine of getting out more, with Michael by her side. It wasn't just about letting herself have a little fun and counter-acting all the stress—networking would be good for her career.

That was why, on a calm Tuesday night at her place, she and Michael sat before a twin stack of mail. One pile was his, the other hers. They were their collected series of invitations. Each of them was invited to at least a dozen functions a month. For obvious reasons, they declined most, but every once in a while something piqued her interest.

"What looks good?" Michael asked as she leafed through the many opulent cards before her.

She had already started a pile of "nos", mostly charity func-tions and weddings. A few industry events were in her "maybe" pile, though she was sure hanging out with a bunch of doctors all night would be pretty dry for Michael. She was just placing an invitation to a film screening in the 'no' pile when Michael caught her wrist.

"Seriously?" he asked.

"It's in Park City," she said reasonably.

"Which is only a three-hour plane ride away," he said, as if she had no understanding of U.S. geography. "Why would you not want to go to Sundance?

"Because it's in Park City," she repeated, not budging an inch.

"It's the *Sundance Film Festival.*"

She shrugged. "I get invited every year. I never go."

"Why the hell not?"

"I don't know," she said a touch defensively. "It seems far."

He shook his head. "You need to get out more."

She took a sip of her wine.

"We should go away together," he said with determination. "I've been thinking about it for a while."

He had?

"You have?"

"I think we could both use a few days away. Don't you?"

"Where did you think we would go?"

It wasn't an answer to his question. She was still turning this over in her mind. It would be amazing to get away. But she'd never even gone anywhere with the men who had been her actual boyfriends. Doing it with Michael would make this more real.

"I don't know—maybe shopping in Milan or in London. And you know we both love Paris."

All of that sounded amazing. She didn't know what to say.

"Before, I used to extend my trips over the weekends…"

"Before what?" she asked absently, having gone back to inspecting the invitation card.

"Before you."

Oh.

"I've always wanted to go to the biggest events around the world. Oktoberfest in Munich. Carnival in Rio. Fashion Week in Paris. The Cannes Film Festival."

"Have you?"

"I've gone to a few of them. They'd have been a lot more fun with you."

It wasn't that she disliked the idea. She liked it a little too much. She liked all of it too much—the unprotected sex, the sleepovers, the intimate gestures, and all the other lines the two of them had crossed. Surrendering, she took the invitation to Sundance and started a new pile—the 'yes' pile.

"I'll book the tickets," she said.

CHAPTER TWENTY-FIVE

THE CHRISTMAS PARTY

DARBY WAS NERVOUS AS SHE AND MICHAEL MADE THEIR way through the lobby of the Hancock building, toward the elevator that would take them to The Signature Room. The Hancock building was the second tallest in Chicago and the hospital had rented out the well-known cocktail lounge on the 95th floor for its annual holiday party. The affair promised heavy hors d'oeuvres, top-shelf liquor and one of the best views of the city.

It also promised the typical sort of holiday party shenanigans Darby preferred to avoid. The awkward introduction of significant others, the small talk that pretended any of them had time for much outside of their insulated hospital-worker lives, and even worse the talk about hospital work itself. It was one thing to grab drinks with her small circle of friends after work once in a while, but quite another to endure a contrived social gathering in which scrubs were traded for cocktail attire.

She usually made an early appearance, and an early exit to an after party with her small crew, but Michael had insisted on coming. She wasn't surprised that he was curious to meet

Huck. If Michael's boss had been described in the same way, she guessed she would have been curious to meet him, too. But since the performance review, Michael had taken an almost obsessive interest in the cast of characters at Darby's job. He hadn't even waited for an invitation—at her first mention of the affair, he'd insisted that he would come.

They exited the elevator with his hand at the small of her back, clearly demonstrating that they were there together but with a gesture so ambiguous that it wouldn't be clear that they were dating. Their public conduct always held well-practiced mystery, denoting some close friendship but making it unclear as to whether they were a couple. When it was just the two of them, their heat was palpable even if they were just looking at one another from twenty feet away, but in a room full of people, they simply appeared as companions and continued to introduce one another as friends.

She scanned the room for Anne, who was typically her 'date' for these kinds of things. She had told Darby in no uncertain terms that she was very much looking forward to meeting Michael. Darby had debated whether to tell Michael that she had revealed their arrangement to her closest girlfriend. Anne's brazenness would give away her knowledge, Darby had decided. It would be better if Michael didn't go in blind. She'd come clean to him the night before.

"So you're the reason for the spring in Darby's step," Anne smiled knowingly after Darby had made introductions.

"I don't know about that..." he said smoothly, shifting an adoring gaze to Darby "...but she's the reason for the spring in mine."

Darby's eyes widened at the ease with which he delivered the line, and the dashing smile he aimed back at Anne a moment later. Swinging her gaze over her friend, she saw that

Anne—who wasn't even attracted to men—looked smitten. She had seen Michael's effect on strangers before, and shouldn't have been surprised. His looks were devastating and he had a natural charisma that simply couldn't be faked. Yet, this was different company. Darby knew he would make an impression on her co-workers, but she saw now that she had underestimated the attention she would receive by bringing Michael to the party.

Going to work on Monday should be interesting, she thought sardonically to herself.

"I hear you're the best labor and delivery nurse this city has ever known," Michael continued, launching into a conversation with her friend. Darby only half-paid attention as she subtly scanned the room to take stock of the situation. Present tonight would not only be the shift staff, but also hospital administrators and members of the Board, some of whom were presiding members of her grant-writing committee.

If there were one other reason why she showed up at these things, that was it—to get a bit of face time with the people whose job it was to decide whether to fund her work. She didn't like that every grant-seeking researcher used events like these to ingratiate themselves to important players. But, likability mattered, and she knew that she would have to say at least a few hellos. And that those hellos would be especially important this year, given her situation with Huck.

"Darby, daaahling…" she broke out of her reverie when she heard the unmistakable English accent. Rich swept her into a light hug and kissed her cheek, their standard greeting for social gatherings.

"Hey," she smiled amicably. "Are we having fun yet?"

He knew how she felt about these kinds of affairs—that she came only out of obligation. Under normal circumstances, he and his wife would be members of the after party crew, but tonight was shaping up differently. For the first time in four years, Lindsay hadn't accompanied Rich. For the first time, Darby had brought a date.

"I've kissed exactly five arses so far and if I'm counting right, I only have three more to go," he admitted in his typical self-deprecating manner. "But, before I do, introduce me to your friend."

She touched Michael's arm.

"Michael Blaine, this is my research partner, Rich, known by some as Richard Graham Leslie Stroh the Fourth."

"You sound like English royalty," Michael commented good-naturedly. "What number in line are you to the throne?"

"One hundred and sixty-six, unfortunately," Rich returned. "Though seven of the ones before me are quite old so I expect to be solidly in the one-fifties by Easter."

Michael laughed. Darby stared in disbelief. From the way Rich said it, she knew he was telling the truth. She had known this man for nearly five years, and never known facts such as this, yet Michael had known him for five seconds and had easily gleaned real information.

"Darby, is this who you've been hiding from us?" he asked, looking between she and Michael with more interest than he had ever displayed. "I knew you were seeing someone, but a famous architect? I never would have thought."

"Michael is a great friend," she lied easily, as she had so many times before. Rich wasn't stupid and she knew that he knew that Michael was her booty call. Still, she didn't want to treat it as public knowledge, so she kept up the act. "I cry on his shoulder when Huck is mean to me and he cries on mine when his designs have structural inefficiencies."

"Good to know," Rich replied, looking at Michael. "The

sound of hearts breaking was audible when the two of you arrived together. The men of Northwestern Memorial will be glad to know you're still on the market. A few women, too." He winked at Anne.

"Keep it a secret," Michael said conspiratorially. "Truth be told, I'm her decoy. It seems that warding off the unwelcome attention of certain colleagues has become a necessity."

"Has it?" Rich asked, turning his gaze back to Darby. Michael was going off script and she had no idea how to respond.

"Some guys just don't know when to give up," Michael said lightly, placing his hand on Darby's neck as he looked at Rich.

Darby was saved from having to speak by yet another interruption, this time from Stacey Kohl. He was in his mid-sixties, yet well-preserved with salt and pepper hair and hazel eyes. He was also the President of the hospital's Board of Directors. She had met him in passing before, but didn't think he knew anyone in their small group.

"Michael," he greeted her date jovially, shaking his hand heartily as if they were old friends who hadn't seen each other in ages.

"Stacey!" Michael greeted back enthusiastically, "It's been awhile. How's Sue?"

"Still singing your praises after what you did for her mother near the end," the older man said more seriously. "And she was very touched that you came to the funeral."

Michael nodded with appropriate somberness. Darby's jaw wanted to drop. Michael had never mentioned that he knew the President of the Board of Directors of her hospital, arguably the most important person to have in her corner given the situation with Huck.

"I didn't know you knew Darby," Stacey continued. "The

work she's doing around opioid treatment could be ground-breaking." Double jaw-drop. Darby figured Stacey knew who she was, if for no reason than the fact that she was the senator's daughter, but she was surprised that he was so familiar with her work.

"It is," Michael agreed smoothly. "And I have more than a passing interest in it. You know medicine's not my specialty, but it reflects the kind of divergent thinking me and my guys in Silicon Valley talk about a lot. We need to be rethinking old problems in new ways, and I think you're well-positioned to support it. It's not just about developing new drug therapies—it's about getting smarter about the things we *think* we know. I know some people who may like to support more projects like Darby's. We should talk more about it, once hers is done. By the way, do you know Dr. Rich Stroh? He's Darby's neuro partner on the research."

"I don't think I do," Stacey admitted. "Pleasure to meet you," he said shaking the other man's hand.

"Sir," Rich replied, looking as flummoxed as Darby felt.

"And this is Anne Higgins, one of the best nurses in labor and delivery from what I've heard," Michael continued.

"Pleasure to make your acquaintance, Anne," Stacey said warmly, shaking her hand.

"That's another area I hear could use some funding," Michael said. "I know a family foundation focused on women's health. We'll talk," he seemed to promise.

When Stacey's attentions were engaged with Anne as he politely inquired about the needs in the maternity ward, Darby gave Michael a 'what the fuck?' look. He just winked, and turned his attention back to the conversation. She knew exactly what he was doing—dangling the promise of funding in front of Stacey so that if, and when, the time came to bargain for Darby's chances, she'd have a chip. It was a pro move on Michael's part—it didn't tie her directly to the string-pulling, especially since it wasn't clear as to whether she and Michael were dating.

"Enjoying the party?" A sixth voice joined the conversation, one she recognized immediately. It was Huck. He held a glass full of something golden, and he edged his way easily into their little circle, settling between Anne and Stacey. He probably wanted to monopolize Stacey's attention—the best way was to cut off his partner in conversation. Anne, a nobody nurse, was nothing more than an obstacle to Huck.

"We were just talking about the game-changing work being done in your department," Stacey said, nodding to Anne in acknowledgment. "And the areas in which we still need help. Have you met Michael Blaine?"

Huck looked up at Michael, recognition in his eyes.

"I haven't," Huck admitted, holding his hand out to shake Michael's. "It's a great pleasure, Mr. Blaine" he continued to Darby's surprise. "I don't follow architecture, but I read an article about you in *The Tribune*. Your accomplishments are impressive. Despite meager beginnings, you're achieving greatness. You remind me of myself."

Darby couldn't believe it—Huck was practically sucking Michael's dick, while still managing to compliment himself. Michael returned the handshake and smiled.

"I hear that you're the developer of Rescutin—that opioid overdose rescue med, right? Darby's spoken highly of your work. Do you have any other projects under development?" he asked with convincing curiosity.

"Actually, I do," Huck began. "I'm working on something that simulates the chemical circumstances of alcohol intoxication in the brain—it's intended to work like Methadone does for opioid addicts, except it targets patients with alcoholism. What makes it unique are the neural pathways the drug works across and a naturally-occurring chemical compound that no one else has looked at before. Not only will it address the phys-iological dependency—it will activate some areas of the brain that may facilitate psychological recovery as well."

"Interesting," Michael said. "That sounds similar to the work that Darby's doing with respect to permanent brain changes from opioids. I'm glad you've been able to transfer the leadership she's shown to other conditions."

"Indeed," Huck said, casting a furtive glance at Darby be-fore paying her a backhanded compliment, "She was lucky to stumble upon such a juicy project."

"I'm sure luck had nothing to do with it," said Michael, making it sound utterly non-confrontational. "But tell me more about what you're doing. In layman's terms, of course."

"It's actually not that complicated, but the specific chem-ical compound, called AB-538, is one that other researchers have overlooked." Huck continued, seeming content to have the spotlight back on himself. "That's my silver bullet, and no-body else knows about it."

"AB-538. Fascinating…but I won't ask you to say more. I'm sure the details such as those are highly confidential and I don't want to present a conflict of interest with other medical concerns I'm supporting. Say any more, and Stacey might ask me to sign an NDA," he quipped.

Ten minutes later, Darby was giving him an incredulous look at the bar.

"Okay," she said. "You've charmed both of my closest hos-pital friends. You know the President of the Board and are dangling the possibility of major funding in front of him. You got Huck to say too much about the work he was doing—so much that he is clearly in violation of his own NDA—and you exposed the fact that his research—which he is getting a ton more money for than me—is based on principles that I brought to the table.

Michael shrugged noncommittally. "And we've only been here for half an hour. You should know by now I'm good."

"If that's your 'good,' I want to see your 'amazing.'"

"Don't worry—you will."

"And what was that thing with Rich? Telling him you were warding off unwelcome attention?"

Michael's eyes hardened a bit.

"He obviously has feelings for you."

"No he doesn't—he's just a friend. And my research partner. I would never date him."

"That doesn't mean *he* doesn't want to date *you*."

"You're way off base." She shook her head.

"You still don't see it," he said, smiling down at her as if she'd done something cute. "You still don't see how men look at you."

He didn't take his eyes off of her, but she found she couldn't keep her eyes on him.

"And the second you realize you *do* want a relationship, you could have your pick of any man in this room."

Not any man, she thought.

CHAPTER TWENTY-SIX

THE IV ANGEL

NO LONGER ABLE TO IGNORE THE GROWLING OF HER stomach, Darby logged out of her laptop and looked at her watch. It was 2PM in Chicago, which meant it was 3PM in Boston. The last time she had eaten had been on her 5AM flight—a small omelet and an even smaller croissant.

But catching up on work all morning had been absolutely necessary. Huck was still burying her in paperwork and she was still being careful to give him no excuse to say she wasn't pulling her weight. It wasn't easy. Since she had also ramped up her job search, she had spent nearly all of her days off flying around the country, quietly taking meetings with hospitals interested in her before flying back.

Huck had known that she would be in Boston to speak at an American Psychiatric Association conference. What he hadn't known was that she'd also met with the Psych Chief at Mass Gen. Michael knew, and had demanded a recap. That was why at the same moment she grabbed her coat, she picked up her phone to dial him.

"How'd it go?" he asked in a weak voice, not picking up

until the third ring. She immediately knew something was wrong.

"It went great," she said with a bit of surprise. "What the hell happened to you?"

"Not sure..." he said, his voice much deeper than usual, "Could be a virus...maybe I ate something wrong, I don't know. Stomach problems are one of the many hidden perks of constant travel."

Michael had also been out of town a lot lately. Between two trips she'd taken to the east coast over the past ten days, and his brief jaunt in São Paulo, their dates had conflicted completely. They hadn't seen each other since the day after The Christmas Party, but they still texted or talked almost daily. Darby had been craving his body and had been looking forward to seeing him that night, but it was clear those plans were shot.

"I'm coming over."

"To watch me throw up? I don't think so."

She rolled her eyes.

"Don't be stupid. I work in a hospital. I see more puke in a week than you've produced in your whole life. I'm impervious."

"I'll be fine. I just have to let it run its course."

"Which pharmacy do you use?" she asked, ignoring him completely. She pressed him until he relented.

Twenty minutes later, she was letting herself into his apartment, a small CVS bag dangling from her fingers. Her purse was full of things she'd pinched from the hospital supply room. She found him on his bed asleep. A mini glass bottle of Canada Dry sat on his bedside table. He looked worse than she had ever seen him—shivering and clutching the covers around him, sweat gleaming on his skin. She touched his forehead, and wasn't surprised to find him burning up.

Her hand must have felt cool to him, because her touch

roused him. "When was the last time you threw up?" she asked caringly when she saw him open his eyes.

"Dunno," he murmured. "An hour. Maybe two."

"Do you think there's anything left in your stomach?"

He shook his head.

"I hope not," he said. Then, "I don't think so."

"Good," she replied. "Then it's probably okay to start you an IV."

She told him to sit up, an act she half-expected him to protest. The fact that he didn't showed her how sick he was. He was completely devoid of energy. Whatever had gotten him, it was nasty.

He took the needle like a champ (Darby knew how many men didn't), and watched her with heavy eyelids as she hung two IV bags, one large, one small, from the corner of his elegant headboard. She eased him back down and had him lie on his left side, then placed a trash can next to the bed, just in case.

She smoothed her hand over his head in what she hoped was a comforting gesture.

"I'll check on you in a few hours," she said quietly.

Before she could rise to head back to work, the hand that didn't have the IV in it reached out to her from under the covers.

"Thank you," he said just as quietly. She squeezed his hand.

Five hours later, she slipped quietly back in. The sun had long since set and his apartment was dark. She set her own dinner down in the kitchen and shrugged off her coat. She was still starving—lunch had been a King Size Snickers bar from CVS—but she wanted to check on Michael again before she tucked into her dinner.

She was pleased to find him sitting up in bed, the dim light of the television illuminating his face. He looked much better.

She noticed that a Gatorade that hadn't been there before sat on his bedside table, which meant he'd gotten up at some point and taken out his IV. When she picked it up, she saw that about half the Gatorade was gone, as was the ginger ale from before. In the trash can were four or five Jolly Rancher wrappers and there were another few on the bedside table. She felt his forehead and was encouraged to find that he no longer felt feverish.

"What the fuck was in that IV?" he asked with a small smile, though his voice remained a bit hoarse.

"Unicorn blood," she smiled back. He was watching *Harry Potter*.

"You're feeling better," she remarked, sitting on the edge of the bed, picking up his wrist so she could feel his pulse.

"I don't know, Dr. Christensen. I think I need an examination," he said cheekily.

"You're definitely feeling better," she smiled, checking on his IV entry point. He'd done a good job taking it out. "Hitting on the doctor is always a sign of improving health."

"Tell me about Mass Gen," he said then, patting her side of the bed in a gesture that said he wanted her to sit next to him.

She kicked off her clogs and climbed over him, sitting Indian-style as she faced him, forgetting about her food for the moment.

"It was amazing," she said. "The facility is state of the art. Their lab technology is the best I've ever seen. They have a much larger cohort of researchers, and the average grant is three times as high as what I'm getting now. They have a larger focus on clinical care, so I wouldn't have to scale back on working with patients. And most of the current work at their addiction center focuses on smoking, but they realize the growing urgency of opioid-related problems, and they sounded eager to expand their focus there."

She could see that Michael was still weak, but he was listening intently. It was clear that he was excited for her.

"What was the chief like?" he asked.

"Really down to earth," Darby reflected. "I'd seen her speak before, and I've read quite a few of her papers. She has high standards, but so do I and it's clear she really cares about the work. I could see myself working with her."

He smiled weakly.

"That's great, cupcake. You're doing the right thing. Maybe all this Huck bullshit is a blessing in disguise."

She'd been thinking the same thing herself. "Everything happens for a reason, right?"

His eyes took on a wistful look, and he squeezed her hand.

"It does," he said in that quiet way of his. "So, what next?"

"She invited me to a research symposium they're having in February. It's the first one they've had on opioids in more than five years. She talked about it kind of casually—said she thought it was something I might enjoy being a part of, but it's really—"

"An interview," he finished for her.

She nodded. "If I were just a clinician, the hiring process would be a lot quicker—I could have someone else's position as soon as they decided to leave. But, with research, it's different. The vetting process is long. But if all goes well with some of the prospects I'm queuing up now," she took a deep breath, "I should have an offer by spring. Which is perfect timing for my current research. My grant runs out in April."

He squeezed her knee, and she smiled, covering his hand with hers.

"How are things at the firm?" she asked then, also curious about Michael's status. "They've had you in Sydney a lot lately, right?"

He nodded, then sighed.

"They're testing me," he admitted. "It's a bit of a problem territory. The guy they brought in to run it is messing up, so they've been farming out some of the accounts to me and a handful of the other junior partners to see who can turn them around."

"So how's it going?" she asked. He threaded his fingers with hers.

"I'm tired," he admitted. "The time difference is punishing. But the client really likes me and Dale is pleased with my work. I'm building strong relationships there and getting great experience. Stomach problems aside, it's been a good thing."

"So what's their endgame?" she asked, "Does the winner get the Sydney office or are they grooming you for something else?"

She asked it casually, though she was eager for details. A transfer meant the end of their arrangement, but he rarely opened up about work. If something like that was coming, she didn't want to be blindsided.

"Hard to tell," he admitted, looking back up at her. "If I make managing partner sooner than later, it'll be a combination of my performance and the details of the individual position. Like, right now, the partner in the Tokyo office is about to retire. But I'd be surprised if I got it—there are other junior partners in line who have a lot more APAC experience than me."

"APAC?"

"Asia Pacific," he smiled in a way that showed he thought it was cute that she didn't understand his jargon.

"So you'll get transferred to somewhere when you make managing partner?"

"I could be transferred to anywhere at any time, promotion

or not. But Sydney's a real possibility. Like I said, I'm doing well. There's no natural frontrunner and I've got a shot at the whole thing."

It was stupid of Darby to resent this, especially since she was orchestrating a transfer of her own. She hated that happiness she should have felt for Michael was overshadowed by an attachment to him she never should have grown.

"Would you want to move there?" she pried.

"I could do a lot worse," he admitted. "The only office I care about one way or the other is Paris—I'd love to go there, but I doubt it'll happen."

"Why wait? You could just go work for a Parisian firm, couldn't you?"

He nodded. "I guess. But I wouldn't consider it until I get promoted. I'll have better leverage if I do it this way."

She yawned at the same moment her stomach growled.

"When was the last time you ate?" he asked, and she could see the beginnings of a frustrated look on his face.

"I picked up dinner on the way here," she defended herself, avoiding his question.

"Eat, please," he said.

She squeezed his hand. "Okay."

CHAPTER TWENTY-SEVEN

THE FIGHT

IT HAD BEEN ANOTHER AWFUL DAY AT WORK. THE HOLIDAYS coming right around the corner meant that Darby was not only busy managing patients on the psych floor, but was also deep in consults from the ER. Starting at around Thanksgiving, drug-related cases abounded, some people just having a little more fun than was good for them, others using drugs to cope with the depression that accompanied the holidays.

Darby understood it. The holidays were the hardest time for her as well. Her mother had loved Christmas and seeing the city decked out in its lights, wreathes, and trees never got easier. Some days, the bright-eyed tourists walking down Michigan Avenue laden with shopping bags made her happy and nostalgic. But at other times, it just sucked.

Today was one of those days. Even the hospital was bursting in holiday cheer. The schedule had just come out and she had to work not only Christmas Eve, but also Christmas Day and New Year's Eve. Not that she had anything better to do, but still. And then there was Huck, whose torture had not relented, despite his smiling face and feigned friendliness at the holiday party.

If anything, he was treating her worse than before. Huck wasn't stupid—he realized he'd been hoisted on his own petard and was taking it out on her. He'd always been condescending to her whenever they spoke in private, but he used to keep things more professional when others were around. Yet, that day, at the planning meeting that the head of neuro had suggested Darby attend, Huck had shown her up in front of some pretty senior people.

Darby's research budget from the previous round had enabled her to purchase analytics software called Tableau in order to help her crunch her data. The grant review board had been so impressed by Darby's presentation of her results that they had asked her to train some of the other researchers on using the tool. As a result, Dr. Scott wanted her further input on other innovations that might make sense. They had been discussing next year's budget, and Dr. Scott had invited Darby to share her opinions on equipment and software that the hospital might want to invest in, in order to support her department.

"What would really help," Darby was saying, "…is a data warehouse. Right now, we're using Tableau for individual efforts, as if all of the data that's being analyzed were in a silo. But if we centralized data from multiple projects to a data warehouse, we would be opening the door to do additional research in areas where individual projects might have future overlaps. It would be a serious investment, but a forward-looking one. It would allow us to not only expand our internal knowledge base—it would position us as an innovation leader and probably get us some media attention."

She was pleased to see nodding heads around the table. It was the only good thing that had happened to her that day and she was hopeful that this would be another point in her favor, to insulate her from the war that Huck was waging against her. She knew that she had to appear fact-based, logical, and dedicated to what was best for the hospital, and her small pitch achieved all three. But she saw the look on Huck's face, and knew he was set to instigate something before he even opened his mouth.

"While I admire your *attempts* at innovative thinking, Dr. Christensen," Huck began authoritatively, "I can assure you that I've read the benchmarking data on this. Most companies that invest in data warehouses find that they are 50% more expensive to implement than original planning estimates, and that they deliver only 35% of the anticipated value. Do you have any direct experience implementing a data warehouse solution for medical research?" he asked.

"No," she admitted evenly. "But I do know that most implementation problems stem from faulty logic during the architecture stage. It would be important to hire a service provider familiar with our space, and to conduct extensive interviewing around possible future uses of the data. If we don't set it up properly, you're right—it will deliver useless results."

"Is that a chance you're willing to take with the hospital's money?" he challenged. "I know that, from where you sit, it seems like there is an endless pool of money for the taking, but this committee doesn't just write the checks—we're accountable for results. Do you feel that you can guarantee results?" His cold gaze pierced her as he attempted to put her on the spot.

"If we make the right hire, and conduct a robust process… yes, I believe the end would justify the means."

Huck nodded slowly. "Uh-huh," he said curtly. "And do you believe that you have time to oversee that given some of the challenges you're experiencing in other areas of your work?"

She bit her tongue then. If they were alone, she would mention that she would have plenty of time to oversee this project if he hadn't gotten her bogged down in so many other things. But they weren't alone, and she couldn't say what she wanted to. The other attendees, she noticed, were watching their interaction with interest and she saw that they were fooling nobody. The tension between them was obvious. Not wanting to appear defiant, she backed off a bit, even though she knew she was right about all of it.

"I believe that we as an organization should be dedicated to taking the steps necessary toward becoming world class, without delay, if that's our goal." She left it at that.

By eight o'clock, she thought she would go blind if she had to read another toxicology report, thought she would go crazy if she had to comfort another distraught family, thought she would punch something if she replayed the events of that horrible meeting again. Making things immeasurably worse was the fact that a patient she'd been rooting for, a teenager who had been in her therapy group six months before, had relapsed the night before, come in in bad condition, and died. The girl, Lacey, reminded Darby of herself in some ways—she had a dead mother, a disinterested father, and was an only child. The father didn't even cry. Not that all men did in these situations, but it infuriated her all the same. When Darby herself had heard the news, she'd gone to her office and sobbed for twenty minutes. She hated herself for having to wonder, if she ever died, whether her own father would cry for her.

She would later realize with the clarity of hindsight that she should have made an excuse and cancelled her plans with Michael, or she should have at least done something to clear her head before going straight from work to the restaurant. But at the time, she was still charged up from her day, and some part of her felt that she had to keep moving. That if she slowed down, she would fall apart.

That was why, twenty minutes after her quick shower in the locker room at work, she was sliding in across from him at Tavern on Rush, ready for a very large drink and, hopefully, for Michael to help take her mind off of things. When he leaned over to kiss her a chaste hello, she noticed that he looked as at ease and put together as usual. It irritated her for some reason—she muttered a greeting and quickly joined him for a drink.

"So was it the kind of shitty day you want to talk about or don't want to talk about?" he asked knowingly, though kept his eyes on the menu. It was pointless—he knew the menu back and forth but always got the same thing. His redundant perusal of the menu irritated her as well.

"Don't want to talk about," she said somewhat tersely.

"Fuck our jobs. I don't want to talk about mine either," he quipped in solidarity, closing his menu abruptly. "What are you up to for Christmas?"

She gave him a look. "I'm working," she replied ironically.

He winced, which she ignored. "What are you up to?"

"Opening presents with my niece in the morning…invited to Bex's in-laws for dinner but I don't really want to go. I was going to see whether you wanted to do something."

"Like what?"

"Have a snowball fight? Watch 24 Hours of A Christmas Story on TBS? Fuck like nobody's business? I don't know."

"Maybe next year," was all she could think to say.

He changed the subject for real then, and she tried to enjoy dinner, though she knew she was being terse with him. The drinks helped. By the time their plates were being cleared, she was thinking less about work and more about blowing off some steam with Michael in bed. But she must've been acting strangely, because, as they stood outside, waiting for an Uber, he turned to face her, his blue eyes piercing her in that way they sometimes did when he had something important to say.

"Don't let him convince you you're weak," he said, clearly suspecting that Huck was behind her bad mood. It wasn't a bad guess—that's what it usually was.

But that's not what it was tonight. At least, not entirely. Her patient had died. She had to work the worst shifts over the holiday, and even if she hadn't, she had no family left to spend her time with. And, yes, the Huck situation was still a problem that felt more painful every day. Sparked by Michael's words, her bad mood returned with a vengeance.

"I know I'm not weak," she said with a touch of bitterness in her voice, "...but I'm not like you, either. Nobody is like you, Michael. You're like Teflon. Everything rolls off of you."

He looked at her strangely.

"Is that what you think?"

But she didn't stop to think. She was on a roll.

"You've never been called to a battle you couldn't win. Never met a problem you couldn't solve. You spend more nights on the red-eye than you do in your own bed, yet somehow you're always perfectly put together. *Your* hard work will get you a promotion. I'm barely holding onto my job. So spare me the advice, please. Reminding myself I'm not weak won't do shit to fix my problems, Michael. I'm not infallible like you."

He seemed taken aback. It wasn't a look she'd seen on him, and before her eyes, his face hardened into a mask. As soon as she'd said the words, she'd known they'd been a mistake, but she couldn't take them back quickly enough.

"You're right," he said, bitter sarcasm tainting his own voice. "What would a god like me know about feeling pain, or love or fear, or any of the other emotions all you humans are allowed to feel?"

The car pulled up then. He looked angry, as he opened the door to let her in. Instead of following her, he bent over and leaned in.

"I'll take a different cab. I'm going home."

Darby didn't go home, though she did get halfway to her house before she realized how big of a mistake she'd made. Rerouting the driver to Michael's address, she knew what she had to do. What had been started had been her fault, and she couldn't end the night this way. She would show up at his house and apologize—she owed him at least that. Not wanting to blindside him with her unexpected arrival, she sent him a text.

I'm sorry. I'm coming over. I'm sure you don't want to see me so I won't stay long. I just want to apologize the right way.

For the rest of the ride, she watched her phone for a reply, but none came.

Waiting in his apartment, five minutes turned into fifteen. Fifteen minutes turned into an hour. An hour turned into her falling asleep on his couch. The sound of elevator doors roused her from her sleep, announcing his arrival. It was 3:00AM. She rubbed sleep out of her eyes and sat upright on the couch. When she looked back up, he was watching her from across the room. His apartment was dark, but in what light there was, she saw that his anger had been replaced with something else. Though whatever it was, was still carefully guarded behind a mask.

"I'm sorry," she said simply, her voice raspy from sleep. "I was feeling shitty for reasons that have nothing to do with you. I had no right to talk to you that way."

Her words hung between them. For long moments, he said nothing in return. She didn't know what he wanted her to do. Maybe the best thing for her to do was to leave. She rose from the sofa then, scanning for where she'd left her coat, unhinged by the niggling idea that this might be the end. Hadn't they said that whenever things got too complicated, or stopped being fun, that one of them would pull the plug? The thought made her want to cry.

"I forgive you," he said in a way that sounded sincere, but still felt strange. "Let's go to bed."

He sounded tired, and it occurred to her then to wonder where he had been. But she was too grateful for her second chance to even consider asking. Five minutes later, they'd stripped down to their underwear and climbed into his large bed together. His body—especially his hands—were frigid even though he'd been inside for minutes by then, and she speculated that he'd been outside in the cold for a long time. He rolled her onto her side so she was faced away from him before circling his arms around to hold her tight. Being close to him again gave her tremendous relief and she held his arms as they held her. But Michael was wide awake—she could feel it in his body. Something was eating at him, and she wished she knew what.

"I'm a good actor, Darby," he said finally, some minutes after she'd been sure he wouldn't speak.

She didn't respond right away.

"You don't have to pretend with me."

"When I'm with you, I'm not pretending. I'm focused on being with you. It feels good to forget the other stuff. I don't even want to think about my own shit, let alone burden you with it."

She rolled over in his arms then, looking up at him. The

lights from the city, which always cast light into his room, even in the middle of the night, dimly illuminated his face.

"Do you wish I wouldn't burden you with my shit?" she asked honestly.

"It's not a burden," he said in a way that said already that he knew where she was going.

"Why would your shit be a burden?"

"You listen to other people's shit all day," he pointed out.

"You're not other people."

She watched his face closely, for a reaction, half-expecting him to formulate another logical retort. But she could see the moment he decided not to form one.

"Not tonight, okay?"

"Okay," she agreed, and snuggled closer to him.

The next morning, when she awoke, she sensed again that he was not sleeping, and feared for a long moment that things between them still weren't right. When he captured her mouth in a long, tender kiss, and breathed a soft "I'm sorry" at the end of it, she knew otherwise, and relished her relief.

His hands moved slowly—first on her body and then in her hair—soothing her in comforting strokes that echoed his words. She leaned into his touch, wanting to lead them back to their sacred place, wanting to complete their connection. He fucked her slowly after that, her back to his front as he whispered how good she felt in her ear. They'd just had their first fight, she realized, when he held her afterward. Not only that, they'd just had their first make-up sex.

CHAPTER TWENTY-EIGHT

MERRY CHRISTMAS, BABE

TEN OVERDOSES. THREE OF THEM WERE DOAs. FOUR WERE psychotic breaks. The icing on the cake was that two psych nurses and one of her MD colleagues had been no-shows for work. She briefly entertained a fantasy of quitting, of not returning to work the next morning, Christmas morning, which would surely deliver much of the same. She had planned on decorating her tree when she got home, but at the moment, she was more than three hours late. She had to be back in just over eight hours. And all she wanted was a huge glass of wine, and her bed.

As she stepped into her kitchen from the garage, two smells hit her immediately. One was garlic, the other hard liquor. Michael appeared, having heard her come in. She hadn't expected him, but she was instantly glad that he was there. He had obviously cooked for her, but what? She mustered a tired smile. It was then that she noticed the glass in his hand. It was a champagne coupe, but instead of being filled with sparkling wine it held something creamy that was almost gone.

"I know you have to work tomorrow," he began, "...but I

wanted to give you your Christmas present." He gestured to her kitchen counter, and she saw the wide, short box, wrapped beautifully in red and white striped paper that reminded her of a candy cane. It was slightly iridescent and sported an elaborate red bow.

She looked back up at him with a watery smile, because her day had been that shitty and to come home to this was everything she hadn't known she had needed.

"I got you something too. Let me grab it."

Two minutes later, she returned to the kitchen with a shiny red gift bag with red and white tissue paper poking out of the top. He poured her something that turned out to be delicious—a Brandy Alexander, he explained. Growing up, his uncle had made them every holiday.

"Open it," he smiled, handing her the box.

"You too," she said shyly, hoping that he would like his gift.

She stalled on opening what he had gotten her in order to observe his reaction, and was gratified by his shining smile when he pulled out the first item—boxer briefs that read "Muggle in the streets, wizard in the sheets."

"Can you imagine?" she asked playfully. "That fancy British underwear company you buy from had never received a request to have custom silk screening put on one of their garments, let alone in Harry Potter font."

He laughed. "I love them." He ran his eyes over them for long moments, before meeting her eyes. "They're perfect," he said, beaming at her and she felt extreme satisfaction. He rummaged around in the bag for the remaining items—Bertie Bott's Every Flavor Beans, a Honeyduke's Chocolate Frog, Drooble's Best Blowing Gum, and a cornucopia of other confections. All were from Harry Potter, and given his sweet tooth, she had guessed correctly that he'd think the novelties were fun.

"Thank you," he said still beaming as he kissed her lips.

She finally opened her own gift. It was a large stack of letter papers held by a simple binder clip. She realized from the cover sheet that it was a screenplay. The title read *Before Midnight*. It was signed in a silver sharpie, in messy cursive. "It's time you find out how it ends. –Richard Linklater"

Michael had gotten her the printed manuscript of the final installment in her favorite movie series, the one she hadn't dared to finish. And he'd had it signed by the writer and director, just for her. After recovering from her gaping surprise, she hugged him fiercely, scarcely comprehending what he might have done to obtain this on her behalf.

"This is amazing," she breathed into his neck. "Thank you," she said and found herself nearly tearing up once again.

Michael fixed her a creamy cocktail and sent her to relax on the sofa with her drink. He had, indeed, been watching *A Christmas Story* as he'd waited for her to return. Knowing how well she loved comfort food at the end of a cold and horrible day, he had made steak frites with a peppercorn cream sauce. They watched together in front of the television until he saw her eyes lull and gently hustled her to her bedroom. When she felt him begin to tuck her in, she realized that he meant to leave, but she didn't want that.

"Stay," she said simply.

And he did. He stripped down to his underwear and slid into bed behind her, holding her in a way that was exactly what she needed.

"Merry Christmas, cupcake," he murmured into her hair before kissing her neck.

"Merry Christmas, babe," she returned a minute before drifting off to sleep.

PART III

THE BEGINNING OF
THE END

CHAPTER TWENTY-NINE

THE REALITY CHECK

"It's been too long," Darby said, smiling into Shirley Whitlock's eyes a moment after they embraced in the secluded bar. They were at The St. Regis at two o'clock on a Tuesday—it was Darby's day off. "Sherlock", as she jokingly called the older woman, had called that morning to say it would be a good idea if the two of them met. Darby wouldn't have taken a call from most of her father's staffers, but she had always liked Shirley and didn't hold it against her that she worked for Frank.

She hadn't needed an explanation to gather why Shirley wanted to meet. "Researcher" was code for "investigator"— Shirley had served in that capacity for Frank Christensen for years. From what Darby had heard, Frank's place on the ticket was becoming more secure. She had no doubt that Shirley's call was the result of marching orders to get Darby aligned with the campaign.

"There's something you should know up front," Darby said after they had caught up a bit and ordered drinks. "I gave Frank a hard limit—three events a year, whether he's campaigning or not."

"Good luck getting him to stick to that," Shirley said flatly.

"Good luck getting me to make any exceptions," Darby retorted. "Whatever he's sent you here to do, you can tell him I decline."

Darby grabbed a small handful of wasabi peas with her fingers.

"He didn't send me," Shirley revealed, giving Darby a pointed look. "I came myself. I'm here with a heads up."

Suddenly insecure, Darby slid a pea into her mouth. "A heads up about what?"

"Your boyfriend? Michael Blaine?"

"He's not my boyfriend."

"Whatever he is, he could be trouble."

If it had anything to do with Michael, she wasn't worried yet. Campaign staff liked to make mountains out of molehills.

"What kind of trouble?" she asked, reserving her alarm.

She knew that Michael did not share her father's political views and figured that the optics of being with Michael would threaten the illusion of Darby's solidarity with her father. Darby almost welcomed the opportunity to see this difference acknowledged. Her own disagreement with his views was part of what had caused her to limit her willingness to participate in his campaigns.

"What do you have on him? Video of him protesting for the other side? Pictures of him burning the flag?"

"Nothing like that," Shirley shook her head as if to appease Darby rather than to take it as its intended joke. "I don't know what's going on between the two of you and I don't care. But I don't want you to be blindsided. You should know—there's been tension between your father's administration and lobbying efforts that are heavily supported by Dewey and Rowe."

Darby's heartbeat quickened. That was the name of Michael's firm.

"It's getting ugly," Shirley continued. "The senator needs his neighborhood redevelopment projects on the South Side to look like a sweeping success. He needs to show that he's delivered on campaign promises. The opposition lobby is fighting him with exactly what you'd expect. They're calling it the most egregious attempt this city has ever seen at self-serving gentrification."

"They're right." Darby said impassively. In this case, her hostility toward her father had more to do with the atrocities he was willing to commit as a policymaker than with the atrocities he had committed as a man. Her father's brand of "neighborhood redevelopment" used public funding to improve housing and amenities to neglected areas while doing nothing to make sure that longtime residents could still afford to live there. She saw the effects of this nearly every day in her work, and even apart from her own observations, the link between drug use and urban displacement was well-understood.

"They're winning," Shirley shot back gently.

"Which Frank can't afford right now," Darby sighed, connecting the dots.

"All the lobby cares about is changing outcomes for the South Side. They don't know about his run."

Shirley didn't need to go on for Darby to understand the implications. Under other circumstances, Frank might have negotiated, but he needed to achieve specific outcomes in order to signal his influence and effectiveness with the party. He couldn't back down. He had to fight and he would do what it took to win.

"How does Michael play into all this?" Darby asked finally. It didn't escape her that Michael was from the South Side and that perhaps his involvement was personal. If that was the case, it would explain the linkage between the lobby and Michael's firm.

"Dewey and Rowe is known for corporate responsibility. Their track record of partnering with local and indigenous people worldwide across construction project ecosystems is… impeccable," Shirley admitted, seeming somewhat in awe. "For all of their work, they set conditions—hire for the build from the impacted community and set long-term controls in place to ensure community stability. And they're sought-after enough to be able to make those kinds of demands. They spend 15% of their work on pro bono projects in the cities where they have offices. Their focus is on helping underserved communities. Michael serves as chair of their corporate responsibility group worldwide."

"That doesn't mean he's close to the lobbying effort," Darby pointed out.

"I'll admit," Shirley hedged. "He's been particularly careful not to criticize the senator directly, which is more than what can be said of other business leaders tied to the lobby."

"But?" Darby knew there was a 'but'.

"But in a few months, someone will make the connection. Reputable papers will juxtapose the senator's position with the position of his daughter's boyfriend. You'll be asked to comment. Whichever side wins will be accused of making a back room deal. If the senator wins, big future successes for Dewey and Rowe in the city of Chicago will look like his doing."

Darby's lips began to tingle.

"The longer it drags out, the more of a problem it becomes that he'll run as part of a national election. Enemies who want to weaken the Republican ticket will pile onto the controversy back here. He'll be under pressure from the party to handle it. And he'll have to protect his interests. If that happens, you know what he'll do."

Shirley's words hit Darby like a punch in the gut. But she didn't dare to speak the words out loud. She didn't need to.

He'll ruin Michael, or his firm, or both.

It took her long moments to let all of it sank in.

"We're not dating, Shirley," she repeated more weakly that time.

"But everyone thinks you are," her friend argued softly. "I know you've fought hard to distance yourself from all this. But if you don't handle it, it's gonna become a thing."

Darby sighed bitterly. Shirley wasn't giving her a hard time. Everything she was being told was absolutely correct.

"I'm not getting him involved in this."

"He's already involved. And if you want to protect both of you, get ahead of it. It's time to come up with a plan."

An hour later, Darby was exiting her car, walking heavily up her back steps, toeing off her boots, and walking dejectedly into her kitchen. Though she'd just downed two martinis at the St. Regis, she found her laptop and poured herself a glass of wine.

She hadn't thought of Googling Michael in several months—not since her dinner with Ben, not since she'd vowed not to let her curiosity take over. With trepidation, she navigated to a query page and typed 'Dewey and Rowe South Side neighborhood development' into a Google search. The picture Shirley had painted came to life.

Most of the articles dated back to months before she and Michael had even met. The majority were feel-good stories about volunteer work the firm was doing in the community.

From employee service days spent building playgrounds, to offering pro bono services to rebuild an apartment complex destroyed by fire, to helping business owners make repairs, it was clear that the firm was deeply committed. They must have had a great PR agency as well, because the dozen projects they had done there over the past three years had gotten a lot of press.

Darby felt an unsettling mixture of pride and betrayal as she read through the articles and watched the video clips. Michael was all over them. She could have guessed that he would be a media darling—in print, his quotes were articulate, on video, he came off as credible and persuasive. But some of the still pictures of him—a dramatic shot of the apartment building he had grown up in rising high behind him, one of him next to railroad tracks with dilapidated buildings all around, a picture of him smiling with neighborhood kids—were stunning. It made for good art—Michael's sparkling beauty against the backdrop of a shabby, neglected place. The stories humanized these neighborhoods and portrayed Michael very well.

But she found more than she bargained for. First there were the pictures of Michael raising money for his foundation—the one Ben had alluded to—the one that helped fund art education for underprivileged kids. There were others of Michael and Darby together, but a far greater number of him alone or with people Darby didn't recognize. She quickly gathered that Michael had been busier than she thought. As she clicked on the events he'd been seen attending without her, she saw that the majority of them were in Chicago. They were precisely the kinds of events she would have expected him to attend—charity auctions and professional functions—they were all recent, and she hadn't been invited to a single one.

Reading these articles hurt. Interviews that focused on Michael revealed deep involvement in the community, beyond what his firm was doing. He was clearly the reason why Dewey and Rowe was so active, but it looked as if he had also been investing funds of his own back into the South Side. In a high profile spread for *Chicago Magazine*, he talked about the first house he had bought back in his old neighborhood—he had completely renovated it, but instead of selling it on the open market, he had sold it back to the tenant on a rent-to-own agreement. Since buying that first property five years before, he had done the same thirteen times. According to the article, he was hailed as a local hero.

How do I not know this?

A sick feeling settled as Darby continued to read. Modesty was one thing, but secrets were another. This was a huge part of Michael's life she knew absolutely nothing about.

Her next search—a similar one on her father's name—found more evidence of what Shirley had told her. The community disliked the senator. Years of bad blood from the days when he was mayor placed him at an automatic disadvantage. And his recent attempts to ingratiate himself to these constituents had fallen flat. At the same time, private initiatives, including those supported by Dewey and Rowe were lobbying against Frank's plan given his track record. Not only that—they had an alternative plan for neighborhood redevelopment that they seemed in a strong position to pull off even without state funding. And if they did, it would draw attention to her father's own plan, which would look bloated and ineffective in comparison.

Her mind went to an unexpected place. A fantasy she hadn't had in a long time—one that involved being vocal about her own political views and publicly opposing her father—re-entered her consciousness. It occurred to her to make a large donation to support the lobby, and she wondered why she had never considered anything like it before. Darby liked the idea of Frank being defeated. He didn't care about those people—all Frank wanted was a feather in his cap and another excuse to throw business to his cronies. But Shirley's words came back to her then.

You know what he'll do.

Darby wasn't so much afraid for herself as she was for Michael. Frank would never do anything to Darby that shattered the illusion of his happy family. He might do something privately to undercut her, something only she would understand. But he would never do anything that prevented her from leading an ostensibly normal life. Michael was a different story and so was his firm. Dewey and Rowe may have been a multi-national company with influence of its own, but it was no match for the unscrupulous methods of Frank Christensen. She spent the rest of the afternoon trying to figure out what to do next.

After a restless night of sleep that left her wide awake at six in the morning, Darby decided to take a very long walk to work. The hospital was several neighborhoods away and the weather was predictably frigid. Some part of her wanted this—wanted the harsh conditions to numb the pain, or maybe to jar her out of her befuddled fog.

She had spent all night trying to talk herself into believing that there could be any good outcome for Michael if he remained with her. By morning, she surrendered to her failure. Because she couldn't forget—not in her gut, or her heart, or her head—the kinds of things that her father had done to people who had stood in his way before. If Frank seemed to be losing a political fight to someone connected to Darby, it would make him look malleable and weak. It would give him incentives to go beyond fighting the lobby as a whole, to make an example of Dewey and Rowe specifically. It would be a signal that nobody—not even somebody close to his own daughter—could undermine his power, and that there would be consequences for anyone who tried.

But there was more. For as much of a shiny little bubble her relationship with Michael existed in, researching him had caused her to face a hard truth. That she knew only parts of Michael, the parts that he wanted her to see. That the parts of him he wanted her to see were narrower than she'd believed. That there was too much she didn't know about the man who, for all intents and purposes, she was dating.

Darby had trouble accepting this. This was a man who had shown up at the hospital during her shift to kiss her to within an inch of her life at the stroke of midnight on New Year's Eve two weeks before. A man who had given her free rein of his apartment. A man who was hiring a private investigator to solve her work problems. A man who was rooting for her. The fact that she had never pressed him to share anything he didn't want to rarely made her feel that she didn't know him. But the truth was, she didn't. And the worst part of all of this was that he knew her.

He knew all her problems with Huck, and about her strained relationship with her father. He had met her friends, and been to her work functions and visited her at her job. He knew about her grief over her dead mother and had given her one of the most cathartic experiences of her life when he'd taken her to the Art Institute. Later that night, he had tasted every inch of her body. When it came to Darby, Michael knew everything.

The thought was crippling, not only because it called into question everything they shared, but because it challenged their agreement. They had said that when it got too complicated, when someone grew feelings or things got even just a little bit messy, that one of them would pull the plug.

Now, here she was, feeling wounded about being left out of parts of Michael's life that he had never agreed to share, feeling guilty about being the reason her father would come down so hard on his firm. This wasn't what either of them had signed up for. And she couldn't deny it anymore. The day to end it had come.

Now, all she had to do was say it.

Snapdragon.

Darby tapped out the word on the screen of her phone, punctuating it with a period, as if to underscore just how final it was. Her fingers still felt stiff and frozen from having spent so much time outside. She stood at the busy corner of Michigan and Chicago Avenues. People rushed by her as she stood still, having ignored the crossing signal that had already told her to walk three times. Her thumb itched. In an instant, it would be over, if only she pressed 'send'.

But it felt wrong. Even though stopping things in exactly this way was what they had agreed to, it suddenly seemed like the stupidest idea Darby had ever had. She knew they couldn't be together anymore, but she didn't want to sever ties to him either. Even if this was getting messy, it didn't mean she never wanted to see him again.

Her thumb moved, but not to the 'send' button, to the backspace key. She erased the word completely and tapped out something different, something that wouldn't throw away what they had together as if it were trash, something that felt more humane.

We need to talk.

She cringed, because that sounded awful, too. But there

was no elegant way to do this. And she could do this. She had to do this. And with just a little bit more courage, she would.

She pocketed her phone again and finally crossed Chicago Avenue, telling herself she could at least wait for a decent hour before she sent the text. Michael was in Sydney, where it would be midnight. She would wait until the next day. But not a full minute after she'd resumed walking, her phone buzzed in her pocket. When she pulled it out, she saw that it was him.

Stopped again, now on the sidewalk, she stared at her phone, not knowing what to do. Not knowing what she was feeling, but knowing she wasn't ready to face him, she slipped the phone back into her pocket. It was the very first time she had ignored his call.

"Hey." He breathed the words in a tone that sounded relieved as he pulled her into his arms for a very long hug. Even through both of their heavy coats, his warmth reached her. She had suggested that they take a walk on the running path on Lake Shore Drive at the entry point closest to his building. Tears stung her eyes from how good he felt, how much like home he smelled, and from the realization that this might be the last time.

"Hey." She managed a weak smile. She could tell that she didn't fool him. His plane had landed two hours earlier. After her vague text and her refusal to discuss what was on her mind over the phone, he'd insisted on meeting as soon as he got back into town.

He took her hand and they began to walk south, toward the empty marina.

"Sorry," she said with genuine regret, knowing that she should say it. "I didn't mean to alarm you, but I thought we should talk face-to-face."

"What's going on?" His question was cautious. It took her a minute to answer.

"There's a lot we don't talk about, isn't there?"

"So, let's talk," he replied after taking in her words. That was Michael. Perfectly reasonable. Perfectly rational. Ever-approachable. But they weren't going to be able to talk their way out of this. "What happened?"

"My father happened," she said, steeling herself. "He's going to announce another run. They've already started to pry into your business—"

"Who's *they*?" he interrupted gently.

"So far, it's my father's research team," she explained evenly. It took effort to calm her voice. "They're stress testing what would come out as part of a real campaign."

"And they found something on me?" he asked, sounding almost amused. "I'm a boy scout."

"A boy scout whose work in South Side neighborhood development has been so effective that it's threatening the senator's campaign."

He stopped walking but his hand stayed firm on hers.

"It's getting complicated," she said, launching into the speech that she had carefully prepared.

"Is it a problem for you that I'm on a different side than your father's?"

"No, it's not that," she said. "You know I am, too."

"Then it's not complicated." He resumed walking.

"He needs this win. He'll do anything to get it. Even if it means blackballing his daughter's boyfriend's firm." She could see his surprise at her use of that word. "He'll make sure that projects Dewey and Rowe touches never get another building permit in Chicago again, and that all of your construction and engineering partners refuse to do business with you. It'll get you off his back and it will send a signal to everyone else who's boss."

But Michael shook his head.

"He's an incumbent senator with a weak democratic opponent. This issue isn't big enough to be a threat to his reelection. He's already won it. He doesn't need to play hardball on this."

This time it was Darby who stopped. "I only said he's running…not that he's running for re-election."

His confusion was only momentary. Soon, understanding dawned on Michael's face.

"Fuck," he commiserated softly. "I'm sorry. That's gotta be the last thing you want."

Tears sprang to her eyes again, and knocked her off of her script. That he knew implicitly that this would be a tragedy for her melted her resolve. Here she was, trying to find a way to break up with him, and he was thinking about how to comfort her.

"It won't be president," she sniffed, trying to get a hold on herself. "He'll be the running mate," she clarified. "But the scale will be the same. The stakes are higher for him this time. He'll do whatever he has to, to win."

She saw the moment Michael admitted to himself what he had probably suspected since she'd sent the text. But she didn't have the courage to deliver the death blow yet. She tried to remember the words she had rehearsed.

"This has nothing to do with us." Michael was indignant. But she came back just as strongly.

"You still don't get it. Being with me makes it worse for you. He can't look like he's caving because his daughter is dating the enemy. If he loses, everyone will say he was swayed because of me or that he made a behind-the-scenes deal with you. Distancing ourselves from one another will be the only thing that gives him incentives to go easier on you."

"No." Michael's eyes blazed. "He doesn't get to dictate who you see. Did his campaign lackey tell you to do this?"

His anger was sparking her own fire.

"I don't give a fuck about his campaign. I give a fuck about you. I don't want to be the reason why his attack is five times worse."

Something in Michael's eyes changed when he realized he had upset her. When he spoke, he was the voice of reason once again.

"Look…I've thought this through. Now that a national election is in play, that'll change the plan a bit. But it's nothing I can't handle."

"You do not know what he is capable of."

"I'm not without resources, Darby."

"You can't beat him," she shot back. "The stories I could tell you would make you sick."

But Michael just shook his head. "I have a plan and I know what I'm doing. Thank you for offering to protect me. But believe me when I tell you I don't need it."

Darby blew out a frustrated breath. Michael's confidence bordered on delusion. Chicago was a crooked town and Frank Christensen was the reigning crook. She had hoped that fact alone would convince Michael that parting ways was a good idea. But it wasn't working and it was time to talk about the rest.

"It's not just that…" she said finally, dropping the second bomb. "It's all of it."

That silenced him.

"All of what?"

She sighed. "All the not talking about important things."

"Look how great that's turning out now."

He shook his head and wiped his gloved hand over his face. She saw then how tired he looked. She had spent days preparing for this conversation. He'd just finished a twenty-one-hour haul from Australia. But his voice, when he spoke, was determined.

"I leave certain things alone because talking about them would only make them more complicated, and complicated is the one thing we promised we wouldn't do. Do you want me to bring up all the events I don't take you to because I don't want to place you in the precarious position of being seen raising funds for a cause that goes against your father? Am I wrong for wanting to save you from uncomfortable questions about his politics? Everything you don't know about has kept you out of the line of fire."

Darby felt tired now too. "I don't need saving, Michael. I need to be told the truth."

The words rang true in her own ears, and in that moment Darby understood why this hurt so much. Hiding parts of himself away from her felt all too familiar. So did always having an angle, always having a plan. Add in the fact that he was so handsome and charismatic as he played his cards, and Darby saw what had really been bothering her. Michael reminded her of her father a little too much.

She knew that they were nothing alike—her father had hidden his own bad deeds. Michael, quite the opposite, had hidden good and noble ones. But it was the secrecy she hated—the manipulation, the veiled message that she didn't factor as important enough to know. The thought knocked the wind out of her for a second. Michael, looking concerned, steadied her body with his hands on her waist. She breathed slowly—two beats in, two beats out—to stave off her panic. Looking into his eyes grounded her. As she calmed, he met her, breath for breath.

"I'm sorry," Michael said then, in a heartbreaking voice. "I shouldn't have decided for you."

And it was the apology of all apologies. It was full of sincerity and remorse. It had nothing to do with the word he had certainly figured out that she'd been ready to say. It wasn't about getting what he wanted. It was about doing the right thing. She could tell in that moment that he understood his mistake. She could tell that he would take this new piece of information he had learned about her and use it to make her happier, just as he had done with every other piece of information he had learned about her. Because that was who he was. Unlike her father, Michael was a good man.

And in that moment, she knew that she didn't have the strength to end it. It was fucked up and complicated and messy as hell, but it was too good—*he* was too good—to give up. She had never had anything this good before, and she had to see it as far as it would go. Even if Michael didn't know what he was in for. Even if it ended on his terms. Even if it broke her heart.

CHAPTER THIRTY

THE FIRING

D ARBY HAD NEVER BEEN ONE TO SHOW EMOTION AT work, yet for the past hour, she'd locked herself in the safety of her lab and sat in the supply closet, bawling. Her face was bathed in hot tears, her nose was running and she held her pounding head in her hands. She had ended her shift a full two hours before, but the devastating blow Huck had dealt with such casual brutality had crushed her.

"It's my duty to inform you that your research project has been transferred." He had said it matter-of-factly the second he closed the door to his office. "Dr. Stroh will stay on as the neurologist, but a new psychopharmacologist will be brought in as your replacement. I wish things had been different, but my hands are tied."

Her immediate reaction had been outrage. But she had scolded herself to keep herself in check. "On what grounds?" she had managed to get out. The fact that Huck was using the passive voice, as if he hadn't been the orchestrator of what had happened, was insulting.

"Your other work is slipping, Darby, and people have

noticed. I tried to protect you from the higher-ups, but you didn't turn things around. Based on your review, other aspects of your employment were already under scrutiny. If I were you, I'd focus on that and try to keep your job."

She'd walked out of his office then, feeling numb as she staggered to her lab one floor below. She had swiped her key card to enter, happy that at least it still worked. After closing the window blinds and forgetting to turn off the lights, she went into her closet and sank down on the floor.

Based on the case Michael was helping her build, she knew she could eventually counteract whatever Huck had planned. But she needed more time, and it appeared that she was out of it. Even if she managed to get herself out of this mess, her reputation would be permanently marked. She had failed, and she didn't know how to forgive herself for that.

So she cried. And cried some more, the room darkening gradually as the sun set outside. It felt like everything was falling apart. Her father's election loomed closer. Things with Michael felt different even though two weeks had passed since their talk. And the one thing that motivated her to come to work anymore—her research—was being taken away.

Her phone vibrated. Once. Twice. Three times, all of them texts. When it finally rang, she reached into the pocket of her lab coat as she recognized the tone. It was Michael calling from Sydney. She had been avoiding him a little, but her heart leapt some at seeing his name on the screen. For all they were going through, his was still the one voice that she wanted to hear. He was probably calling to talk logistics about the weekend—to find out whether they would leave from downtown together on Friday, or whether she would pick him up from O'Hare.

"Hey," she whispered, trying not to sound as devastated as she was, but knowing full well that he would hear her distress.

"Please tell me." His voice was careful, as if it took him effort to remain calm.

"Huck pulled me from my research. I just found out." She sniffled, then sighed shakily, knowing she had to tell him. "And it's not the project they're getting rid of—it's just me."

This invited a fresh round of tears. Darby covered her mouth and bit her lip to keep herself from sobbing again. She heard Michael take measured breaths, and she remembered the look on his face when she'd told him about the performance review.

"Tell me exactly what he said."

She briefed him on their curt conversation.

"I'll handle this," Michael said.

She didn't know what to say. There was no doubt in her mind that he could fix this. They'd both been preparing for it. She wondered whether Michael would speak with the Board President to get her reinstated. She had never liked the idea of Michael pulling this lever and after finding out about how many chess pieces he'd been moving on his own, she felt less and less comfortable accepting his help. Just because she hadn't walked away didn't mean she'd forgotten her reasons for wanting to end things. Not having gone through with it didn't change the fact that things between them were not what she had thought.

Besides, Darby thought, whatever Michael was planning would only be a short-term gain that would win her the battle, but not the war. The real war was still being fought, through HR and private investigators, and every other card Darby had tried to put herself in a position to play.

"Michael—" she began, but he cut her off immediately.

"I'll handle it. By tomorrow, you'll have it back."

And she didn't say anything to try to stop him. Part of her was too weak to protest, part of her wanted—just this once—to be rescued. After all, it was *her* project. She loved it, and Huck was trying to cheat her out of it. In her better moments, Darby was a warrior. She fought hard for her patients. She had given up every chance at a normal life to craft an amazing career, doing work that she cared about deeply. Even if it meant accepting Michael's help, and even if she didn't like using influence like this, she didn't want to walk away without a fight.

Michael hadn't said much after that. He'd only given her instructions to leave her car in the garage and to take a different car that would arrive downstairs in fifteen minutes to pick her up.

"Don't answer your phone, or your door, or your e-mail for anybody but me," he had told her sternly. "And if someone corners you in the hallway on your way out, actively deny that anything's wrong. Do you understand?"

She'd acquiesced, noting his cryptic instructions, but too weak to wonder about his big plan. He promised to call her the next day, and to see her when she fetched him at O'Hare.

At home, she took a long shower, drank a huge glass of red wine, and fell asleep.

She woke up the next day to a hangover, though she guessed she'd asked for it. It hadn't been the smartest idea to fill her large wine glass to the brim and gulp it down with no food in her stomach. She popped a Zofran, donned fresh scrubs, grabbed a ginger ale and slipped on dark glasses. She had planned to hail a cab, but when she walked out into the bright morning light, she found a town car waiting for her, identical to the one Michael had sent the night before.

The ride to the hospital was spent in dreadful anticipation of what was to come: a saved job and a more furious boss.

Even if Huck couldn't prove it, it would be obvious to him that Darby had pulled some strings to save herself. He would find a way to punish her for this. She'd been a daughter of politics long enough to witness unscrupulous men—her own father was a study in stopping at nothing to get what he wanted.

She thought about the other things Huck had said—about Rich staying on. Rich would tell her the second he heard anything about the new lead researcher, so she had to assume that he didn't know. But what about her replacement? It could as easily be one of her colleagues as it could be someone new. She wondered what that person had been told. She didn't even want to think about the grant review board. This kind of change was one that Huck didn't have the authority to pull off on his own. It would have been discussed with a much larger group of stakeholders, meaning that even if Darby got to keep her fellowship, others would already have a negative opinion about her.

Eager to avoid everyone and everything, she took the stairs from the parking garage to her floor instead of taking the elevator. She took a longer way than she needed in order to sneak into her office. Her laptop sat on its dock, still open from the night before. The light on her phone blinked insistently, indicating that she had voicemail. She hit the speaker button to listen as she keyed in her computer's password.

It was time to face the music. Any second now, Huck's grating voice would begin, demanding that she come to his office to either chew her out or make some excuse for her reinstatement that let him save face. God, he was nuts. The fact that she willingly walked into a minefield every day was a testament to how much she cared about her research.

"Bollocks, Darby, where are you?" Rich's recorded voice startled her. "I've texted you ten times. Can you return my call?

I want to talk to you before the meeting. There are rumors they're appointing a new chief. Is it true? If you didn't tell me, I swear I'll..." his voice faltered, revealing the emptiness of his threat. "...I'll be very cross. *Call me*," he finished with emphasis.

Her heart pounded and she was feeling even sicker, but not entirely from the alcohol. There was a new chief? What exactly had happened to Huck? She waited for the second voicemail to begin.

"Hi Darby," a much sweeter voice intoned, one she immediately identified as Huck's boss, the hospital's Chief of Staff, Kelly King. "Dr. Huck has left the hospital rather abruptly, and I'd like to speak with you about what that means. We've been trying to reach you and I apologize—I know it's very short notice—but please come to my office before you begin your shift. We're prepared to make you an offer that I think you'll like."

Darby was floored. The next message was from Anne. "Ding, Dong, the Witch is Dead!" she sang the song from *The Wizard of Oz*, with her version concluding in wicked laughter. The final message was from Michael. Her voicemail had played the most recent one first, so this last one had been left hours before, in the middle of the night Chicago time.

"Congratulations. He's gone." Michael's deep voice said, and she could hear the dull roar of airport sounds in the background. "It didn't go down like you think, so keep quiet about what you know, okay? I'm getting on my plane now. I'll see you when you pick me up."

She took pause long enough to consider that Michael had not only saved her job, but had orchestrated a miracle. Huck had been fired, just like that.

"He pulled it off," she whispered out loud. She'd walked in that day fully expecting her position on her project to be intact. She'd been around politics long enough to know that favors like

this were called in all the time. But for him to be let go overnight meant that Michael either had an astounding level of influence, or some seriously scathing information on Huck. She
couldn't walk into a meeting with the Chief of Staff without
knowing what she was walking into. She had to find out.

She logged onto Facebook, but closed the page as soon as
it loaded, realizing she didn't want to chat with Michael on a
company computer. Right then, he would be somewhere over
the Pacific, but workaholic that he was, he might still be logged
on. Grabbing her phone, she opened her Facebook app and
private messaged him.

What did you do?

She didn't have to wait long for a response.

Me? I didn't do anything.

And a minute later:

But my private investigator…now that's another story.

She forgot to breathe.

Already?

I told you I'd take care of it.

Somehow, she still couldn't believe it.

I'll tell you everything when I land.

As she messaged Michael, more texts were coming in, and
she couldn't handle any of it. She turned off her phone.

With effort, she pulled herself together, shrugged on a
fresh lab coat, removed her sunglasses, put on some makeup,
arranged her hair in a tasteful bun, and made her way to the
executive floor.

"We've had to let Dr. Huck and Dr. Skubic go," Kelly immediately explained. "It was unexpected, but necessary. And
we're looking forward to continuing on with some new leadership," she concluded diplomatically. "We considered appointing an interim chief, but your record is sterling and, as you

know, we like to promote from within. You're young for such a big role, but we feel that you're more than capable. Your track record proves that you can deliver, clinically and otherwise, despite competing priorities. If you'd like the job, it's yours. The Board has been briefed—they're ready to install you immediately should you accept. And if you need more time to consider the offer, we understand."

But Darby didn't need more time. Because being promoted to Chief was better than any of the pending job searches she had on the table. It was better than anything she had even aimed for. She would be crazy to turn it down.

"I accept."

Kelly shook her hand. She didn't remember much of the rest of the conversation other than mentioning that today was her last day in the office until Monday. They agreed to meet the following week to discuss the transition. Darby's body tingled and her head spun as she closed the door behind her.

CHAPTER THIRTY-ONE

LAKE GENEVA

Outside the airport, Darby leaned against her old Range Rover, which was parked on a far curb set back from arrivals. She thought back to so many months before, to that first time that Michael had picked her up from the hospital. He'd been so striking as he leaned up against his Maserati. In all their months together, it had been he who had done the chauffeuring. She imagined that she made quite a different impression now, bundled up in her thick white parka with the fur-lined hood, sidled up against her old car.

She saw him the instant he exited the doors. No matter where he went, he was impossible to miss. He was under-dressed, having come from 80-degree weather, and she could see that his olive skin had deepened into a healthy-looking tan. It contrasted interestingly against the effect that the cold was now having on his skin, which was turning pink in the Chicago weather.

He smiled as he approached, a vision so singularly dazzling that she couldn't help but smile in return. However little she understood things between them these days, the feeling he gave her never faded. He walked right up to her until they were standing close, their height difference exaggerated by the fact that he stood above her on the curb. For a moment, he looked down into her eyes, as if the past few weeks hadn't been drawn with tension, as if she were one of his favorite things in the world. He tore his gaze away long enough to give her car an extended once-over.

"Not what you expected?" she asked.

"You said you had an old SUV—not a Range Rover from the year you were born." He looked like he wanted to laugh.

She shrugged.

"I'm a simple girl, Michael."

"There is nothing simple about you." He opened her driver side door and tucked her inside.

The wedding was in Wisconsin, which was no surprise. Most well-to-do Chicago families had houses on Lake Geneva or some other Wisconsin lake. Darby's family was no exception. She'd confirmed through her father's assistant that the senator would not be staying there, and had the house opened up for she and Michael. The Silberstein home, where the wedding would be held, was right down the road. The estates were so large that they would still need to drive to the festivities.

In good traffic, the ride up to the lake wouldn't have taken more than two hours, but it was Friday midday, and traffic was heavy. Her car was so old that if they wanted to listen to music on their phones, they had to plug a headphone jack into a special tape that sat in her tape deck. The car had neither auxiliary plugins nor a CD player.

"Put something on," she commanded gently, handing him the adapter. He smirked as he took the ancient technology in his hands, but wisely kept his mouth shut.

Darby had no idea how they would begin to approach all

that had happened, but she couldn't endure small talk or silence. Part of her wanted to spend the familiar drive with nothing but music between them. This journey held so many fond memories that she knew the drive itself would find her at ease by the time they arrived. Maybe it would be better that way—to talk in the one place her head had always felt clear.

When they stopped for gas, Darby wasn't surprised that Michael insisted on pumping. She also wasn't surprised when he returned from the mini-mart laden with an arm full of sweets.

He didn't have the decency to look sheepish when she gave him a look as he opened the middle console and dropped his wares inside. She doubted if so much sugar had ever been in her car at once. Picking up a magazine he bought, Michael pretended to read. Her hand was on the key in the ignition, but she didn't start it yet.

"For real?"

She couldn't help herself. He smiled to before he looked up.

"Don't worry, cupcake. Some of them are for you."

Five minutes later, Michael was already digging into the console, and Darby tried not to notice his long beautiful fingers as they played at opening a bright orange packet of Reese's Sticks. Thanks to Michael, she was already familiar with this addictive little candy. They were mini-versions of Nutty Bars, but tasted finer somehow. Secretly, she loved them. Pulling the first one out, he reached over to place it gently in her mouth. She threw him a look that was a cross between petulant and grateful—apparently her love for them wasn't so secret after all.

As they left the gas station, Michael switched from a magnificently mellow playlist to an even mellower Iron & Wine album he knew Darby loved. After polishing off the rest of the Reese's Sticks, which he had savored slowly, he stowed the wrapper, shifted in his seat, and looked right at her.

"So, when are you going to ask?"

She didn't answer right away, keeping her eyes trained on the road and her face deliberately neutral.

"Do I really want to know?"

"My investigator didn't do anything too illegal," he said a bit flippantly. "Huck, on the other hand…"

Now he was just baiting her. But she knew they had to talk about it sooner or later. And they wouldn't be at her house for another hour. Yet for some reason, it was hard for her to spit the question out. When she did speak, her voice sounded insecure, a tone she wasn't used to hearing from herself.

"What did you do, Michael?"

Seeming to sense her discomfort, he straightened. His voice was softer when he finally spoke again.

"Something wasn't right. You're a rising star with a spotless reputation and promising research. You had the potential to make Huck look good. The most logical thing for him to do was let you. He only stood to gain more status by making everyone believe he had groomed you. Even if he didn't like you, distancing himself from someone like you was a move that no ambitious person would make."

Wow, she thought. Already, Michael's logic was impressive.

"He's a smart guy, Darby. Not a good guy, but a smart one. When smart people do dumb things, there's always something else at play. I thought about your theory, that he hates women, or anybody who's not self-made. I thought through how that would play out if that were a pathological obsession. But we looked into that—his record with privileged women like you, and with self-made men like him—and there was no pattern, at least not according to the performance reviews of his other direct reports."

At that, her eyebrows shot up, and she took both eyes off the road for a solid moment to look at him. Michael plowed on, avoiding the topic of how he had gotten hold of the reviews.

"It had to be something specific about you. So I considered everything it could have been. Was he a zealot who hated your father's politics, so much so that you became his target? Was he jealous of your work and afraid that you would surpass him professionally and expose him as an impostor? Was he in love with you and punishing you because you had rebuffed his advances in some way?"

Darby balked. "No, thank God," she muttered.

"Maybe he was in love with someone else, and willing to sink you in order to benefit them."

He spoke those words meaningfully. Darby glanced at him once more, not understanding. She looked back at the road ahead. Then it hit her.

"Yelena," she said quietly.

"They'd been sleeping together for months," he confirmed. "That fact alone was enough to put him in jeopardy—anti-fraternization policies and all."

Darby turned off the radio then. All she wanted to hear was the rough hum of her engine, the gears turning in her own head. How could she have been so blind?

"But I didn't want to take a chance that he would only get a warning," Michael continued. "So I dug up more dirt. If I could prove that he was not only sleeping with her, but also favoring her in some way, there would be more of a case. And there was. Not only was he covering up her mistakes—of all people, he had chosen *her* to take over your research."

"And the exam?" she stammered, the pieces assembling themselves in her head.

"There was no way to prove that he switched the results, but her track record was spotty. Yet, on her last test, miraculously, she only got one question wrong."

"Unbelievable." Darby was floored.

"By the time I figured it out, I had proof enough to get them both fired, but by then I had real concerns about Yelena. She wasn't fit to treat patients. And anyone who would cover up incompetence like hers shouldn't be allowed to practice either. I wanted to—"

"—ruin his career," Darby interrupted.

Michael didn't speak for a moment after that.

"He's a bad guy, Darby. The things he covered up for her... people *died* on her watch—people who didn't need to. I wondered what lengths he had gone to, to hide other things, at other hospitals. The list was long. He did all kinds of horrible shit that had nothing to do with you. By the end, I had so much on him that I didn't even need to bring the situation with you into it. I doubt he'll ever practice medicine in this country again."

Darby took a long breath. That last part was a huge relief.

"I had a scathing dossier on him delivered to legal. It was full of things that spelled out a multi-million-dollar liability for the hospital. It was obvious that an investigator was involved, but I made it look like it was something cooked up by the families of the patients who died. It came off as a veiled threat to press charges in a class-action lawsuit if the hospital didn't settle. Yelena was all over it as well. Not only did the hospital fire them, they're going to compensate the families. There is nothing for you to feel bad about—nothing for you to worry about. It's over. You won."

"Vigilante justice..." Darby recalled Michael's motivation correctly. Maybe he'd started out protecting Darby, but he'd taken it to another level.

"And loyalty," Michael said then, turning to stare heatedly out the window. "I don't like it when people fuck with my friends."

They sat like that, in silence, for a long time, with Darby staring out at the road in front of her, wishing futilely that she could see the look on his face. The familiar hum of tension that had infiltrated her body for the better part of the previous week came back in full force.

"You ruined a man for me, Michael."

He didn't answer right away, and she didn't know whether he would. She glanced over at him briefly to find him unmoving.

"He ruined himself," Michael returned darkly, still staring out the window. "I just gave him his comeuppance."

The house on Lake Geneva had come down through her mother's side of the family. When her father had been back in the city, doing whatever, or *whom*ever, he was doing there, she and her mother had summered happily on the lake. Darby had scattered her mother's ashes in the water, a few years before, but hadn't been back since.

As one of the older and larger mansions in the area, the house came complete with a tasteful stone exterior, shingled roofs, and classic charm. Inside were eight bedrooms, cozy spaces for lounging and living, and grand rooms for entertaining. Out back stood two jetties—Darby remembered which had docked their small boats versus which one she had dove off to swim.

Darby noted that the house had been beautifully kept and she thought of the housekeeper's son, George. Neither she nor her father visited often, but she knew that the Rubens still had something to do with the upkeep of the house. She couldn't help but think of Michael's mother as she recalled Roberta, who had been the head housekeeper. Roberta had been like a second mother to Darby, had died two years before her own, and Darby had cried nearly as hard at her funeral. Last she heard, George still lived in town, and she thought she ought to pay him a visit. It had been too long.

"Memories?" Michael guessed correctly, coming up from behind to wrap her in his arms. It was the first real contact they'd had since she'd picked him up from the airport. She didn't want to think about how much she had craved him while he was gone, not the sex, but this—his arms around her. Things felt right between them now. Things always felt right here.

"Too many to count," she replied, settling into his embrace. She didn't know how long she had been staring out the window, her mind breathing warmth into the cold ground below. The shiver that ran through her had everything to do with being close to Michael. She wanted to turn and kiss him, but she didn't.

"You want to go sit out on the dock?" he asked.

"No." She turned into him so that he would hug her more thoroughly. The truth was that all of it—her being back, him being there—was overwhelming. He hugged her more tightly and she inhaled his scent. Even after twenty-one hours on airplanes, he emanated his comforting smell.

It had begun to snow. The quiet of the house, the feeling of Michael's arms, and the tranquility of being away from the city made Darby feel sleepy and calm. She hadn't gotten much rest that week with so much on her mind. Though the house had been fully heated in preparation for their arrival, she looked wistfully toward the empty hearth, remembering so many hours spent in that house reading or writing in front of a roaring fire.

"Why don't I build us a fire?" Michael asked quietly. He was always so astute—always so tuned into her.

"How about in the library? I'll make cocoa. We can each curl up with a book."

Ten minutes later, Darby was snuggled up with a novel. Michael, however, was sketching. She'd seen the large drafting desk in his office before, but she'd never seen him sit at it. It was strange that, after so many months, she had never seen him draw. It took her mind to that unpleasant place that reminded her again of how much she still didn't know about him.

"What do you draw?" He looked up for a moment and smiled lightly, before returning his eyes to the paper. His hand never stopped moving.

"Anything other than buildings. It helps me calm down when I'm amped up."

"Are you amped up about something?" Some part of her was already feeling bolder. If he wasn't planning to share certain things, she was going to have to ask, and there was no better place to do it than there, where they were away from their everyday lives.

"I'm under a lot of pressure at work," he said vaguely. He'd alluded to as much that night in December when they'd fought, but neither of them had broached the subject since.

She had known him long enough to know not to press the matter, that if he wanted to talk about it, he would. But today, conflict was written on his face. She suspected that part of him wanted to open up to her, but something stopped him. He was definitely the kind of man who did not like to show weakness. But she didn't believe he was the kind of man who didn't know how.

This man had more emotional intelligence than nearly anyone she'd ever known. From the beginning, he had tapped into her deepest emotional needs with an exactitude that frightened her. She'd seen him work Stacey Kohl at the Christmas party, had seen him ward off Rich and manipulate Huck. He wasn't an idiot. If he was shutting her out, he was doing it on purpose.

So Darby trained her eyes back on her book, pretending to read *100 Years of Solitude*. It was a book she had discovered at thirteen and still liked to revisit. But she couldn't slip into the comfort of her old favorite; she felt agitated, even more so because she should be feeling relief.

In her head, Darby broke it all down once again. Huck and Yelena were gone. She was the new Chief of Psych. And Michael, who had stood in solidarity with her for months, had made most of that possible. So why was she suddenly obsessed with knowing what he had sketched in that notebook, and so injured by the fact that he hadn't invited her to see? He had handed her so many other things and he was so laid back in areas where other men could be defensive. But it was clear that the things he cared most about, he kept to himself.

It hurt. And Darby had only herself to blame for that, because before she'd stopped to think how hard it would be to doctor the pain of reality, she'd been eager to nurse the fantasy. He'd never lied to her about it, either. What was it he'd said that night on the beach? That only his companionship was at play. Not his heart. But he was confusing the hell out of her, and in that moment part of her wished he'd been colder. At least then, the boundaries would have felt clear.

So that afternoon, she let him zip her into the dark blue vintage evening gown that had been her mother's, let him help her clasp her necklace, let him stop the hand that held her lipstick brush seconds before it touched her lips so that he could pull her in for a final naked kiss. She let him take her silence in stride, seeming, as always, to know intuitively what she needed.

What she didn't let herself think about was why, if he knew her so well, he permitted her to keep up the ruse.

"Darby! Honey..." the voice came from behind her, the one she'd been dreading all night.

Until that moment, Darby had managed to get over her disquiet long enough to let herself enjoy Michael's company. She'd put on her game face two hours before and had allowed herself to have an otherwise pleasant time at the wedding reception. Michael knew how much she'd been dreading this event, more so now given her knowledge of possible tension about the South Side project, so he'd kept her laughing all night. He was obviously trying to distract her as he forced her to point out some of the more interesting guests and imploring her to gossip viciously about their scandals. She'd just told him about a Mrs. Cait Lawson, who, when she found out her husband was sleeping with her best friend, had extorted them both for millions. She'd gotten her ex-husband to agree to a divorce settlement that was very favorable to her in return for not letting out the skeletons in both of their closets. She'd taken the money and ruined them both anyway—her revenge was the town's worst-kept secret.

"Dad," she said cordially, plastering a smile onto her face and allowing him to lean in to give her a hug. She gained wicked enjoyment from the split second he looked at her and saw her mother's ghost. It was the macabre trick she played on him every time they met—she wore something of her mother's. It caught him a bit off guard every single time.

"This is my friend—"

"Michael Blaine," her father finished for her, and turned to extend his hand to Michael. "It's a pleasure, son," he said, shaking Michael's hand in what would appear to an outsider as sincerity. But Darby knew better.

She had, countless times, seen her father's assistants brief him on the identities of guests seconds before he got an introduction. If things weren't heating up on the South Side project, Darby wouldn't have known whether her father truly recognized Michael or whether he had simply been prepped.

"Senator," Michael said in what would seem to anyone else like warmth, yet she knew him well enough to hear the tinkling of ice chips in his voice.

"None of that senator business, Michael. We're among friends, and more importantly, you're here with my daughter. Call me Frank," he insisted, clapping Michael on the back.

He guided them away from the spot where they had been comfortably watching people, a maneuver Michael accepted with predictable grace. The sprawling tents had created somewhat of a covered outdoor city on the mansion's vast lawns, allowing spectacular views of the lakefront while insulating guests from the cold. Only about a quarter of the space had been transformed into a formal dining room, with another quarter or so being used for the full band, a few bars, and a dance floor. The other half was styled as an enormous lounge, with performers, displays of food, and yet more bars peppered among a large sprinkling of immaculate indoor living rooms.

Darby focused on holding Michael's hand as she listened absently to the conversation between he and her father. Predictably, Frank was buttering Michael up with a mixture of interest in Michael's work and ingratiating talk about himself. He made some specific comments about Michael's reputation and his promising career, and even praised him for his community work. He also threw in a few comments about how proud he was of his little girl, and how important her work was to the world of addiction. Especially after having lost his beloved wife to such a terrible disease.

"Darby's poor mother, God rest her soul, lost the fight," he said in a way that made Darby want to vomit. He had the audacity to turn to her as he spoke. "Darby's got her spirit. I see more and more of your mother in you every day, honey."

Michael wrapped his arm around her, pulling her a bit closer in a way that succeeded at calming her, and gently kissed her jaw. She knew he could tell that her father's talk was making her tense.

"There're somebody who's been waiting to see you," Frank said then, finally stopping in one of the sitting areas. She assumed it would be some crusty donor she was supposed to remember from a lifetime ago. She was only half-right—and when she saw who it actually was, she wished she'd been wrong.

"Darby," came the most unwelcome voice she could conceive of. She hated this voice more than her father's. More than Huck's. For a second, she couldn't breathe. "What a beautiful woman you've become."

Then he came into view—Charlie Sweeney, her father's former Deputy Mayor, and now the Deputy Governor. She shot her father a venomous look. He had some nerve.

In seconds, she was shaking with rage, a rage that couldn't be contained. She couldn't be in the same room with either of them—neither her father, who had swept an unspeakable crime under the rug, nor the pedophile who had committed it. She was over the hurt of knowing how little she meant to her father. Now, it was only his audacity that offended her. In that moment, she knew that she'd been ambushed, that Frank had planned to dangle her in front of Sweeney all along. Not saying a word in response, she turned on her heel and left.

Her father followed her as she stormed inside the mansion.

She navigated the halls easily and found the same library where she had spent so many hours as a child. Darby could hear him hot on her heels. Her hands clenched and unclenched at her sides. She eyed a heavy-looking bookend and imagined the sound it would make as it crashed into his skull.

"This isn't what we agreed to."

He said it seconds after she stopped, because now that she had ducked into a room, she was cornered. Collecting herself, she turned to face him with fury in her eyes.

"I agreed to keep up appearances. I did not volunteer to have you confront me with my attacker so you can raise money for a political campaign," she seethed.

"That's all in the past," he said with matter-of-fact dismissal. "And you'd do well to let it go, honey."

"Well I guess we all wish we could be more like you," she spat. "When I walk in on one of my colleagues forcing himself on my pubescent daughter, I'll be sure that she never speaks about it. I'll protect him and keep her quiet, like you did. It's nothing a little therapy can't fix, right? Luckily I know a few good psychiatrists. They could make a teenage girl right as rain after her father condoned her attempted rape."

"I've learned to forgive, Darby. Why can't you? Human beings make mistakes."

"Why are you making excuses for him? He was forty-five. I was fourteen!"

She was out of wasted breath. Her words didn't seem to penetrate an inch.

"So if you thought you'd come in here and convince me to lower myself to go back out there, you can forget it. And you can forget the rest, too—our agreement is off. I'm not fourteen anymore, old man. If that son of a bitch ever so much as looks at me again, I'll handle things my way."

He looked at her, as cold and calculatingly as ever, and said nothing as he considered his next move. But she headed him off, speaking in a measured but venomous voice.

"And if you ever even mention me, or our farce of a happy family again, I will ruin you. That pervert isn't the only one in this fucked up equation I haven't forgiven."

At that, Frank's mouth widened into a sinister smile.

"And what do you think you're going to do? Go to the press? Tell them your sob story? I own the press, sugar. Nobody will print a single word you say. And, even if they did, you've known me long enough to know what I would do next. So why don't you get your little revenge fantasy out of your system, toughen up, and realize how well my agenda serves us both? You'd be stupid to sacrifice everything you've worked for to get back at me. Two years from now, you'll have everything you've ever wanted."

"The only thing I've ever wanted was for you to get what you deserve."

"You know what I'm capable of. Think twice before trifling with the future President of the United States."

Vice President, she wanted to correct him. *God, he's an egomaniac.*

"Try me," she ground out through gritted teeth.

"Better yet, try me," she heard a third, dark voice chime in. It was Michael's. From the look on his face, she knew he'd heard everything.

Her father had the nerve to smile again then, as if Michael's vow had been the brave words of a fool. But Michael didn't flinch. Frank looked between the two of them, that unshakeable arrogance of his still evident in his smile. But he didn't say anything more, only raised his scotch glass in a final salute before he turned and left.

Left there alone with Michael, and the things he would want her to explain, Darby knew it was only a matter of time.

"Not here," she pleaded softly.

Twenty minutes of silence stretched between them as they got their coats, ordered her car from the valet, and drove the short distance back to her house, his hand in hers all the while. Michael pulled the car into the garage and turned off the engine. Neither of them moved to leave.

Darby had spent the car ride thinking once again about how Michael knew nearly every skeleton in her closet. And now this one—the biggest and scariest one—recalled a story she hadn't told in twenty years, and even then, only to Ben. Before her epiphany about Michael, she would have laid it bare. But giving away even more of herself when she was still so confused about him was something she wouldn't do.

I'm done.

She thought it to herself before opening her mouth to use well-practiced psychiatrist language to draw a boundary. But Michael beat her to it.

"You don't have to tell me anything." He said it resolutely, in a voice that sounded rough and determined.

She looked up at him in surprise. He always made her talk when he knew something was hurting her. It had been the very last thing she'd expected.

"And I know the right thing to do would be to tell you I'm sorry. This is the second time I've interfered in something that you never asked me to be a part of. A decent person would be at least a little ashamed of that."

He turned to her then, his intense blue eyes all over her.

"But I'm not a decent person when it comes to things like

this. Predators like Huck and your father make me lose my shit. I can't control my instinct to get involved, especially when it comes to you. Do you understand what I'm telling you?"

But she didn't speak or nod, because even though she did know by then that Michael had some deep need to defend her, with all that he held back, she didn't understand how it added up.

"I'm not the kind of guy who can hear what I heard tonight, or be privy to the kind of shit Huck pulled, and do nothing about it. And, believe me, I know it's a lot more than you signed up for, but this is who I am."

I know it's a lot more than you signed up for.

She didn't respond for a full minute, not because she needed time to digest what he'd said. Because she needed to figure out how to ask the only question that mattered—why? Why were his instincts to get involved so strong? Why especially when it came to her? What had possessed him to threaten a powerful man, and to ruin a prodigious doctor's career? Why would he give her all of that yet withhold so much else?

"You're an enigma, Michael," were the words that finally fell out of her mouth. His eyes darkened as he comprehended them. "You know my every fear, my every weakness. You come to my rescue. Every time I've needed someone, you've been there. But you hide from me. You don't let me see some of the best parts of you. You never ask me for help. If I had to help you in any...*meaningful* way...I wouldn't know how. And even if I did, I don't think you'd let me."

She didn't think it was possible, but his eyes grew more intense, and his voice more determined in his response.

"You help me more than you know."

But that was the point. She didn't know. He'd said it to her before, but she still didn't know what it meant. He shared his home with her, his bed, and he never seemed to be hiding anything. But there were the things he'd never, ever discussed with her—big parts of his life she'd discovered on her own.

"Fixing your zoning board problems and bringing you Zofran when you're sick doesn't count," she said.

He was quiet then, for a long moment.

"You've never even mentioned your foundation." Darby broke the silence.

"I figured that most people who mention their foundations to you are probably fishing for donations."

"You're not most people," she retorted, a bit of an edge creeping into her voice. "I saw a TV clip of you talking about it. You obviously love it. I've never heard you talk so passionately about anything else."

"If I had mentioned it, would you have donated?"

She cast her eyes out the window, but told the truth. "Yes."

She didn't mention that she had donated anonymously after she'd read up on it. Now wasn't the time. More silence stretched between them. She wasn't going to needle him but she refused to let him escape so easily. It had taken courage for her to say anything about this, to say what she'd said three weeks before, and she wasn't going to gloss over it now.

"I don't talk about the shitty things when I'm with you because I want to milk every last drop of happiness."

She still didn't look at him. It was the same line he'd fed her before. He sighed.

"It's not pretty, Darby."

"I don't need for it to be pretty."

Neither of them spoke. The chill from the open garage was starting to seep into the car, but she didn't move to get out.

"I barely sleep," he said finally, as if he were admitting something grave.

"But—"

"But I sleep like a baby when I'm with you?" He laughed humorlessly. "I know. When I'm not with you…" he continued slowly, "I get two or three hours at the most. And I'm awake hours before sunrise, every single morning."

She proceeded cautiously.

"What do you do?"

"When it's not so bad, I try to meditate; when it's a little worse than that, I draw…"

She hesitated to ask.

"And when it's worse than that?"

He didn't answer, not directly.

"I can't turn off my brain. Every minute I'm awake, I'm thinking…processing. It's one of the reasons why I'm so good at what I do. I obsess over things in my head until I figure them out. But it's not just designs that get stuck in my head—it's every single problem I don't know how to solve. Every tiny weakness. Every little fear."

She recognized her own words turned back on her.

"What are you afraid of?" she whispered, wanting so much to know but afraid of what she might find. Men were secretive animals who hid all manner of things in their caves. Christ, look at what she herself had been hiding. Was there some trauma from his past? Some abuse he had suffered? Some person he had lost? She looked at him then, and for the first time, she saw it—insecurity in his eyes.

"The fall," he said as if it should be obvious. "The day when everyone figures out I'm not some prodigy. The day when it's as clear to everyone else as it is to me that I can't possibly live up to the hype."

And it dawned on her. He felt like an impostor. His fear of failure was crippling, so much so that he hid away a secret inner life. The fact that he couldn't turn off his brain hinted at profound giftedness—she was now certain that he had an off-the-charts IQ. A brain like his had the ability to take in and synthesize astounding amounts of information, but it overwhelmed him and the inability to fully process all that he perceived added to his anxiety.

She felt for him then, for his own sake, but in the same instant her own remorse set in. Because hadn't she been just as guilty as everyone else of putting him up on a pedestal? It was satisfying, somehow, to believe the illusion—to believe that this fairy-tale prince could exist. He was whip-smart, rich, charismatic, a celebrity in his field. He gave oodles of money to charity, comported himself like a gentleman and was tall, dark and sexier than anyone had a right to be. He was the caricature of perfection. Only, he wasn't a caricature. He was a real person. But nobody—maybe not even Darby—had treated him that way. And he was crumbling under the pressure.

"Before I even turned thirty, they were comparing me to Vyatichi. Last week, they called me the next Shah Jahan."

The fact that she had no idea who he was talking about must've shown on her face.

"The first one built the Kremlin. The second built the Taj Mahal."

She winced.

"The interviews, the photo shoots, the awards…the partners at my firm have me on this unstoppable PR nightmare train. At first, I was flattered to be recognized for my work, but it's not about the work anymore. It's turned into a total shit show. Do you know how many times I've been approached for 'Most Eligible Bachelor' stories, or had to turn down features that wanted to portray me as some sort of sex object? *Chicago Magazine* wanted to show me at a construction site, reading plans, wearing a hard hat with no shirt."

"That's terrible," she said, and meant it deeply. A fresh flash of guilt pulsed through her. "And, I'm sorry—that night at Tavern on Rush...I..."

She faltered, and he shook his head.

"I don't blame you for thinking that about me. Why *wouldn't* you think that? I never gave you any reason to believe otherwise. You didn't know any of this shit. I couldn't expect you to understand if I hadn't told you."

Part of her still felt that she owed him an apology. Part of her felt relieved that he had finally admitted to what had been troubling her that entire week. She hadn't understood his reasons for shutting her out and he'd finally copped to the reason why.

"I'm not good at letting people in, Darby. It's not because I don't trust you—I trust you more than nearly anyone. I'm just not used to this. The people closest to me have always had their own shit to deal with. The people I grew up with take so much pride in me. They look up to me, and they have real problems to deal with. I'm not going to complain to them about feeling like a fraud. I mean, fuck—I make half a million dollars a year. People look at me and see a tall, good-looking white guy, which isn't even my story, but which has gotten me a lot farther than I deserve. I sit at a desk all day drawing, which is my favorite thing to do, and I want for nothing. When I think about my mother, who worked herself into an early grave for less than a tenth of what I make..."

He looked broken, and was going into territory she'd never heard him talk about. It was obvious that he carried a lot of guilt.

"Just because you're talented and gorgeous doesn't mean you deserve to feel like this."

He looked out the window. She treaded lightly, unsure of how he would take what she was about to say.

"Have you seen anybody? About your insomnia?"

"No."

"I know a great—"

"No, we're not doing this. Not, no I haven't seen anybody. I don't want you to be Darby my shrink, I want you to be Darby my—"

Darby my what?

Her mind screamed it. But she knew he wouldn't say. And when she calmed down enough, she spared them the conversation she was resigning herself to believe they would never have. Because he'd just told her more than he ever had and she didn't want to make him regret it.

"Your friend," she finished for him in a voice so defeated, that she knew her fight was gone. Whatever she'd realized the week before, however she was feeling about it, however many questions she had, in that instant, she knew they wouldn't all be answered. He looked away then, and she ignored what looked like shame written on his features.

"All I want right now is a hot bath," she said.

He nodded, looking completely dejected.

"See you in bed," she said.

He nodded again.

"I may take a walk."

She opened her little clutch purse, recovered the key ring that was inside and placed it in his hand. But instead of simply taking the key, he held her hand in his, as if asking her not to move, as if he were about to speak.

But he didn't speak. He just stared at their joined hands for a long moment. And he finally let her hand go, sighing as he did. Ten minutes later, her long dress was on a hanger behind the bathroom door, with steam from the bath hovering around it. Darby was neck-deep in hot, scented water, hoping it would wash away thoughts of complicated men.

She was roused from her meditative stupor when she heard him slip open the bathroom door. She cracked open one eye just long enough to catch a glimpse of him. She heard his steps on the tile floor before the shower water started to run. When the shower door closed, she realized she wanted to get out, to be in bed by the time he emerged.

So she did get out, unplugging the stopper that had been holding the now-tepid water inside the tub. After rising, she toweled off. Back in the bedroom, she noticed that he had built a fire in the fireplace. She didn't bother to turn on the light as she rummaged in her suitcase for pajamas.

She felt his presence behind her and absently acknowledged to herself that she'd thought she had more time. Before she could muster the courage to face him, he spoke.

"I don't like feeling like we're fighting."

"You and I aren't supposed to fight, so we don't," she said, not turning toward him.

"We do a lot of things we're not supposed to do."

And when he said it, her rummaging stopped. She was wholly unprepared to have this conversation.

"We're not fighting," she repeated, her voice weaker. "And even if we were, we have to stop. I—" she choked back a sob, thinking about the agony of the past few weeks. "I don't have any more fight left in me."

He stepped toward her and placed both hands on her arms, and bent his head until his forehead rested on her neck.

"I'm sorry."

She reached her hand back until her palm settled on the back of his neck and touched it tenderly. She doubted he knew what he was apologizing for.

"No more talking tonight," she said gently.

They stood like that for a long moment until she dropped her hand and took his, abandoning her plans to find pajamas. When he slipped in bed next to her and folded her in his arms, she snuggled in as close as she could, not wanting to fight, either.

But what had begun as a chaste good night kiss blossomed, slowly, into something more. She'd tipped her head up to him as he'd settled her in the crook of his arm and pressed a soft kiss to his lips. He placed one hand over hers as it rubbed his bare chest, and began to stroke her hair with his other hand. The gesture normally felt comforting, like something that should have lulled her to sleep, but they'd been apart for more than a week and the lust that was bound to build between them was mounting. The uneasiness that had filled the space between them was no match for the magnetism they shared. Their lips met again, as if drawn to one another's. Neither one had initiated it—their touches felt completely inevitable.

When their lips met a third time, the hand on his chest left hers and rose slowly to cup her face. His thumb caressed her cheek as his tongue slipped into her mouth, in search of hers. He moaned a little as their kisses became deeper, as his legs tightened around hers and their bodies pressed closer. Close enough for Darby to feel him, so hard, against her. Though his desire was impossible to ignore, she felt them overpowered by something new, something that slowed their kisses, stole their breath, and invited soft new caresses.

He was breathless when they finally came up for air, staring deeply into her eyes differently than he ever had. Usually, it felt as though he could see to the bottom of her soul. Yet now, he looked like a man who didn't know anything, who was looking to her for answers. She kissed him again. Because being closer *was* the answer. It was the answer to everything.

And, when she did, something in him surrendered. She could feel it in the way his arms tightened around her, in the way his fingers, now splayed across her back as his arms encircled her fully, grasped desperately at her skin. Their movements together remained slow, though she was trembling with desire. Neither did anything to hasten their union but the intensity was building and they were holding each other as if each of them was trying to pull the other into his own body.

When their need for more was unbearable, he took her—so slowly, so deeply—their bodies ablaze in yellows and oranges from the nearby light of the fire. By then, they'd been together a hundred times, but whatever they were doing tonight was something they had never done before. She was too delirious with pleasure to dwell on such things. His every stroke felt like the air she needed to breathe. And when he came in a breathless whimper, he did something he'd never done. He whispered her name.

The next morning as they lounged in bed, she did tell him about Charlie Sweeney. About the night that he had wandered off from the other adults during one of her family's many dinner parties. He had found her in a den, watching TV in her pajamas. She told Michael about the smell of Sweeney's alcohol-soaked breath, and how he had settled in too close to her as he pretended to be interested in what she was watching. She told him how the older man had pulled her down roughly. That he had kept here there forcefully when she tried to excuse herself to go to bed. That he had easily overpowered her and pinned her down under him, that she had tried to scream, but he had covered her mouth and threatened her. He had one hand over her mouth and one hand unbuckling his pants and pulling them down as he told her the sick things he would have her do to him. She was trying desperately to get some leverage—to bite his hand so that he would pull it back and she could scream, or roll him off her. At that moment, her housekeeper had walked in.

As she told the story, she could feel Michael's body humming with emotion and she knew this was difficult for him to hear. It was difficult to talk about. She had nearly been raped in a house full of adults, most of them lawmakers. And her own father had made sure that nobody found out. It was implied at the time that her mother was too drunk that night to see her, but when she was older, Darby realized that she had probably been drugged by Frank. Just as she realized later that the "painkillers" Darby had been given for her bruises probably weren't painkillers at all.

When she would later reflect on the fact that the housekeeper who had found them was the one who had been sent up to help her for a few days afterward, but soon left her father's employ to return to Honduras to "spend more time with her family", that maybe that hadn't been what had happened, and it had it hadn't been voluntary. With the clear perspective of an adult and as somebody who had since been trained in rape behavior and pedophilia, it sickened her more now than it had then to realize what had really gone on. As she relived what had happened, for the first time in so long, she realized how much unfinished business she had with her father.

"Who is this guy again?" Michael asked. Darby had referred to her assailant simply as "he" the whole time.

"Charlie Sweeney. He used to be my dad's campaign manager."

"Charlie Sweeney," Michael repeated with disgust. He seemed to be taking a mental note. Later that night, she dropped him back off at O'Hare. He had to be in New York that week.

It wasn't until much later, until days later, in fact, that Darby realized why Michael had asked to know Sweeney's name.

CHAPTER THIRTY-TWO

SUNDANCE

PLEASURE. EVEN AS SHE SLEPT, DARBY FELT THE GENTLE hum at her center, growing stronger as she began to wake. She didn't consider why her bed felt different or what was making her feel so good. In that halcyon moment, the intensifying hum was all that mattered.

She rubbed her legs together, her body far ahead of her consciousness in its quest to enjoy whatever was happening. It was then that she became aware of her nipple. Not yet wakeful enough to know what was being done to it, she felt the direct connection between it and her core. As whatever amazing thing had been done to one nipple was now being done to the other, the hum became a throb. She panted, just as she felt a wave of heat prickle her skin, creating a light sheen of perspiration.

She arched her back, and rubbed her legs together again. When she heard the muttered curse, she let her eyes fall open and finally let herself come to. She was eager to preserve the dream but her body had begun to comprehend the reality: that Michael was there, and ready to have his way with her.

He didn't see that she was awake at first, which gave her

the rare chance to catch him off his guard. His eyes swept over her body with a mixture of reverence that made her heart hurt, and desire so raw it scared her. As she watched him slip his fingers under the edge of the t-shirt she didn't remember putting on, his fingers splayed to graze a spot above her hip. From the darkening of his eyes and the clench of his jaw she could tell that he was exercising extreme restraint.

"What are you waiting for?" she provoked, her voice raspy with sleep.

His eyes shot to hers and something different welled up inside her as they connected. It was the first time their eyes had met in nearly two weeks and the feeling of him looking into her still stirred her to the tips of her soul.

"Permission."

She moved his hand lower, placing its heel on her pubic bone and curling his fingers so that he would take firm hold over her crotch. By then, she could feel how wet she was, and knew that he would be able to feel it through her underwear. As his fingers squeezed to cup her, he shut his eyes.

She watched him breathe for a few seconds. He was expending effort to collect himself, and she wondered how long he'd been waiting for her to wake up. Eyes still closed, he let his head dip back in toward her and she watched him bite her nipple through the fabric of her shirt with blind precision. She recognized it as the sensation she'd felt a minute earlier when she'd still been groggy. It was more tantalizing, somehow, than if he had bitten her bare skin.

Impatient, she moved his hand again, this time to hook her fingers on the sides of her underwear. Together, they shimmied them off. He rose to his knees so that he could do the same. Before he fell backward on the bed, he brought his arms around Darby and pulled her down on top of him. He guided their hips together quickly and impaled himself on her with such heated force that she whimpered appreciatively at the sensation. When she was on top like this, he usually let her ride him and synced up to her pace, but not then. Instead, he grabbed her hips forcefully and began driving her up and down on his shaft as he pistoned his own hips to meet her thrusts.

She smiled, because he was almost never like this, so turned on that his grip slipped on his usually impeccable control. It was her favorite version of him. Her climax was coming fast, but she could tell from his helpless moans that his was coming faster.

"I wanna see you come," she was barely able to pant because it was so, so good. She knew her words would send him flying over the edge.

And a moment later he did, and it was glorious. His hips rose off the bed and he held her still for a long moment, buried to the hilt inside of her as he throbbed his release. She was seconds behind him, and he resumed his thrusts long enough to let Darby ride hers out. They were both covered in sweat when he released her, placing her gently down on the bed next to him. He slung his arm underneath her head, pulling her to him as they lay together catching their breath. Before she could relax into him fully, he lifted her chin up and kissed her long and slow and deep, as if they hadn't seen each other in months. But it had only been two weeks, two painfully slow weeks.

It wasn't until many moments later that she began to comprehend her surroundings. They were in Park City, for Sundance, in a hotel suite that was more like an apartment. She remembered arriving alone the night before, and spinning around to admire the space. It was a modern duplex, with a sleek kitchen, a powder room and a chic living area below. A long white leather sofa and a polar bear rug complemented the tall fireplace. A modern staircase with no railing led to an elegant loft above. She had been too tired to open the heavy blackout curtain the night before, and had fallen straight to sleep in the darkness.

Bright daylight now shone through the crack between the shades and the wall. The room was very different in the sunlight, with Michael there.

"What time is it?" the words tumbled from her mouth.

She was alarmed by how long she must have slept, because it wasn't morning light that shone in—it looked like afternoon sun. Michael's plane had been scheduled to get in two hours after hers. She'd intended to take a nap, and expected to be awakened when Michael arrived. He stroked her hair languidly and seemed to pull her tighter against him. It felt better than she remembered.

"Nearly noon. Last night you were dead to the world."

It was then that she remembered sleeping heavily on the plane. The flight attendant's motions had awakened her as she'd moved to place Darby's seat back upright. Due to the number of people traveling to Park City that day, she had almost missed out on her First Class seat. It was a luxury she treasured, given her busy travel schedule of late. The First Class seats on domestic flights didn't recline fully as they did on most international runs, but for Darby's three-hour jump from Chicago to Utah, nearly anything would have done. She was so tired that she would have slept like a baby, even in coach.

She'd needed that nap. Since becoming Chief, she had gained a new appreciation for what it meant to be truly, thoroughly exhausted. But if she wanted to do well, she needed to keep her patient care strong while learning her new job. That meant long days. The new schedule was even more grueling than the one she'd kept while juggling her research, looking for a new job and keeping up with her work under Huck. She'd been at the hospital every single day that week. It had been the only way to stay on top of all her responsibilities.

In that sense, Michael's recent travel had aligned perfectly with what her job had in store. They hadn't seen each other since Lake Geneva, which had turned out to be a mixed blessing. It robbed her of their bedroom romps and blissful hours spent lounging in his apartment. But it also spared her having to face all that had been said at the lake.

Time to process everything had been a relief. Not only had she spilled one of her darkest secrets to Michael—she'd been thinking hard about all the things that he had revealed. The pressure he was under, the performance anxiety—everything. Since Lake Geneva, she saw him in a different light.

"I'm sorry." She felt badly about having passed out at the embarrassingly early hour of eight o'clock at night, and sleeping right through his arrival. If his body had adjusted to New York time, he must've been up for hours, a fact that only made her feel more lame.

She started to get up, but he pulled her down and tucked her back in.

"We've already missed two screenings." She looked up at him, feeling panicked as she said the words.

"They don't take attendance." He kissed her hair.

She pushed herself up on her elbow and peered down at him, giving him a look.

"I thought you wanted to watch movies and go to parties all weekend."

"No…" He drew the word out so that it was twice as long. "I wanted to get away with you."

His fingers floated back to her hair, which she guessed was wildly teased by sex and sleep from the way he arranged stray locks behind her ears.

"It's good to see you."

He said it a second before he pulled her in for another kiss.

Her stomach growled, and given his aversion to her being hungry, any hopes of continuing along those lines were obliterated. Whereas seconds before, he was doing everything he could to keep her next to him, he was suddenly pushing her out of the bed, demanding that they shower and do something about lunch.

Though Chicago was cold, it wasn't snowy or mountainous and Darby had been looking forward to the wardrobe she had coordinated for this setting. She wore a three-quarter length shearling in dark green suede, fur-lined snow boots that rose to her knees over a pair of skinny jeans, and a white Sherpa hat with two long tassels. She liked the way Michael took her in with the hint of a smile as they exited the suite.

Any apprehension or awkwardness about her fourteen-hour nap and the missed screenings softened immediately under his charm. At the hospital, she felt like Dr. Darby—the Chief who always had a million things on her plate. But now Michael made her feel like a girl whose only job was to relax with her man and be happy.

And she was happy. Park City was beautiful and buzzing with the excitement of the festival. In place of the stone-faced working stiffs she saw every day in Chicago, the people they passed on the streets here were animated and alive. Overheard snippets of conversation about this project or that excited her, and the vibrant creativity was palpable.

She had no idea how Michael had gotten them into the busiest sushi restaurant for lunch—the place was packed. He seemed to have a reservation, even though she thought the visit was totally spontaneous. She'd learned not to question how he seemed to be so on top of everything. Apparently his influence was limitless, his Carte Blanche good not only in Chicago but elsewhere, too.

"So, this party tonight…"

He didn't need to finish. She knew what he was asking. He was referring to that invitation he'd seen on her coffee table so many weeks before, the first "yes" that had given them the idea to come to Sundance in the first place.

"I'm a producer on a film." She placed a section of shrimp tempura roll into her mouth.

"As in, you're bankrolling it?" He looked impressed.

"Not the whole thing. I just contributed enough to earn a producer title. It's an indie short. It wasn't that much." That might have been an understatement.

"How much?"

"Fifty grand."

He whistled, looking even more impressed.

"You gave fifty thousand dollars to a film project, and you weren't gonna come?"

She polished off another section of the roll.

"It's not like they wouldn't have sent me a copy."

"What else don't I know about you?"

The question caused a tingle in her spine. Hadn't she just been lamenting that he knew everything about her and she knew too little about him? Yet, when presented with the question, she wondered whether she had oversimplified the equation.

"Maybe we should play twenty questions."

There went her mouth again, saying things she'd never given it permission to.

"Maybe we should."

His eyes challenged hers, and she knew he was thinking of their conversation from two weeks before. Ever intense, ever competitive, Michael was telling her he was ready to answer her questions. The thing was, she wasn't good at that, at the grilling part of it. She wanted to know more about him but in her ideal world, he would volunteer information, and she wouldn't have to pry it out of him.

"Alright, then, shoot."

"How many other films have you supported?"

She picked up her phone as she chewed, an act that her manners usually forbade. Looking up her profile page on IMDB, she handed the phone to Michael so that he could see for himself.

"You've produced five short films and two features?" His finger moved to scroll down. "Two of which were nominated for Indie Spirit awards?"

His face registered every bit of surprise she would have expected.

"I'm surprised you didn't know. It's like, one of the first things that comes up when you Google me."

"I've never Googled you." He was still scrolling down with his thumb—still distracted by what he was reading on her profile page when his eyes shot up to hers.

"Wait—have you Googled me?"

Oops.

"Only after Benji told me to."

"You and Ben talk about me?"

"You're really burning through your twenty questions—so far there have been four."

"Yet only two direct answers." He cocked his head to the side.

She liked that he seemed impatient to know. She rarely saw him act impatiently anywhere other than in bed.

"Ben and I talk about everything. We had dinner a few months back. I told him we were seeing each other. He told me to check out how impressive you are."

Darby caught the guarded look on his face.

"Does he know about our arrangement?"

And then, evil psychiatrist that she was, she did a trick she'd done a thousand times—she made him wait longer than she needed to so that she could observe his anticipation.

"Would it bother you if he did?"

"Yes." Michael said it bluntly, and with something serious in his eyes that immediately dissolved the playfulness Darby had intended.

"He thinks that we're dating. I told him it's casual. Our arrangement is none of his business. The only people who I've told are Anne and Rich, both of whom you know about."

At that, the air between them changed. She thought he'd drop it, that he'd ask something as benign as his first questions or that maybe they'd change the subject and just forget this twenty questions thing.

"Why did you tell Rich?"

"He's my friend. We talk."

"Talking is risky for you. Anne is your best girlfriend…I'm asking why you told someone who didn't need to know."

She could've evaded his question again. Could have kept them going around in circles for minutes, but she didn't. She knew what he was asking.

"He bugs me about why I'm not married. I told him it was because I didn't want anything I didn't have. That I was in a relationship that worked."

She held his eyes for just a moment before putting down

her chopsticks and plucking an edamame out of a small bowl.

"That's six," she said as neutrally as she could, as if they hadn't both just figured out that they had license to ask *anything*. "My turn now."

"How many cars do you have?"

"That's your question?"

"Now who's not answering directly?"

"Two."

She waved an empty pod at him as she chewed another one, urging him to elaborate.

"The Maserati and the Tesla."

"I've never seen you in a Tesla."

"Every time we pull into my garage, the Tesla is parked next to the Maserati."

"That white Model S…"

"Is mine."

"You must've gotten one of the first ones off the assembly line. I've still got, like, a year left on the waiting list."

"You can take mine out any time you want."

"Why don't you ever take it out?"

"I do take it out."

"But not with me."

"No, not with you."

She looked at him expectantly, but he shook his head. "Uh-uh. If I'm going to answer it, I'm making you burn a question asking."

"Why don't you ever take me out in the Tesla?"

"Because you like the way I drive the Maserati. And I like it when you like little things I do."

Holy hell.

What had happened at Lake Geneva was happening again. They'd made some silent agreement to break down the barriers.

Except this was five times more dangerous.

"Still wanna play?" he smiled.

"I think I might need a drink for this."

"I think I might need two."

"What about the movies?

"We're at a film festival. There'll be movies tomorrow and again the day after that."

Ten minutes later, the check had been paid and they were on their way to find that drink.

The opulent French sofa at the cozy lounge he'd taken her to faced a fireplace and looked as if it belonged in the Palace of Versailles. As soon as Michael had mentioned his name, they were taken to a little nook and served the drinks that now sat upon its coffee table.

"How do you make stuff like this happen? Tables at jam-packed restaurants with lines out the door, tickets to anything. You can get access anywhere. How do we always end up in the perfect place?"

"I like to be prepared, Darby. We've been doing this for eight months. You know this about me already. So stop asking me questions you know the answer to and ask me something real. You've only got fourteen left."

She said the first thing that came to mind, one of the questions she'd been queuing up in her head.

"Has anyone ever called you anything other than Michael?"

"You needed a drink for that?" His eyes crinkled at the corners. Then he said, "My mom used to call me 'Boo-Boo.'"

"When you were little?"

"Yeah. And when I was, like, twenty."

She laughed out loud.

"I miss it," he admitted it, though he was smiling. "My sister Bex calls me Mikey," he offered a second later.

"Tell me about Ella and Bex," she said then, now thinking about his family. "What do you do with them?"

"Little girl things, mostly. I go to karate tournaments and dance recitals and show up at Ella's school to watch her in historically inaccurate and culturally insensitive plays." He fished his phone out of his pocket and began thumbing around before presenting it to Darby.

On the screen was a gorgeous little raven-haired girl dressed like a Native American. She stood on a stage, shaking the hand of a boy who was dressed like a miniature pilgrim. They looked thrilled to see one another, as evidenced by Ella's wide grin. She had Michael's sparkling blue eyes and was missing her two front teeth. It was one of the cutest things Darby had ever seen.

"Oh, my…" He was right about the cultural insensitivity. "But she is adorable."

Michael looked down at the photo and smiled. "Yeah."

He pocketed his phone and picked his drink back up.

"Bex cooks dinner every Sunday. When I'm in town, I always show up for that. They want to meet you."

"You've told them about me?"

"Yes," he said slowly, as if it were obvious.

"What did you tell them?"

"They know we spend a lot of time together, that's all."

"Have they ever seen any pictures of me?"

"I don't have any pictures of you."

Oh.

"Invite me sometime."

"You always work on Sundays."

She rolled her eyes. "Invite me sometime."

"I will." They held each other's eyes for a beat.

She took another sip of her drink, a house cocktail with bourbon and something sweet that made it delicious. She liked the way they were positioned, as if sidesaddle on the sofa facing each other. They sat in silence, not an awkward one, but a pregnant one, words unspoken thick between them. Both of them knew that the lightweight questions would only take them so far—that things more serious would need to be asked.

"Was seeing Huck get what he deserved the only reason why you hired that private investigator?"

Michael put down his drink, as if preparing himself.

"I hired him because I wanted to protect you. Did you think less of me for wanting to do it?" His voice lacked some of the confidence it had held a minute before.

"No. I thought more of you. I liked that you made me feel protected."

"I told you," he said, and she could tell he was proceeding with caution. "I can't stand by and watch that shit without doing something."

"What are you going to do to Charlie Sweeney?"

He studied her, as if trying to anticipate her response.

She took a breath. "Just tell me."

"I want him to go to jail where he belongs. There were other cases—lewd acts with a minor and attempted rape—but he settled out of court. Since we can't get him for that, we're digging up other dirt. It's still early, but right now the plan is to get him for campaign misconduct and other political misdeeds."

She cast her eyes toward the fire. Michael scooted close to her, slinging an arm around her and pulling her in as close as he could without sitting her on his lap.

"Who's we?"

"The private investigator I told you about is really a friend

I grew up with. He works with private clients in Washington. He handles things like this."

Her heart was still pounding too hard for her to form words.

"Things like what?"

"Bad guys."

She sniffed back tears that were threatening for reasons she couldn't understand.

"You never talk about your friends."

Michael smirked. "Is that a question?"

She rolled her eyes again. "Michael...*why* don't you ever talk about your friends?"

"They all live far away. I rarely see them."

"But you never talk about them either. Just like you never told me you had dinner with Ben the night before I did the last time he was in town."

"Darby, when I'm with you, I'm not thinking about anybody or anything else."

"I envy you that." The words slipped out of her mouth. "Your ability to compartmentalize."

The space remained thick between them, as if the air itself were drunk. It felt as if they were speaking to one another in code.

"What do you want that you can't have?" he asked finally.

"Time, I guess. I always want to be five different places at once. No matter where I am or what I'm doing, I'm always thinking of someplace else. Except when I'm with you. I should probably see someone."

"That bad?" he asked. She realized that she had alarmed him.

"Not bad, just...unresolved."

He waited a minute before he responded.

"Why don't you ever call me?" he asked.

"Because whenever you're not right next to me, you're half a world away."

And what looked like guilt colored his features for a moment before it was replaced with resolve.

"I'm here now. Here is where I've wanted to be all week."

He reached out his hand to hold hers, intertwining their fingers.

"Do you want to know what I love most about this place?" He didn't wait for her to answer. "No one cares who we are."

With her fingers in his, he began stroking the top of her hand with his wayward thumb.

"When was the last time we were in a crowded room and no one was looking at us?"

But she didn't bother to scan the room. She was transfixed by his gaze.

"Never."

"When's the next time we'll be in a crowded room and no one will be looking at us?"

She felt a pang of sadness at the reality. She'd been waiting to tell him, waiting until they were in a truly private place, waiting for the right moment. But the music was loud and they were sitting so close, and he was the one person in the universe she wanted to tell. So, in a gesture that made her feel like she was six years old, she shielded her mouth from prying eyes and whispered in his ear.

"It's locked in. I thought we had more time…but Sanderson's going to announce in a month. My father's going public about his VP spot on the ticket."

Saying it out loud was more emotional than she had anticipated. As soon as she pulled back, she knew that Michael could see her tears threatening to spill over. He was one of two people who knew the real reason why she hated her father so much, and he was the only person who knew how much anxiety his campaigning caused her. Soon there would be no protection from the opposition researchers and paparazzi. Soon, there would be no stopping Frank from whatever he was going to do about the South Side.

He held her tighter then and she felt like he was holding her together. The alcohol wasn't helping to stabilize her emotions, either.

"For once, let's just be free." He whispered as he held her, in a voice so soft as to expose it for the plea it was.

"I don't think I know how." Her words were nearly inaudible.

"I'll show you."

"Thank you," Darby said to the stranger who held the door for her as she exited to the street.

After three loaded cocktails punctuated by as many glasses of water, she had made sure to hit the ladies room before leaving the bar. She squinted as she walked outside, her eyes needing to adjust to the bright sunlight after two hours spent in a pleasantly cavernous retreat. Yet, in that moment, she liked the sunshine, the way that when she looked up to the sky, rays coming down through the clouds were visible. The crispness of the air mixed with the warmth of the sun was a welcome sensation.

Michael had agreed to meet her out front and with the film festival in town, "out front" covered a broad area. Cars still rode through the streets, but had to be careful of the pedestrians that spilled over from the crowded sidewalks. It didn't matter that there were hordes of people walking up and down

Main Street. She immediately saw Michael. He must have been thirty feet in front of her, and there must have been fifteen people in between them. But he was impossible to miss. Even in a town full of famous actors and wealthy patrons and all the other good-looking people, Michael was in a class of his own.

She watched him fish a pair of sunglasses out of the pocket of his fitted leather military jacket, the steampunk one, and which, alone, made him look about ten times more stylish than everyone else. She took in his army-green junker-fitted cargo pants, worn and faded as if he had fought half a war in them. The boots he wore beneath them, also impeccably distressed, pulled together the look.

She shook her head as she got closer to him. Her awe of his fashion sense never faded. He'd been in New York for a week. They would be in Sundance for two more days. He only had a small carry-on and a garment bag that didn't look bulky. How was it even possible for him to be this well-dressed?

"Only you could stand among movie stars and make them look shabby. You're lucky I'm the kind of girl who doesn't mind walking in the shadow of a much better-looking man."

"We're in Sundance. I've gotta stay on my game if I want to head off the competition. I can't let the Hollywood glitterati take you away from me without a fight."

She moved her fingers to gently remove his glasses. Even though she'd spent the past few hours looking directly at his face as they'd talked, something in her still jumped when the glasses lifted to show his eyes. The sunlight made them even more dazzling, and it took her an extra breath to come back with her retort. He didn't protest—didn't ask her why she had taken his glasses off. He just gazed back at her the way he always did, but also with something new that she'd been trying to pinpoint all day. Some new softness or radiating warmth.

"Could it be? Are those blue diamonds turning green?"

"Blue diamonds, huh? So you like my eyes?"

"The answer to that question is so obvious that I'm not going to dignify it with a response."

He quieted then, his face sobering a bit.

"You're the only woman I've ever been with who never talks about my looks."

"Your looks aren't the reason I'm with you."

Then she was afraid she would say something she regretted. So she said the only thing she could think of that would lighten the air between them.

"Your gigantic cock is."

He shook his head and she giggled a bit drunkenly. It felt good to laugh.

Turning them to walk up the road, he hooked his elbow in hers.

"You're lucky you came out when you did," he said, too casually. "I thought I was going to have to send in a search party…"

"Mmm-hmmm." She knew she was being baited.

"And if I had called your phone, what ringtone would I have heard?"

She was laughing again. He had her.

"I don't know. Why don't you call me?" she played along, laughter still in her voice.

He stopped long enough to pull out his phone and pressed a few buttons. As she pulled her own vibrating phone out of her pocket, the opening bars of *Hey Mickey* by Toni Basil began to play.

It took him a few seconds to recognize the song, but once he did, he too came alive with laughter. It set her off again. And again she felt drunk. Or maybe just happy.

Even for those who were new to Sundance, it was clear that the town was transformed. Beyond the restaurants and bars, and shops along the way, all teeming with people, there were other things happening on the street. Pop-up kiosks, signs for parties, both public and private, littered the street. Darby spotted a music venue she had read about online.

"Come on."

She pulled Michael and they walked in.

"During the festival, a lot of big bands come through, unannounced, and play small shows. There could be someone amazing inside," she explained

Dropping their coats off at the coat check, Michael gave the teenager behind the counter a very nice tip, or so Darby assumed from the look in the kid's eyes. Michael took her hand and led her through the crowded room, following the flow of traffic that led to a set of stairs. They descended slowly and already she could hear the beginnings of what sounded like a mellow bluegrass band. She could recognize the twang of banjos and hear soft vocals.

They made their way through the crowd and found a spot in the middle of the floor. When they stopped, Michael coaxed her in front of him so that she could have the better view. He wrapped his arms around her and stood silently with his chin on her temple as the music echoed through them. The crowd was mesmerized by the band, but she was mesmerized by it all—the dulcet tones of the music and the way Michael held her.

It was so simple, the two of them standing together quietly taking in the amazing music. But it felt like so much more. The band was singing about love and it felt as if Michael were pulling her closer, always closer to him. It felt as if they had melted into one another, as if the words of love were being sung just for them. Everything about their day together so far had felt intimate, but this moment most of all. When he began pressing kisses to her hair, they felt possessive in a way that satisfied her beyond measure. And when his kisses moved to her neck, it felt like an affirmation. When he breathed her name into her ear, she thought of that last night with him at the lake.

When the show finished, she felt a sense of loss. These were moments she hadn't wanted to end, but as the band packed up and they'd delivered their applause, they followed the crowds out. She felt punch-drunk as they recovered their coats, everything seeming surreal as they spilled onto the street.

Hands entwined, and closer than they had been when they'd entered less than an hour before, they were halfway soused from all the drinks they had consumed, but not drunk, only pleasantly buzzed. The streets were teeming with people, and Darby suspected that a screening had just let out. They walked up the incline of the street they were on, against the crowd that mostly walked down.

She liked this feeling of being lost in a crowd, like a salmon swimming upstream against the current.

"Where are we going?" She figured Michael had a plan. Michael always had a plan.

"Wherever we want. Remember?"

"What do *you* want?" she asked.

"I told you this morning."

"Let's do something we've never done."

He raised a skeptical eyebrow.

"What's the matter? Spontaneity doesn't factor into your

carefully crafted plan?" she challenged back.

"You want my spontaneous? You can't handle my spontaneous."

"Try me."

No sooner had the words left her mouth than he stopped them in their tracks, a river of people still rushing past them as they worked their way through the crowds. He rounded on her, stopping her in the place she had been walking, and spread his legs enough to shorten his height so that they were eye to eye. His arms went around her and he was holding her now, as if without his embrace, she would fall. And she saw it then. The intention in his eyes. He was going to kiss her.

And it wasn't a wimpy kiss either. Before she could react, he had slid a hand behind her neck and pressed his lips to hers half a second before his tongue probed deeply, longingly but also softly. She felt like he was kissing her for the first time.

The kiss felt infinite. Each time one of them seemed to pull away, the other would coax them back, returning to the fathomless depths of the kiss. Darby was vaguely aware of the cold, of the hordes of people rushing around them, but most of what she registered at that moment was his touch. His thumbs on her cheeks. His body against hers. His breath somehow enraptured. And the way he looked at her when their lips finally parted, what she couldn't comprehend in his eyes, held nothing of the playful tone his voice had just minutes before.

They seemed to be searching hers for something. But she couldn't think about what that might be, because he was running his thumb against her bottom lip. She could feel they were a bit swollen from his kisses.

"God, your lips," he murmured, his gaze resting on them for a long moment before leaning back in to meet hers. Michael noticed everything.

"We should do spontaneous things more often," she declared, out of breath after they had separated once more.

They continued uphill, in the same direction they'd been going in. It was twilight, and the streets seemed emptier than they had minutes before, though Darby realized that they may have been kissing for more than a few minutes. She had no idea where he was taking her and at that moment she didn't care. At the top of the hill was the gondola, which was still running at that hour, though she thought it might close soon. When Michael didn't turn off at the last street that would have kept them in town, she knew they were headed up.

"Are we going skiing?"

"Should we?"

He nodded his head toward the ski shop that stood, its doors open, next to the gondola's base.

"No, let's just go up. I want to freeze my ass off with you at the top of the mountain." She nudged him forward.

He produced two lift tickets from his pocket, stopped and hooked one into the tassel of her jacket. Seconds after walking into the empty car, the doors shut.

It was a large car, with the capacity to carry twenty-five skiers or more. Though there were wooden benches at each end, neither moved to sit. She went to a far window, watching the ground disappear rapidly as they ascended. He came up from behind, wrapping his arms around her, just as she'd hoped he would.

"You hate being cold."

His cheek was against hers and she liked the way his deep voice resonated softly through the car.

"You always keep me warm."

The car rocked as it passed through one of the lower lift stations, but didn't stop. She thought how this was probably one of the last gondolas that would go up that night, and imagined them staying up there until morning, just the two of them, on top of that mountain. It was a ridiculous idea—completely impractical. She then thought of the job she loved most days, the cozy little house she adored, and how empty she would feel when she returned.

"You've got eight questions left." It came out as a whisper. "Are you going to use them or not?"

He didn't answer.

"Isn't there anything you want to know?"

"I already know everything I need to know about you, baby."

Baby. That stopped her wandering mind in its tracks. He had never—not once—called her that.

It emboldened something in her. "Have you ever been in love?" There would be no better time to ask.

"Yes."

"What was she like?"

The gondola was slowing. Moments later, the door opened.

"She was a lot like you."

They were fucking again. Her hair was wet from the shower and hung loosely down to her mid-back, tickling her shoulder blades as they moved in tandem. They had spent languid minutes under the rainfall spray, kissing and touching as they warmed up fully from so much time spent in the cold. Now, in front of the fireplace, they faced one another, her legs wrapped around him as he thrust into her vigorously from below.

The fire was hot, and the dampness that had covered them

when they had arrived from the shower had quickly evaporated. Now the sheen that covered them was hard-earned sweat. He was hitting her deeply, fucking her so good it hurt. So good that with each intensifying thrust, she cried out softly in a mixture of pleasure and pain. His forearm was behind her back, as if he knew she had lost some of her ability to hold herself up. When she tightened around him—so close, but not there yet— he unleashed a guttural moan, and she thought she could have died happy right then.

She let her head fall back because that's how fantastic it felt. When she did, he lowered his mouth and licked a straight line from between her breasts to the dip in her throat. That did it. She came hard, nearly screaming from the pleasure. She felt him pulse and thought that he was coming too. But when she felt herself being flipped over before she caught her breath, she knew he still had more.

The way he hitched one of her legs up to curl behind him reminded her, as it always did, of the first time they had fucked. She wrapped her fingers around his biceps, squeezing hard as he moved over them, and felt swept up once more. Michael cried out, loudly, his control continuing to slip, but he kept driving into her. She felt her next orgasm coming on. She came explosively once more, ending just as his was beginning. He let out an impassioned roar.

He was still pulsing inside her, sporadically now, but he made no move to leave her. They stared at one another, both out of breath, the emotion that passed between them still unspoken, but as naked as their own bodies. They said nothing, because hadn't they said it already?

For the second time that night, Darby felt the impulse to keep him to herself, to stay in the hotel suite until they had to leave Park City. She didn't care about the party they'd already missed or the dozens of screenings she'd been excited to attend. Apart from Michael, Darby had ceased to care about anything at all.

"Do you have to get that?"

His phone buzzed on the nightstand and though they hadn't yet spoken words to each other that morning, each had known the other was awake. It wasn't uncommon, them holding on to one another, clinging really, in the hours of the morning, neither wanting to break the spell by getting up. He kissed her hair and held her tighter, angling his body to more fully cradle hers.

"No."

So they continued to lie like that. Some minutes later—she didn't know how many because she had drifted back to sleep— the buzzing of his phone roused her again.

"Get it," she commanded softly. He didn't move at first. But eventually he succumbed, depositing her gently on the bed before he picked up his phone.

"Dale." He answered neutrally, climbing out of the bed gingerly so as not to disturb her. He mouthed an instruction for her to go back to sleep.

She didn't quite sleep again, though she was groggy, and she liked luxuriating in the warmth of the bed even though he had gone. As she heard his soft footsteps pad down the stairs and listened to his muted conversation, she let herself think about what had happened the night before.

By then, they'd been there for almost two days and hadn't seen a single film. The clock on the nightstand told her that it was nearly noon, but she found that she really didn't want to get out of bed. She wanted to stay there with him, in their bubble, forever. She didn't want to face her father's announcement, and she was not eager to return to the hospital. She wanted this, with Michael, so, so much.

When he returned, he engulfed her back into his arms, placing his phone back where it had been, but not bothering to plug it back in, and she noticed that something about him was tense.

"What did Dale want?" She asked it lightly, knowing better than to push.

"I have to go back to Sydney in a couple of days," was all he said.

So she returned to her own thoughts, because him having to disappear off to where he was needed was nothing new, and if he didn't have to go yet, their time now was good enough for her. So they stayed there, thoughts still swirling in her head, most of them too scary to voice. But the one she could say, she finally said aloud.

"It's going to be a vicious campaign."

He kissed her hair again and said nothing in response.

"They'll look for anything to use against him and he'll play just as hard. I know this must sound paranoid to you, but—"

"I know, baby. I know you're not being paranoid."

There's that word again.

"They'll spin anything into anything. It will be completely invasive," she continued. He only held her tighter. "I wouldn't blame you if—"

"Shhhhh," he soothed, silencing her then. "Don't even think like that."

But she couldn't help it, nor could she help the apology that passed her lips.

"I'm sorry."

He shushed her again.

CHAPTER THIRTY-THREE

MISSED CONNECTIONS

DARBY ENJOYED THE CALM SILENCE OF MICHAEL'S apartment, and was content to lounge in his waterbed as he showered. She relished the way the morning sun—which was not too bright yet—cast light into his room, and the soft sounds of the water hitting the tiles through his open bathroom door. She could have easily joined him, and some mornings she did, but her position on his bed gave her the perfect view of his enormous closet. Watching him get dressed was still one of her favorite things about staying over.

It was like watching a sacred ritual. He wasn't trying to be sexy—he was so into his own dressing routine that she doubted he was even aware that she watched—but to Darby, it felt like soft-core porn. First he put on his underwear: navy boxer briefs that looked like Lycra but felt like the finest silk. Next, he would take a moment to adjust himself. He wore a simple Hanes V-neck undershirt, but it fit in a way that flattered his devastatingly fit body. From there, it was socks, which were always loud and interesting, a quirk she had never asked him about. When he turned the shower off, she smiled to herself in anticipation of the show. Then she heard her phone. The song was *Like a Boss*. It was Kelly, and she had to answer it.

"This is Darby," she said neutrally, managing to mask the slight disappointment in her voice.

"Darby, it's Kelly. I've got good news for you. Some important donors who we've been courting have agreed to meet with us this afternoon. I want to tell them about your research, so I'll need you there. I'll give you some background on a few of them so you can prepare."

The words kicked Darby into gear and she realized she needed to find a pen and paper.

"Hold on, let me find some paper," she said.

But in Michael's apartment, always flawlessly neat and clean, every practical item was put away. Not finding anything in his bedroom, she did another fruitless search of his kitchen before hurrying to his office.

A month had passed since Lake Geneva and he still hadn't shown her any of his drawings. Walking into his office tripped her up. She'd passed by this room before, of course, but she'd never actually been inside. It, too, was as neat as every other room in his apartment. Since she'd become fascinated by what he might be drawing, it felt odd to be in this space, as though she were snooping. But her boss was waiting and she figured there had to be a notepad and pen someplace.

In a stylish leather cup on his drafting table, she found the fanciest pencils she'd ever seen. On his desk, she found a sketch book, and quickly flipped to the last page. Giving Kelly the green light, she took the details down quickly and they said their goodbyes. She held the paper tight and ripped the page she'd written on from its spiral binding.

She was just letting the book fall shut when she caught a glimpse of what was on the earlier pages. They were drawings.

Whatever she'd seen in the blink of an eye was very, very good. She breathed deeply, knowing she should leave it alone—after all, Michael hadn't invited her to look. But she ached to see the kinds of things he drew.

What she saw when she opened the book took her breath away, and she gasped, audibly. These drawings were beautiful, executed with nearly unfathomable skill. Each one contained an emotion that she could barely comprehend. And they were not drafts of buildings—as he'd said, they were everything and anything else. Buckingham Fountain in the summer. Sailboats in the marina. Then, randomly, an octopus that was uncannily realistic.

When she heard the sounds of Michael's shoes against the hardwood floor, she knew she'd been caught. She closed the book, and kept her hands on it as she stared down at the desk for a beat, preparing herself to meet his eyes.

"These are exquisite," she said softly. She found that unshed tears were clouding her vision as she looked up at him. "I didn't mean to pry…I just needed a piece of paper."

She couldn't tell what he was thinking, but he didn't seem upset with her. If anything, he looked a bit vulnerable.

"You can look," he said, and she knew it for what it was—his attempt to be more transparent. She wasn't sure that he *wanted* her to see—only that he felt he should.

But curiosity got the best of her, and she picked up the book a second time, paging through more slowly, eating up one drawing after the other. Flipping from a sketch of a child in the park, to the picture of what, at first glance, looked like a beautiful woman, Darby realized the woman was her.

"You drew this from memory?" she asked, unable to look at him. There wasn't one time when she'd sat for him, not one time she could recall when he'd taken a picture of her like this.

She saw him from her peripheral vision.

"I spend a lot of time looking at you, Darby."

She nodded, still not meeting his eyes.

"It's beautiful," she smiled, no longer turning pages, just looking at the way he'd drawn her face to perfection, her nose, her lips, her hair.

"You're beautiful," he replied simply.

She didn't want to stop looking at it. She wanted to memorize its detail, the emotion it captured. She realized she wanted to keep it, but it would seem rather vain to ask. Thinking along those lines brought her to another realization.

"That painting in your living room…the butterfly…"

"Is mine," he finished for her.

This is what family should be.

Darby thought it at random moments as she sat at Bex's dining room table, conversing fluidly and laughing easily, happier than she'd ever felt at any family dinner of her own. She'd been nervous about meeting Michael's family, obsessing over whether they would like her. Even worse, she had obsessed over what it meant that she was so nervous at all.

Bex was strikingly beautiful. It was strange how strongly they resembled one another given that they were opposite sex fraternal twins. They had the same deep-blue sea eyes. Michael had closely-shaven hair that hinted at a very dark hue, and Bex's impressive mane of wavy black hair gave a sense of what Michael would look like if he ever grew his long. Bex was shorter than Michael, but still a bit taller than Darby, and she had a charisma so strong that it rivaled Michael's. Even Ella, his six-year-old niece, displayed what Darby could only conclude was inherited charm.

Darby was relieved that it felt more like a dinner party among friends than it did a relationship milestone. Alex, Bex's husband who traveled for work, was home for once and a certain joy at his presence was palpable. They talked about things that all adults talked about when they got together: how hard it was to get tickets to *Hamilton*, how ridiculous traffic was on the Dan Ryan, and whether to start or continue watching *Game of Thrones*.

"You were so gracious to bring dessert," Alex said as Bex fetched Darby's cake and placed it on the table. "What a lovely surprise. Michael talks about how hard you work, so we didn't want to put you on the spot to bring something—especially something homemade."

Darby shifted her gaze to Michael, who had explicitly insisted she bring a dessert. Michael shrugged, giving her an unrepentant look at the discovery of his fib.

"Though, the way Michael talks about your baking…" Bex picked up, "I'll admit that I'm eager to try anything you've made."

"Michael does love my baking," she murmured. "I take it he's always loved sweets?"

Bex laughed as she handed Darby the cake-cutting knife and set a sack of dessert plates next to her.

"One time, when he was four, he climbed up onto the kitchen counter and got into the sugar. He just ate it straight from the canister. Mom thought he was napping but he wasn't—he was just scooping sugar by the fistful." She covered Ella's ears as she continued. "He had an epic case of the shits for the next two days."

Darby laughed freely at his expense.

"He's so good at savory food," Bex continued. "If he'd ever wanted to be a chef he'd have been great at it. But he's never been one for baking. The two of you are a great match in that sense."

And there it was—the first reference to them as a couple.

"Very true," Darby agreed smoothly. "I love baking, but before Michael, I rarely baked for myself. If I made a dozen cupcakes, I'd eat a dozen cupcakes. Now, I eat one and Michael eats the other eleven."

Alex laughed. "That sounds about right."

After Michael's entire family had oohed and aahed about the cake, it was time for Ella to go to bed. Darby didn't think she had made much of an impression on the little girl and was surprised when Ella asked if she could be the one to read her bedtime stories.

"Of course, sweetie," Darby agreed, flattered. "I would love that."

"Don't worry, Uncle Michael—you can come too."

And, with that, the little girl led them up to her room.

On deck for that night's stories were *The Cat in the Hat Comes Back* and *Rosie Revere, Engineer*. Despite having no kids of her own, Darby was familiar with these books. On the psych ward, some of her patients were children.

She could see the surprise in Michael's eyes as she read from the books, enchanting Ella at all the right parts with emphasis and making the characters come alive. Ella gave her a huge hug after the last page was read. It was the kind of hug that only a six-year-old could deliver and Darby cherished it.

After bidding Ella sweet dreams and letting Michael take on tooth brushing duty, she made her way down to the kitchen to see whether she could help with cleanup. For the first time that night, she and Bex were alone.

"You have a beautiful family," Darby complimented shyly as she fell in next to Bex to help with the dishes. "Thanks so much for inviting me."

Bex smiled over at her and didn't say anything at first.

"Michael's never brought a girl home, you know. And he's never talked about anyone like he talks about you."

She didn't know what she was supposed to say to that. "I like him a lot."

"I'm glad," Bex said. "Because he needs time."

Darby was afraid to ask.

"Time for what?"

"Time to admit to himself what he really wants, and to rework his plan once he does. Time for him to figure out how to make it work. I hope you're the kind of woman who will wait for him. He's worth it."

Now she really didn't know what to say. She didn't know how much of the truth Bex knew. It was impossible to tell if she was aware of the arrangement, and it would be strange to confide in Michael's twin who she'd just met. And it wasn't just Michael who was holding back—it was her, too.

"It's complicated," she said simply.

"Most relationships are." Bex continued rinsing dishes. "Ella and I barely see Alex these days. It's not ideal, but it's not forever. We pay the price now, but we know what's waiting for us in the end."

Darby said no more, but reflected for the rest of the night on how her situation with Michael was exactly the opposite. They knew what was waiting for them in the end, too. All they had was now, and the price to be paid would come later.

"Thank God I caught you," Michael said with relief, though he didn't sound happy. He sounded like he was moving around, holding the phone between his shoulder and his ear.

"They're about to make me turn my phone off," she said. "What's up?"

The flight attendants were more tolerable of First Class passengers being on their phones, but they'd closed the door and were ready to taxi. A minute later, even she would be asked, however politely, to put her phone in airplane mode.

"I'm so sorry. I can't make it tonight. I've been called to San Francisco and I need to be in the airport in a couple of hours. By the time you get home, I'll be on a plane."

"When do you get back?"

"Not until Friday." Her face fell. It had already been twelve days since she'd seen him.

This was an increasing problem. He was leaving for longer hauls. She was traveling more as well. Three times already, their schedules had kept them apart for long stretches. And she didn't like it at all. They had seen each other only six times over the past two months.

"O'Hare, right?" she asked. She herself was in Washington, D.C. "I'll be there in three hours. When does your flight leave?"

"Not for another five hours," he said, and she could hear that he'd caught on to her idea.

"Why don't we meet there?"

"Are you on Virgin?" he asked.

"Yeah."

"Me, too. So we'll be in Terminal 3." He was an encyclopedia when it came to airports. "Are you a member of the Admiral's Club?"

"No."

"Buy yourself a day pass and meet me in the one on the L concourse."

"Alright," she said, feeling better instantly. "I'll see you there. Travel safe."

By the time she landed, she'd done the math. She'd figured out the flight he was on and knew that they would have just a little over an hour. Not wanting to wait a single minute, she'd bought her Admiral's Club day pass online. She was aching to see him and had been counting the days all week.

The last two times they had gone too many days without seeing each other, they had fallen into bed together—if they even made it to bed at all—and fucked for hours. In some ways, she had loved it. She'd replayed over and over in her mind what it felt like to have Michael slam her against the wall and disrobe them only as much as was necessary to allow him to ram his cock deeply inside her. In those moments, everything felt so raw, so visceral, and his desperation really turned her on. She liked the fantasy that he craved her—and only her—so much that he was never with anyone else. She liked the power of being the only woman who could slake his incredible thirst.

At the same time, she hated it. She missed him when he was gone. And even though being apart gave them incredible moments where pent-up tension was released, she would rather they were together more often. His absence the following week would be agony, though their brief rendezvous in O'Hare was better than nothing.

She wondered whether they would fuck. No doubt, the danger of doing that somewhere they weren't supposed to would only enhance their blazing hot sex. Most of the club lounges had showers, but, O'Hare had four Admiral's Clubs, and she couldn't remember whether the one on L Concourse did.

The second she walked into the lounge, she recognized him from across the room. He sat in a comfortable leather low-back chair, and even from the back, his strong neck and the curve of his shaven head hinted at his beauty. As she walked around to face him, she placed her hand affectionately on his neck.

He followed her with his eyes as she took the seat next to him, blindly turning off his iPad, and slipping it into the messenger bag on his lap.

"Hi," he smiled warmly.

These moments with him were often the most intense—moments when they were in public, and were reticent to be too showy about their affections. She'd found that she was more recognized when she was out among strangers now that buzz about her father's place on the ticket was an item of speculation.

"Hi," she returned, smiling back at him in a way that she knew conveyed her own affection. He took her hand, something he never shied away from. "I'm glad this worked out."

"Me, too."

"So what's in San Francisco?"

"A fire to put out. Not in San Francisco, proper. I'm going to Napa."

She nodded approvingly. That sounded nice.

"One of the former winemakers at Opus One has started his own label and we were hired to build what's basically a small castle. They're sending me in to put out a fire and romance the client. It's not going well," he explained.

"I've always wanted to go there," she admitted.

"Maybe we should go some time," he said. It made her think of Sundance, and she liked the idea of getting away with him again.

"That would be nice," she remarked, not bothering to hide her smile.

"I want to be alone with you," he said bluntly, and not with his usual fire. She would have expected his words to be dripping with innuendo, but they weren't.

"Do they have napping rooms here?" she asked.

He shook his head. "Shower suites," he said. "I've already gotten the key to number four."

"Let's go, then. We only have an hour."

He stood her up then and she didn't bother to pick up her own bag. By then, she knew him well enough to know he wouldn't let her. He slung his duffel and his messenger bag over his shoulder and began to roll her suitcase. Given how late at night it was, the lounge was empty. He let them in and dropped their bags. And they were, finally, alone.

He wrapped his arms around her waist but didn't make a move to kiss her as she expected. Instead, he leaned his forehead down to touch hers.

"All this travel is turning out to be a bitch."

He was right—when they'd first made their arrangement, he had been the one doing all the travel, and much less of it.

"We knew it would be like this," she said.

Michael sighed heavily. "Yeah…we did."

The room was spacious and homey, with an elegantly tiled shower and sink at one side, and a dressing suite on the other. An ironing board and a steamer were mounted on one of the walls, as was a rack that hung towels. A luggage stand was set up so that suitcases could be opened easily. And a long bench was on the opposite wall to provide a space to sit while dressing. Michael took her hand, sat on the bench and pulled her onto his lap.

She knew what was coming next—at least she thought she did. He would start out kissing her and it would turn into something more. He did kiss her then, softly and slowly, but after several blissful minutes of exploring each other's mouths, the something more didn't come. She could feel him hardening beneath her, feel their kisses becoming just a bit more desperate. But he made no move to take things further. It only made her want him more.

"Touch me," she murmured in-between kisses, and she felt him begin to oblige. With the hand that wasn't on her back, steadying her where she sat, he gently cupped her breast from outside her shirt. He could feel her approval and intensified his movements, as he became very hard beneath her. Still kissing him, she began to remove her boots. Next would be her socks and pants.

Soon enough, she had straddled him and was sinking down onto his cock, and he was looking at her in adulation. She didn't make a sound, though she was sure her face showed her pleasure. But they had to be careful to be quiet. She pushed him back, so that her knees were more fully on the bench, placing her in a better position to move. He pulled her sweater over her head and when she saw his eyes widen, she was glad she had chosen that particular bra.

With her hands on his shoulders, she began to ride him. Though she did have the presence of mind to keep them restrained, it felt so good she couldn't stop the sounds that emanated from deep within her. Michael, meanwhile, had closed his eyes and let his head fall forward. She could tell from his own softer sounds that, he too, was holding back.

Inevitably, his hands came to her hips as his own hips began to move with more urgency. Soon he was fucking her from beneath as much as she was riding him from above.

"Fuck, Darby," he ground out softly and so vulnerably. They fucked with rising intensity, but still in that slow, sensual rhythm that always worked.

She wanted it to last forever, to be held with him in that sweet limbo that was gratifying by itself but never enough. When she felt him thumb her clit roughly, it careened her to the edge. He always liked for her to come first, and it was tell-ing that he sped it along. She felt herself tightening in anticipa-tion of her release, and she knew he felt it too. He was the most sensitive person that she'd ever met in that respect. He relished every twitch that she'd ever delivered.

"I'm gonna come all over your cock," she said then, the softness in her voice betraying the filth of her words.

He moaned, louder than he should have. She loved the feeling of him coming inside her. Before Michael, she'd rarely had sex without a condom, but something about him spilling inside her, despite the cleanup that would come afterward, was so, so hot.

"Michael," she gasped, a second before she came.

"Come, baby," he whispered with rough desperation in his voice.

And she did. So did he. It was always more intense when they reached orgasm together. They came down slowly, still moving a bit even after the moment had passed.

When she finally sat still on top of him, his lips returned to hers and they kissed for a long time, even after he had softened. After they'd silently disrobed, she pinned her hair into a bun and stepped in the shower with him. They kissed underneath the warm water for the rest of the hour before bidding one an-other a bittersweet goodbye. She was glad she had seen him, but hated that seeing him had come to that.

"I don't want to go to work," Darby half-groaned, half-whined as she pulled the covers up over her head.

She'd had to go in on both of her days off that week and even after seven good hours of sleep that night, she was exhausted.

"Why don't you just call in sick?"

The thought had never occurred to her, and she was surprised to hear the suggestion coming from Michael.

"When was the last time you called in sick?"

"When I had the flu."

"Not called in sick because you *were* sick—called in sick to play hooky."

She could tell from his face that even though he was taking the time to think about it, it might not have actually ever happened.

"I can't remember," he admitted.

"Mmm-hmm."

"Alright…why don't I call in sick, too?"

It shocked the hell out of her. She couldn't believe that he of all people would just blow off a day of work. It made her wonder whether things with his job were alright, and what he might be trying to avoid. But she didn't ask, and instead jumped at the chance to dodge her own work stress for a while.

It would be nice to have a day off—a real day off—a time when she hadn't scheduled anything and all possibilities were open. She liked the idea of just relaxing with Michael. Lately, they'd had to steal time together during late nights, coming straight from work to see each other, fucking until fatigue took over and then sleeping until they had to get up to go to work the next morning.

Michael rolled his eyes as he eavesdropped on her speaking to the Chief's assistant.

"Pathetic," he mumbled when she got off the phone.

"Alright, let's hear your excuse," she challenged.

His was easy. He dialed, smiling at Darby as he waited for an answer. "I can't come into work today. I'm sick."

He was silent for a minute. "Okay…okay…. that's fine, he can wait…alright, thanks…bye."

Darby shook her head. "Not all of us have assistants that will cover for us," she complained.

"Aww…poor baby," he intoned. "I feel truly sorry for you."

She tossed a pillow at him, and it struck him square in the face. "So what should we do?"

"I don't know," Michael said, plucking a tiny feather from his lip. "Why don't we start by getting a little more sleep?"

Two hours later, they were better-rested, but starving. Neither of them was accustomed to this. Breakfast was the one meal that each of them could usually rely on before their days got too crazy. They debated whether to stay in or go somewhere for brunch, but neither of them wanted to chance being spotted by a co-worker, however unlikely it was.

"What did you used to do on your days off?" she asked. "You know, before you were busy fucking me."

Michael had whipped up amazing egg white omelets and they ate them at his kitchen bar. Despite almost never being home, he had fresh eggs, green and red bell peppers, onions, and spinach lying around.

"Do you really want to know?"

She gave him a look. Since they'd talked about it, he'd been more forthcoming when it came to sharing parts of himself, but she'd also been more assertive about asking. It felt like progress. Apart from the fact that they were seeing each other less, she felt better than ever in their relationship. It felt as if they had hit their stride.

"Should we take the Tesla?" he asked twenty minutes later as they exited the elevator in his garage.

She smiled widely and took his hand. When they reached his parking spot, he bent to kiss her lips before they parted, as if they wouldn't be right next to one another ten seconds later, after they had slid into their respective seats.

"Where are we going?" Darby finally asked after they got on the road. She'd been wondering about this since they had traveled past the end of Lake Shore Drive and exited at the Museum of Science and Industry, slightly south of Hyde Park. They were a few blocks outside the range of the university. It was different from any place he'd ever taken her before. She knew that he had grown up there but had no idea of where they could be headed.

"I'm taking you to my old neighborhood, he explained. "To a place that's special to me, a place where I spent a lot of time as a kid."

Darby just nodded, looking around with trepidation as Michael street-parked the Tesla in a neighborhood that barely had any car nicer than a Toyota. She wasn't put off by the run-down look of the area. She was simply trying to comprehend what Michael might want to show her. He got out of the car and went around to open her door, smiling down at her as he took her hand and helped her out. He then cast his eyes at a building across the street.

The "Heroes and Villains" sign announced the name of the store, and the collection of books on display in the window answered her question.

"A comic book store?" she asked, smiling with delight. "I should've known," she said softly, and he could see that she understood. Of course a kid with a creative imagination who loved stories and drawing would have loved comic books.

"My friend Randy owns it," he explained, leading her across the street. "He's not old enough to be my real father, but growing up, he was kind of like a dad to me. When I was a kid, I came here every single day. He knew I didn't have any money, so he let me sit behind the counter and read. When I was old enough, he gave me my first job. I cleaned the store, stocked the shelves, and did other little things. It helped pay for my drawing supplies and he gave me a deep discount on whatever I wanted."

A wistful smile appeared on her face as they crossed the street. She took a moment to scan over the titles in the window, imagining what a young Michael must have been like. It was something that she'd often wondered, and she was delighted that he was showing her this chapter in his story.

"Will you introduce me?" she asked needlessly.

He held out his hand, inviting her to go in first. She noted that he looked a bit apprehensive.

"Mikey!" Randy's voice boomed as Michael followed Darby into the store. "It's great to see you, kid," the older man said warmly, lumbering over to pull Michael into a fierce hug.

"It's good to be home," he returned, and they pulled back to take in the sight of one another.

Randy was tall—not quite round but definitely not thin—rather sturdy and exactly what you'd picture an aging comic book geek to be. He had long dark hair and a long salt and pepper beard. If he were a few pounds lighter, he would look like a young Gandalf. He had bright green eyes and wore a plain black t-shirt and black jeans. Darby knew immediately that Michael loved this man.

"Don't be rude," Randy chided, swinging his eyes to Darby and smiling. "Introduce me to your lady-friend." For a flash of a moment, something on his face looked like recognition.

"This is Darby," Michael said. "She's a good friend, so no stories about what a brat I was as a kid, okay? I want her to like me."

To her surprise, Randy took Darby's hand and kissed her knuckles.

"It's a pleasure, Darby," he said in a softer voice. "I've

known this kid for more than twenty years and not once has he brought a girl in here. I've been waiting to meet you for a very long time."

Darby blushed deeply. And she thought she caught Michael blushing, too.

"I've been saving a few things for you, Mikey." Randy dashed to the counter and bent down to retrieve something.

"Oh, yeah?" Michael said excitedly, seeming to forget the world for a moment.

"Merry Christmas," Randy said, handing him a large, heavy-looking bag with the Heroes and Villains logo printed on the front. Inside were stacks of graphic novels.

"You've got to let me pay you for these," Michael protested.

"Alright," Randy challenged with a meaningful look. "Then you've got to let me pay *you*."

Michael looked nervously at Darby. He was quick to change the subject.

"Why don't I show you around? Have you ever been in a comic book store?" he asked, leading her away from the contemporary graphic novels toward a wall of collectibles and memorabilia.

"Only once," she admitted. "One of my roommates in college was really into them, and I remember reading a few of hers and really liking them. One time, on a whim, I walked into a store that sold them, hoping to find something else I liked. But I was kind of lost…I didn't really know what to buy, so I never tried again."

"Do you remember what you read before?"

She wracked her brain to recall the name.

"There was this one…it had all the characters from fairy tales in it—The Big Bad Wolf, Little Red Riding Hood—characters everyone reads about when they're kids. But they were living in a modern city, and all their plot lines wove together, like they were all part of the same story."

Michael smiled, recognizing it immediately. "*Fables.*"

"Yes!" she laughed. "That's what it was called. You know it?"

"I know all of them, cupcake. I could recommend some others like it, if you want," he offered.

"I want," she said a bit shyly.

They made their way around the store, both of them checking things out as she peppered him with questions.

"This one looks promising," Darby said as she approached a display. Stacks of the same book were illuminated by a spotlight and had little signs that said "#1 Store Bestseller", "Nationally Ranked", and "Staff Pick." It was called *The Architect*, and she could tell from its summary description that it was about an architect obsessed with building a palace in the hopes of winning the woman he couldn't have.

"If it's a staff pick, I'll bet you've read it. Would I like it? You know I think architects are sexy," she said in a voice that was low enough for only Michael to hear.

"Look at the author's name," he said softly.

"Andrew Dufrain?" He gave her a minute to work it out. But she didn't.

"What's the main character's name in *The Shawshank Redemption*?" he asked.

"Andy Dufresne," she said, still not understanding what he was getting at.

"They're homonyms. It's a pen name," he said then. "It's… *my* pen name."

Her eyes whipped up to his. They stared for a long moment before she picked up the book.

Darby held the object in her hand as if it were something

precious, drinking in the front cover art fully before turning it slowly to inspect the back. "Randy doesn't just own this store—he publishes for a handful of artists he likes. I gave him the exclusive rights for distribution, as a thank you for publishing me..."

"But it's nationally ranked," she nearly stammered.

"He's great at marketing," Michael shrugged. "And the world of graphic novels is small. It's not like fiction. Randy goes to all the Comic-Cons and sells his authors there—that's how it got a national following."

"What's a Comic-Con?" she asked, which made him grin.

"I'll take you to one sometime. San Diego's the big one. It's a huge convention that's targeted to media geeks. Comic artists set up shop there, and they have a huge draw around sci-fi and fantasy TV shows and movies. Some people say it's gotten too Hollywood, but it still has some authentic roots. I think you'd like it."

She nodded, still thinking it all through.

"So...is that what he was talking about before? When he mentioned paying you?"

Michael nodded.

"He wants me to collect my royalty checks, but I won't accept them. I don't need the money and I'd rather he put it back into the store..."

"I want to read it," she said, half-expecting him to protest in some way.

"I'll buy you a copy," he said with a reassuring smile.

Before they left, they spent more time with Randy, who did nothing to heed Michael's warning about not telling embarrassing stories. She hadn't felt the least bit guilty laughing at Michael's expense.

Before they left, Michael autographed a stack of his books

with a metallic silver sharpie. At one point, a teenage kid who was a fan of the series walked in and talked Michael's ear off for a good twenty minutes. Darby took that opportunity to keep chatting with Randy, who obviously adored Michael. Beyond meeting his sister and his niece, this was the closest she had been to other people in his life.

When it came time to leave, she excused herself to the restroom, and returned to the showroom to find Michael and Randy in quiet conversation. They both rose when she approached, focusing on her rather than whatever they had been discussing. That only made her more certain they'd been talking about her. She smiled shyly and Randy hugged Darby again, warmly, just before they left.

Michael clicked the remote to the Tesla to unlock his car and surprised Darby by tossing her the keys.

"You drive," he said simply as he opened her door.

"Thank you," she said softly after he had shut himself into the passenger seat. She looked at him meaningfully as she said it.

"You're welcome," he said in a tone that matched hers. Both of them knew that she wasn't talking about the car.

CHAPTER THIRTY-FOUR

THE BEGINNING OF THE END

T HE SHOWER MUST HAVE BEEN LOUD, BECAUSE SHE HADN'T heard him come in, not the opening and closing of the stall door, nor the steps he took toward her before he wrapped strong arms around her waist. He was hard. Morning wood, most likely, though he could have been watching her through the clear glass doors as she washed herself slowly, absently, thinking of him and the night before.

He said nothing, only held onto her, their bodies pressed together. Michael had a way of holding her more tightly, more impossibly close than anyone had ever held her. Moments before, the warm water had her body feeling soft and pliant, but now she felt a familiar tightening, her nipples puckering and beginning to ache. Michael ran his nose down her cheek, and his mouth down her jaw, so slowly, until his teeth softly bit that magical spot on her neck.

Feeling faint, she raised a hand to steady herself, touching the tile wall, her mouth slacking as she felt Michael's tongue on her shoulder. He snaked a hand down between her legs, the slick wetness he found there entirely different from the water that fell around them. His whimpers made it seem as if it was he, and not she, who had been touched in the most sensitive of places.

He bit her ear as his other hand found her nipple, deft fingers tugging at it in a firm pinch. She gasped, throwing her other hand in front of herself for balance. With her facing the wall, he positioned himself to slip into her. She waited for it, yearned for it—but before she could process what was happening, he was turning her around. In a fluid motion, he hoisted her legs up with ease, had her back against the wall, and pushed inside her. Forearm to forearm, he laced his fingers in hers and breathed heavily as he began to move.

His motions were small, less like the acrobatic fucking she knew that his strong back was capable of. Instead, he ground into her in a way that kept him in constant contact with her clit. His motions were slow, and hard, and oh so deep. She loved it best like this, when she felt he was trying to climb inside her. It was this version of him that owned her fantasies.

His mouth found hers and somehow he kept perfect rhythm below as he kissed her from above. Though he had her pinned in a way that made it nearly impossible for her to move on her own, the intensity compelled her to pull her lips away in order to take a much-needed breath. Her heart pounded as if she were running a marathon and she drank in the humid air greedily. Her senses were overloaded. He took that opportunity to bend his mouth and suck her nipple, grinding into her all the while.

"God, you fuck me so good," she nearly moaned, not loudly and certainly not intentionally, but in moments like this, she had no filter. Her words must have sparked something in him because he bit down on her nipple and seconds later, she felt him pulsing inside her, a needful moan escaping him as they both came.

He lowered her gently to her feet, pressing their foreheads together for a long moment before he captured her mouth in another long, deep kiss.

"You're killing me, Darby…" he said, and she didn't dare to think about what it meant.

Twenty minutes later, he was kissing her again in the morning light as they walked through the front door together. He was off to Sydney again and she was headed to the hospital. Thoughts of what they had just done would keep her warm.

Darby was late for work. It rarely happened, but she had overslept and she was rushing to get dressed, get something in her stomach, and get to work on time. In her fatigue the night before, she'd left her phone in her coat pocket and hadn't heard the daily alarm.

Her mouth was full of a bite of sausage and an Eggo waffle sat, half-eaten, on her plate as she flipped through news channels, catching up on whatever had happened overnight. Finding her father's face on each one, Darby gave up altogether and clicked off the TV.

The doorbell ringing gave her a start. She peeped through the keyhole, praying she wouldn't see paparazzi outside. The media frenzy had already started, and was already becoming difficult to avoid. She'd taken to driving to work every day— sneaking out her back door and escaping through her garage. When she saw that it was Andrew, she relaxed, and opened the door to find him looking more hurried and disorganized than she felt.

"Thank God you're still here. I thought I wouldn't catch you," he said, breathing a dramatic sigh of relief. Everything about Andrew was dramatic.

"Michael wanted me to deliver this to you," he explained, thrusting a small bag into her hands.

The keys. She'd completely forgotten.

"There's been so much to do," Andrew rambled, "with Michael's move and all. I had planned on being here much earlier but I lost track of time," he continued to explain.

Michael's move?

"I'm going to miss him. He's the best boss I've ever had, to tell you the truth. They're going to let me keep managing his Chicago business, but it won't be the same…"

"No…it won't," Darby agreed dumbly, as if she had known.

"Sorry to have to run, honey…" Andrew waved sadly. "My list is a mile long. Take care of yourself, okay? I'm sure we'll see each other again." He retreated down the steps. It took a full minute for Darby to close the door.

Michael's move?

She was an hour late to work. Had she been able to maintain any sense of time, she'd have known that beyond the fifteen minutes she would have been late anyway, she'd spent another twenty standing dumbly in her rotunda, ten minutes backtracking after making wrong turns in her car on the way to work, ten minutes in the parking lot trying not to cry in her car and five minutes touching up her makeup after her attempts had failed.

Whereas she had been looking forward to their plans that weekend—it had been nearly three weeks since they had seen each other—she now dreaded what he would tell her at their rendezvous.

The meaning behind random details she hadn't thought much about as they had happened snapped into focus and she wondered why she hadn't suspected anything before.

The frequent trips to Sydney that got longer every time. The heightened intensity of his touch, and the sadness in his eyes. The way he wanted to see her at every opportunity when he was in town. This weekend wasn't about releasing their bodies' tension after having been apart for so long, or about giving themselves respite from their crazy jobs. This was it. He was being transferred. He'd planned something different because these may be the last days they spent together. And, unbeknownst to Darby, he'd been slowly saying goodbye.

Every hour brought a new realization as she replayed recent conversations. She now saw them—and their overnight retreat, through a new lens. She'd figured he'd booked them a suite at the Drake so that they could pamper themselves at the spa in between lounging—or doing other things—in bed. But she'd only ever heard Michael talk about liking the spa at the Peninsula, and she knew that his favorite hotel brunch was at the St. Regis. The Drake had a different significance—it was the place where they'd gone on their first date.

She'd never called it that before, even in her own mind, when she thought back to the Frigg Foundation Gala. It was hard to believe that nearly a year had passed; she never thought of it in those terms. As she did, she admitted to herself that this had been one of the best years of her life. She had refused to let herself dwell on what had blossomed between them. Whatever it was, it had thrived in a delicate ecosystem. As long as everything between them was good, that had been good enough for her.

But she didn't know what would be good enough for her now. More intense than the knowledge that she would miss him was the desperation to believe that this wouldn't be the end. She didn't want to face the fact that a single word they'd agreed upon nearly a year before could so thoroughly eliminate this thing they'd built. But she had no idea how closely he would stick to the plan.

She wasn't stupid. She knew that he cared for her in ways that had nothing to do with sex. Friendship was a concept Michael didn't take lightly, and no matter how it ended, she would still have some place in his life. She knew that he wouldn't be ending this if he wasn't being transferred. She knew he would miss her. What she needed to know now was what it cost him to let her go.

It doesn't matter, she kept repeating to herself as she slogged through her shift. *He's leaving and finding out the truth would achieve nothing. There's no point in fucking things up now when we've got a shot at ending up as good friends.*

That was what she told herself as she got dressed that night in a pretty black maxi dress Michael liked and a pair of sandals. That's what she replayed, on a loop in her head, as she packed a small bag. That's what she told herself as she slid her room key into a special elevator slot that would take her to one of the hotel's private floors. She almost had herself convinced. Then she opened the hotel suite door.

The room was bursting with color, so much so that it took her a long moment to make sense of what she was seeing. Yellows and oranges, purples and whites, and every color on the spectrum of red to pink covered every surface. Hundreds of blooms that grew like wisteria turned upright sprang out from dozens of vases. They adorned the large suite's every surface, and their fragrance, a bit reminiscent of bubble gum, permeated the large living room. A lump formed in her throat, not only at the fact Michael had done all this for her, but at the unmistakable meaning of the flowers themselves.

"Snapdragons." She closed her eyes as she said the word quietly to herself. Her bags slipped from her fingers and a tear slipped from her eyes. It was tragedy and perfection, all at the same time.

She opened her eyes when she sensed him. He had appeared from deeper within the suite, had possibly emerged from the master bedroom. He walked toward her slowly, appraising her reaction, a storm of emotions rolling across his eyes.

"When do you leave?" she asked.

"Tomorrow," he replied gruffly, approaching her with a bit of caution. "How did you find out?"

"Andrew…he didn't mean to tell me. He thought I knew."

At that, he looked remorseful, but she shook her head, sniffling.

"It's better like this," and she knew he'd know what she meant. "So we have tonight?" she asked softly, as he finally reached her, nodding as he took her hands, intertwining their fingers.

"I missed you when I was gone."

He had never before spoken those words to her.

"I missed you too."

"I miss you every time I go."

"So do I."

They slept an hour past dawn, having spent the better part of the night intertwined with one another in bed. Darby hadn't spoken much, and neither had he. As they made love, so slowly, so desperately, she was sure that her body told him what she wouldn't dare to say out loud.

She awoke to the sensation of him kissing her hair, and she

snuggled more deeply into him, burying her nose into the light tuft of hair on his chest to better-inhale his scent. She wondered how long he'd been up. They lay like that for a long time, each knowing the other was awake, neither of them speaking. As she had done the day before, she debated how to say to him the things she wanted—maybe needed—him to know. Things that could only be said before everything changed.

"Nobody has ever stood up to my father like you did," she whispered finally. "I never thanked you for that."

Michael kissed her forehead again and stroked her hair for a languid moment.

"Like I said, he had it coming."

"Huck, too," she continued, on a roll, as if Michael hadn't spoken.

He stopped stroking her hair then and tipped her chin up to force her to look at him.

"You're worth sticking up for, Darby," he said with a bit of fire. "How does somebody as smart as you not know that?"

She lowered her eyes but he tipped her chin up again.

"I told you. My inner circle is small but there's not much I wouldn't do for the people in it. You're in my inner circle. You have been for a long time. Me moving to Sydney isn't going to change that, so you can stop saying your goodbyes, Darby. This isn't goodbye. You're stuck with me."

His voice was firm, but his hands and eyes were soft, and by the time he finished, his palm was cupping her cheek.

"I guess there are worse people to be stuck with," she conceded, her voice tearing up a bit at his declaration.

Too soon, they were sharing a silent cab ride back to her house. There had been more love making back at the hotel. In the shower, back in bed, after breakfast, after lunch. Every part of her was sore, but she didn't care. She'd taken everything he'd been willing to give, and maybe a little bit more.

He got out of the car with her, helped her inside her house, and took her hand as he led her to her sofa. He kissed her again, until the last minute he could. By the time she had to be ready for work, he'd be at O'Hare, passing through security. She had realized at some point that the two short days he'd come back to Chicago had been only for her.

And then the moment came, both of them standing by her front door, he with his leather jacket and the same small duffel she'd seen him with two dozen times before. He couldn't stop kissing her. She couldn't stop letting him. He might miss his plane. She wished he would.

"You don't have to wait until January to visit," he said finally. At some point that day, they'd talked about her coming then. "You're welcome in my house whenever you want. Show up on my doorstep any time. And I don't care about the time difference, Darby. I want to hear your voice. If you need me, call."

"Of course I'll call," she sniffled. "You're my best friend, Michael. Who else would even listen to all my shit?"

He hugged her fiercely, whispering something she couldn't hear at the very same moment that he pressed something small into her hand. She didn't know how long she stood alone in her rotunda, didn't make a conscious decision to blow off work, didn't hear the loud sounds of her wracking sobs after she'd crawled into bed. She was sure that he had seen tears shining in her eyes as they had stood at her door, but she saved the real tears for after he left.

She also didn't remember sleeping or waking up, only startling to realize that the butterfly that had entered her consciousness was neither a memory nor a dream. It was the drawing from Michael's apartment—the stunning teal and chartreuse-winged creature she had admired a hundred times. And it was hanging over her mantel.

The rendering was exquisite. The wings seemed to shimmer, as if diamond dust and silver had been infused into the paint. It made the room feel complete. The gesture would have been perfect if it hadn't felt so much like goodbye.

AUTHOR'S NOTE

Thank you for reading *Snapdragon*, the first book in the *Love Conquers None* duet. Sorry to leave you hanging, but Darby and Michael's story was too long for a single book. The final volume, *Chrysalis* (a finalist in the Emma Awards), picks up from where *Snapdragon* left off and is told from Michael's point of view. As Darby always suspected, there's much more to Michael's story than he ever let on. There's also much more to Frank Christensen's shenanigans, and, in *Chrysalis*, you'll see some pretty heady suspense that leads to him getting his comeuppance. *Snapdragon* is simply Darby and Michael's origin story—*Chrysalis* will lead them to their happily ever after, and begins their true romance.

A few more notes about *Snapdragon*: words can't express how grateful I am for the amazing accolades it's received. A total of nine award nods as a finalist, and three wins that included 1st Place in the Erotica category in the 2018 NECRWA Readers' Choice Awards, a Bronze Medal in the Romance category in the Independent Publisher Awards (the IPPYs), and an Honorable Mention in the Erotica category in the 2018 Foreword Indie Awards have blown me away. I'm also deeply honored to be the 2018 Emma Award winner for Best Debut Author. This is truly the beginning. I'm looking forward to sharing the rest of my stories with you!

If you like my writing, please consider joining my mailing list (http:/kilbyblades.com/subscribe)—it's the only way to read extended previews of my upcoming titles, to get freebies and outtakes of my stuff, and to win giveaways of other books I love. If you just want to hear me overshare about my crazy life, follow me on Instagram (http://www.instagram.com/kilbyblades). Most importantly, follow me on BookBub (https://www.bookbub.com/authors/kilby-blades) so you'll always know about new releases, and while you're doing that, why not leave a review so that other readers know what to expect?

And speaking of knowing what to expect from my other books, I'm known for what critics and bloggers have called "feminist romance". My books feature empowered heroines and multi-dimensional heroes who are staunch advocates for their women, stepping back from their own spotlights in order to let their women shine. In my angstier books, my characters are dry-witted, but my lighter ones serve up a ton of humor. All of this in the midst of delicious dilemmas and never-before-seen plots.

Apart from Darby and Michael's series, a steamy coming-of-age humor novella, *The Art of Worship,* has been released. It features Reed, an eighteen-year-old virgin with sex on the brain who has yet to exchange V-cards with his steady girlfriend, Aubrey. As it turns out, Reed's father, Preston Whitney—and the other Whitney men before him—have been gatekeepers to a wealth of passed-down wisdom about women and sex. But can Reed survive the awkward embarrassment of instruction from his dad to learn the art of worship?

UPCOMING TITLES

Crocodile Tears (working title) is a soon-to-be-released family feud saga that feels like Hatfields and McCoys meets Romeo and Juliet. Ruby Paige returns home to her small town in Oregon to attend the funeral of Dale Flynn, the patriarch of a family that has feuded with hers for generations. Outing their secret friendship will cause a scandal, but he did her a great kindness that compels her to pay her respects. At the reading of his will, it is revealed that Dale has left her half of his estate, to the chagrin of his estranged son, Wes, and to the utter surprise of Ruby. Dale's multi-million-dollar fortune will be split between them provided they meet one condition: Ruby and Wes have three weeks to demystify the origins of the family feud and learn how the Flynns became sole owners of a wine empire once half-owned by the Paiges. Through Wes and Ruby's journey, we see what it takes to create productive dialogue between people of opposing factions who have been programmed with different information. These themes—often painful, sometimes sweet, and ultimately hopeful—are seen against the backdrop of a road trip taken in a 1969 Chevelle, and felt with the help of a soundtrack that gets them down the road. Beyond tension, it offers enough humor and romance to keep things interesting and leave a sweet taste in readers' mouths. After all, everything is better with wine.

The Secret Ingredient (working title) is a soon-to-be-released contemporary romance featuring Marcella Dawes, a famous television chef who has rented a house in the idyllic seaside town of Longport. Ostensibly, she's there to write her next cookbook—in reality, she's licking her wounds from her latest failed restaurant project and hiding out to escape her predatory agent and an otherwise messy life. When she learns that her next-door-neighbor, Dr. Max Piccarelli is the nephew of the late, famed chef Alessandra Piccarelli, she enlists him to become her kitchen assistant. His aunt died just short of her restaurant earning a Michelin Star and he is an excellent amateur chef. Becoming Cella's assistant is a mixed blessing for Max, who has secret longings to cook professionally, but who has ghosts around the fact that his aunt's award-winning restaurant has sat empty in the five years since her death. Through Max, Cella rediscovers a sense of agency, cuts toxic people from her life, and connects with what she really wants from her career. Through Cella, Max realizes that he needs to abandon his work as a third-world traveling doctor and return to the town (and the people) who desperately need him, and to bring Piccarell's back to its former glory. And, of course, along the way, they fall in love.

The Benefactor is a soon-to-be-released romantic suspense novel featuring an altruistic heroine, Cortez, who lands a coveted job with the elusive Loxley Foundation. It's the most talked-about non-profit in New York City and the brainchild of the elusive Benefactor, a game-changing philanthropist whose identity isn't known, even to the loyal team that works for him.

Enter Kendrick—Cortez's kind-of, sort-of boss—who she's begun to like in an attraction that is clearly mutual. As tension between them builds, so also does Cortez's suspicion that Kendrick is hiding something. What she learns about him plays on her every fear about men and relationships, owing to a devastating betrayal from her past surrounding her ex-boyfriend, Drew. When Cortez follows Kendrick into a dubious situation in which she blows his cover, she places both of them in mortal danger. Can the righteous Cortez accept Kendrick as he is, with a moral compass that leads him in a path apart from hers? More importantly, will they even get out of this mess alive?

CHRYSALIS

CHAPTER ONE
Excerpt: "Leaving on a Jet Plane"

"CAN I BRING YOU SOMETHING TO DRINK, SIR?"

He recognized the flight attendant. He knew them all by now. She'd never offered her name, but he'd heard the other one—Carrie—call her Kim. Everything about this flight was a facsimile of the same leg he'd taken a dozen times before. Flight 187 from ORD to YVR. He was seated in 3A. Left side window. The last row in first class. He usually declined Kim's offer, content to wait until dinner was served to before he ordered a beer, but this flight was different. This time, he did want a drink before takeoff. This time, his ticket was one-way.

"Just water, please."

Her face fell a little when he barely made eye contact. He'd always gone out of his way to be warm with people who others treated as nameless, faceless help. But he'd been dismissive, and he decided he would compensate when she returned. In the meantime, he fished the pill bottle out of the pocket of his jeans. If he didn't take a valium soon, he might just get off the plane. And what would that achieve beyond doing more to fuck up this already-fucked situation?

Talk is cheap.

His mother's mantra repeated itself in his overcrowded mind. This time he believed it. What good would it do for him to tell Darby what he really wanted for them if sacrifices are out of the question? She'd never stand for him giving up his promotion in Sydney. She'd just been through hell to earn Chief of

Psych. So he'd traded a pointless confession for an open-ended goodbye.

"Thank you," he said to Kim and this time, he made eye contact, but he wasted no time after she sets down the glass to pick it back up and swallow his pill. It may have been unwise. The flight to Vancouver was only four hours and he needed to be coherent if he wanted to make his connection. He hated medication, but right then, he need something to knock him into oblivion, to quiet the cacophony of noise inside his mind—something to stop the voices screaming that he was making the biggest mistake of his life.

It was too early for him to recline his seat, so he slipped his headphones over his ears. He started to queue up the Iron and Wine album he usually liked to listen to—Sam Beam's songs played like whispered lullabies that soothed him to sleep—but Darby loved this album and it was more than he could handle. Unable to think clearly enough to choose an alternative, he flipped the headphones on and pulled a black sleep mask over his eyes. He'd settle for noise-cancelled silence instead.

Sleep came quickly, and was mercifully deep, and he might have slept for hours had Carrie not coaxed him awake with instructions to have him place his seat upright for descent. He was dazed as he walked through the Vancouver airport, absently content that the valium was keeping him numb.

He took another half a pill after boarding his flight to Sydney, even though he know for sure he was only supposed to take one at a time. He was still out of it when he met his driver at the airport, but the winter air as he walked outside baggage claim sobered him. By the time he let himself into his apartment, it was midnight, he was lethargic but not tired and the dreaded stretch of a sleepless night loomed.

What he should do was work. He'd been ignoring his

job for days. As shitty as the past forty-eight hours had been, he'd worked hard to make them perfect. It may not have been the right time to tell Darby the truth, but that didn't mean he couldn't leave her clues. He'd closed the door on what they had—gave her as much as his conscience would allow of the ending they'd agreed to—but made absolutely fucking sure she knew this wasn't over.

They both know what this was, even if they'd never said it. He'd nearly slipped a dozen times. But what kind of dick would he have been to say it a second before he walked out the door? He'd thought they had more time. Time to break down the last barriers that stood between them. Time to figure things out on their own. To choose one another willingly. Not because the transfer forced their hands. Not because he was moving to Sydney. Not like this.

He knew that leaving had left both of them broken, but contriving some shit-show of a long distance relationship until they figured out something better could break things between them even more. Each of them had kept secrets. Both of them had told lies. Both of them had kept up the charade. And, because they weren't idiots, each of them had known the other one was doing it.

He wasn't proud of all the rules he'd broken—all the half-truths he'd let her believe. He'd done what every guy who likes a girl does: showed her the best parts of himself to get her to like him back. Fixing things between them now wasn't just about overcoming the distance—it was about overcoming the lies. But he'd hidden more than she had. And there were things she wanted to know. She'd been right about him all along.

ACKNOWLEDGMENTS

Writing a book is one thing. Seeing it come together is another. Maintaining a sense of sanity and well-being while you're doing it is a third. A huge thanks to my pro team, Tasha, Sabrina, Carrie, Kerri, Stacey, Jada and Anya for helping *Snapdragon* come together. Another big one to Nicole, Leslie and Rose for making sure I didn't fall apart.

ABOUT THE AUTHOR

Kilby Blades is a fresh new voice in smart contemporary romantic fiction. A business executive by day, by night she writes dynamic characters in to (and out of) tantalizingly complex predicaments. Critics laud her "feminist romance", noting empowered heroines and multi-dimensional heroes who are staunch advocates for their partners, stepping back from their own spotlights in order to let their women shine. From dry wit in her angstier books, to blatant humor in her lighter ones, her characters are resplendent in their witty repartee. All her stories, regardless of genre, serve up delicious dilemmas and never-before-seen plots.

Her debut novel, "Snapdragon", was a nine-time finalist and a three-time winner for honors including the IPPYs, the Publisher's Weekly BookLife Prize for Fiction, the Foreword Indie Award, the HOLT Medallion, the New England Reader's Choice Award and the OKRWA National Reader's Choice award. Its sequel, "Chrysalis", was a finalist in the Emma Awards. Her novella, "The Art of Worship" was an IndieReader winner, a HOLT Medallion finalist, and a Passionate Plume finalist. Two of her three soon-to-be-released titles were 2018

Stiletto Contest finalists and the third was a finalist in the CIMRWA awards. She is also the 2018 recipient of Best Debut Author in RSJ's Emma Awards.

When she's not writing, Kilby goes to movie matinees alone, where she eats Chocolate Pocky and buttered popcorn and usually smuggles in not-a-little-bit of red wine. Kilby is a mother, a social-justice fighter, and above all else, a glutton for a good story.

TITLES BY KILBY BLADES

Fiction
Snapdragon (2017)
Chrysalis (2017)
The Art of Worship (2017)

Non-Fiction
Marketing Steamy Romance (2018)

CPSIA information can be obtained
at www.ICGtesting.com
Printed in the USA
FSHW01n0644080918
51900FS